D0445589

ALSO BY HANNAH ROTHSCHILD

The Improbability of Love
The Baroness: The Search for Nica, the Rebellious Rothschild

House of Trelawney

HOUSE OF TRELAWNEY

Hannah Rothschild

ALFRED A. KNOPF
New York
2020

THIS IS A BORZOI BOOK
PUBLISHED BY ALFRED A. KNOPF

www.aaknopf.com

Knopf, Borzoi Books, and the colophon are registered trademarks of Penguin Random House LLC.

Library of Congress Cataloging-in-Publication Data
Names: Rothschild, Hannah, [date] - author.
Title: House of Trelawney / Hannah Rothschild.
Description: London : Bloomsbury Publishing, 2020.
Identifiers: LCCN 2019028762 (print) | LCCN 2019028763 (ebook) |
ISBN 9780525654919 (hardcover) | ISBN 9780525654926 (ebook) |
ISBN 9781524711757 (open market)
Subjects: LCSH: Domestic fiction.
Classification: LCC PR6118.08755 H68 2020 (print) | LCC PR6118.08755 (ebook) |
DDC 823/.92—dc23
LC record available at https://lccn.loc.gov/2019028762
LC ebook record available at https://lccn.loc.gov/2019028763

Jacket illustration by Sacha Floch Poliakoff
Jacket design by Megan Wilson

Manufactured in the United States of America
First American Edition

To Yoav

House of Trelawney

1

Trelawney Castle

WEDNESDAY 4TH JUNE 2008

Trelawney Castle, home to the same family for eight hundred years, sits on a bluff of land overlooking the South Cornish sea. Since their ennoblement in 1179, the Earls of Trelawney used wealth and stealth to stay on the winning side of history; ruthlessly and unscrupulously switching allegiances or bribing their way to safety and positions of authority. The castle was their three-dimensional calling card, the physical embodiment of their wealth and influence. Each Earl added an extension until it was declared the grandest, if not the finest, stately home in the county of Cornwall.

In summer months, until the First World War, it was the custom of the family and guests to take the Trelawney barge from the Trelawney boathouse, through Trelawney land, past Trelawney follies and temples, to Trelawney Cove where they could use the seaside house (Little Trelawney Castle) or sail the yacht (the *Trelawney*). In the winter, the same ilk would hunt with the Trelawney foxhounds or shoot game raised on the Trelawney Estate. At that time, the family were so landed and powerful that they could travel from Trelawney to Bath, from the south coast to the Bristol Channel, without stepping off their own domain. This swathe of England became known as Trelawneyshire, an area of 500,000 acres including forty miles of coastline. With the advent of the railway, those family members who chose to go as far as London (most refused and who could blame them) would travel from Trelawney Station in a private train stamped inside and out with the Trelawney coat of arms.

By the early nineteenth century, the castle had expanded sufficiently to have a room for each day of the year, eleven staircases and four miles of hallways. After King George III's favourite mistress became hopelessly lost in the maze of corridors and nearly died from hypothermia, guests were, thenceforth, given a miniature crested silver casket containing different-coloured confetti to sprinkle on the floor, so as to leave a personal trail to and from their bedrooms.

The Victorian diarist Rudyard Johnson, a regular guest, wrote: "The castle is made of four main blocks, each built a century apart in markedly different styles. Part of the amusement of Trelawney is sleeping in an Elizabethan bedroom, breakfasting in a Jacobean hall, taking tea in a Regency conservatory and dancing in a Georgian ballroom. For those who like a morning constitutional, the battlement walk is a perfect 400-yard perambulation." The respected eighteenth-century architectural historian J. M. Babcock dismissed the castle as "a vomitorium of conflicting architectural styles, reflecting the whims of wealthy, ill-educated and self-indulgent aristocrats."

Until the early twentieth century, rooms were lit by candle or oil lamps and warmed by open fires. Hot water was prepared in vast cauldrons on stoves in the basement and carried in buckets to the bathrooms. Even human waste, kept in porcelain dishes mounted in wooden boxes or cupboards, was disposed of by (a servant's) hand. Eighty-five members of domestic staff were employed to carry out those tasks, including a butler, housekeeper, kitchen maids, footmen, chars and a clock man; outside there were sixty more, ranging from gardeners and grooms to mole catchers and coachmen, and even a bear and camel keeper. In 1920 the decision was taken to instal central heating, plumbing and electricity. It was a Sisyphean task, started but never finished. Only the Georgian wing was modernised, providing nine bathrooms for eighty-four bedrooms and a total of eleven radiators.

The castle made its own music: pipes hissed and gurgled; house-parties filled the septic tanks under the cellars; and a constant plop and gurgle underscored every activity. Wide wooden floorboards let out little squeaks and groans as they shrank and expanded in changing temperatures. Wind whistled round the crenellations, storms rattled windowpanes. The huge boilers in the basement shuddered while the water tanks in the attics bubbled and whooshed. Little wonder that the family thought of their home as a sentient being: in their eyes, Trelawney was far more than bricks and mortar.

The beauty of the interiors paled next to Trelawney's setting. To the north of the castle were four hundred acres of medieval oak woods, set in deep cushions of moss laced with streams chasing over granite boulders. In the heart of the forest there was a perfectly round and deep lake, fed by a waterfall. At different times of the year, the glades were carpeted with flowers—crocuses, snowdrops, bluebells, wild garlic and rare orchids. In these Elysian settings lived native fallow, roe and red deer, thirty types of songbird, thirty-four varieties of butterfly, sixteen different species of moths, as well as foxes, badgers, otters, stoats, weasels, mice, voles, moles, slow-worms and snakes.

To the east and west were undulating meadows dotted with sheep and cows and also arable fields. For eight centuries this rich and fertile area was the breadbasket of the West Country and provided added income to the family's coffers. It was the southern perimeter, however—some sixty acres of landscaped garden leading down to the estuary—which guests recalled with awe. Successive generations of Earls and their wives had tamed and reshaped the terrain, creating walks and waterways, avenues, terraces, sunken gardens, raised beds, topiary, wild-flower meadows, exotic palmeries, carpet bedding and a 24-acre walled kitchen garden. Wending through the pleasure grounds were streams, waterfalls and, to the south, a vast rhododendron and azalea forest surrounded by ancient laurels. Vistas and views were punctuated with Doric temples and triumphal arches. There were secret grottos and fierce fountains that, by an ingenious natural system of displacement, shot jets of water more than fifty feet into the air. The combination of the manicured and the wild, the conflagration of man's determined hand and nature's attributes, created an unforgettable experience. Trelawney was, everyone agreed, the most captivating setting in the British Isles.

As the centuries tripped by, the Earls of Trelawney, their senses and ambition dulled by years of pampered living, failed to develop other skills. Of the twenty-four Earls, the last eight had been dissolute and bereft of any business acumen. Their financial ineptitude, along with two world wars, the Wall Street Crash, three divorces and inheritance taxes, had dissipated the family's fortune. Bit by bit the accoutrements of wealth disappeared. Servants went to war, not to be replaced. Farms were sold along with the London mansion. The private train and barge were left to rust and rot. Wings of the castle were closed up. Little Trelawney Castle was sold and became a hotel.

The good paintings and furniture were auctioned off and all that remained were their scars: discoloured squares and rectangles on walls or awkward absences in rooms. The only objects left were those without financial value, testaments to the whims and enthusiasms of generations of Trelawneys—such as the enormous stuffed polar bear in the west entrance hall, its fur and fangs turned yellow by time.

The tapestries in the Great Hall and corridors, formerly a riot of vibrantly coloured woven silks, had faded to monochromic pastels and hung in shreds. Worn-through carpets revealed wooden floorboards. Horsehair stuffing and rusty springs poked out of sofas. Broken chairs lay where last used, wooden corpses in a losing battle against maintenance. Red velvet curtains, burnt by sunlight, had turned a uniform grey. Windows were obscured by the march of ivy and bramble on the outer walls. In some places the ceilings had fallen in, exposing floors above. Swathes of wallpaper flapped disconsolately in draughty rooms. The present incumbents chose to avoid setting foot in most of the castle. For them locking doors meant keeping decay at bay. Occasionally a great crash of avalanching plaster could be heard falling like a tree in a faraway wood. Once a child had nearly plummeted through a first-floor landing into the morning room below, but these occurrences were quickly forgotten, stashed away in the department of unhelpful memories.

Nowhere was the reversal of the family fortunes more evident than in the once-famous gardens: nature had slowly and inexorably taken back her land. The waterways were choked with lily pads; the ponds silted up; the hedges, now unclipped, spread across paths; the carefully manicured beds had gone to seed; the yew and beech hedges were blowsy; the rhododendron and azalea, fighting each other for light, had grown tall and raggedy. The fountains spluttered. Buddleia ran amok. The kitchen-garden vegetables had bolted years before. The temples and arches were covered with ivies and vines.

Amidst the chaos and decrepitude inside and out, one relatively small patch of garden remained beautifully and obsessively tended, and on this June afternoon of 2008, Jane, the Viscountess Tremayne, daughter-in-law of the 24th Earl of Trelawney, wife of the heir Kitto, worked diligently amongst the roses, refusing to admit defeat against the army of encroaching weeds. For her, keeping control of this area of garden was a form of therapy; she found double-digging and deadheading calming. That morning, a seemingly innocuous letter, written on two sheets of airmail onion paper, had been so upsetting that she'd taken the first opportunity to come outside with a trowel and a pair of clippers.

Jane Tremayne was forty-one. Her figure was kept trim by the endless stairs of the castle, by tending the garden, seeing to most of the domestic chores, looking after her ageing parents-in-law and her three children, as well as riding and mucking out the last horse in the stables. With fine brown hair beginning to grey around the temples, Jane had pale skin, eyes nearer the colour of grey than blue and weather-beaten rosy cheeks. Had she bothered to take the slightest interest in her appearance, she might have passed as a handsome woman. As it was, with her badly cut hair (kitchen scissors), faded overalls and rough, unmanicured hands, she looked more like a labourer than most people's idea of an aristocrat.

The family's Labrador lay supine by the box hedge, occasionally raising its handsome black head to snap half-heartedly at a passing fly. A trained gun dog, Pooter spent most winter weekends with Jane's husband at someone else's pheasant shoot (their own had been abandoned in the late 1980s). Though he could not return invitations, Kitto was a valued guest in circles that admired a distinguished title, a first-class shot and a keen drinker. When his master was home, Pooter ignored Jane except at mealtimes. Jane's three children took much the same line as the Labrador, using their mother as a glorified taxi and meal service. Her elder son Ambrose was in his last year at Harrow but, due to exorbitant public-school fees, her younger son Toby and daughter Arabella had been sent to the local comprehensive.

The letter, when it arrived after breakfast, had sat glaring at her from the fruit bowl on the kitchen table. Jane tried covering it with bananas, a dishcloth and other post. She knew from the elegant writing and the sender's address who and where it was from. Some sixth sense told her that it was better left unopened or forgotten. Curiosity won; Jane ripped open the envelope. Seeing the writing was as disturbing as walking through a spider's web; the invisible silken fronds unnerving, repulsive. Turning the pages over, she saw the script started small but became increasingly large and erratic. At school, its author had always won the Best Presentation Award and most other things. There had been prize days when only one child was called up to the podium to collect everything, from the gym to the maths and the history cup.

Jane sat down, cleared a space on the table and spread the pages out in front of her.

Dear Jane, I have often thought about you, Blaze and Trelawney over the last twenty years. Closing her eyes, Jane could hear Anastasia's lilting voice, so quiet and conspiratorial that you had to lean in, letting her sweet breath brush your face and ears.

I have been living in a magnificent Indian palace called Balakpur, several hundred miles north of Delhi, with my husband the Maharaja and eight of his eleven children. I have two children but my own son is the youngest and won't inherit the title.

Jane thought about her second son Toby, in many ways a more suitable candidate for the earldom than her firstborn but destined by birth to be the runner-up at Trelawney.

After such a long time, you must be wondering why I'm writing, Anastasia continued. *Jane, I need your help desperately, even if it's only for old times' sake, for sentimentality, for human kindness, for the Three Musketeers.* Jane's heart contracted at the mention of their old nickname.

I am dying. Dengue fever has shut down my organs one after another, like lights failing on a dashboard. My husband died a few months ago. On the day of his death, his palace Balakpur, and all chattels, passed to his eldest son. The new Maharaja has banished me and my daughter Ayesha to a tiny cottage hospital on the outskirts of Calcutta. He has kept my son, Ayesha's half-brother Sachan; I doubt I will ever see my darling boy again.

Jane tried to summon compassion for her friend and her children, but felt nothing other than a sense of foreboding.

As you know, dear Jane, I have no family, no parents, no siblings. You and Blaze and Trelawney will forever be my home. Ayesha has nowhere to go and I am flinging myself on your mercy. Please take her.

Jane read the last paragraph three times. Was Anastasia asking her and Kitto to take on her child? After twenty years? After all that had happened? Jane laughed out loud. There was no way that the daughter was coming to stay. She and Kitto could hardly afford to feed their own children, let alone anyone else's. Besides, Jane didn't believe that Anastasia was dying; she probably wanted a holiday from parenthood and who, Jane thought, could blame her.

Now, in the peace and tranquillity of the garden, Jane took out her anger on deadheading roses, including some wild snips at perfectly healthy blooms. Looking at the clipped rose heads around her feet, she decided they were metaphors for lost friendships which, once snipped, couldn't simply be reattached. Real intimacy was a delicate cloth of shared experiences stitched together by tiny accretions of time, mutual trust and support. It wasn't something that could be folded, put away and shaken out when the need presented itself. Whatever the three women once enjoyed had lain fallow and untended for so many years that it had shrunk and corroded. At best their friendship was like an old postcard, a tinted seaside scene, imbued only with memory and sentimentality. She, Anastasia and Blaze would never recapture their earlier affinity; their lives and circumstances were too disparate. Whatever Anastasia was implying in her letter, Jane owed her nothing. She also decided not to tell her husband. The less Kitto thought about Anastasia, the more confident Jane felt.

Pleased that she had resolved this issue so quickly and effectively, Jane looked over the rose bed towards the west wing of Trelawney Castle. The windows had turned golden in the late-afternoon sun and the whole of one wall, three storeys high and a hundred and fifty feet long, was covered with the last flowers of the purple wisteria. She listened to the hum of bees feeding on the pendulous blooms and caught sight of a flash of yellow as a goldfinch darted into a nest. A pair of curlews flew over, calling to each other—theirs was Jane's favourite sound, part giggle, part siren. In the far distance a cow bellowed, perhaps to its calf, and in the village two miles down the estuary an ice-cream van played "Greensleeves" through a tinny loudspeaker. Looking around, Jane felt her heart swell with love. This was her husband Kitto's Trelawney and one day it would belong to her eldest son Ambrose. It would never be her castle; this Viscountess, like many before her, was nothing more than a faint shadow passing over its history.

Her mobile phone rang. The screen said "Clarissa," her mother-in-law. Tempted not to answer, Jane, impelled by duty and habit, took the call.

"We will have supper early tonight. The Earl is feeling a little wan." Her mother-in-law hung up without saying goodbye.

Jane had become the house skivvy and had no one to blame but herself; always eager to please, she had been far too accommodating. At least old Aunt Tuffy kept to herself in a cottage in the park; Jane occasionally saw her scuttling around corners, both women keen to avoid each other.

She put the gardening gloves, clippers and trowel in the wooden trug and set off towards the kitchen. The smell of warm grass drifting on the breeze reminded her of her old life again: running over menus with Cook, discussing seeds and borders with the gardener, ordering fresh flowers for the bedrooms, going to London twice a year to buy new clothes. It was a relief to have lost contact with old friends; there was no one to witness what had become of her life.

She walked around the west wing of the castle, past the collapsed greenhouses and outhouses, along the cobbled pathways sprouting with dock and ragwort, until she reached the peeling side door. It was never locked; the key had been lost many years earlier. Even the walls of the inner passage were lined with moss. Rogue buddleia self-seeded in the cracks; Jane took comfort in the prettiness of its purple flowers. She followed the family custom of kicking her shoes into the mountain of wellingtons and trainers in the boot room.

In the kitchen, she put the clippers back on the dresser along with all the other detritus of family life: school reports, cricket balls, teapots, cracked plates, aspirin bottles, old photographs, keys to forgotten doors, incomplete packs of cards and a stuffed, moth-eaten rabbit (provenance unknown). To stave off winter gloom, when the Cornish sun hardly rose above the escarpment, Jane had painted the whole room an electric pea-green with a wide border of intertwined honeysuckle, wild roses and clematis; those who looked carefully could pick out tiny field mice and bumblebees hidden in the foliage. On the pine table, a radio with an aerial made from a coat hanger sat permanently emanating the comforting if barely audible sounds of Radio 4. The washing-up—saucepans and cups—stood upended on the scrubbed wooden draining board and, in the sink, there was a pile of broad beans, carrots and new potatoes dug up that morning from the kitchen garden. Wiping her hands on her trousers, Jane turned on the tap and scrubbed earth from the potatoes, cut them into chunky medallions and laid them in rows over the top of the minced meat. It was the third time in one week that they had eaten a variation on cottage pie. Jane was an incompetent cook, bereft of ideas and patience. On Monday mornings she bought a catering-sized pack of mince and a bumper carton of tinned tuna from the local cash and carry. For her, cooking was a duty that had to be endured. Spare minutes, and there weren't many, were spent in her studio designing and printing wallpaper. This activity was her lifeline to sanity. The process of painstakingly transferring her ideas on to paper, etching into blocks and printing in a phantasmagoria of colours, was intensely satisfying. Here at least she could complete a task; in other areas of her life, the chores were seemingly endless.

Her phone pinged with a text from Kitto: he had an important meeting and would stay in London. Taking a carrot and a large knife, Jane chopped the vegetable with gusto. Pooter, eyeing her nervously, slunk off to sit in the corridor. No wonder Kitto wasn't coming home; if only she could have a mini-break from this life of drudgery. She felt envious of his job as Chairman of the bank, Acorn, the tiny flat in Pimlico and the tedious business dinners. It brought in a necessary income, but there was an unfortunate consequence: Kitto's time in the City inflamed his tendency to invest in unlikely schemes. A few weeks earlier, her husband had bounced through the kitchen door, slung his briefcase on the table and, grabbing his wife by her waist, planted messy kisses on her neck. Things were finally going to change, he assured her. He'd made a "fail-safe, blue-chip, pukka, five-star investment" in some kind of "bond." He couldn't explain what this "thingamajig" did—something to do with housing and mortgages. The more he told her it was bombproof, the greater her feeling of dread.

Jane had heard this kind of talk before: always a different concept, always the same result. Kitto had turned five hundred prime acres over to growing strawberries at a time when Spain was mass-producing the fruit at a fraction of the cost. His idea to host organic burials had led to a massive and expensive advertising campaign and only three takers. He built and self-funded a housing development but failed to get the proper permissions from the local authority: the buildings' shells still stood empty. His hydroelectric scheme had cost many hundreds of thousands to implement but had lacked sufficient water pressure to make it viable. One Christmas he had bought the family expensive metal detectors on the assumption that, after eight hundred years, there was bound to be hidden treasure. After four days of divining and a lot of holes dug, the most exciting object found had been an engraved trowel which was valued by the local auction house at less than £20. Later, there was the sizeable investment in rare-breed animals that turned out to be rare because no one wanted them.

And now some new idea and a bigger mortgage. Frustrated, Jane banged the saucepan so hard that the handle broke. It was one of her last good pans, a wedding present given by a distant cousin. Looking at it, she wondered if it could be soldered back on. She had become good at mending things; the tractor, her car, the lawnmower had all been coaxed back into service. Filling the armless saucepan with cold water, she put it on to the Aga and noticed that neither of the hobs was hot. She bent down to check the pilot light and found that it had gone out. Taking a match, Jane tried to get it going: nothing happened. She turned on the electric oven, put the pie in and went downstairs to the cellar to check the oil tank. Flicking on the light, she walked along the musty corridor to the boiler room. Don't panic, she told herself, four huge tanks can't have run dry. She took out her phone and held it up against the oil gauge on Tank One. It was empty. She held the light up to the second tank and then the third and the fourth. There was no oil in any of them. No oil, no Aga, no heating, no hot water. At least it's June, she thought miserably, and we still have electricity. The children can have showers at school. I can carry hot water to my in-laws. And as for herself and Kitto, they could take soap down to the estuary and pass it off as a newfangled health cure.

Fighting feelings of doom and despondency, Jane went back upstairs and turned left into the scullery to empty the washing machine. With Ambrose and Kitto away, at least there was less laundry. Emptying the machine, she put the wet clothes into a basket and took it out to the back courtyard to hang the things up to dry.

With the washing on the line and fifteen minutes to spare before the pie was cooked, Jane steeled herself for the inevitable. Spirits sinking, she went along the flagstone corridor to the office. Since they let the estate manager go, four years earlier, Jane had assumed the role of family accountant. In the beginning, she'd attacked the tasks with alacrity but, as the bills mounted and the possibility of paying them lessened, her enthusiasm for sorting waned. Her filing system was split into three categories: urgent, desperate and cataclysmic. It had started as a joke; Jane had never imagined that these words would be so prophetic or that their troubles could escalate as quickly and steadily as a platoon of ants marching up a sugary bun. Over the last few months, the "cataclysmic" tray had become as large as "urgent" and, if she were being honest, many of the "desperates" needed to be upgraded. Jane picked up the top unopened letter and tore out the contents. It was English Heritage threatening, for the third time that year, to put a condemned notice on Trelawney. *We have repeatedly warned you that the upkeep of this Grade I listed building is falling short of even the most basic requirements. On our last visit, we counted fifty-six windows in urgent need of replacement. The buttresses on the east and the south wings were clearly subsiding. The Elizabethan roof is falling in.* How did that esteemed body think the family could pay for the renovations? Crumpling the letter into a ball, she threw it across the room behind the filing cabinet. The next two letters were from banks offering interest-free credit cards for withdrawals up to £10,000. Jane slipped them into a drawer. Flicking through the other envelopes, she found one headed "West Country Fuels." There, in red capitals, was the word "Arrears." Her eyes spun down to the figure: minus £88,000. Minus £88,000! They had to be joking. She was about to sit down and write a holding letter when she remembered the cottage pie. Wearily, she got up and went to the kitchen.

Her younger son and her daughter, fresh and hungry from school, came bounding in. Jane's genes hardly showed in her children, who all had their father's auburn hair and hazel eyes.

"Oh no, not bloody cottage boring pie again." Arabella slung her bag on the kitchen table and kicked off her shoes.

"We haven't had it for ages." Jane picked up the trainers and threw them on to the shoe mountain.

"Not since last night anyway," Toby said, shooting a warning look at his younger sister. Jane smiled gratefully at her son.

"This kind of food could stunt my growth. It's 4 per cent meat and 98 per cent fur and foot," Arabella said, piling her plate high with grey cooked meat and slightly burnt potatoes.

"That makes 102 per cent." Toby took a smaller helping and cut himself three large slices of bread.

"Please leave some for your grandparents," Jane said.

"They never eat anything." Arabella sat down at the table and squeezed the tomato ketchup bottle until all the mince was covered.

"Gross," Toby said, smearing salad cream on his bread.

"It's so I can't taste it." Arabella looked reproachfully at her mother.

"Maybe tomorrow I'll make tomato ketchup pie and you can sprinkle some mince on it."

"Remind me to laugh."

Jane bit her tongue. For five years, she'd been waiting for her daughter to pass out of this phase. It was no comfort that the teachers at school also found her impossible. Wolfing down the food in a few minutes, Arabella dumped her unwashed plate in the sink and left the room.

"How was your day, darling?" Jane asked Toby. After the shock of oil tanks and Anastasia's letter, she longed to have a conversation with someone other than Pooter.

"All right."

"Who did you hang out with?"

"No one." Toby wiped the last of the pie up with a piece of bread, got up, kissed his mother on the cheek and vanished.

Jane looked at the leftover corner of the pie: just enough for her parents-in-law. To fill in the silence, she started to sing; and to work out some of her irritation, she beat the tops of the pans with a wooden spoon.

In the television room down the corridor, Arabella and Toby listened to their mother and rolled their eyes. "It's the gizzards and intestines they mash into that cheap mince. It gets into your brain and sends you tonto," Arabella said knowingly.

"Mad cow disease," Toby agreed.

"Do you think we're going to be orphaned?"

"No such luck."

On the ground floor in another part of the castle, known as the Mistresses' Wing, Enyon and Clarissa, the Earl and Countess of Trelawney, sat side by side on a small sofa in front of a four-bar electric fire. Even in June, the room was cold and Clarissa had flung a fur coat over a tweed skirt and twinset. Her husband wore a corduroy suit with leather patches at the elbow, buttoned up over a thick woollen sweater and two scarves. Above the fire there was a mantelpiece with a clock and a family portrait of an ancestor, the 12th Earl. On the lintel, there were rows of stiff, wildly out-of-date invitations as well as some old Christmas cards. On the right, a side table was piled with books and papers, a small boxed television set, and sherry and gin in cut-glass decanters. In another corner, there was a roll-top desk over which were more family portraits. The windows were framed by green velvet curtains: one ripped, one intact, both faded brown by sunlight on the inner edges. The well-trodden Turkish carpet had been worn through in certain places and there was a dog basket for a long-departed canine friend.

"I'll redo my will tomorrow," Enyon said.

"Have your thoughts changed since yesterday?" Clarissa asked, not unkindly.

"I'm going to leave the Gainsborough portrait to Bella."

"Who's Bella?" She didn't remind her husband that the Gainsboroughs had been sold a long time ago.

"My granddaughter, you silly old bat. Honestly, Clarissa, I do wonder about you."

"You don't have a granddaughter called Bella," the Countess said. "Ambrose, Toby and Arabella."

"Who the devil is Bella?" the Earl said crossly.

"Come to think of it, it might be Arabella."

"Ha! There's life in the old boy yet." Enyon slapped his thigh. "Come here and I will search you, all over, particularly in those nice lace knickers."

"I haven't worn lace knickers since 1962," the Countess giggled. She was eighty, while her husband was eighty-five. Today, his wrinkled face and gizzardy neck stuck out of a collar many sizes too large, making him look like an old tortoise. In his youth, Enyon had been a towering man with a neck as thick as a telegraph pole, who'd thought nothing of lifting up small heifers and could exhaust three fresh horses on a day's hunting. His roar of laughter or shout of displeasure could be heard half a mile away. During their long marriage, the Earl had been constitutionally, almost pathologically, unfaithful. The combination of great looks, supreme self-confidence, a title and a monumental libido meant that few were safe; over the years his conquests included wives of friends, actresses, housemaids, girl grooms—so many that his nickname had been the Earl of Tres-horney. Nevertheless, his wife, determined to turn a blind eye, counted their marriage as uncommonly happy and content. There had only been one near-irreversible mistake, when both her husband and the girl had lost their heads and threatened to elope. The young lady, like a few others before her, had been dispatched to the Colonies with a sizeable pay-off. Now, looking at her beloved, shrunken, desiccated version of her husband, Clarissa knew that she'd been right to disregard the peccadilloes. How lucky for her that she had been born without any romantic aspirations.

"Is the yardarm at the right place?" Enyon asked.

"It's 5 p.m. One hour to go."

"Can't we pretend it's 6?"

"Standards, darling. Standards."

The cold wrapped itself around their old bones so viciously that neither could move.

"Is it just me or is time going particularly slowly today?"

"Maybe a little slower," Clarissa had to admit.

Their lives had been narrowed by age and infirmity. They rose at 7, washed and took a short constitutional walk around the castle's perimeter. After that they sat by the small fire and had a race to complete *The Times* crossword (they lived in hope). The monotony was broken by a stiff sherry at 12 and the lunchtime news at 1 p.m. There followed a brief nap and then "correspondence" (largely letters of condolences). There was a second constitutional at 3 p.m., a flannel bath at 5, another "snifter" at 6 p.m., supper at 7 and bed by 8:30 p.m.

"What do you think Mulligan will prepare tonight?" Enyon knew perfectly well that there was no cook but couldn't bear to break his wife's heart. Clarissa minded desperately about standards and staff. Enyon knew this was a woman's lot; they didn't have the brains or brawn to do more than worry about domestic life. Looking over at his wife, he thought how damned lucky he'd been. Clarissa had kept her figure and her counsel; a husband couldn't ask for more than that.

"Let's hope we don't get wretched cottage pie again."

She had never told her husband that the chef these days was their daughter-in-law. Mrs. Mulligan, the cook, had retired nearly ten years ago, but Clarissa was pleased that the Earl imagined a significant number of staff in the kitchen.

"Shall we change for dinner?" she asked. It took at least sixty minutes for them to get out of their day and into the evening clothes.

"Do we have to, darling? It's so damn cold."

"If we let things slip, what hope is there for the next generation?"

What hope indeed? Clarissa thought silently. She knew that the future of Trelawney hung on a thread that might break at any moment. She prayed her husband would die before seeing the entire castle sold to a foreigner and she had resolved some time ago to place a pillow over his head rather than let him hear the death knell on eight hundred years of tradition. If only Enyon hadn't been such a philanderer; all those women they'd had to pay off. Damn her stupid, self-indulgent son for failing to make something of his life; all that time footling around with unpublishable poetry and that ridiculous bank job. Marrying Jane was the best thing Kitto had done, even if her fortune had not been as large as they all hoped.

She patted her husband's arm. "Come on, darling."

Enyon tried to struggle to his feet but his knees gave way and he slumped back in his chair. "The most important thing is to make sure that the next generation has a clean slate and no surprises."

"Did I ever tell you what a good and kind man you are?" the Countess said, kissing her husband on the cheek.

"Maybe I should leave the Gainsborough to Blaze. Is she coming down soon? I do miss my girl."

The Countess's heart gave a lurch at the mention of their daughter. It had been twenty years since they had last seen her in London for their annual tea, on her birthday at Fortnum and Mason. Since the Earl refused to leave Trelawney and Blaze refused to visit the castle, contact had dwindled to a phone call at Christmas.

"I will try to persuade her to come soon. But you know how busy she is with work."

"She's breaking my heart," the Earl said.

"I know," the Countess echoed.

"What did she and Kitto row about?" Enyon asked.

"It was the bedroom issue again."

The Earl's face flared with anger. "Why can't the bloody spares realise that this is a family tradition. If we didn't move the spinsters and second sons along, this place would be a Tower of Babel, choked up with unmarried siblings."

"She thought that Kitto and Jane might be more modern."

The Earl snorted. "Where the blinkers has modern got anyone?"

"Couldn't agree more."

"Twenty years is an awfully long time to hold a grudge about a bedroom," he said sadly. Blaze—stronger, braver and more substantive than her brother—was her father's favourite; he'd often wondered if his son's and daughter's genes had got mixed up.

Enyon and Clarissa sat in silence, looking at the four glowing bars on the heater.

"What will you wear tonight?" the Earl asked eventually.

"The long green taffeta and the diamanté, I think."

"We might even put the wireless on after dinner and have a dance," the Earl suggested.

"That would be divine, darling."

Enyon wrapped the blanket around his knees.

"Have you seen Tuffy recently?" he asked.

Clarissa thought for a few minutes. "Not for at least a year."

"Do you think she's dead?"

"Wouldn't we have heard?"

"Who'd tell us?"

Clarissa hesitated, trying to remember if Tuffy spoke to Jane or Kitto. Her husband's sister was, even by family standards, deeply eccentric. She had been the first female member of the dynasty to have a job. No one knew what it was, but rumour had it that it was something to do with a university and insects. When she was at home, Tuffy stomped around the park armed with a butterfly net and a collection of plastic bags, picking over carrion with glee.

"I'm sure she's fine."

"Shall we send the butler over to check on her tomorrow?" the Earl asked.

"I think I'll mention it to the farm manager—he's not the squeamish type." Clarissa had no idea if her son employed such a person, but she liked finding a decent answer to any problem.

"Jolly good idea. Jolly good."

A bug flew into one of the fire's electric bars, sending up tiny sparks and a faint smell of burning.

"Do you ever think about death?" the Earl asked his wife.

"Certainly not." She glanced sideways at her husband. It was unlike him to ask a direct question on such a maudlin subject. "Why?"

"This isn't much fun, is it?"

"What isn't?"

The old man flapped his mottled hands. "All this. Everything hurts and there's so little to look forward to."

The Countess found the conversation most perturbing. She wasn't sure whether to comfort or scold her husband. "The purpose of life is to keep on going," she said matter-of-factly.

"The only thing that keeps me alive is the fear of death," Enyon said.

Fifty minutes later Jane carried a tray into her parents-in-laws' wing, finding them dressed for dinner. The Earl was in a green velvet smoking jacket, a black tie and embroidered slippers, and his wife in taffeta. Jane noticed that Enyon's nose was bright red and Clarissa shook slightly.

"Why don't you come and have supper in the main kitchen, it's lovely and warm," Jane offered.

"What'd the servants say?" the Earl said. "They'd think it awfully rum if we pitched up."

Jane wondered again why they had to go through this charade; they both knew there were no more servants, apart from cross Mrs. Sparrow who was supposed to cook supper on Tuesday and Thursday evenings but hadn't turned up for a fortnight.

"Why didn't Barnes bring dinner through?" the Earl said, looking at his daughter-in-law.

"Shouldn't you be changing for dinner, darling? Kitto will wonder what happened to you." Clarissa glanced knowingly at Jane, willing her to play along.

Jane wasn't in the mood to pretend that night. She put the tray down on the side. "Can you manage, Clarissa?" Her mother-in-law nodded. Jane looked at her, this woman, once so powerful and wealthy, now so thin and cold and consumed with maintaining the pathetic fallacy. She felt overwhelmed with pity.

"Leave them there, Barnes will come in to clear after you have gone to bed," Jane said, laying two places on the polished table. She also set out some wine glasses, although it had been some time since they'd been able to afford a bottle of anything decent.

"I better go and change," she added.

The Countess smiled gratefully.

"Pour me a gin, darling," the Earl said. "Three fingers—I need something to chase the cold away."

"I think I will join you tonight," the Countess said. "Never known such a cold June. Never."

Tuffy Scott had to admit that the mice population in her cottage had become too large and a solution had to be found. On her return to Trelawney from two weeks away, her bed was littered with tiny droppings, her cereal packets had been torn apart and the loo paper shredded (she found the nest later in an old suitcase). Luckily, as the rodents couldn't open the tins of beans and lentils, there was something to eat. For a woman who survived on Rice Krispies, Weetabix and pulses, the loss of two-thirds of her normal diet was a bore, particularly when she had hoped to spend the next fortnight working on a new hypothesis instead of navigating Cornwall's woefully inadequate public-transport system in search of basic provisions.

Tuffy used to encourage the mice. Living alone, she liked hearing their tiny claws scampering through the rafters or across the floor. Recently the scamper had become a stampede and a few little friends had turned into battalions. Tuffy wanted to understand why, after so many years of easy cohabitation, this sudden population explosion had occurred. It was her job, as one of the world's leading entomologists specialising in the effects of climate change on insects, to investigate changes in natural phenomena. If there were several thousand mice in her own home, there were bound to be several billion fleas living on their bodies. And nothing excited Tuffy more than living, breathing, jumping and multiplying Siphonaptera.

The mouse droppings were only part of the problem. There were also the birds; every year, from mid April to the end of summer, she left all the windows open so swallows could make their nests between the beams of her sitting room and bedroom. At first only a few had availed themselves of the offer. In recent years, more than ten pairs had set up home and each produced bewildering quantities of excrement. Tuffy didn't have the heart to close the windows again but nor did she have the time to clear up after her feathered friends.

Tuffy had always preferred the company of animals to humans and on her sixteenth birthday, in 1950, she eschewed the consumption of any animal products, from meat to milk (not difficult as the iron grip of rationing was still in place). She had from then on refused to wear any leather products which might endanger or harm the natural world. She wore gym shoes and tunics in the summer and wellington boots, corduroy trousers and tweed jackets in the winter. The family tradition was not to waste education on girls; their youth was simply a holding pattern before marriage. With no interest in the opposite (or indeed the same) sex and a fascination with the natural world, Tuffy decided to take the highly unusual (for a Trelawney) step of enrolling in further education with a view to finding a career. Her interest in fleas began when the insects decimated her beloved pet chicken; Tuffy's first (and, as it happened, only) taste of heartbreak had unexpected consequences.

In the post-war muddle and mayhem, no one in her family asked why the youngest daughter went by bus to Plymouth every day or shut herself in her room for hours at a time. A maiden aunt left her a small stipend. Over the next few years, Tuffy, already a mature student, gained qualification after qualification; degrees and doctorates. A modest income was supplemented by academic fellowships. When her elder brother enacted the family tradition of evicting his siblings from the castle, Tuffy barricaded herself in a semi-derelict cottage on the far side of the park and had remained there ever since.

As she sat eating baked beans and peaches from the tin (less washing up), chased down by a bottle of stout and a multivitamin pill, Tuffy wondered how to bring the rodent population under control. Poisoning or trapping were out of the question. She toyed with the idea of introducing a cat but that, she decided, was simply murder by displacement. Looking around the room, she considered how many of her belongings were essential. There were about forty yards of scientific journals; several different microscopes; two computers; some 28,000 specimens of fleas and other insects; kitchen equipment (a kettle, a tin opener, two bowls and some cutlery); and maybe two suitcases' worth of clothing and shoes. It was, she had to admit, an absolute dump but it was her dump.

"One of us has to go," Tuffy said to a mouse who had sauntered out of a cereal box and looked calmly at her with glittering black eyes, "and, as I am seriously outnumbered, that has to be me."

Although Tuffy knew she would have to leave her home of fifty-five years, there weren't many options. The cottage, set in a dell in the park, was wonderfully private. The thought of moving closer to civilisation was an anathema. At some point in the near future she would have to walk to the castle where her nephew and his wife lived (Tuffy was sure she was called Jane) and ask if they could rehouse her.

Sweeping aside the tiny droppings from her sheets, Tuffy climbed into bed. To her annoyance, she found a nest of baby mice in both of her pillows and their constant squeaking and wriggling made sleep impossible. Taking a plastic bag from her bedside table, she evicted the babies and popped their cocoon (made from loo paper and her favourite jumper) inside, hoping to find a few resident fleas. She then got up, went over to her desk and spent the night making notes to form the basis of a new paper: "The effects of climate change on the population of *Mus musculus*." Among the sections worthy of exploration, she jotted down "early mild spring," "beech tree seeds" and "poor farming practice."

On a separate piece of paper, she wrote the heading "Why give shelter to an aged aunt." The responses included extreme low maintenance; few possessions; frequent travel; death imminent (she was old); substantial rent offered (with few overheads, she had accumulated a tidy amount in prizes and fees from her doctoral posts). She'd take any room they offered and would put down four years' rent in cash in advance, providing it was far away from her brother and his (forgettable) wife.

2

Moonshot Wharf

MONDAY 30TH JUNE 2008

Blaze Scott stood on her apartment's wraparound terrace overlooking Tower Bridge. It was 9 p.m. and still light and warm. Below her, ant-sized drinkers spilled from pubs onto pavements; in a nearby flat, a group of friends were having a barbecue on a roof garden; through an open window she saw a family eating dinner; two lovers in an adjacent apartment lay entwined on a red sofa; and in a small park at street level, there was a wildly uncompetitive game of rounders. Lighting a cigarette, inhaling deeply, she watched its end sputter and glow a vibrant orange and wished her own life burned as fiercely. The sudden inhalation of acrid smoke made her cough, but she didn't bother to put her hand over her mouth; there was no one to criticise, no one was watching her.

Since she'd acquired Number 5, Moonshot Wharf in 1998 for £250,000, it had quadrupled in value. She hadn't bought it as an investment or for the view; its main attraction was that it had come as an "instant home," fully equipped with everything an owner needed, and a lot they didn't, from silver-plated teaspoons to a four-person Jacuzzi, from the finest Egyptian sheets to a baby grand piano. The apartment was the antithesis of her childhood home Trelawney—another reason Blaze chose it; best to have as few reminders as possible.

When her brother took over the castle in 1988, Blaze, like all daughters and younger sons before her, had been sent away to find a husband or some other life. Arriving at Paddington Station, she'd had nothing: a small suitcase, £50 in cash, a first-class maths degree from Oxford and no idea what to do next.

She looked south towards Canary Wharf. A white plastic bag caught on a breeze wafted perilously close to the water's surface. The tide was low and the shoreline glistened in the late evening's gloaming. Two mudlarkers foraged; each carried a bucket and sifted through the flotsam and jetsam left by the receding water. Blaze had once been down for a closer look and had found an odd shoe, a golf ball and a dead cat. Since then she'd preferred to see the river from up high—looking down on people hurrying to work; buses and taxis delivering their fares; and the boats, from battleships to rubbish barges, passing back and forth. The breeze changed direction, bringing the smell of sulphur and algae up to the penthouse floor. She wished it was later and she could go to bed; she wanted to finish today and get the next over and done with. She decided that one small vodka wouldn't hurt. Just one. In the kitchen she poured a shot and knocked it back, loving the burning feeling in her throat, the rush of tears to her eyes. One more, she decided, and took the second shot back out on the terrace and made an imaginary toast to success in her presentation the following morning when Kerkyra Capital's new owner, the American activist Thomlinson Sleet, would decide which of the senior partners to retain. Blaze had been bitterly opposed to Sleet's takeover; on paper, the deal looked lucrative, each of the key players awarded substantial share options, but in reality, these were realisable only after five years and meant little if her fund tanked during that time. Her concerns were taken on board but overruled by a vote of five senior partners to one.

Over the last year, Blaze had been haemorrhaging money and clients. Once considered the star of Kerkyra Capital and one of the City's most successful stock pickers, she was increasingly written off as an eccentric outlier and a misguided peddler of doom-laden predictions. For twelve months she had been forecasting a massive financial correction, but the markets had kept on rising. When the French bank BNP Paribas froze three of its funds in August 2007, she said it harked back to the origins of the Great Crash of 1929. Nothing changed. A little over a month later there was the first run on a British bank, Northern Rock. Again Blaze foresaw collapse, placing her own and her clients' money into gold only to watch the precious metal's price rise and fall again. She also missed out on a surge of soaring stock-market prices; a share she sold in 2006 for $142 climbed to $235 in October 2007.

Financial markets had always sailed on tides of bravura and promise, but Blaze was convinced the waters were now so shallow and currents so vicious that even the largest and most buoyant institutions should have run aground. Tomorrow's presentation represented the last chance to convince her remaining clients that her intuition was correct: she also had to convince herself. The banks, she'd argue, had borrowed too much. International institutions were too interdependent to withstand the failure of any major institution. There had been a fatal marriage of deregulation and technology; anyone could invent new products but few understood the underlying risks. Blaze had made this speech before but her credibility had been steadily eroded. In 2005 she'd had £2 billion under management; now she was down to less than £1 billion. Her most important clients had migrated to JW Inc., the hedge fund run by the brilliant and reclusive Joshua Wolfe who regularly and consistently outperformed her and the world indices. If her assets under management dipped much lower, she'd be demoted from senior partner to associate. Like others at Kerkyra, her bonus was more significant than her salary; this year she'd be lucky to take anything home.

Blaze went back inside, dragging her toes through the thick white carpet, unstained and still pristine, soft and warm underfoot. Walking through the open-plan living room—a harmony in beige and taupe—past the kitchen with its black marble surfaces and white fitted units, she stopped in the sitting area and looked sadly at a pyramid of rose quartz, a staggeringly expensive and apparently fail-safe way of attracting love, now six years old and yet to work.

Her stomach rumbled and she opened the fridge, hoping the contents would surprise her. They didn't. She was confronted with face products, bottles of vintage champagne, neatly stacked rows of dark chocolate. There was no point buying food just to watch it rot. Most days, Blaze ate lunch and dinner at her office desk. She rarely socialised;

work took precedence over friendships and, without the common currency of spouses, children and hobbies, her conversational arsenal had become impoverished. It was easier to pay shrinks to listen, masseurs to touch her, and, although she knew better, she often mistook her trainer and hairdresser's solicitude for genuine concern. Over the last years, she had pollarded her emotional life, hacking off the limbs of hope and desire and tenderness one by one; even, occasionally, believing this was the life she wanted. A permanent sense of guilt hovered over Blaze like a dank cloud, obliterating most of the rays of her success; she was unjustifiably privileged, her good fortune the result of a freakish mathematical ability. To fend off those feelings, she buried herself in work and, when she wasn't working, she exercised.

Closing the fridge door, Blaze got a sudden glimpse of herself and turned away. Even after forty years, she had yet to get used to the scarred birthmark that ran from below her left eye across her cheek and down her neck. Her father, on seeing his daughter's disfigurement for the first time, had tried to make light of it by naming her after a racehorse that had an irregular blaze across its face. Her mother, appalled by the affliction, scrubbed her baby's cheeks with a mixture of lemon juice and bicarbonate of soda which caused painful lesions. Hearing of a doctor in Plymouth able to treat these conditions, Clarissa allowed him to experiment on her six-year-old child. The skin graft went horribly wrong. The ensuing scarring was worse than the original blight. Corrective surgery and laser treatment had failed. The right side of Blaze's face was beautiful, her hair luxurious, her figure lovely; but, looking at herself in the mirror, all Blaze could see reflected in the door was her puckered skin and her mother's abject disappointment. Tears brimmed in her eyes and spilled on to her cheeks. She dug her nails into the soft flesh of her palm; self-pity was worse even than loneliness.

She had been in love once, in her early twenties, with another mathematician, Tom Barnabus, who had died of cancer. She'd had affairs since then, some longer and more successful than others: the libidinous civil servant who lived in the East End and referred to himself as the Stepney Stallion; the Viennese arms dealer who cried like a baby at the sight of an injured animal; the American documentary film-maker, handsomer and vainer than a matinee idol, who left when she refused to fund his next project; the cross-dressing hedge-funder; the philosopher who kept a cat called Wittgenstein; the younger men who claimed her wrinkles were sexy, the older ones who said the same lines reminded them of their wives or mothers.

As the years passed, Blaze's sense of adventure had become ossified by work and responsibilities, making it harder to meet anyone. Men asked her out but they were inevitably the married, not the marrying, kind. She rarely got a call for a second date; perhaps her need to be loved was too palpable, her loneliness as real and off-putting as a third person in the room. Who, she began to wonder, would mourn her passing? What traces would she leave behind? She had never planted a tree, given birth to a child or put up a building. She wasn't worthy of an obituary and only the dutiful, bored or alcoholics in search of a sherry would attend her funeral. Her cadaver would be interred in the family plot set aside for maiden aunts. Even her career was nebulous: the art of conjuring profits from dreams and failures, trading in stocks and shares, an activity that was invisible to the naked eye and involved moving money from point A to point B for the benefit of a tiny fraction of the population.

She had made weekdays manageable but weekends were a kind of purgatory; what the hell was one supposed to do between Friday night and Monday morning? Occasionally she tried foreign mini-breaks but faced all the same issues with different scenery. For a few months she had volunteered at a homeless hostel until a man complained that the sight of her disfigured face put him off his dinner. Occasionally, Blaze thought about having a child, if only to give her life some non-negotiable coordinates and structure. The regularity of school terms might be comforting and there'd be blessed relief of having something other than oneself to think about. Sense would prevail as she remembered the accompanying mess, noise and detritus, not to mention the utter tedium of bedtime stories, sandpits and play dates. No wonder her mother had outsourced the upbringing of her children to members of staff. After a couple of minutes of agonising, Blaze always reached the same conclusion: better to keep one's figure and the last vestiges of sanity.

Wandering aimlessly through her apartment, Blaze went to her library and looked through the shelves of unread novels, self-help books and biographies bought in fits of unsustained enthusiasm for their given subjects. Glancing down the spines of her collection of one thousand DVDs, she failed to find a title that tickled her imagination. She made a list of all the people she'd slept with (short) and those who'd rejected her (almost the same length) and stalked them on Facebook. She read half an article about how sandwiches were eating culture, which made her feel hungry. In the kitchen cupboard, there was a box of Frosties, well beyond its sell-by date but preserved by sugar. With no milk, she added vodka, a delicious combination, and, in the highly unlikely event that she ever gave a dinner party, Blaze resolved to serve "Froska" as a pudding.

It was only 9:15 p.m., too early to take a sleeping pill. She eyed the bottle of vodka, considering taking another shot. Only then, she noticed the letter, left presumably by her cleaner, which had slipped down behind a bowl. The handwriting was a ghostly echo from another time. She read the sender's name, Anastasia, and a shadow raced over her heart. Images from their last encounter, twenty years ago, flashed across her mind. Unable to face the onslaught of memories, let alone the contents, Blaze crumpled the letter in her hand and dropped it into the bin.

The "Froska" pudding had made her drunk and, holding lightly on to furniture for support, she went back out onto the terrace. She tried to conjure up numbers and figures for the next day's presentation, but all she could see was the blue envelope. Against her better judgement, she fished it out of the rubbish and smoothed it on the marble worktop. The postmark said Balakpur, Orissa. Tearing open the envelope, Blaze sat down at the kitchen counter and read.

Dear Blaze,

Thanks to the internet, I have followed your many successes. Businesswoman of the Year two years in a row, youngest senior partner of Kerkyra Capital, guest speaker at important international conferences, panel member and leader in the world of finance. Each time I see one of these accolades, I feel a stab of undeserved, vicarious pride. I've not been able to find out much about your personal life; maybe you have married, maybe you have children.

I suspect Jane is following in the noble tradition of all Trelawney countesses, sitting under the watchful eye of a great Gainsborough in Trelawney's dining room, ordering an egg, reading an ironed newspaper, discussing menus with Cook, working out the evening's placement. Once I yearned for that kind of life, now it seems like death by boredom.

Since we last saw each other I've had many adventures. I worked in a refugee camp, lived like a gypsy, walked over the Himalayas, wrote four books (unpublished) and, as you know, I married a maharaja (I was sorry you couldn't attend our wedding—it was quite a spectacle). It wasn't the scenario I imagined or wanted but it's been interesting. Now that I find myself so perilously close to death, I cling to life with a savage desperation. I thought something big would get me—a war or an avalanche, not a disease eating my insides out. I am not ready. I am far from ready.

Blaze put the letter down. It had been a long time since she had thought about Anastasia. Since "the incident," Blaze had tried to erase her erstwhile friend from her mind—now Anastasia had the nerve to try and inveigle herself back into her life. Did the woman think that she would be welcome, after all that had happened? Blaze shook with fury and the words blurred. She turned the pages quickly, her eyes skipping over various paragraphs until the last line. *I am imploring you to take in my daughter.* Blaze jumped back as if scalded and tore the letter into tiny pieces, ran outside and threw them off her terrace, watched the tiny shreds of paper flutter away on a passing breeze. Gone, she thought, good riddance. Her heart was beating fast and the effects of the vodka dispelled. After nearly twenty years of determined exorcism, Anastasia was back in her thoughts.

Blaze needed to talk to someone, but who apart from the main protagonists would understand? Her next therapy appointment was not until Friday, four days away, so she called her American psychic. Madame Alvira. Blaze regarded mediums as many agnostics considered God: with equal degrees of hope and scepticism.

"Shall I put the charge to your American Express?" Madame Alvira asked through a mouthful of food.

"Yes."

"Whaddya need to know?" Alvira's accent betrayed a Bronx background.

"A long-lost dying friend has written, asking me to bring up her child. I don't know what to do."

"Let me consult the oracles." Alvira rustled noisily among some papers. After a few minutes she spoke in her "I'm doing a reading" sing-song voice. "There's a young fox that has nearly crossed the stream when its tail gets wet. Firm correctness leads to good fortune. Let him stir himself up as if he were invading the demon's region where for three years rewards will come from the great kingdom."

Blaze wrote down what the psychic said.

"There might be progress and success if he shows me sincerity that makes recourse to divination. Or there might be trouble. There might be stillness and warmth or there might be danger in the unknown." The medium stopped. "D'you get that?" she asked, reverting to her Bronx accent.

"I don't understand what it means?" Blaze was confused.

"You asked me to consult the oracles, not to give advice. If you want advice, that'll be another $500. Now, I have another call waiting so can you make your mind up?"

"I'd like your advice."

"Shall I charge the same American Express?"

"Yes."

"What do you know about the kid?" Alvira asked.

"I don't even know how old it is."

"Sounds like a very bad idea indeed."

"That's what I thought."

"Maybe it would be nice to extend your circle? What about your family? You strike me as kind of lonely."

Blaze didn't respond.

"My family drives me nuts but they're the only thing I got," Alvira said.

Thinking about her parents and brother made Blaze's throat contract and her heart beat faster. Was it possible to hate and miss people simultaneously?

"You have an opportunity to help someone, and if there's one thing I've learned in life," Alvira continued, "it's better to be needed than wanted. Desire and romantic love pass, leaving little trace. But dependency has an afterglow, the satisfaction of having done something good." She shuffled some papers on her desk. "Is there anything else?"

Blaze hesitated. "I wonder if you could look at my romantic life?"

"It's best to let a few weeks pass before doing that again. Don't want to annoy the oracles."

"I suppose not."

"I have to go." The psychic hung up.

Putting down the telephone, Blaze felt a peculiar heaviness. Twenty years had passed since she'd seen Anastasia or her brother and sister-in-law; wasn't time supposed to heal? If only she could let those images go. She looked at her phone: it was ten o'clock. Going into her dressing room, she pushed open the sliding doors to her wardrobe and looked at the rows of almost identical black suits and white silk shirts. Perhaps, if she got through tomorrow, she might go shopping for another colour. She laughed at herself, knowing that would never happen. She ran through her notes for tomorrow's presentation one last time, got into bed, took two sleeping pills and turned out the light.

3

The Train Journey

TUESDAY 1ST JULY 2008

As the train passed into a tunnel, Kitto, who had been looking out of the window, was confronted with his own reflection. Once considered extremely handsome, beautiful even, the middle-aged man with the lined face, bloodshot eyes and thinning hair who stared back at him was so unexpected that he winced and shrank into his second-class seat. He was only forty-three years old; who was this cadaver? What had happened to the luxuriant auburn hair, the hazel eyes, the high cheekbones and wide, slightly fleshy mouth? Kitto felt like a person who had mistakenly wandered into a fairground attraction, a hall of distorting mirrors. The only comfort was that she wasn't here to witness his decline; he hoped her memories of him were preserved in the aspic of time.

The train left the tunnel and the monstrous image disappeared. Passing from Cornwall into Devon, the carriages rumbled along only a few feet from the seashore, travelling through small coastal towns. Kitto watched a lacy tide lapping a pebbly beach, a couple throwing a ball into the water for their dog to fetch and moored sailboats bobbing on a slight swell. He remembered days out to Teignmouth with his sister Blaze and their nanny, riding donkeys and crabbing in rock pools, and wished he had spent more time with his own children following similar pursuits. The train track turned inland and the coastline was replaced by hedgerows fluffy with hawthorn flowers, verges stacked with swaying cow parsley and grasses, lambs playing in acid-green fields laced with buttercups. Two horses, frightened by the train, wheeled around in their paddock and galloped away, their hooves throwing up clods of soft ground. Inside Carriage C, the temperature was kept at a constant 18 degrees; outside it looked considerably warmer. If only this train were going the other way—towards home, to Cornwall. He was the first Trelawney who had had to seek employment outside the estates or the House of Lords. It was dashed unfair but at least the drudgery was about to end.

In the next seat a young woman was listening to music, and a tinny noise relentlessly bled out of her headphones. Kitto looked at his watch—it was two and a half hours to London. He wanted a cup of tea but at £2.20 it seemed like a luxury too far. As Chairman of Acorn, the West Country bank, he was entitled to first-class railway tickets and, though he claimed this perk, he travelled in second and pocketed the difference, a useful £6,000 per year. As soon as my new investments come good, he thought, stretching out his legs as far as the second-class seat would permit, I'll be back in First Class. His father and grandparents used to hitch the family's own coach on to the London train, loaded up with retainers, clothes, bedlinen and the best china to make their town mansion appear a little bit like home. The Earls and their families hated leaving Cornwall but it was, at times, a necessary evil: when the House of Lords was sitting or a child needed to find an eligible spouse.

Outside the window, the sun, rising over gentle hills, cast long shadows and the trees were unruffled by wind. His family had once owned thousands of acres of this fertile land, all lost in one night on the gambling table. "Just make sure the sun doesn't set on your watch," Kitto's father had warned him over and over again. "Don't let the pride and glory of twenty-five generations end with you." To make his point, the old man pinched Kitto's arm so hard that the bruise lasted for weeks. If only his threat had also faded from black to purple to green and yellow, but it hung like a noxious vapour over his son's life.

When Enyon had handed the running of the estate over to his son and heir ten years earlier, Kitto found that the cupboard was almost empty; there was no money and few easily disposable assets. He was presiding over the end of a dynasty and eight hundred years of hegemony, and, as the last man standing, knew he'd be blamed. He felt powerless but not culpable: someone had given him a beautiful toy without batteries included. Unsuited to remaking the fortune, Kitto had done the next best thing: he had married for money—and compromised his own right to be happy for the sake of the house. Blaze resented her brother for inheriting Trelawney; he envied her for breaking free.

The train rolled on, mile after mile, until, looking out of the window, Kitto saw the familiar shape of Reading Gaol and, lined up in the station car park, neat formations: rows of black or silver Mercedes, Range Rovers and Bentleys. His own car was a ten-year-old Passat.

He really wanted the tea. If he walked from Paddington to the office, he'd save the Tube fare—about the same amount of money. Tapping his neighbour on her shoulder, he got out of his seat and made his way through the carriages, past the businessmen hunched over their computers, the young lovers entwined, the dummied toddlers, wriggling babies and an elderly woman engrossed in a copy of *The Lady.* At the buffet car, the queue was mercifully short. Looking towards First Class, Kitto saw a stack of unread *Times* newspapers. Surely no one would mind, he thought, edging towards them. Just as he reached out to take the top copy, a hand clapped on his shoulder with such force that Kitto's legs nearly gave way.

"Hello, mate," a voice behind him boomed.

Mate? Kitto wondered if this was how the train police tried to sound contemporary.

"Kitto? It *is* you, isn't it?" the voice asked.

Very slowly, Kitto turned around. The man before him was dressed in the uniform of the international super-rich: jeans and a jacket. It was beautifully cut cashmere but couldn't hide the rolls of fat. The man wore a gold Rolex and, on his pinkie finger, a signet ring. He had short hair, a lightly tanned face and beady little eyes set in undistinguished features. Kitto knew with absolute certainty that the package—the jacket, the tan, the white T-shirt, the firm hand—reeked of importance. Whoever this person was—he was a somebody.

"Thomlinson Sleet, we met at Oxford. March 22nd, 1988. I was a pimply Rhodes scholar, hot off the boat from the U.S. A day I'll never forget."

"Of course, of course," Kitto said, although he had no recollection.

"I didn't see you, must have walked straight past. Come and have a spot of breakfast," Sleet said and, without waiting for an answer, turned and headed back towards First Class. Kitto wanted to say no—he wanted to turn and run, tea-less, back to the safety and anonymity of Carriage C. Instead he followed. Sleet had sequestered two facing seats in the Pullman car.

"Jim," Sleet called over the waiter. "This is Viscount Tremayne—bring him the works, please."

Kitto saw a moment's hesitation in Jim's face—he had been trained to spot an interloper from Second Class—but whatever reservations he had were quickly overcome.

"Sit down, sit down, tell me about the last two decades. Who did you marry in the end? I assume it was the beauteous Anastasia."

Kitto swallowed hard. "She went to India and never came back."

"Did she marry a prince?"

"I heard she married a maharaja."

"You keep in touch?"

"Only through the gossip columns." Anastasia never responded to his letters but he'd never stopped writing.

Sleet hesitated. "What was it about her brand of beauty that was so bewitching? I suppose it was that Russian blood. And her backstory: weren't her parents spies, killed in mysterious circumstances?"

"A plane crash," Kitto said. "When she was eleven." Nearly twenty years had passed since their last meeting, but his obsession had hardly dimmed with time.

"There are plenty of pretty girls . . . what was it about her?" Sleet leaned across the table and jabbed his finger at Kitto. "The two of you together were a poster for perfection. You dark and moodily aristocratic, her a perfect golden spirit."

"It might have looked like that from the outside." Kitto could only remember his increasingly desperate attempts to persuade Anastasia to love him and his ultimate failure.

Both men fell silent. Sleet tapped the table hard with his fork.

"You don't remember, do you? That makes it even worse." He clenched and unclenched his fist and, for a moment, Kitto thought Sleet might strike him.

"I'm sorry—I don't know what you're talking about."

Sleet shook his head and didn't answer. Jim brought a full English breakfast. "Tea or coffee?"

"Tea—thank you."

Sleet speared some blueberries on a fork and dipped them in a pot of yoghurt.

"Aren't you having a cooked breakfast?" Kitto asked.

"Fuck, no. My trainer would kill me and the wife would run off with him. That's the problem with being married to a younger woman—you have to keep up with them."

"How old is she?"

"Twenty-eight—you've heard of her? Calypso Newsome—exVictoria's Secret. Now Lady Sleet."

"You're a knight?"

"Can't you tell?" He used his fork to imitate a sword and pretended to ennoble his coffee pot, touching it on the right, the left and then on the lid.

"What did you get it for?"

"For services to industry, which as we all know means giving funds to the dear old Tory party."

"Well done, you." Kitto raised his cup.

"I'd rather be a viscount or an earl but any amount of money doesn't buy that now."

"I'd sell it to you happily," Kitto said, wondering if his titles were worth anything.

"Who did you marry?"

"Jane Browne."

"Plain Jane Browne? The dumpy one?" Sleet looked surprised. "Are you still married?"

"We are."

Sleet looked even more surprised. "You've done better than me—I'm on number three. A different mother for each brace."

"What are you doing in this part of the world?"

"I own an enormous house near Reading. Not as big as yours, but a few more mod cons and a hell of a lot more acres. How's your farm?"

"Difficult," Kitto admitted.

"It's all a question of scale, isn't it?" Sleet said, as if reading Kitto's thoughts. "I have fifty thousand acres spread all over the world."

"Fifty thousand?" Kitto repeated, trying not to spray his host with half-digested eggs.

"Fifty-three thousand four hundred, to be precise. It's all about IHT for me."

"IHT?"

"Inheritance tax." Sleet skewered a few more blueberries. "I can recommend a good tax planner if you want; she's saved me a fortune."

Oh, to need a tax planner or have millions to save, Kitto grimaced. He broke the yolk of his egg and used his sausage to mop it up. If he ate enough breakfast, he might skip the lunchtime sandwich. His thoughts turned to his eldest son's school fees and the oil bill—both unpaid.

"Land is one of the most cost-effective ways of leaving money to the next generation. But farming's such a bloody awful business that I have diversified by buying in different parts of the world. I have farms in Australia, Europe, America, the West Indies, just about anywhere. I grow all sorts, from hazelnuts to blueberries to corn."

"Have you been to them all?" Kitto asked.

"Only if there's an Aman hotel nearby." Sleet roared with laughter. "In fact I own a few parcels of your old estates."

"You do?" Kitto didn't remember selling any of the land to a man named Sleet and supposed it would all have been done via a company.

"Remind me how you made your money in the first place?"

"I'm a prize cunt, otherwise known as an activist." Sleet laughed at his own joke. "I buy flabby old businesses, break them up, rescue the good bits and flog off the dregs. If I can't buy something then I look for distressed situations. If there's money to be made off other people's messes, I'm the first in."

Kitto wondered if great success only came to odious individuals.

"What are you up to, apart from farming?" Sleet asked.

Kitto leaned back in his seat and pressed his hands together, wondering how to make his own portfolio of activities sound more impressive. "I've diversified over the years. I've created housing estates; I'm big in strawberries, given the Spanish a good run for their money; have a few hydroelectric plants, that kind of thing. Recently I became Chairman of Acorn Bank, the oldest institution in the West Country."

"I've heard of it," Sleet said half-heartedly "It was a building society that turned itself into a bank? Most of its funding comes from the wholesale market."

Kitto nodded. "We made pre-tax profits last year of £52 million."

"What's your AUM?"

Kitto swallowed hard. He found financial terminology confusing. Over the centuries, the City had developed its own language, a patois sprinkled with acronyms and arcane shorthand. At first Kitto had been in awe of those who spoke it fluently, but realised quickly that the highfalutin words and terms were a way to aggrandise simple ideas and confuse outsiders. Though he'd made a huge effort to learn the lexicon, the misunderstanding of one simple term could render a whole conversation meaningless.

"We manage approximately £2 billion." He hoped that was the right amount.

"Mostly from retail depositors?"

Kitto nodded. Tiny beads of sweat broke out on his neck. Please don't let him ask any more technical questions, I am only the Chairman, he thought.

"You must have shat your pants after the collapse of Northern Rock?"

"Why do you say that?"

"Your portfolios are similar, lots of CDOs, sub-primes, issues with debt covenants; all the usual stuff," Sleet said, helping himself to Kitto's toast and smothering it with marmalade.

"Obviously," Kitto said, making a mental note to ask his CEO to translate this jargon.

"Coincidentally, I've just bought your sister's company. On my way there now to shake things up a little."

"Blaze?" Kitto's hand froze, leaving his fork loaded with egg and sausage hovering between his plate and mouth.

"Careful," Sleet said, as a drip of yolk fell on to Kitto's shirt. "Too late." Sleet waved at Jim. "Bring him a damp cloth."

Kitto took the proffered cloth and dabbed furiously at his shirt; he'd only brought one spare to last the week.

Sleet leaned towards Kitto. "What's the intel on Blaze? She used to have a great reputation. Sharp as a tack. One of the best in the business, but she's lost her touch. Are there personal issues? Death of a child? Cocaine? I've got to think whether to keep her on."

"What's she calling wrong?" Kitto asked, wishing he was close enough to his sister to ask her advice.

"She keeps giving interviews saying the markets, particularly the banks, are in deep shit, that we're in a bubble that's about to pop."

Kitto felt even larger beads of sweat prickle on his back and hairline. The yolk had become an insignificant problem; all his worldly goods and a lot of borrowed assets were in a property bond named FG1, which he'd been assured was from a 100 per cent safe income-yielding fund.

"Is there anything in what she says?" he asked, trying to keep his voice level.

Sleet shrugged nonchalantly. "Maybe. I look at every prevailing wind as an opportunity to make money. If there's a crash, I'll scalp the schmucks."

Reaching into his briefcase, Sleet took out a business card embossed with a coronet and his name, Thomlinson Sleet. There were no numbers or email addresses. Kitto looked at it closely. Under the name, in very small letters, he read: "And who the fuck are you?" Sleet bellowed with laughter.

"Genius, no? Wedding present from the third Lady Sleet. Now you see why I married her." He hesitated. "For you, I'll do the unthinkable and give you my PA's number." He whipped the card away and, turning it over, wrote a mobile number on the back.

"Can I ask you a favour?" Kitto said. "My son Ambrose needs some work experience this summer. Would you have anything? It doesn't matter how menial." He could only imagine how furious his eldest would be, having to forgo a summer at home in Cornwall.

Sleet smiled. "I love the idea of having a posh git fetching me tea and coffee. He can start whenever. Call my secretary. She'll fix it."

"Thanks."

Sleet glanced at his watch. "Got to do a bit of work now. See you later. Chin-chin." He looked down at his papers.

Realising he was being dismissed, Kitto got to his feet. Yolk-stained, humiliated and frightened, he made his way back to his seat. By the time he sat down, the train was trundling through the outskirts of London, past row upon row of red-brick houses. Was his sister correct? Had he, like so many others, bought into a worthless bond? Was it possible that he stood to lose everything? He thought momentarily about cashing in his investments but was reminded that he was Chairman of Acorn Bank, a person of discernment, a man who operated above and beyond tittle-tattle heard on a train to London.

It had been some time since Kitto had thought about Blaze. Occasionally he saw her profile in one of the financial pages and looked with interest at her photograph: where had the wild-haired, farouche woman gone? Was she buried under the highly packaged corporate façade of a sharp suit and lacquered hair? If it wasn't for her face, he wouldn't have recognised her. He missed her but knew that Blaze would never take his call. If only she'd tried harder to understand that he had never abandoned her; it was only a bedroom, an old aristocratic tradition. It hadn't been personal.

The train slowed slightly and the carriage filled with the acrid smell of diesel on brakes. The girl next to him pulled her polo neck over her nose. Kitto wondered whether to change into his one clean shirt in the train or wait until he reached the office. At Paddington, he walked across the park to St. James's. Although it was only the end of June, the grass had turned bare and yellow, and was littered with leftover picnics, beer bottles and rubbish. A woman tried unsuccessfully to control the greedy impulses of her dog. Two young policemen circled a comatose tramp. As he walked, Kitto thought about Sleet's prediction. "Most fuckers will lose their shirts, a few will cream it." Please, dear God, Kitto prayed, don't let me be one of the fuckers.

4

The Presentation

TUESDAY 1ST JULY 2008

Following her daily 55-minute workout, Blaze walked into Kerkyra Capital at 7:10 a.m. The offices were built around a thirty-floor glass atrium. There were full-sized palm trees, a waterfall and the piped sound of the jungle. When the building had been opened by a minor royal four years earlier, there had been real birds but this had proved unhygienic. Inside the reception area, ten elegantly dressed women sat behind a sixty-foot desk made from carved marble moulded into the shape of galloping horses. "Good morning, Blaze," the receptionists cried out in unison.

Blaze nodded curtly. At the security barrier, her PA Donna waited with the day's files, briefing her as the lift shot up to the nineteenth floor where her senior adviser, TiLing Tang, was checking through the morning's presentation.

"Nothing to report from the Far East," TiLing said, passing over printouts from the early-morning trades in the Japanese markets.

"How's Joshua Wolfe doing?" Blaze asked, dreading the answer. Wolfe was the unofficial benchmark against whom she measured her performance. His daring calls, his split-second timing and audacious decisions were legendary. Five years earlier, she and Wolfe had been neck and neck, two great stars watched by all, but in recent times he had steadily and inexorably outperformed her.

"He called it right again. Up another 5 per cent this week." TiLing, like Blaze, was obsessed by Wolfe and spent many hours checking and cross-checking his investments.

"How?"

"As far as I can tell, by the usual combination of market and stock-specific judgement calls." TiLing shrugged. Without full access to Wolfe's portfolio, it was impossible to find out what the maverick investor was up to.

Blaze groaned with irritation, wondering if Wolfe had some kind of insider information. He never seemed to put a foot wrong.

They spent the next couple of hours going over Blaze's presentation, cross-referencing her notes and arguments. At two minutes to eleven, the receptionist buzzed upstairs to say that most of the clients had arrived. Blaze checked her make-up in a small compact mirror and applied another layer of cover-up over her scar. At 11 a.m. precisely she entered the auditorium, then, looking calm and strikingly beautiful, walked across the stage and smiled at the audience.

She had just begun her presentation when Thomlinson Sleet came into the room.

"Don't mind me!" he shouted out, and brought her talk to a halt while he spent a few minutes greeting and shaking the hands of many guests. Making his way to the front of the auditorium, he stood directly in front of Blaze and made an announcement. "As most of you know, I just bought Kerkyra Capital, so its £30 billion under management is now part of the Sleet Empire and so are its pretty little slaves." Looking at Blaze, he winked. She blushed deeply. Her discomfort made him laugh. "Kerkyra has done well, but it's going to do a hell of a lot better. Year on year this hedge fund has outperformed its rivals, delivering Alpha to its clients. But what is a hedge fund? It doesn't own anything. Its USP is built on two things—the quality of its employees and its track record. I intend to make it the best. We'll blow Joshua Wolfe out of the market; the guy's had a run of good luck but he's dead meat. Kerkyra is going to be even bigger than BlackRock; I'm going to turn this business into the greatest money-management company in the world."

His speech was greeted with applause. Sleet raised his hands and, smiling, turned to Blaze.

"Haven't seen you for a few years. Glad you've kept your figure. Guess you're still riding those horses." Pleased by his own innuendo, Sleet laughed again, accompanied this time by the mostly male audience. Blaze flushed red from embarrassment. She couldn't remember meeting the man before.

It took a few minutes to regain her composure and for the room to settle. Standing at the front of the stage, Blaze hoped the microphone couldn't pick up her clattering heart. Clearing her throat and fixing her features in a smile, she started again.

"The City is full of brilliant people. Many are here today, but have we been too clever? Have we created the means to destroy ourselves?" She had got their attention. "Think of markets as an old-fashioned steam engine needing an endless supply of logs to make it run. Those logs can be made of wood, or stocks and shares, of gold or currency. These instruments are finite, so clever people thought: why not free the markets from antiquated metrics and create something synthetic and endlessly malleable?" Blaze spoke in a low voice, wanting her audience to strain to catch her words, to have to concentrate.

"The most audacious examples of these new creations are CDOs, or Collateralised Debt Obligations. What the hell does that mean? How many here can explain it?" She looked around the room at the many blank faces.

Sleet jumped to his feet. "Stop treating us like schoolchildren; get to the point, if you have one." A smattering of laughter broke out. Blaze flushed with irritation. Just because the man had bought the company didn't give him the right to heckle the staff.

"Sir Thomlinson," she said in a polite but icy tone, "perhaps you'd tell us what a CDO is? Or a sub-prime mortgage, given that you bought several million pounds' worth only yesterday?" There was a sharp intake of breath from her colleagues, unable to believe that Blaze was challenging their new owner so brazenly and in public.

"I don't give a damn what it is," Sleet said, laughing. "All I care is that it keeps on going up in value."

Blaze shook her head ruefully. "There are hundreds of billions' worth of CDOs in the market and yet hardly anyone knows what they are or what they do. I am not—don't worry—going to give you a boring lecture, but a CDO is a bundle of disparate loans which yield interest. All well and good until the underlying value collapses and you're left with no income and no asset." Out of the corner of her eye Blaze saw Sleet's expression darken. She wondered if she should soften her stance—after all, the man had the power to fire her—but she had spent so long preparing her pitch, and was too keen to prove her point, to alter her course.

She cleared her throat. "One of the world's oldest and most venerable invesment banks, Bear Stearns, bought two hedge funds specialising in CDOs. In 2007 its shares were valued at $172; just over a year later you could buy them for $2. That was the end of the Bear; nearly eighty-five years of history eviscerated. And yet the lesson wasn't heeded; Lehman Brothers, the fourth-largest bank in the sector, has borrowed over thirty times its capital. Every single day it has to raise millions just to pay the interest. All their energies, their profits and, more worryingly, some of their assets have to go into restructuring their borrowings. Employees go home each night not knowing if there'll be enough money to trade the following day."

Looking around the room, Blaze saw concerned faces staring back at her. Even Sleet was momentarily lost for words.

Blaze swallowed. "The whole system is perilously close to collapse. I don't think this is the eve of the dot-com crisis or the Tuesday before Black Wednesday: this is an abyss as dark as 1929."

There was an outburst in the room.

"Hang on, hang on!" Sleet stood up slowly from his chair like an omnipotent Neptune rising above a sea of worried faces. "How do you explain that the stock market hit a seven-year high last year, followed by an all-time high on the Dow last fall?" He sat down heavily.

Blaze looked at him without blinking. "Everyone has puffed up their earnings and underplayed their losses."

"Everyone?" Sleet sneered.

"I don't think Lehman will last till Christmas. I'd put Goldman on the critical list."

There was a gasp of horror at the mention of Goldman Sachs, long seen as the ultimate blue-chip safe bank managed by titans of the universe.

In two great bounds, Sleet left his seat and climbed onto the stage. He didn't speak at first but shook his head in mock disbelief. As his chin moved side to side, the rolls of his stomach undulated. Taking a handkerchief from his pocket, he mopped his damp brow.

"My name, as you all know, is Thomlinson Sleet. I'm the adopted son of a Catholic vacuum salesman from Delaware. I was not born in a castle, like my colleague Lady Blaze Scott. My family were so poor that I didn't own a pair of shoes until I was thirteen. Four of my seven brothers ended up in jail. Three of my nine sisters got knocked up before their fourteenth birthday. I didn't get a double first in mathematics at Oxford like her but I did get to that venerable university on a Rhodes Scholarship to read physics. Do you remember the last time we met, Lady Blaze?"

Blaze shook her head, unable to recall anyone matching his description.

"Odd how a single shared event can transform one life and leave no trace on another's." Shrugging, Sleet returned to his main theme.

"I don't want to do a colleague down, but let's compare results. Last year my investment portfolio was up 32 per cent and Miss—sorry, Lady—Scott's was a bit stagnant at 9 per cent. This year, and it's only July and things have been a bit tricky; yeah, I am up 18 per cent and she is down 2 per cent. Apart from the fact that I own this company, these are my qualifications: my crenellations."

The room roared its approval. Sleet held up his hand to quiet everyone. Blaze wanted to walk out of the auditorium but sat in her chair with a fixed smile.

"Lady Scott is a doom merchant. Last year she took her money off the table and missed out on the biggest rises in the market." Sleet made a mock sympathetic smile towards Blaze. "Now, gentlemen—and let's accept it, nearly all of you here are gentlemen—what our lovely friend doesn't know is anything about team sports. Let's talk about something we blokes have in common; let's talk about soccer."

Blaze could hardly believe what she was hearing. Was Sleet intent on presenting a serious financial meltdown in footballing terms? Casting a glance around the audience, she saw many leaning forward with a look of delighted anticipation.

"We men like to back teams, through thick and thin, and that's why the U.S. Treasury will never let their side go down. The boys from Goldman Sachs run the world. Guess where Bush's Treasury Secretary Hank Paulson and his Chief of Staff Joshua Bolten were trained? And John Thain at Merrill? And the Governor of New Jersey? And Robert Zoellick, head of the World Bank? And Mario Draghi, head of the Bank of Italy? Tito Mboweni, Governor of the South African Reserve Bank? And Mark Carney, Governor of the Bank of Canada? Yes, Team bloody Goldman. Guess where I was trained and where I made my first million? Same place. We are the best and we are not going to let our own kind go down."

The crowd bellowed with laughter and the atmosphere in the room changed. Blaze saw that the worried faces had gone; Sleet had reassured them.

Sleet paused. "There are a few little issues but, as my friend Hank said the other day, 'I do believe that the worst is likely to be behind us.' In the meantime, what do we do?"

He paused again for dramatic effect. He walked around the stage. His audience were mesmerised.

"I'll tell you what we do—we'll go out there and make loads of money."

The room burst into spontaneous applause. One or two got to their feet.

"What is the Chinese definition of the word crisis? It is opportunity and, fuck me, there is a whole load of opportunity begging to be taken. I love a bit of volatility; that's how, as you Brits like to say, we make dosh."

The audience stood as one and stamped their feet. Blaze's colleagues, with whom she had worked and built the company for the last fifteen years, turned their backs on her. Unable to stand it a moment longer, Blaze left the auditorium with as much dignity as she could muster. Her face burned red and she traced her fingers along the wall to steady herself. Pushing open the door, she made it through and, out of sight, waited to see if any of her clients would follow. Only TiLing came. They walked in silence back to her office.

"I am—" TiLing said.

Blaze raised her hand. "Please don't say anything."

TiLing nodded.

They sat in Blaze's office, waiting for the phone to ring or for another colleague to put their head around the door to offer words of consolation. At 12 p.m., a client emailed to say that they were moving their portfolio, valued at £50 million, from Blaze's account to another senior partner recommended by Sleet. Throughout the afternoon, others confirmed their decision to look for alternative management within the firm. By 5 p.m., all but one of Blaze's eighteen clients, worth a total of £270 million, had moved. Without any portfolios to look after, her income would cease.

With little else to do but wait, she googled Thomlinson Sleet and was confronted by walls of images of Sleet with beautiful women, larger and larger boats; or with captains of industry and political leaders. She put in the name Tommy B. Sleet and a smudged image from a college yearbook came up. She leaned in close to study the man's features, to find the grown-up in the pudgy, ginger-haired, spotty youth wearing an ill-fitting suit, a shirt whose collar was a size too small and a tie the shape of a Dover sole. In a flash, the incident came back to her: Oxford, June 1988—Kitto had been visiting his sister and her friends Jane and Anastasia, and the four of them were drinking in Anastasia's third-floor room. There was a frantic tapping and rustling at the open window. A young man, bulbous in shape, dressed in synthetic trousers and a brown shirt with a rose clamped between his teeth, slithered through the narrow gap and landed on the floor at their feet. Apparently unperturbed by his inelegant arrival or the presence of three other people in the room, the would-be suitor heaved himself up on to one knee and, swishing his rose to the left and right, declared undying love to Anastasia. He held out his token of admiration but the rose, exhausted by its journey, drooped and its petals fell off into a desultory little heap at her feet. Twenty years later, Blaze couldn't remember which of them laughed first but, once they started, it had been impossible to stop. The suitor got slowly and painfully to his feet, brushed the dust off his trousers and tried to cajole his hair back into some kind of order. He went to the door and, before leaving, very solemnly told Anastasia, "The name is Tommy B. Sleet. Don't forget it."

Blaze pushed her chair back. No wonder the man disliked her.

At that moment, Sleet walked into her office. He didn't say hello or even wave a hand in greeting. Instead he looked around as if he owned the place; which, of course, he did.

"Interesting that you have no mementos, no pictures of loved ones or personal effects," he said, glancing at the empty shelves and surfaces.

"I like to concentrate on work," Blaze replied. Once or twice she'd been tempted to bring in a framed photograph of a handsome stranger for appearance's sake.

"Do you live up to your nickname? A Blaze Runner? Are you like Ridley Scott's automatons, a person with no feelings or emotions?"

Blaze winced; if only it were true.

Sleet sat down on the edge of her desk, his corpulent behind spreading over her paperwork. Idly, he picked up a pencil and snapped it in half. "By keeping your portfolio liquid, you've missed out on a great rise in the market. If I'd put £100 million in your fund a year ago, I'd have lost a fortune."

"I don't count fantasy numbers," Blaze said. "You're referring to a lost opportunity. If those games were real, we'd all be multibillionaires."

"I *am* a multibillionaire," he replied. "And, for the record, I don't play games." He leaned in towards her, apparently smiling, but although his mouth stretched to reveal white, even teeth, his eyes were hard and unblinking.

"I presume you're firing me," Blaze said, making a huge effort to keep her voice steadier than her spirits.

"Making money is not about calling it right, it's about calling it at the right time." He grinned. Picking up a second pencil, he broke it into three pieces and lined them up in a neat row in front of Blaze.

"I'm busy, why don't you get to the point?" She rearranged the broken pencils into a triangle.

"I'm cutting your bonus to ten basis points."

Blaze grimaced. With her fund down to less than £30 million, her bonus would be reduced to £30,000 a year. Less than she spent on personal trainers, shrinks and Madame Alvira.

"That's insulting. My colleagues are on a hundred basis points."

"Take it or leave it."

"I'll leave it."

Sleet paused for the first time. When he did speak, he leaned forward, his breath smelling of hamburger. "Getting flouncy doesn't suit you."

"Is this about the Anastasia incident?" Blaze asked. "It was a long time ago."

"You finally remembered."

"There were so many men . . ." Blaze said.

Sleet threw back his head and roared with laughter. "For you and your ilk, it was an amusing little incident; for me, it was life-defining: it made me who I am today. Walking away from those college rooms, I promised myself never, ever to let anyone belittle me again. You should rethink my offer, Blaze; you won't get a better one." He got up and walked out of the room.

Blaze didn't have time to reflect. Seconds later, TiLing put her head around the door and, hardly able to contain her excitement, said, "I've got Joshua Wolfe on the line."

"Are you sure?" Blaze asked. Wolfe was a recluse who lived, as far as anyone knew, in a guarded estate near Aylesbury. The only definite information was that he was in his fifties and had come to the UK as a young man. There was one smudgy photograph of him on the internet, and all his staff had to sign privacy notices agreeing not to disclose any information about their employer or his practices. Rumours abounded that he was a hunchback or a cripple, that he suffered an allergy to light and lived like a troglodyte in the cellar of his stately home.

"It could be a prank," TiLing admitted.

"Put him through." What was one more humiliation, to add to all the others? She picked up the receiver on her desk.

"Blaze Scott?" the voice asked. "This is Joshua Wolfe."

"How can I help you?" she said curtly.

"I didn't like the way Sleet spoke to you earlier," Wolfe continued, dispensing with any further introduction.

"Were you in the audience?" Blaze hadn't seen his name on the list of attendees.

"That's irrelevant," Wolfe said. "There are two types of investor: the market chasers, and those who take a longer and more considered view. I like the second type and I liked your analysis." He paused. "The winds are changing. I think your predictions are correct. Would you be interested in teaming up on some joint investments?"

Blaze inhaled slowly. It was a tempting offer. "I have a non-compete clause with this company and would automatically forfeit my bonus and options if I leave."

"Those golden handcuffs will be worthless if your colleagues maintain their present course and, from what I hear, your sails have been trimmed."

"You're startlingly well-informed, Mr. Wolfe." Where, she wondered, was he getting this information? She looked enquiringly at TiLing who shrugged her shoulders.

For the first time in the conversation, Wolfe hesitated. "Come have lunch with me and we'll discuss it further."

"That would be a pleasure," Blaze replied, intrigued.

"I'm busy with the harvest at the moment but I'll be in touch when I have most of the wheat in."

Blaze wondered if he was teasing her. What would a man like Wolfe know about cereal crops?

"Agreed?" he asked.

"I look forward to it," Blaze said. Meeting the reclusive investor would make a good story, even if nothing else came of it.

5

Attics

TUESDAY 8TH JULY 2008

Jane took the ninth of eleven staircases up to the attic floor to her studio. As usual, she carried a duster, a torch and a bucket useful for emptying the pots and pans strategically placed to catch incoming rainfall. There was never a moment, in summer or winter, when some part of Trelawney Castle's one-acre roof wasn't leaking. Reaching the top floor, she turned left along a corridor known for many centuries as Housemaids' West Wing.

It had been nearly three weeks since Jane had had time to go to her studio. Swinging her duster like a scythe, she swept away the gossamer cobwebs hanging across her path. A recent storm had poured in through a hole in the roof, leaving the pale floorboards below dark and soaked. Rounding a corner, she saw that the stone lintels on either side of the window had cracked and the architrave was buckling. Its collapse might block access to her studio and Jane's heart contracted. She couldn't imagine a life worth living without this creative outlet. Weeks passed without making the long trek upstairs, but its very existence and the promise of another session sustained her.

Jane had found the printing press ten years earlier while trying to locate the source of a leak in the third ballroom. She'd never been to that section of the fourth floor before and was amazed to discover thirty nearly identical rooms, each almost bare save for twin iron beds and a small cupboard—the staple furniture of junior domestic staff. Opening the door of Room 128, Jane wondered why, and for that matter how, anyone would heave a laundry mangle to the attic so far from the washing rooms downstairs. Forgetting the search for the leak, she examined the heavy cast-iron table with a large metal roller at one end. Using all her strength, she managed to turn it around, forcing the roller majestically and rustily from one end to another. The contraption must have weighed half a ton. Intrigued, Jane opened the neatly stacked wooden crates lining the wall. They contained blocks of typefaces and letters in different fonts and dried-out bottles of ink. In a nearby cupboard she found some fading printed posters, all relating to the suffragette movement and specifically to a women's march from Penzance to London on 19th June 1913. Jane laughed out loud. Someone had deliberately hidden the press in the farthest maid's room in the attic, where neither the butler nor any member of the family would dream of venturing. It made her happy to think that, deep within the heart of this ancient bastion of absolute male hegemony, there had existed a small and defiant opposition: a group of feminists prepared to risk their jobs and livelihood for the rights of their own sex.

The following day Jane returned with some oil and set to work dismantling the old machine, lubricating and cleaning each of its parts. It took three weeks. She bought some inks, carving tools and lino blocks in a local art shop and made her first drawing since school: a fox running through a cornfield. It took many attempts to reproduce the drawing on a piece of lino; at first, her etching lines were wobbly and inept. To her, the image had none of the elan of a child's drawing and lacked the sophistication and surety of an adult's, but a touchpaper was lit. From then on, she spent every spare moment trying to improve, working for hours at a time, neglecting other duties. Six months later she produced an image worth printing.

The same afternoon, Jane inked her design and, covering it with a piece of paper, cranked the roller over it and held her breath. Slowly, she peeled the paper away from the linocut. Her heart quickened and soared as she saw her fox in brown ink sneaking through an imaginary garden. It was a naive, inept print but it was a start, a clarion call. Room 128 became her exclusive world, independent of Trelawney and the overwhelming burden of her husband's inheritance. Her printmaking was a safe space to explore her own feelings and to be herself. Her inspiration was the Cornish landscape; her drawings were, ostensibly, of the local flora and topography. Had any of her family (who occasionally wandered into her studio) looked closely, they would have detected a strong autobiographical element. Her nearest kin were transformed into trees and plants: her mother-in-law was an all-pervasive and poisonous ragwort; her father-in-law, an overblown elder; Arabella, a wild rose; Ambrose, a stocky privet; Kitto, an elegant ash; and Toby, a kindly oak. For herself, Jane chose a series of wild weeds: a usurper, tenaciously clinging to the rocks.

With time, she learned how to print and overprint and create layers of colour bringing depth and life to the studies. The simple images evolved into complicated, dense designs, reflecting her mood and waning sense of optimism. As she became more proficient in technique and style, she graduated from linocuts to woodblocks, and then to etching. For the first few years, she hung the finished prints to dry on a makeshift washing line strung along the wall before stacking them in neat piles beside the old suffragette posters in the cupboards. Soon, unable to express her ideas on single pieces of paper, she graduated to rolls of wallpaper, printing her phantasmagorical landscapes onto strips measuring fifteen feet by four. She bought wallpaper paste and plastered her creations around the walls until they covered most of the rooms in the attic corridor. When a room was fully papered, from the skirting board and often over the ceilings too, she locked the door and hid the key.

Anastasia's letter, though discarded, had triggered an overwhelming urge to make a new print. So it was on that Tuesday afternoon in July that Jane took a box of old photographs to her studio and, looking through the images of her erstwhile friend, wondered how to depict her.

"Mum, Mum, are you up there?" Toby's voice rang out from a distant corridor. Jane was tempted not to reply. He'd want food or the answer to a question.

"Mum!" The voice was insistent now and she heard footsteps.

"Here," Jane called.

"Why didn't you answer?" Toby said, stopping to brush dust off his grey school trousers. "What are you doing?" He looked around the room and at his mother sitting on the floor.

"Going through some old things. Are you OK?" She looked up at her son, already freckled by the weak summer sun, too tall for his trousers, which flapped around his ankles. Like his siblings and father, Toby had the Trelawney auburn hair and hazel eyes.

"I want to go out tonight. Is that OK?" he asked.

"A date?" Jane said, teasing, never imagining that her sixteen-year-old son had any interest in the opposite sex. To her, he was unformed physically and emotionally.

Toby went bright red but said nothing. He sat down heavily on the floor, sending eddies of dust into the air. Jane laughed.

"Toby Scott, have you got something to tell me?"

Toby traced a smiley face in the dust.

"I hope she's good enough for you," Jane said fondly. There was something deeply sympathetic and touching about her middle child. Unlike the other two, he noticed people's feelings.

"She's nice." His tone of voice closed the conversation down.

Jane smiled at her son. "If you ever want to talk about it . . ."

Toby shrugged and shook his head. "There is something I want to ask."

"Anything, darling." Jane looked forward to dispensing maternal advice.

"Why don't we have any hot water?"

This was the question Jane dreaded: how to explain their dire circumstances to the children? The unexpected appearance of Kitto's Aunt Tuffy yesterday morning had staved off, temporarily at least, total penury. Jane hadn't recognised the fluffy-haired woman with eyebrows like white animated caterpillars who was wearing a moth-eaten sweater and pulling two suitcases. Trelawney, Jane thought, was a long way for a tramp to come. It was only when Tuffy spoke in a deep voice and held out three plastic Lidl bags of £50 notes that Jane took the visit seriously. The old lady's cottage had become infested and she wanted to move into rooms in the castle. Rent would be paid on the first Monday of the month and the only stipulation was that no one would, under any circumstances, invade her private space. In return she would pay the family £400 a month in cash. Jane would have offered her the whole castle but Tuffy chose the former butler's apartment which had its own entrance. Jane celebrated the windfall with a bar of her favourite Floris Rose Geranium bath essence, a luxury given up many years earlier. She also bought small bunches of red and green grapes and stopped off at the butcher for an organic chicken. On her way home she had dropped by and paid her cleaning lady, Glenda Sparrow, four weeks' back wages and another three in advance.

Determined to reassure her son if not herself, Jane said in a bright voice, "Things are going to change. Your father's been very clever and got us into a special kind of investment. Over the last eighteen months our money has grown by 18 per cent. We're going to hang on to the thingy until Christmas and then sell up."

"What makes him so sure?"

Jane didn't tell her son that she had asked Kitto the same question.

"I thought we didn't have any money." Toby was confused.

"We have a second mortgage." Jane tried to stifle her sense of foreboding.

"Who's going to pay the first one? Isn't that robbing Peter to pay Paul?"

"Your father says debt is an asset class." Jane repeated Kitto's maxim with confidence if not conviction.

"Might we go on holiday?"

"Once we've filled the oil tanks and done a few other things, of course."

Toby didn't look convinced but was distracted by something on the floor.

"Who's this? She's well fit," he said, picking up a faded photograph. Even at fifteen, in a grey, shapeless school uniform, one sock up, the other down, Anastasia's beauty had the power to shock. She was standing on the back of Blaze's horse, holding an imaginary telescope. She wore white breeches and a green felt jacket and matching hat with a large pheasant feather at a jaunty angle. Her long blonde hair hung in two thick plaits. Jane held the pony's bridle and tried to look insouciant (she had been frightened of horses in those days). Blaze had taken the photograph and her elongated shadow made a stripe across the bottom right-hand corner of the frame.

"That is Anastasia Kabakov. Her beauty could stop traffic." Jane remembered her former friend, dressed in a flimsy white sundress, golden hair on bronzed shoulders, crossing King's Road on a July evening. Two men jumped out of their cars and tried to persuade her to go for dinner. Anastasia had laughed prettily and refused.

"We were close friends for over ten years," Jane told her son. "We spent holidays together, here, and called ourselves the Three Musketeers: Anastasia, your Aunt Blaze and me. From the ages of eleven to twenty-one we were inseparable. It was inconceivable that anything or anyone would dent our friendship."

"So what happened?"

Jane picked up a photograph showing the three young women lying in the sun, their legs and arms entwined, laughing and squinting. It had been Blaze's birthday, a hot summer's day, and they'd spent hours swimming in the estuary. Jane remembered the tightness of her sunburned shoulders and the lightness of spirit.

"She lives in India." Jane was unable to explain how events had unfolded.

"That's only a nine-hour flight," Toby said.

"We lost touch," Jane replied.

"Why?"

"These things happen," Jane said with finality.

From outside came the mournful cry of the rooks returning to their roost. The light was fading. Jane switched on the lamp, which cast a flickering, half-hearted pool of yellow light on the floor. "Shouldn't you be going to see the girl?"

Toby looked at his watch and scrambled to his feet. Giving his mother a quick peck on the cheek, he took off along the corridor at great speed.

"Bye," Jane whispered after him.

She picked up a photograph of Anastasia, wondering what kind of plant or animal her childhood friend should become. A rare rose? An exotic orchid? Taking her sketchbook, Jane started to draw and play with different images, but only one depiction seemed to vivify on the page; Anastasia would be the kind of ivy whose tendrils threatened to choke all in its path.

A few hours later, Jane tore herself away from her work and went downstairs to make supper for her in-laws and Arabella. She felt constantly guilty about her fifteen-year-old daughter, who needed far more time and maternal support than Jane was able to give. Opening the fridge, she hoped that there was something to reheat but only found the remains of yesterday's mince, the meat greying in its package. She decided to hide it under a tomato sauce and a topping of stale breadcrumbs, minced carrots and chopped nuts. Pooter nudged her leg: she'd forgotten to feed him; worse still, she'd forgotten to buy any more dog biscuits. She gave him the mince and made the others a Spanish omelette. Arabella came into the kitchen and sat down at the table to eat her supper.

"Where's Toby?"

"He's gone to see a girl."

"Celia."

"Oh, you knew."

Arabella snorted. "Everyone knows."

"I didn't."

"You don't notice anything."

Jane felt stricken. Was there something her daughter was hiding? "Darling Bells, you can tell me anything you know."

Arabella looked up in surprise. "Like what?"

Jane sat down next to her and took her hand. "Is there something you're worried about?"

Arabella snatched her hand away. "I'm worried that I might have to eat mince again."

Jane laughed. Her daughter didn't.

"Or eggs," Arabella added.

Jane hesitated. "Arabella, could I talk to you, seriously, just for a few minutes?"

Most of the time a cloud of curly auburn hair covered Arabella's pretty freckled face. Now, pushing her hair out of the way and cupping her chin in her hands, she looked at her mother suspiciously.

"You've got cancer!" Arabella said.

"No," Jane laughed.

"You and Dad are getting a divorce. Like we all saw that coming."

"We are not! We're very happy, actually." Jane gave a defensive cough.

"So what is it?"

"I thought we ought to have a little chat about—" Jane struggled to find the right words "—about contraception."

Arabella recoiled. "That is so gross."

"It's natural. Nothing to worry about."

Arabella pushed her chair away and stood up. "We learned about all that three years ago in PD."

"PD?"

"Personal development. Silly, as Helena Diggs and Sabine O'Grady had been having sex for years."

"Aged twelve? Isn't that a bit young?" Jane felt the blood rush out of her face. How could she be so out of touch with her daughter and her friends? She knew Sabine and Helena: sweet, pint-sized girls who seemed to like horses and dolls.

"It's 2008, not the Middle Ages." Arabella went towards the door.

"Arabella, come back here," Jane said. Flashing her mother a broad grin, Arabella left the room.

Later, Jane wiped the kitchen surfaces for the last time, turned off the lights and climbed the stairs to her bedroom. Sixteen generations of Trelawneys had slept in the huge Elizabethan four-poster. Jane and Kitto had invested in a new mattress as a wedding present to themselves but, two decades on, the springs poked through and, when her husband was at home, Jane had trained herself to lie in a "S" shape to avoid them. With no hot water, Jane washed herself with a flannel and brushed her teeth. Though she had bought her children duvets, she preferred the weight of blankets and even in July she needed two. Their room was one of many without heating and, in the depths of winter, husband and wife would close the heavy tapestry curtains around their bed to try, vainly for the most part, to keep out the icy Cornish winds that worked their way under lintels, down the old chimneys, under the doors and through cracks in the windowpanes. For eight months of the year, Jane undressed in bed under the covers to conserve heat. From November to March she wore socks and in January and February flannel pyjamas and a jumper to sleep in.

At least they had electricity, she thought, undressing and putting on a white cotton nightdress. She got into bed and pulled the blankets up to her chin. It had been a long day; she was tired. Flicking the light switch off, Jane lay in the dark for a while with her eyes closed but then, unable to sleep, she got up and looked out into the garden below, at her tiny patch of tended roses and beyond to the muddle of misshapen topiary, remembering how, nearly thirty years earlier, the three friends were still schoolchildren playing jumping competitions, each on an imaginary pony, each vying to win a national event, and being chased out by the head gardener. Looking over to the far right, she saw the falling-down Temple of Dawn where she, Blaze and Anastasia had carved their initials framed by a heart into the remaining column. As she rested her forehead against the cold pane, a lump of emotion hardened in Jane's throat. Anastasia's letter had made her realise something: Jane didn't miss wealth, or youth; what she missed desperately was friendship.

6

Fleas and Sparrows

TUESDAY 12TH AUGUST 2008

When the gangly young woman put her head around the door, Aunt Tuffy sat as still as a rock, pretending to be asleep. The girl had to be one of Kitto's children and, for Tuffy, the only good relation was a dead relation.

"I know you're not asleep or dead," Arabella said.

"How?" Tuffy opened one eye.

"Because I listened to you shuffling about." Arabella crossed over and looked at her great-aunt's work table, which was, in contrast to the rest of the room, extremely neat. "What are you doing?"

"What does it bloody well look like?" Tuffy answered.

"Can I see?" Arabella advanced without an invitation. With nothing to do, and her family preoccupied with other business, she'd taken to shadowing her great-aunt's early-morning rambles and longed to know why Tuffy spent so many hours pootling through birds' nests and rotting carcasses, putting finds into plastic bags and specimen boxes. During one of the old woman's rare trips into town the previous week, Arabella had crept into her room and poked around her possessions. There were neat stacks of notes and carefully labelled bags of insects, dead and alive. Arabella skimmed through the names, her heart quickening with excitement; she didn't know the difference between an *Archaeopsylla erinacei* or a *Ceratophyllus fringillae* but knew that it mattered. At school, elementary biology lessons were restricted to photosynthesis and the life cycle of a tapeworm. Some innate inner sense told Arabella that within this room, inside these plastic bags and through the large microscope on the desk, lay a form of salvation.

"Was it you who moved my things around last Saturday?" Tuffy had returned from St. Austell to find bags of agitated fleas.

"I didn't touch anything."

It was pointless lying to this woman. "Don't do it again." (Or I might commit my first murder.)

"I'm sorry. I was interested."

Arabella looked so dejected that Tuffy decided to lessen her sentence from murder to grievous bodily harm.

"I looked up *Spilopsyllus cuniculi* and found out that it's one of sixty different types of flea in this country." Arabella's eyes shone with excitement. "I thought there was just one kind and it bit you."

"There are over two thousand varieties in the world," Tuffy said airily. "I have discovered four new species in my lifetime—if you look them up, you'll find them under the sub-classification of Trelawnii."

"That is the coolest thing I've ever heard." Arabella meant it.

Tuffy softened and gestured to her microscope. "Would you like to see a flea close-up?" Arabella nodded vigorously. Tuffy made space for the girl at her table. It took Arabella a moment or two to see through the lens; her long eyelashes kept getting in the way and she moved to the left and right trying to find anything at all in the white circles, but, shifting her gaze, she eventually managed to bring the highly magnified insect into focus.

"I thought they were just made up of shiny little tubes with long legs attached to the sides," she said.

"A common mistake," Tuffy said. "Its back isn't smooth, it's made up of thousands of tiny serrated hairs, acting like Velcro anchors against anything trying to dislodge them."

"Sick!"

"Now look at its mouth. Do you see all those spines? Together they create a fierce and highly effective biting machine. There are two saw-like laciniae for cutting the skin as well as a saliva channel. The longer, thinner one is the epipharynx which, along with the labial palps, creates a kind of needle for puncturing."

"Why doesn't the army adapt this as a weapon?"

"Our weapons are frightfully naive and unsophisticated." Tuffy sniffed. "Humans have only been killing each other for tens of thousands of years; nature's been at it for three billion."

"I read that a flea can jump up to thirteen inches—the equivalent of a human jumping over the Statue of Liberty."

"Only if they were twenty-five foot tall. Most fleas jump one hundred times their own height."

Arabella hesitated. "If I had their legs, I could leap over the roof of Trelawney with room to spare."

"Correct." Used to most people recoiling in horror at the word flea, let alone the insect itself, Tuffy was pleasantly surprised by her great-niece's enthusiasm.

"Imagine if we could copy the piston action of their legs and extract the resilin."

"Resilin?"

"It's the rubbery elastomeric protein found in many insects and arthropods, the magic ingredient that helps fleas jump, bees sting, crickets saw and the wings of dragonflies spin. It uses little energy and never wears out."

"So this is why you need so many fleas? To extract resilin?" Arabella leaned back and looked from her great-aunt to all the specimen boxes.

"There are billions of fleas in the world, and it would take many billions more to harvest a significant amount, but if we could extract the DNA sequencing of resilin and graft that into a plant, we could make limitless amounts."

"Imagine if I had resilin trainers: I'd be on all the sports teams!"

Tuffy smiled. "Why bother with shoes? We could just inject it straight into your joints."

"Wicked." Arabella continued to look down the microscope, fascinated by the fleas' long, almost transparent legs.

"'Wicked' isn't a scientific word; we might have to work on an alternative." (There was something endearing about the child which reminded Tuffy of herself at that age: all legs and arms and lacking in confidence.)

"What are you working on?" Arabella asked, raising her head from the microscope to look at her great-aunt.

"I had an infestation of mice. Mice carry fleas. Fleas carry disease. Why did the mice population explode? Do their fleas harbour anything unexpected?" (This is bound to bore the girl to pieces and hopefully she'll bugger off and leave me to get on with my work.)

"It was the mild winter. A cold snap kills off the young ones. I noticed many more voles and mice in the woods this year."

"As it happens, I agree with you." (Could it be that this girl is less of a dunderhead than most of my relations?) "It's vitally important to establish a link between rising temperatures and the proliferation of disease-bearing insects."

"Is this about climate change?"

"As a matter of fact it is." (Well, knock me down with a feather.) "How old are you?"

"Fifteen."

Tuffy remembered herself at the same age; it was the year she caught her first salmon on a family holiday in Scotland. She had put the animal straight back after scraping the sea lice from its mouth and skin. Later she had caught sand fleas on the beach. The holiday became even more interesting when she realised that the insects found there differed from those she extracted from the feathers of a dead chicken. A lifetime obsession was born.

Arabella noticed Tuffy's absent but blissful expression and wanted more than anything to have a front-row seat in her amphitheatre of knowledge.

"Do you want me to bring you some more nests? I know where most are."

"Why do you think I'm interested?" (She's been spying on me.)

"There's a fresh dead deer in North Woods teeming with insects. I could collect it."

Tuffy looked at the girl. While her common sense told her to desist, greed for fresh carrion overruled her desire for privacy. "I could give you some specimen bags."

Arabella detected the note of excitement in her voice. "Or I could show you?" She wanted desperately to learn more.

"Privacy is the most important element of my work," Tuffy said firmly.

"Do you think people could steal your ideas?"

"And intrude on my time." (She'll get the hint now.)

"I won't tell anyone. I swear on Pooter's head."

"Pooter?"

"Our dog. He's my best friend." Sometimes Arabella thought he was her only friend, but was too proud to admit that.

Hearing the sadness in the young woman's voice, Tuffy, against all her instincts, weakened.

"I'll meet you at the back door at six tomorrow morning." (That will put her right off.)

"I can't wait." Before Tuffy could change her mind, Arabella ran out of the room.

In a small semi-detached house on the outskirts of the Trelawney Estate, Glenda Sparrow was making dinner for her husband Gordon and their eldest grandchild Mark. She was a fine and adventurous cook and tonight was making organic lamb with rosemary, lemon and *zucchero rosato* followed by caramelised pumpkin pie. Mark was helping Gordon fix some tiles on the roof and she could hear, through the open window, the familiar banter between grandfather and grandson. BBC Radio Two played in the background and, opening the oven door, Glenda basted the meat. When Jane had come to the house with her back wages, pulling £50 notes out of a plastic bag, Glenda had been too surprised to complain about her bad hip and all the other excuses. Besides, there were few employers in Cornwall and, until Gordon cashed in their pension the following year, they needed the extra money. Nor could Glenda imagine life without the job at Trelawney; her mother, her grandmother and many great-great-grandparents had been in service at the castle. When she'd started, aged sixteen, as a scullery maid in the 1950s, there had been over sixty staff. One by one they left and Glenda had worked her way up to head lady's maid to the Countess and eventually as cook. She'd seen things at the castle that she'd have preferred to forget.

Glenda couldn't understand why the family were clinging on to the place. Trelawney was a dank, miserable death trap and a deep hole into which to sink a fortune without any obvious return. She wondered if the Earl and Countess would make it through another winter; their room could get so cold that Glenda occasionally had to break the ice in their lavatory. They should be moved to an old people's home; it was sinful, keeping them in near-arctic conditions for the sake of appearances or to save a few pennies. To add to all the mayhem, mad Aunt Tuffy had moved into the butler's apartment, bringing plastic bags full of live, hopping fleas. Bumping into her in the corridor, Glenda had screamed with horror and Tuffy had looked almost hurt. "I only ask that you don't touch them," she said.

Mark came in first. He was twenty-seven years old, handsome, with broad shoulders set off by a slim waist and long legs, black curly hair and brown eyes in sleepy almond-shaped eyelids. Twice a week he drove from Bristol to Trelawney to see his grandparents, parents and younger sister Celia. Glenda wished he'd give up computing, whatever that meant, and get a proper job nearer to home in a bank or an office. Playing around with games was hardly a career, particularly when he had a first-class undergraduate degree, a Masters and a PhD.

Her husband Gordon, wiry-framed, came in next. He had small, black, deep-set eyes and an almost bald, shiny head.

"Smells good, Gran," Mark said, kicking off his boots by the door.

"Mark," Glenda said sternly.

He picked up his boots and placed them neatly in the corner.

"How's your sister getting on?" Glenda asked, setting the table for three. "Still top of the class?"

"Celia's got her heart set on a place at Oxford to study politics, philosophy and economics." Mark washed his hands in the sink and from his bag took a bunch of flowers wrapped in brown paper for his grandmother.

"Thank you, love," Glenda said, and put them in a jug on the table. "Don't waste your money on me, though. You should be setting it aside for your wedding."

"I don't even have a girlfriend!" Mark laughed. His grandparents would be shocked to hear how much money he earned; more in a week than his grandmother took home in a month. Mark had risen quickly through the ranks of the firm to become Chief Technical Officer.

"Celia brought Toby Scott home the other day," Mark said to change the subject.

"How did she meet him?" Gordon asked.

"They're at the same school."

"A bloody toff at the comp. Fuck me sideways," Gordon said.

"Language, Gordon!" Glenda admonished, flicking him with a tea towel. "What did you think of him?"

"He was awkward but nice. Celia's going to the cinema with him tonight," Mark said.

Glenda stopped stirring and looked at her grandson in astonishment. "You don't mean that they're sweet on each other?"

Mark shrugged.

"That's not right," Glenda tutted.

"Why not?" Mark couldn't understand why his gran saw a divide between the Trelawneys and other people.

"I work for his parents and grandparents." Glenda beat eggs, milk and cream into the pumpkin mixture, then added a sprinkle of cinnamon before pouring it into the pastry shell. Taking the lamb out of the oven, she left the meat to rest on the counter.

"You know Celia: she'll do what she likes and when," Mark said.

"I'll have to resign." Glenda pursed her lips.

"'Bout bloody time," Gordon said. "Don't know why you go there; it's not good for your leg or your shoulder."

"It gets me out of the house." Glenda put the zucchini into a dish.

"I just said they were friends." Mark wished he had never raised the subject.

Glenda hesitated. "It won't work, Mark. You should warn Celia off before her heart gets done in." She bent down to put the pie into the oven.

"Our Celia can take care of herself. If you scratch the Trelawneys, the same blood comes out."

Glenda straightened slowly, to prevent her hip twingeing. "Even our Celia doesn't stand a hope when faced with someone with eight hundred years of superiority bred into them. That family has only ever looked out over fields that they owned, lived in houses they controlled and drank their own spring water. Eight hundred years of being better, richer and more powerful than any of your neighbours gets into the fabric of a person. It's been reinforced by the servants that take away their shit and by the Parliament that listens to their speeches."

"They don't look out on their own fields any more," Mark said. "I hear it all belongs to the bank."

Glenda took three plates out of the oven and placed them on the kitchen counter.

"When I was a girl we had to curtsy when the Earl's carriage passed by. My dad had to take off his cloth cap. In church, we stood up when the Trelawneys came in. My whole family worked for them, my nan and great-gran too. Perhaps that's why I scrub their baths; serving's as much in my blood as bossing is in theirs."

"It's about time society changed, and it should start here, with that family," Mark said.

"There's those who want to lead and those that want to serve. Most people just want pay packets and none of the responsibility. If you were to offer me Trelawney Castle and all those millions, I'd run a mile." Glenda shook her head. "The Viscountess works herself to the bone already. She looks so tired that my heart breaks."

"Jane Tremayne is not your problem," Gordon said.

"The oil tank hasn't been filled since March. It ran dry last month."

"No hot water or heating?" Mark's voice rose in astonishment.

"Three times a week she carries buckets of boiling water all the way from the kitchen to her parents-in-laws' rooms for them to wash. She buys bumper packs of mince from Freezer World on a Monday and makes it last for a week."

"I wouldn't feed a dog that stuff," Mark said.

"You don't have a dog," Gordon pointed out.

"I said to her: 'Why don't you sell up and buy a nice flat in Fowey?' "

"The meat looks beautiful," Mark said.

Gordon took his place at the head of the table with his wife on his right. The kitchen was so narrow that Mark had to flatten himself against the wall to reach his chair. Gordon opened two bottles of beer and passed one to his grandson.

"She said it would kill Kitto and his parents to move, since the family has been there for eight hundred years and it would be letting the side down. Said none of them would forgive themselves. They had to keep going somehow."

"They'll freeze to death next winter without any fuel." Mark shivered thinking about it.

"Kitto Tremayne is Chairman of Acorn," Gordon said.

"Where your grandfather keeps his money," Glenda added.

"Our nest egg." Gordon smiled proudly. "Your gran won't have to work for much longer. Next year I can cash in the pension, tax-free. Forty-three years I've been contributing to that pot." He looked at his wife. "All so that you and I can have a nice retirement."

"You're a fine man, Gordon Sparrow." Glenda smiled at her husband.

"Are you sure you should put all your eggs in one basket?" Mark asked.

"If it's good enough for the Trelawneys, it's good enough for the Sparrows," Gordon said with finality.

"I just wonder if you should diversify—why not sell some of Acorn's shares and put the money into another business?"

"Banks are safe as houses."

"I invest all my savings in technology," Mark said. He owned shares in Apple and Facebook and was waiting for the IPOs of several new start-ups in the worlds of car- and house-sharing. Mark predicted that in future most would care more about having an iPhone than a house; ownership would be considered anachronistic and constrictive; the internet guaranteed freedom and choice. If his own work, teaching a computer about cognitive thought processes, was successful, he stood to make a fortune. It was, he believed, a matter of time before artificial intelligence replaced humans in many areas of life.

"The internet's only a passing fad," Gordon said.

"It'll never catch on," Glenda agreed. "This country is built on solid things like the monarchy, the National Health Service, the Royal Mail, Lloyds and so on. Why would you trust something you can't touch or see?"

Gordon and Glenda were educated and informed. Gordon knew the name of every wild flower and most domestic species in both Latin and English. Glenda kept and reread the collected works of Dickens, Walter Scott, Thackeray and Thomas Hardy. In their spare time they sang at the local choral society and made two outings a year to see a production at the Royal Shakespeare Company. Nevertheless, Mark knew that his grandparents would dismiss as folly the trials of automated driverless lorries in California. Nor would they believe that, in the future, Glenda's fridge would decide what shopping was needed and that all groceries would be delivered by drones.

"Will you carve?" Glenda asked her grandson.

Mark cut the meat into neat red medallions and laid it in fans on white china plates. "When I make my fortune, I'm going to set you up with your own restaurant. People will come from miles around. You'll become the new Nigella."

"Don't be so daft." Glenda beamed and sprinkled freshly chopped parsley over the potato dauphinoise. Then she arranged spoonfuls of redcurrant jelly and mint sauce next to the cut lamb, making glistening patterns of white, pink, red and green.

The three looked appreciatively at their lunch and then began to eat.

"This meal is beautiful, Glenda," Gordon remarked, mouth full. "Maybe marrying our Celia would be a step up for the Trelawneys."

They all laughed.

7

Blaze Takes a Trip

MONDAY 1ST SEPTEMBER 2008

Blaze walked into the restaurant in Piccadilly at 9 a.m. to meet her uncle, Tony Scott. The Wolseley, like Tony, was grand, flamboyant and frequently made over. In previous incarnations, it had been a car showroom and a bank. In former careers, her uncle had been a paid "companion," but for the last fifteen years he had found his most fulfilling and lucrative role as a private art adviser acting as the conduit between an owner's needs and a purchaser's desires.

As a younger son of the Earl of Trelawney, Tony had, in line with family custom, been evicted from his childhood home on his eighteenth birthday, leaving with nothing but a present from his parents: a book bound in wax paper tied with a yellow ribbon. It was assumed he'd conform to the aristocratic tradition of following "spare" sons into either the Army or the Church, but neither institution wanted such an ostentatious homosexual. "We have some of those deviants here, but none who carry this appalling and embarrassing affliction with pride," a commanding officer wrote.

Bound by their mutual experience of expulsion and fondness for each other, Tony and Blaze met monthly for breakfast. On the surface, Tony was the antithesis of what the aristocracy represented but he was also, in Blaze's opinion, a true Trelawney. If her family shared a common trait, it was to conceal an anarchic streak under a conventional veneer.

Perhaps it was something in the Cornish water, or living so far from a major metropolis, or an almost feral upbringing with little parental supervision, but Trelawneys never conformed. Their family history was saturated with examples of eccentricity. Until the last two generations there had been enough money to cover up any scandals or peccadilloes.

"Lady Blaze Scott?" A smart, besuited gentleman, the maître d', bowed slightly.

"My name's just Blaze." She never used her title, even to get a table at a restaurant.

"Mr. Scott is waiting for you in the bar." Her uncle, dressed in a white linen suit paired with a bright yellow cravat, raised his glass of champagne in greeting.

"You are a ray of sunshine, darling uncle," Blaze said, kissing him on the cheek. He returned her kiss and, taking a step back, looked his niece up and down.

"And you, dearest, are too old to be so thin; a bit of fat is far better than Botox or fillers. Women are supposed to put on one pound a year from the age of forty."

"Please don't kick off. I'm having a rough time."

"Black makes you look dressed for court and it's so ageing. Try something a little more feminine. Who wants to bed a spider?" Though his comments were cutting, Blaze knew he meant well. "The whole world," he said, waving his arm in the direction of the diners, "will think I'm meeting my lawyer and imagine the worst."

"I'm dressed for work. People who eat here probably don't know what that is." Blaze was tetchy. "Remind me to refuse your next invitation," she continued, looking around and hoping that no one had overheard their conversation. "Anyway, who says I want carnal diversions? Don't tell me you're still up to all that?"

Tony rolled his eyes. "I'm nearly eighty. Ten years ago my testosterone fell off the cliff—such a relief. Who was it that said it was like being untethered from a lunatic?"

"Kenneth Williams?"

"I so miss Kenneth. Why does the Almighty take all the good ones?"

"He was old."

"He was only sixty-two!"

The barman leaned towards them. "A drink, madam?"

"Murray, bring her a Bloody Mary," Tony said.

"I don't drink at breakfast!"

"You need one."

"I don't want one."

"Live a little, I dare you."

Murray placed a Bloody Mary on the bar.

Blaze took it.

The maître d' led them across the black-and-white chevron-tiled floor to a table in the centre of the room. As they made their way, several people waved or called out to Tony. One woman, dressed in pink tweed Chanel, leapt out of her chair and rushed towards them.

"Here comes Cappuccino Joan," Tony said to Blaze. "I'll give you one guess how she earned her sobriquet." Blaze looked at the woman whose hair had been teased into a frothy mass of blonde curls on top of her head.

"Tony, Tony," Joan called out.

"Joan, my dear," Tony said and air-kissed her on both cheeks.

"I need a new Picasso for Gstaad; my decorator says it has to be blue."

"The Blue Period is so gloomy—I keep telling you that. What's more important, the wall colour or the canvas?"

The woman looked crestfallen. "But it's specially woven silk from Palermo."

"New silk versus new Picasso—hardly a contest."

Joan shook her head ruefully and slunk back to her seat.

"Tony, Tony, you never return my calls." A dapper man wearing a black suit with wide white pinstripes now approached.

"That's because your bank bounces your cheques. The Dambusters has nothing on your line of credit," Tony said loudly.

Mr. Pinstripe puffed with indignation, turned his back and marched out of the door.

Blaze sat down at Tony's usual table, trying to look relaxed and insouciant. While her uncle circumnavigated his various acquaintances, she looked surreptitiously at other women's clothes and saw that Tony was right: only the waiters were wearing black. Glancing to the left and right, she noticed women with tousled hair, smudgy eyes, sun-kissed skin and loose-cut suits; handbags were brightly coloured, nails painted in pretty pastels and shoes open-toed. Blaze longed to write them off as ladies who lunched or breakfasted but recognised a well-known literary agent, a theatre impresario, a magazine editor and a deputy governor at the Bank of England. Blaze had always thought restricting her wardrobe to black trousers and white shirts was a kind of freedom from choice; now she wondered if her "uniform" was a kind of sartorial straitjacket. Perhaps colours could be used to create a mood or set an atmosphere? Maybe different styles or fabrics could be liberating? She tried to imagine herself in a soft-pink dress with unvarnished nails and a looser hairstyle, maybe to cover up her face.

Sensing her discomfort, the maître d' returned with a copy of the day's *Times.* Blaze smiled gratefully and laid the paper out in front of her. One headline dealt with the Chancellor's precarious position in the Cabinet, another with the exodus of the wealthier inhabitants of New Orleans ahead of a hurricane. Turning to the business pages, she saw that President Bush had signed a decree guaranteeing up to $300 billion to support troubled mortgages; the author congratulated the Americans for putting an end to a period of instability. Blaze snorted derisively; this was a drop in the ocean, hardly likely to fill the pond of debt and particularly insignificant when one considered the rumours that the biggest mortgage lenders, Fannie Mae and Freddie Mac, were in serious trouble. What, she wondered, would it take to bring the whole house of cards tumbling down? Or had she got it wrong? Her predictions at Kerkyra's shareholders' meeting had not come true and since then markets had risen again. For Blaze it wasn't simply a loss of face; if she couldn't trust numbers and logic, she was a woman adrift without any kind of coordinates or belief system.

"I can't frequent this place any more; look around, it's full of people with a past meeting those with no future," Tony announced, finally joining her at the table.

He sat down and unfolded his napkin with three brisk flicks. "Why does anyone want a Blue Period Picasso?"

"Because it screams Picasso."

"He did the first forty in one night before a show. The paint wasn't even dry when the doors opened. A couple are all right, but hardly worth the money. Regardless, in today's market they fetch over £10 million a pop. That means each brushstroke earned Picasso £100,000. No wonder he painted so much." He laid his napkin over his knees. Turning to Blaze, he asked, "What are you looking so thunderously cross about?"

Blaze pushed the paper in his direction and stabbed her finger at the mortgage report. Tony took a pair of tortoiseshell pince-nez out of his top pocket and peered at the headline. " 'Presidential intervention ends housing instability,' " he read aloud. "One of the most exciting headlines ever," he said with irony. "I thought you owned your flat?"

"This isn't about me, it's the world economy."

"I can't spend my life worrying about intangibles; looking after myself is hard enough."

"This will change all financial, political and social structures."

Tony pushed the paper away and pursed his lips.

"I was born in the embers of 1929. I've lived through more crashes than you've had falls out hunting. It all rights itself in the end. History is like waves on a seashore: tides come and go but nothing really changes."

"Not this time. The world is so interconnected that a financial crash will reverberate across every corner of the world, through all sections of society."

"You're being a catastrophist. All that will happen is those who own stocks and shares will be a lot poorer."

"It will decimate jobs, industries, communities and pensions." As she spoke, Blaze heard a messianic desperation in her voice.

Tony smiled benignly at his niece. "You've been banging on about this financial Armageddon for well over a year and nothing has happened."

"That's because you haven't tried to understand it."

"I read all those long dreary articles you sent me after our last breakfast," Tony said tiredly. "I wasted a whole afternoon and continue to think a derivative is a type of biscuit and a CDO is a cross between a protest group and a venereal disease."

Blaze didn't smile; she didn't think anything about the present situation was funny.

Tony, seeing his niece's displeasure, tried a different tack. "The art world is getting stronger and stronger. Take Damien Hirst—he's having an enormous sale in a fortnight, it'll smash auction-house records. I can't decide whether to go to that or a party in Moscow."

"The world is teetering on a precipice and the super-rich are going shopping. Ordinary people were told that all this wealth would be spread about, not concentrated in the hands of a few. There'll be a revolution."

"We don't do revolt in England; we're not like the French." Tony waved at the waiter. He'd had enough.

"It may not take the form of sticks and stones or result in immediate action, but if the collapse is as big as I fear, then old orders will be replaced."

"Crashes are like laxatives. There is nothing like a good round of bankruptcies to get the art market flowing. People like me live off the three Ds: debt, death and divorce."

The two sat in silence for a few minutes, one imagining opportunities, the other foreseeing disaster.

"Have you been consulting people on the other side?" Tony knew about Blaze's penchant for psychics.

Blaze flushed. "I wish I'd never told you about that."

"I suppose Madame Jojo's been looking into her crystal ball . . ."

"I don't ask them about work-related issues."

"Them?" Tony snorted. "How many do you have?"

Blaze didn't answer.

"If the world is about to end, I'm going to disobey my doctor and order eggs Benedict. He says I should only eat the whites. Can you imagine anything more repulsive? Anyway, at my age who cares about a bit of chlamydia if the end is nigh?"

"I think you mean cholesterol," Blaze laughed. It was impossible to stay cross with Tony for any length of time.

"Same difference; it's all an invention of the pharmaceutical companies trying to make you buy their drugs and the GPs attempting to stay in work. The private doctors have to see enough patients to pay the rent, the National Health ones need to meet quotas."

"What would your prescription be?"

"A long walk and a stiff willy. Or vice Versace."

Blaze giggled and Tony, seeing her change in mood, glowed with pleasure. He loved Blaze for her awkwardness and lack of guile. He often wondered how, with all her success and business acumen, she had failed to develop better mechanisms for coping with life. Only a fragile membrane separated her feelings from the outside world. She was beautiful but could only see the ugly scar on her face. She polished her cleverness like a shield until it shone so brightly that others had to protect their minds from its piercing rays.

"Your need to be certain, to predict the outcome, whether through numbers and sums or prophesy, is touching but I wonder if you might consider a more relaxed attitude? As the youth say: 'Let it all hang out.' "

"I like clarity." Blaze tried not to sound defensive.

"What about waking up one morning and saying: 'I don't know what I'll do today' or 'Where will it take me?' "

Blaze's look of horror gave Tony his answer. This time it was she who waved impatiently for the waiter.

The young man hurried over. He took Tony's order first while Blaze studied the menu.

"Summer fruits and yoghurt," she said, making her usual choice.

"You will have a full English," said Tony, and nodded at the waiter. "Honestly, darling, I am serious: you look all blue; like Casagemas in his coffin."

He waited for Blaze to say something. She remained silent. Tony leaned towards her. "Now, tell me what's actually going on."

Blaze folded and unfolded her white linen napkin, unsure what to say. She shrugged her shoulders.

Tony put his hand on hers. "Are things that bad?"

Unused to kindness, Blaze felt tears rush to her eyes.

"Oh my darling, of all people in the entire world, you deserve happiness. I've never known anyone have such a bad run."

Blaze swallowed hard and stared across the restaurant, willing herself not to cry. She could cope with anything but sympathy.

"A love affair, I assume?"

Blaze shook her head.

"What the hell else is there to cry about?"

Blaze said nothing.

"The only thing worse than love is lack of love."

Blaze wiped her nose on the back of her hand. Tony tried not to react; ladies shouldn't behave in this way.

"Why don't you go down to the big house? See your parents, reconnect with your old life. I have often found that denying something gives it too much weight."

At the mention of Trelawney, Blaze's shoulders slumped.

"Please don't look upset—people will think it's my fault," Tony said, glancing around the restaurant nervously. "My USP is a rudimentary knowledge of art and an advanced degree in life enhancement. Your long face will besmirch my reputation."

Blaze laughed, in spite of herself.

"You are still pretty," Tony continued. "Now, make my day: tell me you want to spend millions of your pounds on art."

"It might be a better investment than stocks or commodities."

"What's the point in having money if you don't spend it? And you can't frame a share certificate or hang futures in Japanese yen on the wall."

"I don't know anything about art."

Tony roared with laughter. "If people who bought art knew about it, I wouldn't have a job!"

"It's just not my thing."

Tony shook his head sorrowfully. If he'd had Blaze's money, he'd have built a fine collection; as it was, he owned some good prints and a few minor oil sketches. His niece was always happy to supplement his income when business was slow; he wished he could take this money as a commission on a beautiful asset rather than a handout.

Sipping his champagne, he changed the subject.

"One of my clients, a ghastly man called Sleet, has been boasting about buying land around Trelawney."

"Thomlinson Sleet?"

"There can only be one."

"What a coincidence! He bought my business."

"Have you met him?"

"Unfortunately, I have," Blaze said, thinking about her presentation. "I'd forgotten we were undergraduates together at Oxford; he was one of the many men in love with Anastasia Kabakov."

"That woman is still dominating the conversation?"

"You remember her?"

"Few could forget her—the most bewitching flower of your generation; perhaps any generation. What happened to her?"

Blaze twisted in her chair. "She's dying."

"Dying, like dead?" Tony's mouth fell open. "What of?"

"Dengue fever. She's written to me asking if I'll look after her daughter."

"I didn't know she had children."

"Nor did I."

"You don't want to be saddled with a heartbroken orphan. Frightfully trying."

"My thoughts exactly." Blaze was relieved that Tony saw it her way. "Jane and Kitto can have it."

"How old is the thing?"

Blaze shrugged. "I never asked. Apparently there are two children—a boy and a girl—but the boy gets to stay in India."

"Why India?"

"She married a maharaja."

"Of course she did. How romantic." Tony hesitated. "I wonder which one. I had a little dalliance with one who had eyelashes like a camel and a thingy like a donkey."

Blaze held up her hands in protest. "Tell me more about Sleet."

"He telephones from his treadmill, no doubt sweating out buckets of Romanée-Conti."

"He doesn't look like he exercises," Blaze said, thinking of Sleet's corpulent figure.

"Once he was so out of breath that I thought he said buy the Manet when he actually meant the Monet. I realised my mistake too late and nearly had a heart attack—thought I'd be saddled with a multimillion-pound picture."

"What happened?"

"Needless to say, the Manet was a better picture and he made millions. People like that always come out on top."

"Do you like him?" Blaze asked.

"He's 100 per cent ghastly. He thinks that owning art will bring him class. Even the most exquisite works couldn't whitewash his vulgarity."

"If you hate him, why have anything to do with him?"

Tony wriggled uncomfortably. "I don't have the luxury of choosing my clients."

Blaze grimaced. "I thought you'd cleared up that issue." Seven years earlier, Tony had made a bad mistake, buying what he thought was a Camille Pissarro at a high price only to find out it was a fake.

"I'm not sure who'll live longer, the debt or myself."

"You know I'll help you."

"You've already done enough."

The waiter brought their food. Blaze dipped a sausage into the poached egg.

"This is delicious."

"What are we going to do with you?" Tony asked.

"If I could think of another job, another way of living, I'd jump at it."

"I know a nice retired French marquis."

"Anything except love," Blaze said firmly.

"It is an option."

"I'm over love and it's been years since anyone showed any interest."

"I imagine they're terrified of you."

Blaze took a sip of tea and buttered some toast. The food was making her feel better. Since the presentation in July she had spent weeks trying to find new clients, but her reputation put many off. She wished that she'd devoted more time to cultivating friendships in the investment world; remarkably few would take her calls. She wanted to leave Kerkyra, but had no idea where to go.

"What else have you heard about Trelawney?" she asked.

"Kitto has been selling like crazy; the darling old place has gone to wrack and ruin. He should get rid of it before the roof goes."

"Let eight hundred years of history go to some foreigner?"

"There's a bigger problem: who the hell would want it? Stately homes are so last century. No one wants miles of corridors and bad plumbing any more. Easier to start from scratch, build to spec, than try and adapt some old monstrosity."

Blaze was shocked. "It was your home too—you must love it."

"I've had sixty years to get over that love affair. When I was young and expelled from Eden, as you were, it broke my heart. I moved on; it's about time you did too."

"It's the only place I ever felt at home," Blaze said, reaching for Tony's handkerchief. "Aren't we formed by the landscape we came from? I am a product of that earth and of the water that bubbles up from the springs. I can feel the floorboards under my feet, picture the rafters over my head, which came from the woods we played in. At night my dreams are full of the ghosts and echoes of my forebears; I am woken by their laughter and sighs. At Trelawney, I was part of a continuum, a pattern, but here in London I am nothing, no one. My tap water has been through eight other bodies, none of whom I will know or ever meet. Maybe I walk past them in the street, maybe not. I eat food grown in a country I'll never visit. At Trelawney I had an identity. Here I am simply a statistic." Her tears flowed freely now. "I hate Kitto and Jane for living the life I was meant to enjoy."

"Don't assume they're happy. They are probably just as desperate."

"Miserable in luxury."

"Still miserable, only with better, older china." Tony looked at her sympathetically. "Plus you don't have their shame of failing to make the most of a wonderful life. Yours is a blank canvas. What a pity you never appreciated that freedom."

"It's not what I wanted."

Tony leaned back in his chair. "You are my favourite relation: stronger, braver, kinder and cleverer than the rest of them put together. Why haven't those attributes and your amazing success translated into a happy life?"

Blaze started to remonstrate but thought better of it.

"When did you last have a holiday?"

Blaze blew her nose loudly.

Tony winced. "Could you try and be a bit more ladylike? Next time I'll take you to a working-man's cafeteria."

"I can't go abroad when the world's about to end."

"A watched kettle never boils," Tony said. "Besides, there's a newfangled thing called the internet and the mobile telephone."

"I wouldn't know where to go," Blaze said in a small voice. "I can't face sitting in a spa or on a beach on my own."

"You can come with me on Tikki's yacht. Lots of lovely octogenarians."

"That sounds depressing."

"Now who's being a body fascist? We are young people trapped in old skin."

"It's not the bodies, it's the endless chat about people I don't know."

"You must have other options?"

"Literally none."

"Do some charity work. Being desired brings transitory pleasures, being essential brings lasting joy."

"That's what my psychic said. The economics don't stack up. I give 10 per cent of my earnings to good causes. It makes more sense for the charity to keep me at work than have me out in the field."

"Once a mathematician, always a mathematician," Tony said. "You must stop trying to control; leave some things to chance. Live a little. I dare you."

Later that morning, Blaze took a train to Buckinghamshire. As the train trundled through the outskirts of London, she thought how dreary this part of England was compared to her beloved Cornwall. Here, uniform red-brick villages were bordered by neat little fields. Valleys which must once have been beautiful were bisected by ugly dual carriageways and scarred by long rows of pylons carrying electricity to new towns and superstores. Blaze imagined the constant thrum of traffic above the hedgerows and at night an orange phosphorescence from street lights hovering over the fields.

She had received Wolfe's invitation to lunch a few days earlier, but had no idea where he lived. His email had said: *You'll be met at Haddenham Station.* She hatched clear ideas about Wolfe's house and grounds: a gated, long tarmac road lined with young trees would lead in a straight line to a huge mock–Queen Anne mansion. Mrs. Wolfe, encased in a velvet tracksuit and dripping with gold jewellery and diamonds, would shout at indulged miniature dogs and obsequious Filipino servants. Wolfe himself would wear luxuriously soft cashmere tweeds and pastel-coloured cashmere pullovers. Both would be "watching their weight." Mrs. W would talk about box sets, Mr. W would discuss the market fluctuations. She'd be fearful of foreigners, he of crime. After lunch there would be a short potter around the six-acre garden to admire Mrs. W's roses followed by a visit to his study for some "serious talk." There, underneath a late chocolate-box Renoir ("bought for a song when you could buy art"), he'd be condescending about her market analysis and give her a few useless tips.

As the train pulled into Haddenham Station, she was tempted to cross the platform and take the next service back to London. Curiosity triumphed—just. At the station car park there were five large Rovers and a purring BMW. Blaze walked towards them but, one by one, her fellow passengers overtook her and got into those cars. Blaze stood and glanced around. In the far corner there was a beaten-up Land Rover. She looked in its direction and, to her surprise, the driver flashed his lights twice. The door opened and out stepped a man wearing jeans and a wax coat.

"Blaze Scott?" he called.

Blaze smiled and walked towards the car. Wolfe must have sent a farm worker to pick her up.

The man held out a hand and Blaze shook it, feeling the rough calloused skin of a manual labourer. He didn't introduce himself. "You should have worn less formal clothes," he said. "Those shoes won't last long out here. What size are you?"

"Six," Blaze said. She went round to the passenger side of the car and saw a large unbrushed collie sitting on the seat.

"Queenie, back, now." The dog jumped onto the back seat, shooting Blaze a reproachful look.

"I haven't made a friend there," she said.

"One-man dog. You never stood a chance," he laughed.

Blaze tried to brush the hairs and mud from the seat, knowing her black suit would pick up every spot of dirt. What, she wondered, would Wolfe think?

The man put the car into first gear and it lurched into action. Blaze held on to the side of the door and laughed. "I learned to drive in a car like this," she said. "My father sent us out as soon as we could see over the steering wheel." She looked around at the dashboard and on the floor at an assortment of random objects. "It had much of the same stuff—string, binder twine, wire cutters and gloves."

"The essentials of country living."

"I never thought of this area as country. More Metroland."

"Next to the wilds of Cornwall, it must be tame."

She thought it odd that a farmhand was so well informed.

They drove in silence for a few miles before turning off the road down a track that ran through a tangled wood. The Land Rover bucked and skidded in the deep, bumpy lanes and Blaze hung on to the dashboard.

"The best way to deter visitors," he said, navigating potholes and fallen trunks. After a while they came through a clearing and emerged in a deep cleft of a valley whose high banks were covered in wild flowers and grasses. Blaze gasped; it was enchanting. There was an open pasture planted with mature oaks and beech trees and through the middle a meandering river with sheep grazing on one side, cattle on the other. Occasionally there was a break in the ribbon of green made by a drystone wall, a rambling hedge or a small copse, but otherwise the valley seemed endless.

"This is unexpected," Blaze shouted over the noise of the engine.

"It was in the same family for six hundred years," the driver shouted back. "Never had a drop of fertiliser or a chemical near it. It's the most perfectly preserved natural environment in southern England. Of course we can't stop the birds and other wild animals bringing progress in on their coats or in their shit, but we like to think that once here, they won't ever leave."

"I'm not sure I would either," Blaze said, as the Land Rover bounced over a wide track.

After a few more miles they reached a farmhouse and two large stone barns. Two more dogs appeared, barking wildly. Blaze saw an old red tractor, a 1960s model that she recognised from her childhood, and horses' heads sticking out from a stable. Other pieces of antiquated farm machinery lay here and there and, most incongruously, a small merry-go-round. The farmhand parked the car outside the front door and got out.

"I'll let the lady out," he said.

Blaze waited for him to open her door but he let down the tailgate and Queenie jumped to the ground.

Blaze got out of the car and stepped into a puddle. Her smart kitten-heeled shoes kept her heels dry, but her toes were immediately sodden. Looking down at her suit, she saw it was covered in white dog hairs.

"Is there somewhere I can wash before meeting Mr. Wolfe?" she asked.

He looked at her in confusion and roared with laughter. "I'm Wolfe; call me Joshua."

Blaze couldn't remember ever being so embarrassed.

"Would your wife have any shoes I could borrow?"

"No," he said and, without waiting, walked into the house.

Amazed by his rudeness, she followed him inside.

"I'll find you something to wear." Looking her up and down, he added, "You're a size ten."

"Eight, actually."

"I'll lend you a belt."

While he was gone, Blaze took in a low-ceilinged room with white-washed walls and a worn flagstone floor. There was an open fire, unlaid, and next to it two baggy chintz-covered armchairs. One wall was lined with shelves, painted red and loaded with assorted bowls and cups. A plate rack hung over a long white ceramic sink and the pine draining board had been scrubbed so hard that it was almost white in colour. Seeing two recently washed mugs, Blaze wondered where Mrs. Wolfe had got to. The table, also scrubbed pine, was set for two, an earthenware jug spilling over with wild flowers in the centre. On the sideboard there was a loaf of bread, some salad in a bowl and a large glass carafe of water. The room was untidy but the acceptable side of clean. Wolfe returned with a pair of boots and some clothes.

"Do you ride?" he asked.

"I haven't for a long while."

"Let's eat before we take the horses out. Do you have to be back by any particular time?"

"I have a life," she said testily. Already Wolfe had made too many presumptions.

Over lunch she had a chance to study her host more closely. She put his age between forty-five and fifty-five. He was about six feet tall, with long legs and wide shoulders. His face had turned a deep brown in the sun, but she could see from the flesh peeking out below the neckline of his shirt that it was naturally white and slightly freckled. He had hooded eyes and deep blue irises. His hair, greying at the temples, was a dark brown and thinning slightly over the top. His features were slightly too large for his face—he had a big nose, made larger by a prominent break, and a sharp jawline. The ageing of his skin and the deepening of lines around his eyes and mouth made his facial architecture softer; as a young man he'd never have been called good-looking, but he was certainly middle-aged handsome. His voice was surprisingly soft, low and with a slight Canadian twang.

He moved around the kitchen with considerable grace, sidestepping Queenie and an old lurcher, who both followed his movements devotedly.

"How did you end up here?" Blaze asked.

"I was born on a small farm in Canada. I'm what's known as second generation, the child of two German Holocaust survivors who thought they were going to America to begin a new life and got as far as Toronto."

"Where had they been interned?"

"Belsen. They were twelve when they went in, and clung to each other for the rest of their lives. Their tragedy is that, while they didn't die, they never learned how to live."

"I don't understand?"

"They tried to shut their memories behind a door of silence; denial isn't the same as forgetting."

"They never spoke about their experience?"

Wolfe shook his head. "Not once. But if we left the house they both held my hands so hard that the blood stopped in my fingers. Not one day passed, often one hour, even minutes, when they didn't tell me how much I meant to them, how I was their only reason for living."

Blaze tried to remember either of her parents touching her, beyond the awkward hugs before the chauffeur took her back to school and a handshake from her father when she got into Oxford. Neither had ever said they loved her.

As if reading her mind, Wolfe added, "The weight of love can be crushing. A child is too young to bear the burden of a generation's dreams."

"Which is worse? One child smothered or the other starved by the absence of love?" Blaze shifted awkwardly in her chair. "What an oddly personal conversation."

"It's often easier to talk to strangers."

Blaze wondered if that was right; she was many full moons away from any kind of intimacy. "How did you end up in England?"

"My parents died within two days of each other; I was eighteen and left Canada with a couple of books, a change of clothes and no direction. I travelled around the world for about seven years, working on ships, factories, farms, anything. I joined a travelling circus in France, fell in love with a trapeze artist, followed her to England, and, when the troop moved on, I stayed behind."

"That's all I'm going to get?" Blaze asked.

"For now, yes; I want something for you to come back for."

Blaze looked up; he held her glance. Her heart gave a lurch, like a magnet pulled by gravity towards a pole. Get a grip, she chided herself and, feeling a blush creeping up from her neck to her face, pretended to cough.

"Are you OK?" he asked and poured her a glass of water.

Blaze drank it in greedy gulps, hoping he thought her redness was coincidental.

Wolfe cut two large slices of bread on a scrubbed board and, fetching a large hunk of cheese from the larder, set it down on the table.

"Keep an eye on Queenie. She loves Cheddar."

Blaze looked at the dog who eyeballed her back; the animal wasn't thinking about cheese.

Wolfe opened the fridge and took out a bottle of white wine.

"I forgot to ask Molly to make any soup," he said. Blaze felt a stab of disappointment; of course, there had to be a Molly in the background: doubtless her own polar opposite, a slight, beautiful, blonde girl just the right side of thirty.

"So it's your turn. I know you're from a grand Cornish family."

Blaze tried to think of a story to tell—anything but the banal truth. She wanted to impress him, to invent a colourful hinterland, but she was out of practice talking about herself. In the financial world there were few women, and most men were only interested in their own lives and opinions. For her, conversation was a withered, underused muscle.

"We're a really close family. Probably spend far too much time in each other's company," she lied.

"When you're not out dancing."

Blaze laughed out loud: a hollow, tinkly sound. Uncomfortable under the spotlight of his gaze, she tried to steer the conversation away from herself. "How did you get started?"

"Making the first ten thousand was harder than anything else. I never thought I would break free of abject poverty. I got very lucky; someone needed to sell a business quickly and I happened to know another who needed it. Did it a few more times, built up some capital, bought and sold a few things, diversified. Right time, right place. One of the most unfair things about capitalism is that once you've made a lot of money, it becomes easier to make more: the wealthy don't have to do a lot."

"You and I know there's more to it than that."

"I employ incredibly talented people who have helped me build the world's most sophisticated computers and the fastest internet router in England."

"Algorithms are only as good as the information you feed them."

"Do you want to know the real secret of my success?" he asked.

"Of course."

"It's spending hours on a tractor ploughing a field or herding sheep or churning butter."

Blaze, irritated, didn't laugh; how typical of a man to be so condescending, assuming that she might not understand complicated financial systems or be interested.

Wolfe leaned towards her. "You think I'm being facetious; but the mundanity of those chores, the repetition, acts as a kind of meditation. I start each day with a series of numbers and questions written on a piece of paper, put them in my pocket and get on with the business of farming. By mid morning the answers are clear."

Blaze looked to see if he was teasing, but his face was serious. "It can't be that simple."

"It works for me."

He got up and, taking the bowl from the sideboard, tossed the salad with two large wooden spoons. Blaze liked watching him work; there was a sensuality to his movements.

"If I had this farm, I'd never leave," she said.

"It's hard sometimes." He put the bowl on the table. "I always attend your presentations. Even I have to get out of the valley."

"I never saw you."

"Maybe you didn't know where to look." He sat down again.

"Your argument was compelling and your colleagues' behaviour repellent." Wolfe pushed the salad towards her.

Blaze didn't reply—she was touched by his show of support but wished fervently he hadn't witnessed her humiliation. "I don't understand why stocks aren't tumbling. Those businesses are telling whopping lies; their balance sheets should be written down by a huge percentage."

"Maybe the collective desire for things to remain the same is overriding the reality," Wolfe suggested. He scooped some salad onto her plate and then grated slivers of Parmesan over the top. Blaze smiled and speared a piece of lettuce with her fork. It was home-grown and so fresh that she could detect the taste of warm earth and sunshine.

"The less charitable explanation is that the culture of the city is outperforming the hard facts; that financiers, drunk on years of success, believe they can outrun and outwit reality."

Wolfe let out a low whistle. "You have a very low opinion of us."

"I am culpable too. I've been part of the system." She ate some more leaves. "I have always found comfort in numbers but they are letting me down; two plus two no longer equals four. Instead, clever and successful people are doing the same sums and finding out that the answer is actually forty."

"Have some more." Wolfe pushed the bowl towards her.

"If only I had the space." She smiled. "That was the most delicious lunch I have eaten for a long time. Thank you."

"You have to have some home-made pie and home-produced cream."

Probably made by Molly, Blaze thought.

Wolfe removed the pie from the warming oven and the kitchen was filled with the smell of pastry and scented apples. Taking two small red plates from the rack, he put one in front of Blaze and fetched a spoon from the drawer.

"Help yourself, please."

Blaze couldn't resist. Fetching a small jug from the fridge, he put a dollop of thick cream on the side of her plate before serving himself.

"I know how lonely it can be swimming against the crowd. Perhaps you and I could exchange ideas or even work together." He hesitated. "On the condition that it would be done independently, away from Kerkyra Capital and Sleet."

Blaze was startled. "You don't need me; you regularly outperform my fund by a significant margin."

"It's easy making money in bull markets; but when the shit hits the fan—which if you're right, it will soon—then two brains are better than one." He hesitated and added, "Maybe I need an excuse to see you." He leaned towards her. Blaze's breath caught in her throat; was he flirting with her? How disgraceful, given the other woman, Molly, in his life. She pushed her chair back.

"Would you like some coffee?" Wolfe asked, attempting to bring the conversation round to neutral.

"Thank you."

He turned his back on her again and, taking a jar from a cupboard, tipped some grounds into a cafetière. Blaze looked around the room at the tired furniture, old television and flagstone floor. There were no obvious accoutrements of wealth; she wondered what he did with his money.

"While it brews, why don't you put those on?" he said, pointing to the small pile of clothes on a chair. "If you go upstairs, there's a spare room on the left and a bathroom off that."

Blaze took the clothes and went up to change. She longed to snoop around the upper floor, but was worried creaking footsteps might give her away. The spare room was decorated in a pretty faded chintz. There was a big brass bed covered with a quilt. Above a small fireplace there was a painting: a pot of cyclamen next to a silver jug. Blaze looked closely at it and saw the signature "William Nicholson"; she smiled, knowing that the artist commanded high prices at auction. She had found one chink in her host's parsimony. The clothes, though slightly too large, fitted well. She wondered if they belonged to Molly or another woman.

As she came downstairs, he glanced at her and smiled.

"Much better than a black suit." He handed her a cup of coffee.

They saddled up the two horses and rode out of the yard, leaving the pecking hens and a lazy marmalade-coloured cat sunning herself on the wall. Blaze was relieved that Wolfe had chosen the friskier animal, a gelding who pranced sideways and whinnied at the slightest opportunity. He rode well, like an American cowboy, with long stirrups and reins held in one hand. The sun was high and Blaze tilted her face upwards to catch its warmth. They headed away from the house up a small incline to a long stretch of meadow grazed by sheep and cows.

"Faster?" Wolfe asked.

Blaze nodded, praying she wouldn't fall off. As a young woman, she had been a fearless and accomplished rider but twenty years had passed since she'd got on a horse.

He set off at a great pace, his animal's hooves throwing up clods of earth. Blaze urged her mare into an easy canter. She was several lengths behind and, loosening her reins, she squeezed her horse's flanks. Soon they were galloping side by side through long grass laced with wild daisies and buttercups. Blood pulsing through her veins, Blaze felt an absurd lightness of spirit. This was what she had been missing, cooped up in her ascetic white apartment and her beige office. Leaning down over her horse's neck, she urged it on. The animal flattened its ears and pushed forward. She and Wolfe were neck and neck. He also leaned forward and for ten strides they raced, flushed with exhilaration. There was a wooden fence in front of them and Wolfe raised his hand in warning. He collected his horse and steadied into a canter. He took the fence well and flew over it. Blaze, glad there hadn't been time to think, clutched the mare's mane and only just stayed on. The landscape rose sharply and the horses, blowing hard, slowed to a trot and then a walk, their flanks wet with sweat and their sides heaving. Wolfe jumped off and held out his hand to help Blaze down. His fingers touched hers for a little longer than necessary. They walked side by side, leading their animals, until they reached the top of the hill.

As they looked back over the valley, Blaze thought about an alternative life for herself on a farm, with horses and other animals, living off the land with a man like Wolfe. She dismissed the fantasy immediately; love was the preserve of the young, or of demented optimists, and she was a middle-aged rationalist.

They rode the horses home in silence. The sun lowered in the sky and the afternoon peace was broken by cooing wood pigeons and the sound of their horses' hooves brushing against the stubble of recently cut corn.

"Would you like to stay for dinner?" Wolfe asked.

"I have a dinner in town." She didn't, but was tired and keen to be back in her own surroundings.

"Of course you do." Wolfe shook his head.

Later he dropped her back at the station. Blaze held out her hand and, with an amused look, he shook it.

"I thoroughly enjoyed myself," he said, squeezing her fingers in his.

Blaze removed her hand quickly. "A most unconventional meeting," she replied.

"Will you come back? Soon?" he asked.

"I wouldn't want to impinge on paradise."

"You'd be adding to it," he said.

What, Blaze wondered crossly, would Molly make of this flirtatious banter? Maybe the two of them would laugh about it together after she'd gone.

"I hope you'll consider my offer."

"Goodbye, Mr. Wolfe," she replied, "thank you for lunch." Then, smiling curtly, she turned and headed for the bridge to take her over to the London-bound platform.

8

The Arrival

SUNDAY 7TH SEPTEMBER 2008

Jane stood at the sink, her hands immersed in soapy water. Glancing over her shoulder, she smiled with pride and satisfaction at the sight of her family sitting in relative harmony around the kitchen table. It was ten in the morning, and there hadn't even been a major row, partly as her sons were engaged in a game of FIFA and her daughter was reading a nature magazine.

"I love family time," she said.

Ambrose, leaning forward, arched his back and let out a large belch.

"Gross," Arabella said without looking up.

"Better out than in." Half rising from his chair, he farted loudly. Since starting as an intern for Thomlinson Sleet, Ambrose had become even more entitled. His employer's sense of self-importance had transferred seamlessly, osmotically, to the younger man.

"Ambrose!" Jane said.

"It's your cooking," her son replied, and belched again. "Death by overcooked mince."

"I hope you die," Arabella said, waving the noxious smell away with the magazine.

Kitto flicked the outside edge of his *Sunday Times.* "There are indications that the Americans will bail out Fannie Mae and Freddie Mac. What a relief."

"Are they film stars?" Jane said, making a feeble attempt at a joke.

She found her husband's and son's recent obsession with all things financial trying.

Ambrose laughed condescendingly. "They are the U.S.'s biggest mortgage brokers."

"Why do they need rescuing?" Jane asked.

"Sleet says the Fed will never let the system collapse," Ambrose said without taking his eyes off FIFA.

"Sleet says this and Sleet says that. At this rate we won't be able to do anything without Sir Thomlinson's opinions," Arabella retorted.

"If you say one word against—" Ambrose raised his fist at his sister.

"Stop it, now." Jane flicked soapy water at her son. The suds missed him and landed on the floor.

"Our investment will be safe," Kitto said.

"Sleet says CDOs are rock-solid," Ambrose agreed.

Jane wondered how two men, both new to the world of finance, could be so certain.

"What's so genius," Ambrose said, "is that Sleet keeps inventing new things to sell to people. This week he bundled up a whole East Asian debt, mixed in a bit of Detroit housing, topped it off with some oil futures, called it XT129, and there was a stampede to buy it. We laughed ourselves sick and drank champagne."

"Why would anyone buy something if they didn't understand what it was?" Arabella asked.

"The Emperor's new clothes," Jane suggested.

Kitto and Ambrose looked at each other and rolled their eyes. "Better stick to making wallpaper, Mum," Ambrose said, scratching his head with a kitchen spoon.

"Mum, tell him not to do that," Arabella whined. "It's unhygienic."

"This whole house is a health hazard," Ambrose countered and, with one easy swipe, knocked the magazine out of his sister's hand.

"Don't do that," Arabella shouted. Toby took advantage of the hiatus to initiate a sneaky move in the game. The fragile peace accord between the brothers shattered.

"You fuckwit," Ambrose yelled, snatching the computer away. "That's cheating."

Jane put her soapy hands over her ears.

"When you make a good move, it's skill, but if I do something clever . . ." Toby leaned back in his chair.

"Boys—I am concentrating on our future," Kitto said, waving the newspaper at his sons.

The phone rang in the small scullery off the kitchen.

"Can someone answer it?" Jane asked, looking around for something on which to dry her hands.

No one moved.

"One of you!" Jane repeated.

"It'll be someone wanting money." Ambrose reluctantly placed the computer back on the table so that his brother could see the screen.

"Or trying to sell us something we can't afford," Toby added.

"No one uses landlines any more," Arabella opined. "It'll stop soon."

The phone rang insistently and Jane, wiping her hands on her jeans, went out into the passage to answer it. "Hello, hello," she said, raising her voice. All she could hear was a wild crackle.

"Told you," Arabella said. "One of those Bangalore call centres."

"Shh," Jane hissed. "Can you speak up, I can't hear you." She listened. "Yes, this is Lady Tremayne. Who is it?" She put a finger in the other ear to hear better what the person on the other end of the line was saying.

"Oh, how awful," Jane said. "When did it happen? I am so sorry."

She hesitated and listened again. "No! I never said I'd have the child."

She paused and then spoke very clearly, enunciating each syllable. "I already have three children. I don't want any more. Do you hear me? I do not want any more children."

Pause.

"Call Blaze Scott. She doesn't have any." Jane's voice rose an octave. "And no, I don't have a number for her."

By now all three children were on their feet and crowding around their mother, trying to work out what and who she was talking about.

"You can give me as many flight details as you like. I won't be meeting any of them." Jane put her hand over the receiver. "Someone pass me a pen, quickly quickly."

Toby ran over to the dresser and found an old pencil and a used envelope and took them to his mother.

"BA 4712. Lands Heathrow at 11:40 p.m. on Thursday the 11th of September," Jane said out loud and wrote down the information.

"I want to make it quite clear. This child is not my responsibility. Thank you, goodbye." Slowly she replaced the receiver and leaned back against the wall.

"What's happened?" Kitto asked, putting the paper down and getting up from his chair. When Jane didn't say anything, he took her by the arms and shook her slightly.

"Anastasia's dead," she said.

Kitto looked at his wife then shouted, "No, no, she can't be."

"Who is Anastasia?" Ambrose asked.

"Some friend of Mum's," Toby said. All three children looked nervously from one parent to another.

Kitto tried to make sense of the news, but could only hear the noise of his own blood whooshing in his ears. The idea of life without Anastasia was unbearable. Her physical absence had made her emotional presence in his life even stronger; he thought of her constantly. They hadn't met for nearly twenty years but she was his mirage, the point on the horizon that he aimed for and dreamed of. He knew his redemption lay in their eventual reunion. He started to agitate and shout.

Jane looked back at him in astonishment. His reaction—flailing his arms, keening, grabbing at chairs—was frightening. Had her husband and Anastasia been more than friends?

She refound her voice. "There's more. Anastasia had a child and it's got nowhere to go."

"What kind of child?" Arabella asked.

"How old is it?" Toby shook his head. Rations were already sparse.

"It's a girl, but I forgot to ask anything else."

"It can't come here," Ambrose said.

Kitto banged his forehead on the wall, over and over again. "We can't abandon her child."

"Dad's upset," Arabella observed.

"I can see that," Jane replied tersely.

The fate of the child precipitated a tremendous argument between husband and wife.

Jane: It's unreasonable for a man who eats business lunches and dinners in London during the week to foist another person on his wife.

Kitto: You should be charitable.

Jane: I've sunk everything I owned—all my money, all my parents' hard work and my own prospects—into this place; don't talk to me about charity.

Kitto: I thought you did it for love?

Jane: I thought you married me for love; now I'm beginning to think it was just for my money.

Kitto: When your money ran out, I didn't.

Jane: You had nowhere to go.

Kitto: Why didn't you leave then?

Jane: I ask myself daily.

Kitto: Unlike Anastasia, you always lacked imagination.

Jane: Perhaps you should have married her.

Kitto didn't answer.

Jane ran from the room and spent the night working in her studio.

Kitto left for London the following morning without saying goodbye. He didn't, as he usually did, call from the train or to say he'd arrived. Jane was relieved, wanting only to erase the argument from the record, to rescind the hurtful things they had said to each other. After much agonising, she decided to meet the plane. The child was destitute; Jane didn't feel able to ignore her plight. As the hours before the arrival loomed, so did Jane's anxiety; she hadn't been to London for five years. Her life had been gradually eroded into smaller and smaller pieces. She was a virtual prisoner of Trelawney, hardly venturing outside the castle's grounds. If she went to a shop, it was the supermarket on the outskirts of St. Austell: the local fishmonger, butcher and baker were too expensive. Most days, aside from cursory exchanges with her family, she spoke to no one. She was years away from the last decent conversation. The struggle to save Trelawney was so all-encompassing that it had eclipsed Jane's independence.

The morning before her trip to Heathrow, Jane fainted; clutching the washing machine for support, she slid to the floor, gasping for breath. Mrs. Sparrow found her and put her into bed with a cup of sweet tea.

"It's bound to be the change. It gets us all," the older woman said.

Please, dear God, don't let things change, Jane thought miserably.

She arrived at the newly opened Terminal 5 with a few hours to spare. In the harsh neon-lit arrivals hall so far from Trelawney and all things familiar, she felt shipwrecked, an insignificant vessel adrift on a foreign sea. The only comfort was that the child, bereft of her mother and wider family, would feel worse; and Jane, though unqualified for many things, could provide a loving and dependable ballast. She foresaw the younger woman bundled up in a sari and colourful shawls, shivering with cold in Britain's weak autumn sun. She imagined wrapping her arms around Anastasia's daughter and explaining all things British, their idiosyncrasies and mores. Jane, cheered up by the thought of being useful, bought herself a cup of coffee and, sitting at a fluorescent-orange table, made a list of things to show and tell Ayesha, about local plants and landmarks. Maybe the young woman's innocence and sweetness would rub off on Arabella; the three of them might go shopping or cook together. After the Indian food even mince would be a delicacy.

Jane's daydreams were interrupted by the sight of her sister-in-law walking towards her; their first encounter in twenty years. The two women kissed awkwardly, keeping their bodies far apart, their cheeks brushing. She's let herself go, Blaze thought, scanning Jane's ill-fitting velour tracksuit, the unfashionable haircut, the trainers (a son's cast-offs), unmanicured nails and faux-leather handbag. No amount of make-up could hide the weathered skin or tired, ageing face.

Half woman, half praying mantis, Jane thought, looking at Blaze's just-the-wrong-side-of-thin limbs encased in black, her blood-red nails, her ironed-straight auburn hair and pale skin. Had she known her sister-in-law was coming, she'd have made more of an effort.

"Why are you here?" Jane asked.

"Curiosity, guilt? And the knowledge that you'd take the child," Blaze said.

"Why were you so sure I'd have her?"

"Because you always do the right thing."

Jane wondered why the apparent compliment sounded like an insult.

"I wonder if the flight is on time?" Blaze squinted at the arrivals noticeboard.

"It's only a few minutes late."

"What a bore."

Blaze's mobile phone rang. There was no caller ID but, pleased at the sudden interruption, she turned away from her sister-in-law. "Hello."

"Have I done something to offend you?" Wolfe dispensed with normal pleasantries.

"No." Blaze felt a flutter of panic. He was the one person she craved but also dreaded hearing from.

"Do you normally ignore people who ask you out to dinner? I have sent you four texts."

Trying to buy time and collect her thoughts, Blaze looked across the brightly lit concourse. What could she say to him? That she treasured and polished the memory of their afternoon spent together like a rare and precious shell?

"Are you there?" Wolfe asked.

"Yes," Blaze said.

"Do you have an answer to my question?"

Blaze decided to match bluntness with bluntness. "What would Molly think?"

"Molly?"

"The woman you live with." Blaze knew that by mentioning Molly she'd killed any hope of a relationship with Wolfe; for her anyway, infidelity was the death knell of desire.

There was a pause and Wolfe let out a great shout. Blaze held the phone away from her ear. He was laughing. She couldn't believe his insensitivity, or the gall of his hiding bad behaviour behind a veil of humour.

"Molly is the most wonderful woman, one of the best," Wolfe said. "She is, however, married to my farm manager Bert and has been for forty-six years. Twice a week she comes in to help clean my house and is kind enough to leave the odd stew or bowl of soup."

Blaze was glad Wolfe couldn't see her discomfort.

"Now, how about my invitation?"

"Let me look at my diary," she said, flicking through an imaginary calendar filled with other assignations and wondering how many weeks it would take to bring about a total physical and mental transformation. "I've got a lot going on at the moment. Can I get in touch when things settle?"

"I understand." Wolfe sounded disappointed. "Could I telephone you or maybe take you to lunch?"

"Let's talk on the phone," Blaze said, trying to sound nonchalant.

"I look forward to it." He hung up.

Blaze walked across the concourse to a small water fountain and splashed her burning face with cold water. If only she could begin the conversation all over again, do the whole thing differently. She shook her head. A few weeks ago Wolfe had been a distant, mythical figure, but those few short hours spent in his company had been a lens into another world. She wanted to get to know him, but fear outweighed intrigue. Experience had taught her that intimacy only led to abandonment. Besides, affairs were things that happened to other people.

Leaning against the wall, she tried to breathe deeply to steady her nerves. Her eyes flicked back to the arrivals gate and she saw Jane gesticulating towards the board. The flight must have landed. Blaze walked back to her sister-in-law and sat down at the small Formica table.

"She'll be through any moment," Jane said.

Blaze's mobile rang again and, seeing that it was TiLing, she pressed answer. "Hi, any news of Lehman? There are a lot of rumours," she asked. "The mezzanine RMBS synthetic CDO? I want to know the second you hear anything; it doesn't matter what time of day or night. QE2 on M3?"

Seeing that Jane was listening, Blaze couldn't resist adding, "Did you see Acorn's latest figures? They think the effects of bond-yield retardation will soften the blow or that you can securitise air? Oh, sure, one plus one equals two thousand."

Jane jumped on hearing the name of her husband's firm; if only she could understand what her sister-in-law was saying. Blaze, it seemed, was speaking in a foreign language.

Blaze registered Jane's pained expression. She felt a shiver of delight as she sowed further seeds of doubt in the other woman's mind. Let her have a taste of fear, she thought.

"Why would anyone go on putting money into a housing market when foreclosures are spiralling? Did you see the news from Detroit last night? That's just one city—I got the stats from Atlanta, Memphis, St. Louis . . . I could go on. Unemployment in high single digits and rising as fast as vacancies in rental and homeownership." Blaze shook her head in amazement.

Jane thought about telephoning Kitto to tell him what she'd heard. Would he even listen? Unlikely. She felt a sudden frisson: what if the worst happened? Would they lose Trelawney? After the safety of her three children, this was Jane's single greatest fear.

"What's the EBITDA multiple on that?" Blaze said.

Keeping one eye on the travellers pouring through the doors, Jane pretended to read a text on her own phone.

"How much damage are they saying Hurricane Ike will cause in Texas? Is there money to be made there? Should we try and buy into a local construction firm? Can you find out who the blue-chip companies are in Galveston, Houston and surrounding areas?"

Jane sent a text to Arabella saying *Hi* for something to do. Arabella texted back immediately. *Whot?*

Blaze continued to talk loudly. "Thailand is clearly taking a beating; see what you can find to short there, particularly anything to do with tourism. A state of emergency is never a USP for a great holiday. Call me if you hear anything." She hung up and, pushing her chair back, angled her body away from Jane.

They sat in silence for a few minutes. Jane, unable to bear it any longer, asked, "Blaze, why are you so angry with me? What did I do?"

"You don't know?"

"It can't still be about a bedroom."

Blaze shook her head in disbelief. "Of course it's not just that. It's about you elbowing me out after I had taken you into my family home and shared my childhood with you."

Jane took a deep breath. "If I ever made you feel unwelcome or excluded, that was absolutely unforgivable and I deeply, bitterly regret it."

Blaze slowly exhaled but didn't reply.

"Is there anything else you want to say?" Jane asked. "It would be good to wipe the slate clean."

"What is there to say?" Blaze checked her watch and the arrivals board. "She must have been held up in Customs." She looked at her phone again for any updates.

"Did you talk to Anastasia over the last few years?" Jane asked, making another attempt at conversation.

"No. You?"

"Christmas-card relationship. I wonder why her death feels so discombobulating. Can you miss someone you haven't seen for longer than you knew them? Maybe we rue the time not the person. It was so simple then, so joyous," Jane said, chuffed with her analysis.

Blaze snorted derisively. "Believe me, it wasn't. There were things you didn't know."

"Like what?"

Blaze pursed her lips. Whatever events she alluded to were staying a secret.

Jane, irritated, examined her tatty fingernails. "None of us wants to look after the girl."

Blaze let out a hollow, unconvincing laugh. "You've got a huge house, servants and all that. What's so hard? Don't forget we took you in."

Jane imagined Blaze's horrified reaction if she ever saw Trelawney's decay or her parents' living conditions, and hoped her sister-in-law would never witness their dire circumstances. At least Anastasia's daughter, used to living in a Third World country, would be overwhelmed with gratitude and cowed by Trelawney's grandeur.

The silence between the two women was like static on an untuned radio. Blaze sipped her coffee. It tasted acrid. "I'm sure my brother would want to take her child in."

"Meaning?"

Blaze said nothing.

Jane guessed what Blaze was implying. "There was nothing between Kitto and Anastasia. Nothing. Your brother fell in love with me and I loved him from the first second. The proof of our love has been its longevity and our three glorious children. Though not easy, it's been a great success, a real love story." As she spoke, fury burned through Jane's veins. "If your brother only married me for my money, he'd have left me when it ran out, years ago. You're jealous because, for all your worldly success, you've failed to have children or get married and you begrudge other people's happiness." Jane got to her feet. "Now let's go. The least we can do is put on a united front."

Blaze, stung by her sister-in-law's remark, wondered how quickly she could dispense with the introductions and return to her office. Maybe simply a quick kiss, or at worst an interminable cup of tea?

The two women stood side by side, bristling with anger, watching travellers, befuddled and bewildered, step cautiously from a bright-white corridor into the cavernous arrivals hall. Many, Jane noticed, looked around anxiously for a familiar face. The lucky few were met by entire families waving banners and flowers.

Three wayward luggage trolleys piled high with suitcases and pushed by three young men burst through the exit.

"Do be careful," an imperious female voice rang out. "Those are all my worldly possessions."

The young men, clearly co-opted fellow travellers, grimaced at each other: the pleasure of doing someone a favour had worn thin.

"Where are the porters?" the voice resounded again. "Wait here," and from behind the mounds of luggage stepped a slim figure wearing skintight jeans and a white Chanel tweed jacket with a matching tweed baseball cap. Around her neck and on her delicate wrists were a mass of golden chains and bangles.

"What does one have to do to get decent service around here?" the girl asked.

Blaze knew the type: a spoiled Upper East Side teenager sent to London with her father's credit card to put distance between her and an unsuitable boyfriend. Jane felt grateful that Arabella wasn't that bad.

The new arrival scanned the crowd and, catching sight of Blaze, she waved. Jane cast her eyes around to find the object of the girl's interest. To her surprise, the young woman marched up to her.

"You must be Jane. My mother described you perfectly," she said, looking the older woman up and down condescendingly.

Turning to Blaze, Ayesha smiled graciously. "By process of elimination, that makes you Blaze." She spoke in a cut-glass English accent with the barest and most charming Indian inflections. "My mother also had you down to a T."

Jane and Blaze stared at the girl in astonishment: the heart-shaped face, high slanted cheekbones, translucent skin and the palest blue eyes; their old friend lived on in a seemingly identical copy. A sudden flood of emotion reduced both to silence. They were transported back to younger, purer, more innocent and hopeful versions of themselves. Like a movie in reverse, memories spooled through their minds. Glancing at Blaze, Jane saw that her eyes too were brimming with tears.

"What an odd way to greet someone," the girl remarked.

"You are most welcome here," Jane said, trying to contain her incredulity. She could only suppose that the young woman was hiding her bereavement and feelings of displacement behind this haughty exterior.

"How kind. My name is Ayesha. Now be good enough to find some porters. These young men have other lives to get to." She waved her arms towards her fellow passengers who, seeing an opportunity to flee, sidled off towards the Underground.

"There aren't porters at Terminal 5," Jane said, staring at the piles of suitcases and wondering how they'd manage the 16:45 to Penzance the following afternoon.

Ayesha looked around. "Where are your people?"

"People?" Jane asked.

"Servants."

"I'm sure we can cope," Jane said firmly, "between the three of us."

Blaze had temporarily forgotten about the office and was even more relieved that Ayesha wouldn't be her problem. Although her daughter was physically similar, Anastasia had been mysterious, not imperious. She charmed others into doing her bidding. She never raised her voice; indeed, even from her two closest friends, she hid her feelings well away. Part of her allure was to keep those close to her in a state of permanent suspense, never giving a clue about how she'd react or what she was thinking. Her daughter—brash, uncouth, demanding—was a monster.

"I thought we could stay in London tonight and make our way to Cornwall tomorrow," Jane said.

Ayesha shook her head. "It would be more amusing to pass a few weeks in the city."

"That's not possible; we no longer keep a town house."

Ayesha shrugged. "I'm told Claridge's is comfortable."

Blaze and Jane exchanged looks.

"I would like to use the bathroom," Ayesha said.

"I'll show you where it is." Jane pointed to a sign across the concourse.

"You'll be kind enough to watch my luggage?" Ayesha said to Blaze.

Jane led the way to the ladies, followed by Ayesha. Blaze watched them depart. Looking at the piles of suitcases, she saw that each was stamped with a crest and the initials "A. B." Of course, Blaze thought, Princess Anastasia, the Maharani of Balakpur, and she wondered what her life had been like.

Blaze's reverie was interrupted by the sight of Jane striding towards her. Alone now, her face was bright red. "I'm not having that girl anywhere near my house or my family. She's your problem."

"What the hell's happened?" Blaze asked, looking towards the ladies.

"Go in there, you'll see," Jane said, pulling on her coat and tucking her handbag under her arm. "I'm going back to Trelawney, without her." Turning, she marched in the direction of the Underground.

"Wait! You can't leave me alone with her!" Blaze ran after her sister-in-law. "I don't do children. I have a job." Catching up, she saw tears pouring down Jane's face.

Jane wiped a hand over her cheeks and kept walking. "I have a job too. A bigger one than you might imagine."

Blaze reached out and touched Jane's arm.

"What happened?"

"You go in there," Jane shrugged away Blaze's hand and gestured over her shoulder, "you'll see."

Watching her sister-in-law disappear down the ramp towards the Underground, Blaze realised that she'd left the luggage unattended. A security officer was circling. She ran towards him and then pushed and pulled the trolleys to the lavatories where she found Ayesha standing before a full-length mirror, touching up her make-up. It wasn't the young woman's figure or face that Blaze noticed; it was her hair. No longer hidden by the baseball cap, it tumbled down her back in thick curls, the exact shade of Trelawney auburn. Taking a step closer, she saw that the shape of Ayesha's face was much like her own, and the younger woman's hands were carbon copies too, with long, thin and slightly masculine fingers. Anastasia's fingers had been tiny and delicate.

"Is Jane all right?" Ayesha asked. "She left suddenly. Maybe I remind her of Mummy."

"How old are you, Ayesha?" Blaze asked.

"I'm nineteen. I was born in May 1989."

"Did your mother ever tell you the name of your father?"

"He's an aristocrat called Scott. I am going to find him." Ayesha spoke quietly. "I have his address." She passed Blaze a piece of folded paper. On it was written "Trelawney Castle, Cornwall."

"Does your father know about you?"

"I am not sure," Ayesha said and, for the first time, she seemed vulnerable.

Blaze leaned against a basin and looked at the young woman; she'd had no idea that the affair had resulted in a pregnancy.

"You look as if you've seen a ghost," Ayesha said.

"Of Christmas Past and Christmas Future," Blaze said.

"I did Dickens at A level. Frightfully overrated author."

"You did A levels?" Blaze asked.

"You'd be surprised what you can do in India these days," Ayesha said cuttingly. "We have hospitals too. Like most British, you think we are a nation of punkah wallahs and coolies."

"I never said that!"

Ayesha shrugged.

"You will of course take me to my father. I have looked forward to this moment for as long as I can remember. I can't tell you how excited I am."

Blaze wished she could share the young woman's optimism.

9

Kitto Unleashed

FRIDAY 12TH SEPTEMBER 2008

Looking at Jane's list of instructions pinned to the fridge, Kitto felt a mixture of tenderness and exasperation. Each chore, and there were many, had been ordered and allotted a certain amount of time. Kitto wondered how they had stayed married for so long: how she could have borne such a life; how he could bear such a wife. Did she imagine he'd stick to this kind of script, this awful mundanity? Did she know anything about him?

Waves of indignation washed away any feelings of personal responsibility. It was, perhaps, too painful and humiliating to accept that he was to blame for their penury; it was easier to blame Jane's lack of imagination. Looking at the suggested menus, he felt deeply sorry for his children having to eat the same things at the same time week after week. Where was the spirit of adventure, the sense of occasion? What was the point in living in such a beautiful house, in a peerless setting, only to sit down, night after night, between homework and bed, to a dish made of mince? His wife, Kitto reflected sadly, was and forever would be a product of suburbia. Anastasia said once that, asked to choose between a natural lake and a municipal pool, Jane would choose the chlorinated option, with narrow allocated lanes and warning signs clearly laid out. It had been a cruel but prophetic indictment. Kitto regretted, once again, putting duty before happiness. Thinking about Anastasia, his heart turned inside out. When she had been alive, he had managed to contain his longing; but in death, she was all-pervasive, infecting his thoughts. The day before, she'd appeared like an apparition on the far-distant horizon, and he'd held out his hand to her; but, as their fingers were about to touch, her image disintegrated. Three nights earlier he'd woken to feel her hot breath on his cheek and had lain still, not moving, inhaling her scent. Finally he'd opened his eyes and felt the crushing disappointment of her absence. Her only rival had been Trelawney; and ultimately the castle had won. Love, his father told him, was for ordinary people; the Earls of Trelawney had a more important calling and Kitto had to put duty before desire. Women would come and go. There would be other Anastasias, other passions. If Kitto couldn't make money, he had to marry it. So Kitto proposed to Jane and thenceforth ruined his and Anastasia's lives. Worse than that, he was failing to save Trelawney.

It was a beautiful evening and Kitto decided to take his children foraging. Over the next few days—even when Jane returned—he'd teach them how to be self-sufficient and live off the land, something that he longed to do as a child but Nanny Smith had forbidden. Earlier that day he'd prepared a fire by the estuary and left a frying pan and various utensils in wait. Homework be damned! They could get up half an hour earlier or deliver the kind of excuses that all children and parents fall back on.

Pooter nudged his leg and whined. Kitto realised he'd forgotten to feed him. Opening the cupboard, he found a packet of dried biscuits. How much did the dog get? A bowlful? Two? Was it mixed with anything else? Reading the back of the pack, he saw that dogs weighing over ten kilograms should have 900 grams a day. What did Pooter weigh? Kitto picked him up like a baby. He was pretty heavy—certainly more than ten kilograms. He measured out one and a half bowlfuls, hoping that was about right.

The clock on the wall struck five. Kitto went down the long east corridor to the gunroom and picked out two twelve-bore shotguns, made specially for him by the gunsmiths James Purdey and Sons, engraved with the family coat of arms. They were worth nearly £50,000 on the open market. He had often thought of selling them, but his grandfather's maxim came back: "Judge any man by the quality of his guns."

The imminent reversal of his fortunes made Kitto smile. His colleagues had guaranteed a £2 million profit on the sub-prime fund. Once he'd made the roof of the house watertight, filled the oil tanks, placed £100,000 in a deposit account as an inheritance for each of his younger children and taken Jane on a "hot" holiday, he'd reopen the Trelawney shoot. He'd stay on in the City; men like him were rare and hard to find. From a separate cupboard, he picked out two fishing rods and a box of flies. If they used spinners, the children would be sure to catch something, but that would defeat the purpose of the adventure: hunger would make them better shots, keener fishermen.

"Dad, are you there?" Toby called down the hall.

"In the gunroom," Kitto replied. "Come and help me with this clobber."

Toby's large feet echoed down the long corridor, slap-slapping all the way from the kitchen. His shadow loomed before he arrived, backlit by a bare bulb which made him appear taller, thinner and menacing. Kitto smiled to himself: no one would ever accuse his middle child of being frightening. Toby emanated kindness and bonhomie.

"What are you doing?" Toby asked, looking at the array of guns, cartridges, fishing tackle, knives, flies and nets laid out on the table.

"We're going to catch or kill dinner and build a fire and cook it."

"And if we don't?"

"There's nothing else in the fridge."

Toby's face broke into a broad grin. "Can we use your Purdeys?" he said, picking up one of the guns. Normally, the children had the use of older, less distinguished firearms.

The sound of other footsteps echoed down the flagstone corridor.

"Dad? Toby?" Arabella called.

"Pretend to be dead," Kitto told Toby. "I'll stand over you with a shotgun."

Toby looked uncomfortable.

"Oh, just lie down—do it," Kitto insisted.

Toby lay face down on the floor just before his sister arrived.

Arabella walked in, looked at the guns, her father's stricken face and her prostrate brother.

"Very funny," she said, aiming a kick at Toby's flank.

"How did you know?" Kitto asked.

"You get older, your jokes don't," Arabella said. "What's for supper?"

Toby got up and brushed dust off his school trousers.

"Up to you," Kitto replied, handing Arabella a rod.

"I've got homework."

"Tell your teacher the dog ate it."

"Can't use that one again," Arabella said.

"Or that a piece of the battlement fell on it?"

"And crushed my skull into a thousand pieces!" Arabella grinned, imagining Miss Bell's horrified expression.

"There was a flood in the east wing and we had to clear it out by hand."

"The portrait of the 3rd Marquess fell off the wall and crushed Granny."

"Come on, we're wasting hunting time," Kitto said, giving Arabella a box of flies and her brother some cartridges. "Get your coats and we'll head down to the estuary. Arabella, you'll try and catch a fish."

"I'll get a sea bass," Arabella said.

"Not in a river, you pillock," piped Toby.

"You're a pollock."

Arabella tried to hit her brother but Toby jumped out of the way.

"Hey, hey!" Kitto held up his hands. "Save your killing instincts for dinner. Toby, you and I will take the guns up to the oak wood."

"I hope you're not going to kill anything," Arabella said, lip quavering. Aunt Tuffy believed the animal kingdom needed protection.

"What's the point of living in the country and eating from packets? We need to put the adventure back into our lives." Kitto slapped his hands together. He hadn't felt so invigorated for a long time. "We'll meet back at the ruined temple."

"Which ruined temple?" Arabella said. "The whole place is full of falling-down, rotting buildings."

"The one at the end of the rhododendron walk."

"What's a rhododendron?"

"Big bushes with vulgar flowers."

"It only flowers in the late spring. How will she know?"

"She couldn't forget the enormous purple and pink frilly thing."

Arabella wasn't worried about getting lost; she was hungry. "If we fail?" she asked.

"We won't," Kitto said.

As he walked side by side with his son, Kitto compared his style of parenting with his own upbringing. Enyon and Clarissa had been neglectful; for them children were to be seen, not heard, and preferably neither. Their son, stung by his own parents' lack of interest, had promised to be different, but for him fatherhood had come to mean the odd walk, not losing his temper, keeping the oil tank full and remembering birthdays. In recent years, he'd failed most of these tests.

"Did you do this kind of thing with your father?" Toby, reading Kitto's mind, called out across the small brook that ran between them.

"Your grandfather was far too busy!"

"Doing what?" Toby asked. As far as he knew, "Gramps" had never had a job.

"Attending the House of Lords, seeing to matters of the estate, house-parties. I don't think he knew where the nursery was."

"Was Gran the same?"

"She was even busier: three houses to run, menus, servants, friends, organising, organising, organising—that was her clarion call." A pair of partridges flew up in front of them. Kitto shot them both with a left and right before Toby had managed to lift his gun. Pooter looked at his master expectantly and, when Kitto nodded, the dog ran to pick up the dead birds.

"First course!" Kitto said, holding up the brace. Toby jumped the brook and followed his father into the undergrowth where he found him bent over something large and white, the size of a football.

"What's that?" Toby asked.

"A puffball mushroom—delicious."

"They're everywhere." Toby pointed through the gloaming wood littered with white globes.

"Enough food for a week," Kitto said. "We're going to eat like kings."

"Are you sure they're not poisonous?" Toby sounded doubtful.

"How could you live in the country and not understand the basics?" Kitto straightened his back and placed the puffball carefully into his shooting bag.

"How do you know this stuff?" Toby asked.

"I spent the holidays with our gamekeeper, a wonderful man—his name was Peter Daw. There wasn't a corner of this estate—a tree, a deer, a rabbit warren—that he didn't know. He taught Blaze and me to shoot, fish and forage, as well as all the Cornish songs."

"I'd like to learn." Toby didn't, but would do almost anything to prolong his father's attention.

Kitto sang as he gathered three more puffballs.

"A good sword and a trusty hand!
A merry heart and true!
King James's men shall understand
What Cornish lads can do!

And shall Trelawny live?
Or shall Trelawny die?
Here's twenty thousand Cornish men
Will know the reason why!"

As he sang he strode ahead of his son into the woods. Toby hurried to keep up. With this noise, he thought, there'd be no game to shoot and he was getting hungry.

"That's the Cornish anthem—we sing it at school. Was that written about our family?"

"It's spelt differently, but it's about us. One of our relatives was imprisoned in the Tower for supporting the King back in the seventeenth century. There was always a Trelawney at key battles and important moments in Cornish history." Kitto stopped. Toby watched his father deflate suddenly; Kitto's shoulders sagged, his chin dropped.

"What's wrong, Dad?" Toby felt a shiver of fear; his father looked old and frail.

"I've been a frightful failure."

Unsure how to respond, Toby touched his father's arm.

Kitto gulped hard, trying to swallow the lump in his throat. "I thought being the oldest son was about sitting tight. Turns out that wasn't nearly good enough."

Toby tried to change the subject. "I'm hungry."

Kitto looked at his younger son. "You'll never understand: you can escape."

Toby had no idea what his father was talking about. "Arabella will wonder what's happened to us."

"You and Bella are so lucky. Ambrose and I have been dealt an impossible hand."

"I need some food." Toby hadn't eaten since lunchtime and his stomach was rumbling.

Kitto pulled himself together. "Let's stay parallel and walk up through this section of wood. With any luck we'll get a couple of pigeons or a rabbit."

They walked silently through the stunted oaks that lined the river. The ground underneath was covered with a thick mossy carpet broken only by the odd outcrop of granite. The small valley was steep-sided and tree-lined. The sun had sunk over the top of the hill and a faint damp mist steamed from beneath the ground. The river hissed and bucked over great rocks. Up ahead on a far bank, a heron, grey, etiolated, waited patiently for a fish to rise. In the distance they could hear rooks coming home to their nests, their mournful cries soaring above all other noises. Toby saw a movement out of the corner of one eye. Raising his gun, he slipped off the safety catch. Seconds later a pale brown head poked out behind a tree. Toby saw innocent brown eyes, a white throat and two buds of antlers: it was a young fallow deer. He lined the muzzle of his gun up between the deer's eyes and stroked the trigger with his right finger. It was an easy shot, but Toby couldn't bring himself to kill the animal: he'd rather go hungry. A loud report rang out to his left. Toby's heart contracted. Had his father seen the deer? A pigeon fell to the ground some distance away and Pooter bounded after it. Toby hoped the deer was a long way off by now.

The light fell and scents trembled on a gentle breeze: the musk of a fox, the ripening winter wheat, a distant bonfire. The family sat in companionable silence by a small fire, frying slabs of puffball mushrooms and the breasts of pigeon and partridge. They had not bothered to pluck the birds; Kitto showed them how to slit the chest and extract the tender meat: he called it the lazy hunter's dinner. Arabella had failed to catch a fish, but had picked two big pocketfuls of blackberries for pudding. She was so hungry that she decided to delay becoming a vegetarian until the following day.

"Aunt Tuffy told me about a friend who went mushroom picking. He died and the rest of his family are on kidney dialysis forever," she said.

"You need to know what you're looking for."

"Aunt Tuffy said there are thirteen different types of worm you can get from eating wild animals. Tapeworm, roundworm, bovine TB."

Kitto held up his hand. "Stop! You're ruining my dinner. Anyway, what does she eat?"

"Only things from packets. Not because she likes what she calls 'that crap,' but because it saves valuable time shopping and washing-up."

Kitto roared with laughter. "We should bring her with us one evening. Feed her something proper."

Arabella said nothing; she didn't want to share her new best friend with anyone.

Earlier, Kitto had put a bottle of Meursault into the estuary to cool and he drank it straight from the bottle. They lay on their backs listening to the calls of evening: the song of the wood pigeon and thrush nightingale, a mating toad, the last rooks and some squabbling magpies.

"Dad?" Toby nudged his father. "Are you awake?"

"Yes, just thinking," Kitto said.

"What about Grandad and Grandma?" Toby sounded anxious.

"What about them?"

"Their dinner—Mum gives it to them at seven."

Kitto sat bolt upright. He had forgotten about his parents. Jane's list swam into vision: "Replace used logs in their log bin; lay their fire; take hot water at 6 p.m. for their bath; light their fire and close the curtains; bring their supper at 7 p.m. sharp and collect dirty plates at 8 p.m. Try not to let Enyon see you complete these tasks."

He looked at the empty frying pan and the scraped plates, hoping against hope that some morsel was left.

"What are we going to do?" Toby asked. "Is there any food in the house?" He knew there wasn't—all the kitchen cupboards were empty.

Kitto jumped to his feet. "Let's go to the local Chinese."

"Great, I'll have some sweet and sour and some dim sum," said Arabella, not full enough after their wild dinner.

Kitto kicked away the last logs and stamped on the embers. "Just to be sure, fill that pan and pour it on the remains," he told Toby. "I'll run up and get the car. Cut across the field and meet me at the corner."

It was 9:40 p.m. when they arrived at the Earl and Countess's apartment. Enyon and Clarissa were dressed in black tie, sitting side by side in front of the four-bar fire. Clarissa was wearing a fur stole and her husband had a blanket across his knees.

"You should fire Mullion," Kitto's mother said crossly. "This is the second night he has forgotten to feed us. We might starve." Her voice cracked slightly, her hands shook and the end of her nose was red with cold. The mangy fur wrap slung over a tulle dress and pearls offered little protection against the elements.

"Mother, you look freezing," Kitto said, and went to her room to fetch a blanket. The bed had not been made, but his parents were so thin that their bodies left only a light indent on either side. Their curtains had been half drawn and, when Kitto went to close them, the material disintegrated in his hand. It was September yet a bitter draught whistled through the loose window frames. Next door, he saw his children helping their grandparents to the table and was touched by their solicitude and gentleness. Toby took two slightly grubby napkins from the sideboard and laid them across their laps. Arabella undid the cartons of food and spooned the contents on to two plates.

"Is this a colour found in nature?" the Earl asked, peering at the bright-orange sweet and sour prawns.

"It's Chinese," Toby explained.

"Chinese?"

"Chinese food."

"Do you have a new chef?" the Countess said, poking at some noodles with her fork. "I don't like spaghetti."

"It's noodles—the Chinese invented them." Arabella moved the noodles around in their polystyrene tub.

"Most of the British population love Chinese food," Toby added, hoping there would be leftovers.

"We are not and never will be most of the British population," the Earl said.

"I thought you might like to see how the other 95 per cent live," Kitto said, trying to make a joke.

"You thought wrong. I am not interested in common people and this is simply disgusting," the Earl said, pushing his plate away.

"You're obviously trying to kill us." Clarissa drew her wrap further around her shoulders.

"There would be quicker and easier ways," Kitto said.

"Grandfather, try the crispy shredded beef," Toby urged. "It's my favourite." The Earl nibbled a bit, but it was too tough for his old teeth.

"I'm so hungry," the Countess said. "I have to eat something. So do you, darling," she said to her husband.

"Try the rice," Toby said. "It's fried with egg, and soft." Here finally was something his grandparents could manage and they ate it quickly. "These are bamboo shoots in oyster sauce—also delicious," he encouraged.

"This is just edible," the Countess said, some colour returning to her blanched cheeks.

"Tell Mullion not to prepare this muck again," the Earl said crossly. "Just because others like it, doesn't mean we have to."

Behind them, the log fire laid by Arabella sputtered into life and the licking flames cast shadows on the wall. Kitto stood by the door watching his children help his parents. Even with heating and hot water, Enyon and Clarissa were too old to fend for themselves and Jane was too busy to look after them. Until now, he'd failed to take in how dependent and frail his parents had become. His mother, once the finest horsewoman in the county, a little shy of six foot and broad and strong as a young oak, had shrunk and withered. Her skin was mottled and papery, and liver spots stood out on her cheeks, while the low-cut neckline of her dress revealed a latticework of broken veins and ribs like scaffolding on her chest. Enyon's eyes, once hazel, were covered in a milky film; the hands that had once controlled great horses shook in his lap; the formerly luxuriant auburn hair hung in forlorn wisps around his ears. Kitto knew that moving his parents out of Trelawney might kill them; keeping them at the castle through winter would be another kind of death.

A novel thought came to Kitto: he wished his wife was there; dependable, devoted, kind, protective Jane. Since the age of fourteen, she had adored him—which explained, perhaps, why he had never bothered to develop any independent feelings for her. She had always been there, always would be there. He took her entirely for granted and, although he'd never been in love with her, he could see that she was a fine woman. More than that, he realised that he couldn't manage without her.

"When does your mother get back?" he asked Toby.

"She's supposed to be coming later," Toby said. "With the girl."

Kitto wondered how on earth they were going to feed and care for another person and, more importantly, how he'd cope with the constant reminder of the love of his life.

10

Volcanoes

SUNDAY 14TH SEPTEMBER 2008

All fourteen of Ayesha's suitcases were mini-volcanoes, spewing assortments of shoes, books and clothes over the Moonshot Wharf apartment's pristine white and beige interiors.

"What is this?" Blaze held up a tiny leather minidress. "Did your mother let you go out like that?" She was astonished.

"She insisted!" Ayesha laughed. "Her great hope was that I might induce heart attacks in old men."

Blaze knew it wasn't a joke; titillating ageing aristocrats was a game Anastasia had played at Trelawney house-parties.

Any suggestion that Ayesha might like to tidy her possessions or clear up after herself was met with total bewilderment.

"What is the point of tidying, only to untidy moments later?" Ayesha said. Blaze anticipated (correctly) that her own cleaning lady would resign upon seeing the state of the flat.

"When can we go to Cornwall?" Ayesha asked over and over again. "Mama made the Trelawney way of life sound like paradise. She never stopped complaining about Balakpur: the crumbling palace, hopeless servants, the damp and the heat." She looked around her. "At least it was colourful—this place is so drab."

Blaze accepted that her apartment, like her life, was made up of a limited palette. She couldn't get angry with the younger woman; she recognised that her polished demeanour was a veneer—Ayesha's confidence spun like a weathervane in high winds. One moment she was imperious and spoilt; the next awkward, curmudgeonly and spiky. For several nights, Blaze lay awake listening to her crying softly. Once she went into her room.

"Are you missing your mother?"

"And my brother. It's so quiet here," Ayesha sobbed. "At home there are hundreds of people running around." Sitting up in bed, she asked, "Why doesn't my father come for me? Doesn't he know I'm here? Doesn't he want me?" Her shoulders shook and she bent over her knees in misery. "If he knew how many years I have dreamed of meeting him."

Blaze put an arm around Ayesha and pulled her close. Raising her left hand tentatively, she stroked her niece's hair, wondering if this was how mothers behaved.

"How well do you know my father?" Ayesha leaned in to Blaze's embrace.

Blaze didn't know how to respond. "What did your mother tell you about him?"

"That she loved him more than she thought it was possible to love any man." Ayesha burst into tears again.

Blaze shifted uncomfortably. "Did she tell you why their relationship ended?" she asked, trying to keep her voice even.

"She never properly explained." Ayesha wiped her eyes with the back of her hand. She looked up at Blaze intently. "Will you?"

Blaze shook her head. "What happens between two people is mystifying; the opposite of what you think can be closer to the truth."

"That doesn't make any sense."

"I'm not sure love makes sense even to those who are involved. If we could simply explain it like an algorithm or a theory, we might lose interest."

"That's such a cliché." Ayesha laughed dismissively. "Have you ever been in love?"

Perhaps it was the comforting cloak of darkness, but to her surprise Blaze answered the question. "Yes, twice. Once with a house, a way of life; once with a man. Trelawney was my whole life, and then my fiancé

Tom. Both were taken away: one by my brother, the other by cancer. Love and loss are so inextricably linked in my mind that I do everything I can not to feel."

"Mama said that regret was the only thing to be frightened of. Her refrain was: 'Passion wounds, regret kills.' She taught me to evaluate every situation with a matrix, to add up the pluses and minuses in different columns. Even love was a mathematical problem, something to be solved."

After Ayesha had fallen asleep, Blaze lay awake thinking about the eighteen-year-old Anastasia. Had she been a seductress or a victim? Could or should Blaze have done more to protect her friend?

A few days later, over breakfast, Ayesha made an announcement.

"I am down to my last £200 and an emerald ring, and my options are limited," she said without any preamble.

"I can give you money if you need it," Blaze replied.

"That is generous, but would only be a short-term solution." Ayesha smiled as graciously as a duchess opening a garden party. She took a piece of paper from her pocket and handed it to her aunt. There, in her neat handwriting, was a list of options. Scanning it, Blaze saw three choices: *1. University. 2. Job. 3. Marriage.* The last one was underlined in red ink.

"You've put things in the right order," Blaze said.

"Poppycock," Ayesha snorted. "I intend to marry for money."

Blaze laughed nervously. "I'm not playing this game, Ayesha. It's stupid and demeaning."

"In my culture, it's perfectly normal to have arranged marriages. Indeed, it works better than your so-called love matches. Imagine if you'd had one."

Blaze flushed. "This is not about me."

"Are you prepared to help?"

Blaze shook her head. "You are nineteen years old. You have good A levels; now you need a degree. That would give you options. Otherwise, I will help you find a job and until then I'll support you."

"I will accept short-term support, but my mind is made up." Ayesha nodded at her aunt and, scooping up her coat and bag, left the apartment.

Blaze sat down heavily. What was she supposed to do now with her willful, anachronistic niece? Her mobile phone rang; it was TiLing.

"The Deputy Governor of the Bank of England has been alerting major financial institutions that Lehman's will be declared bankrupt tomorrow. The Barclays acquisition failed. It's all going tits up."

Blaze could hardly believe what she was hearing. Though she had foreseen the failure of market confidence, the idea that the U.S. government would allow such a totemic bank to collapse was almost unthinkable. Her prediction was wrong: there would be no correction, only collapse.

"Surely the Fed will step in?"

"My sources say Lehman's will file for Chapter 11 in the morning."

Blaze jumped to her feet. "I'll be at the office in half an hour." She ran to her bedroom and pulled on a pair of black trousers and a white T-shirt. She put two clean pairs of underwear and her spongebag into an overnight case, anticipating that she wouldn't be home for a few days. Hurrying out of the apartment, she caught sight of herself in the mirror. Her face was flushed with excitement and her eyes shone. After years of ridicule and ostracism, she had been proved right. Now she had to do the thing she was trained for: make money.

11

Big Shot

MONDAY 15TH SEPTEMBER 2008

Jane gave no reason for delaying her return to Cornwall; Kitto was too busy to ask for one. By Sunday night he and the children had shot and eaten deer, partridge and rabbit over an open fire. There had been enough to feed his parents and he'd remembered to light their fires and bring buckets of hot water. Shortly after first light on Monday morning, the rain came. The storm arrived with heavy banks of cloud, grey upon grey, rolling in from the sea up the estuary towards the house, signalling a long spell of wet weather. Kitto woke to a familiar drumming of water on the York stones outside. While the children were sleeping, he went to the local Co-op and bought a catering-size pack of forty frankfurters, three bags of oven chips and a week's supply of dog biscuits. The hens had laid five eggs and he planned to boil them for breakfast. His office mobile phone rang constantly; he ignored it—didn't they understand the meaning of "time off"?

Arabella was the first downstairs. Kitto suggested walking to the old oak wood to find mushrooms and maybe shoot some breakfast.

"Have you looked outside the window? Even the stupidest deer, the keenest rabbit, will be cowering behind a rock or in its burrow," she said, watching the rain running down the glass in wide rivulets.

Toby appeared a few minutes later.

"You better do the buckets on the top floor," he advised his father. "Mum empties them out on days like this."

"Check the tarpaulins in the Carolean ballroom—last time it rained this hard a whole section of cornice fell in." Arabella poured some cereal into a bowl and ate it standing up.

Ignoring his children, Kitto grabbed his gun and, followed by Pooter, strode out of the house, past Jane's roses and down to the once formal, now decidedly wayward garden. The rain was horizontal, driving into his eyes and running with abandon below his collar. Determined to ignore the elements, he marched on past the ruined temples to the estuary. The tide was out and the mud glistened like patent leather. Walking along the bank, he hoped that a fish or two might have mistimed the tides and got trapped. Once, in the 1970s, a whole shoal of mackerel had become marooned; the story made the local paper. Wiping the rain out of his eyes, Kitto looked left and right, unsure which way to go. His clothes were so wet that walking was difficult; his coat and trousers stuck to his flesh like cling film and his boots sloshed. Even Pooter was dejected, head hanging and tail drooping between his legs.

As in a dream, a doe and her fawn poked their heads out of a small spinney and cautiously made their way towards the estuary. Even in the rain, the mother was beautiful, with long neck and ears and a white rump. Her baby hopped beside her on spindly legs. Pooter growled softly. The deer and fawn came even closer. It was an unmissable shot. Slowly, Kitto lifted his gun, took aim, squeezed the trigger and fired. Perhaps it was the rain in his eyes, but he watched in amazement as the mother and fawn leapt, unscathed, across the field and into the wood. He put his gun down, hoping no one had been watching.

The miss of such an easy shot was unsettling. If he couldn't aim true in the arena he was born and bred for, what hope did he have in any others? In his pocket, his mobile buzzed again and he felt a shiver of fear about his recent investment. What if his sights were off there too; what if missing the deer was a sign? What if his colleagues were wrong; what if he lost more money? He shook uncontrollably and tried to reassure himself that it was only a reaction to the rain, rather than a premonition.

Taking the phone out of his pocket, he saw eight missed calls. Putting the safety catch on his gun, he turned towards the house. Then he tossed his handset into a puddle and made a decision: he would redeem his investments that morning.

His boots were full of water, yet Kitto felt a lightness in his step; he'd regained the initiative. Emboldened by his own decisiveness, he made another decision: to pull Ambrose out of Harrow. His eldest son had no aptitude for academia (or much else) and no gratitude for the sacrifices his parents and siblings were making to keep him in the private system. At the end of each term he returned with a dreadful report and more airs and graces. Since his internship with Thomlinson Sleet, the boy had become insufferable, telling anyone who would listen that Sleet, in his opinion, was a God amongst men. His conversation was littered with "Sleetisms," or endless banal slogans that the financier used, such as "Hope is a shitty hedge" or "Real men don't need liquidity." Sleet had a boat, a trophy wife, a big bank balance. Sleet didn't care about the little people; he concentrated on the big picture. Ambrose watched the film *Wall Street* over and over again and slicked his hair back to look like Gordon Gekko. Kitto rued the day he had asked Sleet to take his son on. From Christmas, Ambrose could enroll at the local comprehensive school along with the other two.

Walking with renewed purpose, Kitto strode back to the castle and into the kitchen. He didn't mind the rain any more, letting it soak through his clothes, down the nape of his neck and into his boots. He would remember this walk as one of the happiest in his life. By the time he arrived home, his children had finished breakfast and, as far as he could tell, had used most of the kitchenware to cook five eggs and half the frankfurters. The sink was piled high with unwashed pans and crockery. Furious, Kitto picked up a dirty plate and smashed it on the floor. He was about to smash the second plate when the landline rang.

"Hello?" Kitto said, hoping it was Jane ringing from the station.

"Kitto? It's John," the CEO of Acorn said.

"John, old boy. You might recall that I've got a few days' leave." Kitto held the plate in the air.

"Cancel it. The news from New York is bad. Lehman's is filing for

Chapter 11 bankruptcy. The U.S. government has washed its hands of the problem."

"I'm a bit busy here," Kitto said, peering into the sink.

"You need to get back to London at once. We have to put out a statement."

Kitto made a face at the telephone. "How does the failure of an American bank affect us?"

"We have similar sub-prime exposure to Lehman's." The CEO hesitated. "Our share price is tanking."

"Tanking? Going down?" Kitto repeated. "And our funds?"

"We borrowed too much. Can't repay the debt. The money's pouring out. People are queuing up to get their savings. We're finished. I'm sorry, Kitto—it could have happened to anyone," the CEO said. "Get on the next train to London."

Kitto put the telephone down. "It could have happened to anyone," he repeated, "but it didn't, it happened to me." Only a few weeks earlier he had taken out a second £1 million mortgage against the castle; that money had been supposed to triple in value. Holding on to furniture for support, Kitto made his way back towards the sink and, turning on the tap, splashed his face with cold water, hoping it might unite his body to his mind, which seemed strangely numb and absent. "It could have happened to anyone," he said again. "Anyone." Picking up a plate, he threw it at the wall where it smashed, showering shards of china all over the floor.

Toby walked into the kitchen, dressed for school.

"What are you doing, Dad?"

"Avoiding washing-up. It's a family game."

Toby gave his father a withering look. "Grandad's not well; he's got pains in his chest."

All Kitto could hear were the words "bankrupt," "finished," "over."

"We took them breakfast. Arabella was telling them about Anastasia's death and the daughter coming to stay. Grandad clutched his heart and fell down. You better get the car." Toby pushed his father towards the door.

Kitto carried Enyon to the car; the old man weighed less than the dog. Arabella tried to keep him dry by holding a raincoat over her grandfather's body. Clarissa, still in her nightdress, got into the back seat and cradled her husband's head in her hands. Toby climbed into the front seat. Arabella and Pooter were left at the castle.

Most of the twenty-minute drive to A&E was passed in silence. The only noise was the slap-slap of the windscreen wipers and the drumming of the rain on the roof of the car.

"Stop the car, stop!" Clarissa said suddenly.

"What's happening?" Kitto asked, pulling over to the side.

"Turn the engine off at once." Clarissa's tone of voice, normally deep and measured, had risen to a tremulous staccato. "He's trying to say something but I can't hear."

Kitto turned the key and the engine fell silent. He, Toby and Clarissa strained to hear Enyon's words.

"Tell her to come back."

"Who's he talking about?" Toby asked.

"Ignore him," Clarissa said, her face set in a line of disapproval.

"I love her," Enyon rasped.

"Kitto, drive on." Clarissa's voice was icy.

Assuming his father was referring to Blaze only added to Kitto's despair. How typical, he thought bitterly, that it was his sister the old man had asked for: the one that had got away, who had spent the last twenty years doing exactly what she wanted, who eschewed all responsibility, who'd been set free to make something of her life. While he, the eldest son, who had relinquished his dreams, was not even in his father's last thoughts. If only he'd persuaded Anastasia to marry him; if only she hadn't run away. Slamming the car into gear, Kitto put his foot down on the accelerator.

He set the windscreen wipers on to full speed and drove faster. Next to him he saw Toby looking across nervously, his fingers whitening as they clung on to the seat.

"You're driving too fast."

"You frightened?" Kitto said.

"A little, yes."

"Being frightened is good; it sets the heart on fire." Kitto laughed manically.

"Dad, you missed the turning." Toby's voice jerked him back to the present. "The hospital was up to the right."

Without thinking or looking to the left or right, Kitto wrenched the wheel to make a U-turn. There was a terrible screech as a large lorry slammed on its brakes. The last thing they heard was the sound of tearing metal and a loud bang. Then there was silence.

12

The Date

THURSDAY 25TH SEPTEMBER 2008

Blaze and Wolfe met at a small French restaurant in Soho. Away from the farm, dressed in a suit and an open-necked shirt, he appeared less handsome and ill at ease. Blaze, wearing black trousers and a white silk shirt, held out her hand awkwardly. He ignored the gesture and leaned forward and kissed her on her unblemished cheek. Blaze, worried that he'd press his lips to the other side and feel her puckered skin, stepped back.

They looked at each other awkwardly until a waiter appeared and led them to a corner table.

"Would you like a drink?" Wolfe asked once they had both sat down.

"A Martini please," Blaze said. She had already had a shot of vodka at home and, when the aperitifs arrived, resolved not to drink hers too fast. Be cool, she told herself. Pretend this is normal. The contents of the menu swam before her eyes and, when the waiter took their order, she asked for the first things from each section.

"I must thank you," Wolfe said. "I heeded the advice you gave at the Kerkyra presentation. As a result, my portfolio weathered the last few weeks pretty well. You saved me and my investors from huge losses."

Blaze tried to hide her disappointment; this was a thank-you dinner. Romance was not on the table.

"I'm pleased someone was listening." She downed her Martini in one gulp. They sat in uncomfortable silence for a few minutes until Wolfe asked a question.

"You'll want red wine?" he said.

"Why?"

"Because you ordered bresaola followed by steak."

"I did?" Oh, for goodness' sake, get a grip, she told herself. "Of course, red wine would be lovely."

"Do you like Merlot?"

"Please choose."

"Are you OK?" he asked. "You've gone a bit pink. Do you need some air?"

Blaze let out an involuntary high-pitched laugh. "No. I was just thinking about the crisis. I think we are just in the foothills of the real crash. I imagine it will take months to understand what's happening and to see who else will be brought down."

She could hear herself babbling and, glancing across the table, she saw Wolfe looking intently at her.

"What are you staring at?" she asked, running her tongue over her teeth to make sure they were clean.

"I was thinking how beautiful you are."

Blaze instinctively placed a hand over her left cheek. He probably felt sorry for her or was one of those types who traded on other people's vulnerability. She'd eat her food and leave. She decided to keep talking about the markets, a relatively safe area.

"A friend of mine said that Detroit looks like a horror film: deserted streets, abandoned buildings and homeless people." Blaze pushed her starter around her plate. "I know it sounds odd but, on September the 15th, when Lehman's collapsed, I had this strong premonition that the world had changed and the consequences of what's happening will reverberate for many years." Now on familiar ground, she felt her heart calm and her breathing return to something near normal. She continued to talk, hoping that words would allay any possibility of an awkward silence between them. "There will be change; there has to be. Ordinary people will be furious that governments are putting the fates of failing banks before their own countries."

"Ordinary people? Sounds a bit condescending."

"I consider myself ordinary," Blaze said briskly.

Wolfe laughed. "You are far from ordinary."

"You think I'm ridiculous," she replied.

"Not at all." Wolfe smiled. "I wonder if we could explore something else."

Blaze assumed he wanted an update on her investment decisions. "I've decided to stay liquid for now. Prices are bound to keep falling. At some point I will go back into the market. I can't believe the casualties—they say that Woolworths is teetering on the verge of bankruptcy. I couldn't imagine my childhood or any high street without Woolies, can you?"

"It didn't get as far as my hometown," Wolfe said. Like Blaze he had ordered bresaola and, like her, was hardly eating.

"Even though interest rates are supposed to be slashed, I suspect none of the banks will be lending."

Wolfe refilled her glass and Blaze downed it in one. He topped it up again.

"I'm considering taking a position in a road-haulage firm—we'll never stop needing goods taken from A to B."

"Can we change the subject?" he asked again. But Blaze didn't dare.

"Since seeing the opening of the Beijing Olympics and China's mighty display of pomp and ceremony, maybe we should just learn Mandarin, sit back and wait for their invasion. Clearly it's coming. Perhaps the democratic nominee Barack Obama will get elected and deliver on his campaign promises." Blaze could hear herself talking far too quickly and took a large gulp of wine to try to slow herself down. Wolfe opened his mouth to say something and she quickly jumped in. "I'm interested by the Large Hadron Collider, aren't you?" She didn't give him time to reply. "I keep hearing about all these tech disrupter companies—apparently they'll change the way we live and work. Apple continues to be a fantastic investment; sales of their iPhones are killing the competition."

This time Wolfe leaned over and placed one finger on her mouth to stop her from talking. "Tell me about yourself."

Blaze was staggered by the intimacy of his gesture; her heart contracted.

"Could you go first?" Why did her voice sound so odd?

Wolfe smiled. "Ask me a question."

"Why aren't you married?"

Wolfe sat back in his chair. "You don't believe in small talk!"

Blaze's hand flew to her mouth; if she could have caught her words, she would have pushed them back in.

"You don't have to answer," she said.

Wolfe shook his head. "I have had three long-term relationships with wonderful women, each of whom I would gladly have shared my life with." He hesitated. "But there was a consistent stumbling block: I don't want and never have wanted children. And they all did."

"Why are you so certain about that?"

"I told you about my parents. Their past hung over our lives like a noxious cloud. When they died, I made a conscious decision to leave their pain and their history behind. Having children would bring those feelings up again, and I'd be frightened of infecting them with everything that's happened." He spoke softly, without any sadness or introspection. Blaze wished she could face down her own past with as much clarity.

"I tried looking you up on the internet," she said. "I got my office to search the press cuttings. There's practically nothing on you—no trace, no gossip, not even in the financial pages."

"I take precautions."

"How does that work?" Blaze had heard of public figures using court orders to suppress stories.

"I make generous donations to editors' and newspaper owners' pet charities and make sure they know about it."

"Is that bribery?"

"It's for a good cause." He smiled.

"Yours or theirs?"

They both laughed.

"Your turn," he said. "Where are your skeletons kept?"

Blaze squirmed in her chair. There was no alternative but to tell him a version of the truth.

"I was born with a silver spoon in my mouth which was later wrenched out. Luckily, I had a facility for numbers, became an analyst, then a fund manager and have hardly left my desk for twenty years."

"No one's life could be that dull." Wolfe grimaced but, seeing Blaze wince and hoping to make her feel better, added, "I could make mine sound equally banal."

"I've put all my energy into my work and not enough into creating new relationships. I live in one place but dream of being in another. I have nothing to tell you about. I live alone, I dine alone, I sleep alone." Looking down at her plate, she realised she'd been far too honest and felt ashamed; he'd see her for the imperfect and pathetic human being she was. Unable to bear the humiliation, she reached for her bag under the table and was about to stand up and leave when she saw his expression. Far from disgust and pity, Wolfe looked sympathetic and, in that second, Blaze felt an enormous sense of relief. He was still there. He didn't seem horrified. Emboldened by his response, she continued to talk.

"The same day as the markets crashed, my father died. Even though it was a coincidence, I can't separate the events: both dreaded and anticipated, both with awful consequences." She thought about her mother's telephone call: *Your father's dead, a heart attack, and your idiot brother has lost everything and brought ruin upon the family. The funeral's on the 27th. I expect you to attend.*

Wolfe looked at her in astonishment. "I'm so sorry. If I'd known, I would have asked to postpone our dinner."

Blaze thought about her father's obituary in the *Telegraph. Enyon Trelawney made hunting and fishing into an art form.* She realised that Wolfe had asked a question. "Sorry, what did you say?"

"Were you close?"

"I hadn't seen him for a long time; there was a horrible row." Blaze twisted her napkin in her hands and looked into her glass of wine. "My sense of loss seems unreasonable, out of proportion. I never saw him but my emotions are wrung out." Her voice cracked slightly and, letting go of the napkin, she drove the fingernails of one hand into the other palm in an attempt to transform mental anguish into physical pain. Wolfe must not see any more vulnerability.

"Is it about lack of closure, unfinished business?" he asked. "Or perhaps that, whether people are with us or not, the relationship keeps on going. The dead only leave the room; they remain firmly in our lives."

The knot in Blaze's vocal cords prevented her from saying anything.

They ate their main courses in silence. As soon as she'd finished hers, Wolfe gestured to the waiter for the bill. She felt exposed, awkward. Wolfe moved the table and held out his hand. The waiter brought their coats. Blaze burned with mortification; if only she'd kept to her original story. Outside the restaurant the air was biting cold. Blaze held out her hand. "Thank you for dinner. I'm sorry that I wasn't good company." She turned away and started walking.

"Blaze, wait," he called out.

She stopped and stood immobile on the pavement, then heard his footsteps behind her. He put a hand on her right shoulder and swivelled her round to face him.

"I didn't ask for the bill to get away from you. I couldn't sit opposite you for a moment longer without doing this."

He stepped forward and kissed her on the mouth. Blaze stood with her arms by her side, not daring to move, feeling his lips against her own.

"I think you ought to breathe," he suggested.

She gulped for air.

Holding her face in his hands, Wolfe kissed her again, parting her lips with his tongue. This time she responded, leaning into his body, exploring his mouth, revelling in his taste. After some time, he drew away and, wrapping his arm around her, pulled her into the crook of his left shoulder. She leaned her head against his chest, thrilled by the sensation of touch.

"Shall we walk for a bit?" he asked, after kissing her once more. Blaze didn't want to move; she wanted to stay there for the rest of her life, feeling his warm breath on the crown of her head, the muscles of his arms through his overcoat, the rise and fall of his chest.

It began to rain. Small, hard drops at first and then a downpour. The two of them stepped back to shelter under the restaurant's awning, hand in hand, watching the raindrops bouncing in the headlamps of oncoming cars. In the distance they saw the shimmering orange light of a taxi. Wolfe, putting his coat over his head, ran towards it. The driver flashed and pulled over. Running back to Blaze, Wolfe held his coat above her head to shelter her from the rain.

"Where do you live?" he asked.

"Near Tower Bridge."

Once in the back of the taxi they kissed again. This time with more abandon.

"My niece is at home," Blaze said, remembering to breathe.

Wolfe laughed. "I would never presume anything like that on the first date."

Leaning into his arms, surrendering to his mouth again, she caught glimpses of a soft, milk-coloured moon rising above buildings and the glow of lights through a rain-smeared window.

The taxi made its way through Victoria and turned onto the Embankment along the Thames. Lights from nearby buildings bounced off the river's surface.

"I have to go to Cornwall tomorrow. For the funeral."

"When will you be back?"

"As soon as possible."

"Or I'll have to come and get you."

Blaze laughed. "Do you even know how to get to Cornwall?"

"Actually, I have a lot to thank the West Country for. I shorted Acorn Bank shares. It was a good call. It crashed nearly as far as Lloyds, down 62 per cent. Unlike Lloyds, though, the government can't be bothered to rescue it."

Although Blaze knew that this was normal City banter—language that she might have used herself in different circumstances—the realisation that Wolfe was one of the people who had brought about the collapse of her brother's business was shocking. The press had confirmed her mother's accusation: Acorn had gone into receivership, Kitto was bankrupt and the castle would have to be sold. The same touch that, minutes earlier, had been so delightful was now repulsive. She shrank from Wolfe, keen only to get out of the cab and away from him as quickly as possible.

"Could you stop the taxi please?"

"What's happened?" Wolfe asked, tapping on the glass and asking the driver to pull over.

"I need some air," Blaze said. The moment the vehicle came to a halt, she yanked on the door handle and jumped out.

"Let me pay, I'll walk with you," Wolfe offered.

"No," she said firmly. "Goodnight." She ran up a side street.

"Blaze, wait," Wolfe shouted. But, by the time he'd given the cabbie some money, Blaze had disappeared. Only then did he realise: Scott was the family name; her father was the Earl of Trelawney; and her brother, who went by another name he couldn't remember, was the hapless Chairman of Acorn. How, he wondered, had he been so stupid and slow on the uptake? Taking out his phone, he dialled her number. It went straight to voicemail. "Blaze, I can't tell you how sorry I am."

An hour later, Blaze, drenched by rain, arrived back at Moonshot and listened to his message. She didn't believe him. How could a person so well informed and sophisticated have failed to know Kitto was her brother? She pressed delete and blocked his number.

13

The Burial

SATURDAY 27TH SEPTEMBER 2008

The morning of the funeral, there was hardly a break between the sky and the landscape; both were the colour of soft-lead pencils. As the nominal head of the family, Kitto, now the Earl of Trelawney, walked at the front of the procession, his head bowed against the prevailing wind, his dark suit soaked through by drizzle. Since the car crash, he had lost a significant amount of weight and both his clothes and skin, also grey in colour, hung from his bones. Ten feet behind him, his three children walked side by side—Ambrose in the middle, flanked by Arabella and Toby—all dressed in their old school uniforms and dark green wellington boots (even Clarissa had conceded that the ground was too wet for normal footwear). Behind them, on a cart pulled by a grey horse, led by the former Trelawney groom Manshanks, the Dowager Countess sat on a padded cushion beside her husband's coffin. Following the cart, the incoming Countess, Jane, walked alone. Behind her, the Earl's female next of kin—his newly discovered relation Ayesha, his daughter Blaze—and, between them, the old Earl's brother Tony and sister Tuffy. The rear was brought up by a motley group of neighbours, relations and local stalwarts.

Clarissa Trelawney tried to bring dignity to her ignominious position on the back of a cart. Sitting up tall, head held high, she was determined to act the part of the widow of a nobleman. Her leg, broken in the car crash, was in plaster. Her body was shrouded in black velvet while a heavy veil obscured her face. As the cart bumped over the soft, rutted ground, throwing her slightly to the left and right, Clarissa recalled her father-in-law's funeral, when the estate workers and household staff, some three hundred in total, each dressed in their respective uniforms, had waved white handkerchiefs and lined the entire two-mile avenue of beech trees that ran from the castle steps to Vanbrugh's rotunda. The footmen wore Trelawney livery: tailcoats of deep crimson with purple frogging and glinting polished-brass buttons stamped with the family's coats of arms; the gamekeepers were in their green worsted plus fours, the grooms in hunting best, the housemaids in white starched pinafores and the labourers in tweed. Four bay plumed horses had pulled the glass-sided carriage and the pallbearers had been dressed in black crêpe with high top hats, while huntsmen dressed in pink led the Earl's hounds across the park, sounding "Gone Away" on his horn.

Hundreds of mourners had lined the drive to see off her father-in-law. The wake had lasted for a whole week. The kitchen staff struggled to feed guests and relatives who came from all over the world and included two former prime ministers, the Queen Mother, three royal princesses and one royal prince. It had taken place just after the Second World War and so many families, demented and decimated by loss and bereavement, had come to Trelawney in hope. Here, they all thought, was a family rich enough to withstand taxes, wars, divorces and death duties, whose stupendous wealth would act as ballast against outside forces. Clarissa was glad that so many of that generation, now entombed in their own mossy graves, were unable to witness how the mighty roar of the House of Trelawney had faded to this tiny whimper.

Looking out from the privacy of her veil, she noted a few locals had turned up to gawk. In the old days all the men from the village bowed and the women had curtsied to the Earl and Countess. She caught sight of Alf Gander, a long-retired former stable boy, now in his eighties, wearing a threadbare tweed suit and poorly ironed shirt. As she passed, he doffed his cap and this unexpected measure of civility brought a lump to her throat. She would not cry for the loss of her beloved husband or the way of life that had ended with him. As the last bastion of the age of deference, she intended to maintain standards. Dignity was all she had left. At least Enyon was not there to see this motley raggle-taggle procession.

Clarissa looked at the mourners bringing up the rear. Where were you when we needed you? she thought bitterly, watching their fake expressions of sadness. They had only come to witness a spectacle and for a free glass of sherry. First in line was the Duke of Swindon, whose own fortune had been denuded by a court case with yet another housemaid, this one Lithuanian, seeking support for another illegitimate child; Swindon must have nine out of wedlock by now. Windy's breath was as famous as his libido—fourteen-day-old Stilton had nothing on his halitosis; few blamed his wife for outsourcing her conjugal duty. Walking behind Windy was Earl Beachendon, masquerading as a mourner but here mainly as an envoy for Monachorum and Sons, the auction house. No doubt Beachendon was after the Van Dyck, the only great painting left in the family's collection. The noble lord was attended by three chinless daughters. Clarissa tried to remember their names. Something Shakespearean: Olivia, Ophelia and Desdemona. With those looks, she thought, their names were unfortunate; they should be Ethel, Doris and Doreen.

Hot on their heels were a ragbag of aristocrats: the Wellington d'Aresbys, the Smith-Gore-Browns and the Plantagenet-Parkers. Not one had bothered to visit the Earl and Countess over the last few years. Clarissa took delight in seeing them slither and stumble on the muddy track, ruining their shoes. Let's hope it's your last good pair and may you rot in hell, she thought.

Her attention turned to her daughter. If only Blaze had found happiness. For a woman, wealth was a poor relation to marital bliss. It was such bad luck to be born with that birthmark. God knows, Clarissa had tried to put it right, even taking her to Harley Street. Such a pity that the local charlatan had botched the job. Blaze could have been a great beauty but, at forty-one, she was past it; no one decent would want her now. Maybe she could bag a widowed duke—that would be nice; a title was so reassuring. It was all Blaze's fault for rejecting convention, refusing to learn the piano or ballet, needlework or ballroom dancing. No wonder no decent man would marry her. Thank heavens she was beyond child-bearing age. Enyon had heeded his wife's advice and made Blaze the temporary custodian of Trelawney, bypassing Kitto altogether.

Their children had had the best in life: the right schools, nannies and ponies and dances. Kitto had been given a pair of Purdeys for his eighteenth birthday and Blaze a pearl necklace. What more could they ask for? Clarissa smarted at their ingratitude; I was too nice to them, she mused. Spoiled them. Should have sent them on more holidays with Nanny to her family in Northern Ireland.

Clarissa knew she wasn't liked, even by her children. But, having survived the war which had claimed her four brothers, being liked came low on her list of priorities. Her mother had taken the easy route out, drowning her sorrows and then herself. Clarissa was not going to let Hitler win. For her, victory was about survival and the perpetuation of the old order. Her father and her brothers had lost their lives to preserve a certain kind of England and she'd do anything to honour their sacrifice. She had equally set views about marriage. It was for life: for better, for worse, for richer, for poorer. She was luckier than most; she loved her husband but, even if she hadn't, her attitude to the union would have been the same—to make it work.

At the front of the procession, thirty feet in front of his mother, Kitto was leading the mourners towards the escarpment. He kept his eyes fixed on the golden orb above the Vanbrugh rotunda which glinted in the low autumn light, sending refracted rays across the latticework of hedge dividing arable and grass fields. The morning's heavy early mist had lifted and, though the rain held off for now, the ground was sodden and squelched beneath his feet. Kitto felt his family's eyes boring into his back and the weight of his mother's blood-curdling disappointment on his shoulders.

The revelation that he and Anastasia had had a daughter only deepened his feelings of misery and shame; how could he not have known, why hadn't she told him? Now the child had come back to mock and witness his ineptitude. When they met, Kitto couldn't bring himself to look at his daughter; her likeness to her mother was too painful. Conversation proved impossible; all they had in common were withered expectations and bereavement.

Following the crash, Kitto had been banished by Jane from home and was living in the flat in Pimlico. Facing charges, including causing injury by careless driving when under the influence of alcohol, falsifying records of ownership, intention to defraud and theft, he spent his days trying to marshal a defence. He'd argue that, for eight hundred years, land and property had always gone to the eldest son. He had been as shocked as anyone that his own father had disinherited him in favour of Ambrose, with Blaze as an interim custodian.

Debt collectors acting on behalf of the now insolvent Acorn Bank would claim a first charge on the estate and castle: Kitto had used the property as collateral against his last disastrous investment in their subprime mortgage fund and his family must now honour those debts. Ambrose publicly disowned his father, refusing even to pay his solicitor's fees. Blaze, who had been appointed as custodian of the Trelawney Estate until her nephew reached the age of eighteen, also declined to cover her brother's debts. Jane, as the wife of a bankrupt and therefore also liable, was forced to sell her last pieces of jewellery and to liquidate a small pension scheme.

Jane was also concentrating on not falling over, but it had little to do with the mud. Since the events of the last few weeks, she mistrusted even the ground beneath her feet. The appearance of Ayesha, with the same mouth and hair as her own husband and children, had come as an appalling shock; she'd known that Kitto and Anastasia had liked each other but never imagined it had led to anything serious. All those years after their marriage, Jane replayed the innuendoes. Her father-in-law's wedding speech praising her fortune and wide hips. Anastasia's decision not to attend. Her husband's copious tears (despair not joy). Now the awful revelation that he had spent their marriage dreaming of someone else; and not just any other woman, but her best friend.

Jane had gone straight from the airport to a small hotel in Victoria, where she'd spent four days considering her options only to realise that she didn't have any: she had always been at someone else's mercy—first her father, then her husband—living and abiding by other people's rules. And now she was a 41-year-old woman with an ancient degree. Hardly hot property in the jobs market. She imagined her CV: *Middle-aged woman, can clean, muck out, drive. Dependable, steady and kind.* She couldn't imagine anyone beating the door down to employ her. There was another worrying aspect; what did she want now? She couldn't leave her children and had no way of supporting herself or them. This sense of crushing failure had been followed by a series of short, sharp jabs: the death of her father-in-law, Kitto's disinheritance and Blaze's appointment as regent over Trelawney. Jane was no longer the chatelaine; she was a guest, a usurper. Twenty years ago, she'd got what she wanted—Kitto, the prestige and the most beautiful house in England. Plain Jane Browne, the also-ran, far inferior to her two glamorous friends, had triumphed. She remembered walking up the aisle, her head held high on a feeling of smug superiority. But time proved she'd not been good enough to keep any of it. No doubt, Jane thought bitterly, Anastasia would have made it work.

She could not look at her mother-in-law, sitting upright only a few feet in front of her. Nor could she look thirty feet beyond the cart at her husband's back. She kept her eyes fixed on her feet and the slap-slap-slap of her shoes against the mud. This, she thought, is the sound of shame.

"Do you find it unbearably cold?" Tony asked Ayesha. His nose, turned violet by the weather conditions, was running.

"Balakpur was freezing in winter," Ayesha said.

"What are your first impressions?" Tony asked.

Ayesha, after only a few weeks in England, had learned to keep her true feelings hidden. "It's rather different to how I imagined and not at all as my mother painted it." Anastasia had described Trelawney as a wonderland. But what Ayesha saw was crumbling buildings, faint vestiges of glamour and a desperate attempt by its inhabitants to hang on to a past way of life.

Tony lost his footing, stumbled and fell.

"My best bloody suit," he said as Blaze, Tuffy and Ayesha peeled him off the ground. Behind them the funeral procession came to an unwieldy halt. In front, Clarissa rapped on Enyon's coffin and Manshanks slowed the pony and cart.

"Shift my husband forward and we'll put Anthony on the other side," she told the groom.

Tony allowed himself to be helped onto the cart. Without looking at her brother-in-law, Clarissa handed him a large white handkerchief.

"Get a grip, for all of our sakes."

Tony fumed. He loathed his sister-in-law and her unbearable airs and graces. There was never anything so appalling as a truly common woman elevated above her station.

Toby was thinking about his girlfriend Celia; nowadays he thought about little else. Even when his father's car had hit the lorry, amidst the noise of screaming, crushing metal, tyres skidding, while they were careering towards certain death, Toby's mind was consumed by Celia. What if I die and never see her again? The absence of her frightened him more than the loss of his own life. Was his body large enough to contain all the emotions she inspired in him? There were occasions when his heart swelled and beat so fast that he thought the tsunami of feelings might burst out of his skin.

The funeral arrangements had caused their first argument: Glenda Sparrow was not invited.

"Your grandmother suggested she wave the coffin off from the back door," Celia said, unable to disguise her indignation.

"She comes from a different generation," Toby said, unsure whether to defend Clarissa or make the Sparrows feel better about the slight.

"This is 2008, not the 1900s. We have all sorts of things now like the wheel, the washing machine and lipstick in a tube."

"If it were up to me—" Toby said, but Celia wouldn't let him finish.

"She cleaned his house for forty years and washed his plates and his underwear. Our families have been neighbours for generations. What planet are you lot on? You're big-house people with small-fry manners. You know the worst of it? She's going to come and prepare stuff for all of you to eat after the funeral. Service is so ingrained in her that she can't stop."

Toby didn't dare tell her that his grandmother would be shocked and appalled by the revelation of an affair between a Trelawney and the grandchild of one of their staff.

"You're all the same—so intent on saving this house and following some antiquated moral code that you forget what actually matters."

Toby tried to think of a good explanation: anything at all. He couldn't. It was the first time he'd heard anyone question the way things were done in his family and he felt unable to marshal any defence.

"People matter, places shouldn't. And the worst thing of all is just to keep on doing things because that's what was done before. You lot aren't even old-fashioned or quaint. You're myopic Jurassic has-beens," Celia said before leaving the castle, slamming the door behind her. He'd seen her at school but she had ignored him.

Ambrose, reliably irritating, hummed the opening bars to an Eminem song, over and over again. Arabella moaned and grumbled. She hated wearing her school uniform.

"Tuffy doesn't have to wear a skirt."

"Tuffy's an old dyke," Ambrose taunted.

Arabella was full of indignation. "Just because she thinks about things other than sex doesn't mean she's that way inclined."

"Dykey dykey doo doo," Ambrose chanted. He'd never had a way with words.

"Ignore him, Bells," Toby urged. But Arabella couldn't and, picking up a clod of wet earth, shoved it into her eldest brother's face. There followed an unseemly tussle, ending with the cortège waiting while Toby helped his flattened, muddied sister get to her feet and dry her face on her coat.

Gordon Sparrow watched the funeral procession from behind the hedge. That week he'd had a letter from the chief executive of Acorn Bank explaining the "unfortunate" situation. Acorn had a liquidity issue brought on by the financial crisis. Seventy-five per cent of its retail depositors had decided to withdraw their cash, leaving the bank insolvent, and the board of trustees were asking the government to step in. Gordon had invested £123,575 into Acorn's share-save scheme, having been promised it was fail-safe. Now he read that he'd only get £2,000 in compensation, with the slim possibility of a further £25,000 from a government guarantee scheme.

Gordon reread the letter so many times that it fell to pieces in his hands. Fifty years working in a job he hated; fifty years of saving and scraping; fifty years dreaming of retirement; fifty years wasted. There was nothing "unfortunate" about the situation. How dare anyone use such bland language? How could he tell his beloved wife that he'd failed her, that she wouldn't be able to retire after all? He'd have to keep working. His job wasn't a means to an end; it was the bitter end.

His eyes followed the Trelawneys as they walked up the track towards the brow of the hill. They would not get away with this. Not as long as he had breath in his body. If he'd owned a gun, he'd have stepped out in front of Kitto and blown the man's brains out.

The Trelawney hilltop burial ground was bare and windswept, sandblasted by centuries of salt spray from the sea below. As with the rest of the estate, it had become overgrown and fallen into disrepair. As the family made their way up by foot, they were unsure what lay ahead. Two local gravediggers and an architectural historian had been sent in advance to prise open the Vanbrugh vault and find space for the 24th Earl, the first for seven generations not to build his own sarcophagus. Over ten centuries, the burial ground had expanded into a confusing but delightful smorgasbord of obelisks, gazebos, sugar loaves, sham ruins, pagodas, kiosks, screens, temples, grottoes, hermitages, towers, roundhouses, menageries, cascades and pavilions, built in a variety of styles—Egyptian, Chinese, Druidical, Indian, rural, Moorish, grotesque and even occasionally classical—all purloined and adapted by their lordships in an attempt to keep up with or, better still, outdo their ancestors; to leave their mark or occasionally just to add to a noble tradition.

The congregation traipsed through the assortment of buildings and stood by the door to the Vanbrugh rotunda as Kitto and his children lifted the coffin from the cart and shuffled it inside. The interior was cavernous and elaborate. Vanbrugh, inspired by the grand Mogul tombs he had seen on a visit to Surat in 1683, had indulged the memory. Standing nearly one hundred feet high, it consisted of fifty columns surrounding a domed cylindrical cone. It held the graves of the 18th Earl, his wife and daughters, leaving plenty of room for others.

Blaze followed the coffin into the mausoleum. She looked up at the mighty blocks of stone and took comfort in the fact that this edifice was strong, unlike so many areas of her life. Her father's will had left her in charge of Trelawney until her nephew turned eighteen. There was no income attached; the Earl had inherited many millions but died a pauper. Blaze wondered about the business of death and if there was money to be made from selling plots in the burial ground to rich Americans or Chinese. Was it possible over the next months to create a stream of income to enable Ambrose and his heirs to keep the house? For a while she would support Kitto, his family and her mother, but could not meet her brother's sizeable debts. Her most useful contribution would be to make the estate into a viable concern.

"Blaze, Blaze," her mother said, bringing her back to the present.

Looking around, she saw fifty faces gazing expectantly at her and suddenly remembered the poem chosen by her father. Walking into the semicircle of mourners, she took the piece of paper out of her pocket.

"My father left instructions for me to read this sonnet by Shakespeare." Blaze couldn't remember Enyon ever reading a book or expressing any interest in literature and had been taken aback.

"Who will believe my verse in time to come,
If it were fill'd with your most high deserts?
Though yet, heaven knows, it is but as a tomb
Which hides your life and shows not half your parts.
If I could write the beauty of your eyes
And in fresh numbers number all your graces,
The age to come would say 'This poet lies:
Such heavenly touches ne'er touch'd earthly faces.'
So should my papers yellow'd with their age
Be scorn'd like old men of less truth than tongue,
And your true rights be term'd a poet's rage
And stretched metre of an antique song:
—But were some child of yours alive that time,
—You should live twice; in it and in my rhyme."

She had never thought of her father as a sensitive person; he was far too vital, too full of activity and energy. This poem, an acknowledgement of a deep secret passion, surprised her and, for the first time, she thought of Enyon as a fallible, susceptible human being rather than a distant and altogether frightening figure of authority. Had she seen him in this light before, maybe she would have forgiven his transgressions. Maybe things could have been different. A bubble of emotion caught in her throat; she would never see her father again or make up for lost time.

Startled by a loud wail, she looked up to see Kitto stumbling out of the mausoleum, keening into the wind and rain before resting his head against a red porphyry column. The congregation, their sensibilities honed by centuries of aristocratic propriety, pretended not to notice. But Blaze didn't see the man; she remembered the child who had come to his sister's rescue when she had fallen off her pony or got lost in the dark, and the years of resentment fell away. She ran through the tufts of grass and clumps of bramble until she reached her brother. Dropping to her knees, she peeled his fingers away from the great stone column and wrapped her arms around him so that his head rested on her shoulder. His tears trickled down her neck and she felt his slight, bony arms fasten around her back.

"Thank you," he whispered. "Thank you."

She didn't answer, but held him closer. Through his clothes, Kitto's body felt childlike; there was little hint of muscle or fat. Blaze felt unbearably sad. They had spent the last twenty years separated by mutual distrust. Far from making any of them rich, wealth had impoverished them all.

Blaze looked up and saw her mother coming towards them, a velvet-clad figure on crutches bent in the wind. "You are making a spectacle of yourselves," Clarissa hissed at her children. "Come away now."

Kitto winced.

"We're going back to the castle," Blaze told her mother, and pulled Kitto to his feet. Behind Clarissa she could see her nephews and niece looking anxiously towards them. Blaze smiled reassuringly and, with a free hand, motioned for them to stay. Jane kept her eyes on the ground, resolutely uninvolved.

Brother and sister stumbled down the slippery track, Kitto holding her hand tightly.

"Did you know about Ayesha?" Blaze asked.

Kitto stopped and looked at his sister in amazement. "I had no idea; I would never have left her. Did you?"

Blaze shook her head.

"We only made love once," Kitto said. "I don't think she liked it."

"When did it happen?"

"On my twentieth birthday."

Blaze did the maths, hoping in vain for a different answer.

Arriving at the castle, Blaze led Kitto into the kitchen, a no-go area which, being Cook's domain, had always been strictly out of bounds to the family. Now the window blind hung in ribbons. The copper saucepans and jelly moulds had turned green from lack of polish. The mighty pine table was piled high with detritus. The chairs were like wounded soldiers, all held together with bits of masking tape and twine. The windows were dirty and moss grew out of the sills. On the side, covered with newspaper, were trays of cocktail sausages to feed the guests. Also lined up were bottles of port and cheap white wine. Blaze wondered how anyone could live in such squalor.

Glenda Sparrow came out of the storeroom, dressed in black with a red apron. She looked at Kitto and at Blaze.

"Lady Blaze, haven't seen you round these parts for a long time." Twenty years had passed since their last meeting following the event neither wanted to witness.

The clock on the kitchen wall said 1:55. "I think you should leave before the mourners return," Blaze told Kitto. "I've got a car outside. I'll ask my driver to drop you at the station and come back for me and Ayesha."

Kitto went towards the door. "I've got a place in Pimlico. Will you come and see me?"

"I'll come tomorrow."

"And the next day?"

"And the one after that."

Kitto threw his arms around his sister's neck.

"Do you ever wish you'd been born someone else?" he whispered into her ear.

Blaze nodded. A lump was building in her throat. Equal in height, the siblings rested their heads together.

"I'm sorry, darling. I shouldn't have stayed away so long," she said.

"I'm even sorrier, Blazey. I should have known better."

Disentangling from each other, they walked out of the kitchen and down the back corridor. Blaze's driver got out of the car and opened the door.

"Please take my brother to St. Austell and put him on the London train. Here's money for his ticket," Blaze said, handing over two £50 notes.

As the car set off down the drive, Blaze could see Kitto's white face pressed against the window and his hand raised in a gentle wave.

14

The Wake

SATURDAY 27TH SEPTEMBER 2008

Summoning up her courage, Blaze walked around to the front of the castle and, pushing open the massive oak doors, stepped into the hall. Her first impression was that little had changed. As usual, during summer or winter, a huge open fire burned. The chimneypiece, measuring at least ten foot by ten foot, was framed on each side by half-naked Nubian gods carved in marble. On the wall to the right hung the Van Dyck portrait of the 16th Earl and his family, surrounded by hundreds of sporting trophies, ancient weapons and plates of armour.

Put another log on the bloody fire if you're passing, her father's voice called through time, and Blaze, from habit, dragged a large log from a pile by the door and threw it on to the embers. The fire licked appreciatively and she stepped back to avoid the sparks.

With a deep breath, she went through the second set of mahogany doors, into the smaller hall and up the main stairs. The first thing she noticed was a damp, musty smell. Looking down at the stair treads, she saw that the once-red carpet was worn to white threads and in the middle was frayed right through to the wooden steps. Up to the left and right, many of the picture frames had slipped and the canvases had bowed or sagged, making generations of noblemen and women appear drunk and misshapen. Reaching the landing, she noticed that the Turkish carpet was stained in huge patches like dirty clouds and, on the ceiling thirty feet above, chunks of beautiful woodwork, intricately carved by Grinling Gibbons, had fallen away, with the sky visible in places.

At the top of the stairs she turned right into the library. In the dim autumn light she was relieved to find her favourite book-lined room looked the same. The huge sofas covered in green velvet bowed in the middle and the material had worn away to the palest lime; it was almost exactly as she remembered it. Glancing towards the far door, she pictured the sixteen-year-old Anastasia, wearing a red silk slip, making her first grand entrance and silencing the room.

Rounding the corner, Blaze had to push hard against the double doors into the first of the great ballrooms. After some persuasion she managed to slip through a narrow opening. Her breath caught in her throat. The cut-velvet curtains hung in ribbons, the French eighteenth-century panelling had split. The only hint of paintings were from dark square or rectangular outlines on the walls. Some pieces of furniture remained; the huge side tables were covered in a layer of dust and detritus, and a grand piano sat in a pool of water. Ivy had inveigled its way through the glass and spread its tendrils around the shutters and into the room, a beautiful, menacing acid-green foliage creeping over the floor. Blaze walked faster, through that room and into the next and then the next. As door after door was pushed open to reveal stories of decay and dilapidation, she felt a rising sense of panic and confusion. What had happened? And so quickly? Could time and three children have done this? Was nature this angry and powerful? She imagined the ivy wrapping its leaves around her feet and pulling her back down into the earth.

Through the window she saw the mourners returning and retraced her steps. In the second ballroom there was her mother hobbling on crutches towards her, a diminutive, emaciated figure whose imperious deportment made her appear far taller and more stately than she actually was. Clarissa stopped three feet in front of her daughter but didn't lift the heavy veil which covered her face.

"Has he gone?"

"About half an hour ago," Blaze answered.

"Thank God. I was worried he might hang around and attract even more attention."

"He's having some kind of breakdown."

"As long as it happens elsewhere." Clarissa turned and walked away.

"Mother, wait," Blaze said. "We haven't even spoken about Father."

Clarissa stopped but didn't face her daughter. Her shoulders and back remained erect.

"What is there to say?"

"Words of comfort, perhaps," Blaze said. "You've lost a husband, I've lost a father."

"You lost a father the day you walked out of here."

"I didn't walk out," Blaze shouted. Trying to control herself, she said more quietly, "Are you going to deny what happened that day?"

Clarissa turned around slowly and lifted her veil. "Nothing happened."

"How can you say that?" Blaze shook her head in astonishment.

"Because it's true," Clarissa said with finality, shifting her weight on her crutches. "Now come along, we have people to entertain."

"Good God, girl, you haven't aged a bit," a large man said to Ayesha. "Is there a portrait in the attic?" He roared with laughter at his own joke, showering the young woman with shards of sausage roll. He had a strange face, with each part looking like it belonged to another—a narrow chin, pendulous cheeks and beady little eyes. He reminded Ayesha of a game called Consequences that she used to play with her mother: each person had to draw a section of a face and fold it over.

"You think I am my mother, Anastasia."

"Aren't you?"

"I'm her daughter, Ayesha."

"Where's she?"

"She died."

"What a waste." He looked her up and down slowly. "Who's your father?"

"Kitto," Ayesha said.

This revelation led to a fresh blast of sausage-roll pieces. "Jesus H. Christ," the man said. "I'm Peter Plantagenet-Parker, by the way. Call me Planty-Pal."

Ayesha smiled politely and picked shards of pastry out of her hair.

"Windy, Windy, come here," the sausage-sprayer shouted.

Another man, equally florid and flaccid-jawed, came over.

"You're jolly pretty," Windy said. His breath was so rancid that Ayesha had to step backwards quickly. "The Duke of Swindon at your service." He took her hand and kissed it wetly.

"Who does she remind you of?" Plantagenet-Parker asked.

"That girlfriend of Blaze's."

"A hole in one, old bean. Guess who her father is?"

"I wish it had been me! I fancied that girl rotten—we all did."

"Her father is Kitto."

"Lucky fucker."

"Are you older or younger than Ambrose?" Plantagenet-Parker asked Ayesha.

"Older," Ayesha said. She wanted to run away from these two men and their innuendoes.

"Just as well primogeniture is firmly in place. How many children do you have the wrong side of the blanket, Windy?" Plantagenet-Parker enquired.

"Get stuffed."

"They all did!" Plantagenet-Parker roared with laughter at his own joke. Swindon tried, playfully, to hit him.

"Will you excuse me?" Ayesha said and, without waiting for an answer, she slipped between the two men and worked her way towards the door.

"Ayesha, my dear, come here," Great-Uncle Tony called. He was talking to a tall, thin woman with a velvet beret clamped over long, grey, waist-length hair. She wore wellington boots and a thick overcoat even though the fire was chucking off heat.

"Lady Wellington d'Aresby, meet my great-niece Ayesha Scott."

Her Ladyship held out a hand which Ayesha shook.

"We were trying to decide whether we like weddings or funerals better," Tony explained. "I think weddings are depressing because you know that they're going to go wrong and all the misery is ahead. With funerals, all the hell of living is over."

"Marriages don't always go wrong," Lady Wellington remonstrated.

"Show me one happy one," Tony challenged her.

"Clarissa and Enyon's was pretty good."

"Hardly."

"Do tell."

Tony looked knowingly at Lady Wellington and then at Ayesha. *"Pas devant l'enfant,"* he said.

"Will you excuse me?" Ayesha ran out of the castle and into the drive and didn't stop until she reached the huge Cedar of Lebanon some two hundred yards up the hill. Resting her head against its gnarled bark, she took several large gulps of clean air and realised that she was crying.

"Are you OK?" someone asked.

Ayesha hadn't noticed anyone by the tree and, looking up, saw a strikingly handsome young man in jeans and a faded shirt. "I didn't mean to alarm you," he said. His voice was deep and gentle. Ayesha liked his broad face framed by unruly sandy hair and his gold-flecked eyes. Realising there were tears on her cheeks, she wiped them away with the back of her hand. The man took a clean handkerchief from his pocket and offered it to her.

"Thank you," she said and blew her nose loudly. She remembered her mother telling her off for this "unladylike" habit of "trumpeting" her colds and checked to see if the man was shocked. To her surprise he was looking at her solicitously and with great kindness, unlike most of the people she'd encountered since coming to England.

"Were you close to the Earl?"

"He was my grandfather but I never met him."

After a moment of confusion, the man nodded.

"You must be Ayesha."

Ayesha was taken aback. How did this total stranger know who she was?

Reading her mind, he answered, "This is a small place, news travels fast. I'm Mark Sparrow. Glenda, the cook, is my grandmother. I came to see if she needed any help."

"The cook?" Ayesha's heart sank. Her mother had warned her against wasting time on people of no consequence.

"There's a pub in the village—would you like a drink?"

"I would like a cup of tea," she said and, turning, set off down the drive. Mark hurried after her. At the pub, he found them a table in a corner and tried not to stare too intently. He had never seen a more beautiful woman. She caught his admiring glance and smiled back at him. Mark knocked his glass of water over and they both reached for it at the same time. Their hands overlapped. Instinctively he closed his fingers around hers. Ayesha tried and failed not to be aroused. They stared at each other. She heard her mother's reproving tones but it was too late.

"What do you do?" she asked.

"I work in computers. Games." He hesitated, desperate to try and make himself sound more accomplished, more desirable. "I'm finishing a PhD in Cognitive Neuroscience in my spare time."

"Is that a hobby?"

"The better I can understand the human brain, the greater the chance of inventing a machine to copy and replicate it. I run a team who are working on the Memristor, a memory transistor which will help computers store and process data even when they are turned off. In the past, they lost memory; now, like human brains, they'll be able to retain and analyse information at all times."

Ayesha's pulse quickened. She'd read how inventors like Mark were on the cusp of creating the fourth Industrial Revolution.

"If we are successful, and I believe we will be, it will transform the future of the world; it'll enable computers to supplement and, in many cases, replace the human mind."

"Will you own the patent?" Ayesha asked.

"I'm not sure if you can copyright progress."

"Do it and I'll never leave you."

Mark sat back and looked at her, unsure whether to be shocked by her avarice or thrilled by her directness.

"This is only the beginning," he said with quiet authority.

Ayesha squeezed his fingers. A shadow passed over the table.

"Someone said they'd seen you and a man go into the pub." Blaze loomed above them. Mark and Ayesha scrambled to their feet.

"I'm so sorry, Aunt Blaze," Ayesha said, flustered.

"Who are you?" Blaze asked Mark.

He put out his hand. "Mark Sparrow, Glenda's grandson." Something about this woman made him ill at ease.

"How do you do." Blaze shook hands. "Your grandmother has been kind to my family."

Mark nodded.

"Ayesha, we need to go," Blaze said and, in case there was any doubt at all, added, "now."

Ayesha turned to face Mark. "Thank you for the tea."

"Where are you going?" Mark asked. He could not bear the thought of losing this young woman so soon after they had met. Taking a pen from his pocket, he scribbled his telephone number on the back of a beer mat and handed it to her.

Ayesha put it in her pocket and, smiling shyly at Mark, followed her aunt to the door.

When the port ran out, so did the last guests. Before they left, Windy Swindon and Peter Plantagenet-Parker both offered to "comfort" Jane.

"You'll be needing to keep things supple down there," Windy said, looking over his shoulder to check that his wife was out of earshot.

"I'm a fine swordsman, you'll not complain." Planty-Pal patted her bottom. Jane slipped away. Carrying a tray of dirty glasses to the kitchen, she realised she was ill-equipped to deal either with heartbreak or lascivious men.

"Here, let me take that." Toby came down the Great Staircase towards her.

"Thank you, darling." Jane handed him the tray and picked up the last of the empty serving plates. The house, designed for many servants, was hopelessly laid out for this kind of event. Mother and son had to walk down two long corridors and two flights of stairs to reach the scullery. Toby went ahead, his trousers flapping around his ankles and the long tear in his shirt stretching from shoulder to waistband.

"What happened to your shirt?"

"It tore."

"I can see that."

Toby didn't answer. Jane could see from the slope of his shoulder that her son was upset.

"I'm desperate for a cup of tea. Would you like one?" she asked when they reached the kitchen.

Toby nodded and sat down heavily. Jane put the kettle on the Aga, now working again thanks to Blaze's patronage. The fridge and cupboards were full once more and all eleven radiators were on. As long as you ran from heated room to heated room, ignoring the icy passages, living at Trelawney during the coming winter would be reasonably comfortable.

"My girlfriend is Mrs. Sparrow's granddaughter," Toby said.

"Cross Mrs. Sparrow, our cook?"

Toby traced the grain of the pine table with his finger.

"Did you meet her at school?" Jane hoped that Clarissa wouldn't find out; she could only imagine the volley of disapproving asides. "Is she nice to you?"

"She's angry that we didn't ask her gran to the funeral."

"She has a point." Jane carefully took the glasses off the tray and put them into the sink to wash. Filling the basin with warm water, she handed her son a tea towel. "Will you dry, please?"

Toby stood beside her.

"Celia says this house is the tyrant and it's manipulating all of us. We are living 'anchrone' somethings."

"Anachronisms."

"Why don't we just leave, walk away?" Toby asked.

"We may not have a choice."

"Will Blaze chuck us out?"

"The house is hers until your brother is eighteen—until then she can do whatever she likes."

Toby put the glass he was drying down and looked at his mother. "What's going to happen? Now that Grandad's gone and Dad's . . ." He hesitated. "Why did you ask him to leave?"

Jane looked out of the window, as if the answer lay in the distance. It was a question she asked herself repeatedly.

"I was hurt and angry."

"That 'thing' happened ages ago, before you were married."

"He should have told me."

"He didn't know." Toby's voice rose and broke slightly. Jane reached her hand across the sink to touch his but he shied away.

"Do you miss him?" she asked.

Toby didn't answer.

"I miss him dreadfully," she said.

Toby snorted derisively. "It's your fault: you've got to sort it out."

"I'm trying." Jane knew how pathetic she sounded.

"Try harder." As Toby ran out of the kitchen, he knocked two chairs over and didn't stop to pick them up.

Jane righted the chairs and sat down at the table. Pooter nudged her leg and rested his head on her knee. Absently she stroked behind his ears. He whined slightly and looked at her with kindly brown eyes. At least someone loves me, she thought. He nudged her firmly; all he wanted was an evening walk. Rising stiffly to her feet, she took her coat from a peg on the wall and headed out into the rain.

15

Picking Up the Pieces

MONDAY 27TH OCTOBER 2008

Looking into the mirror, Blaze saw a white-faced woman with deep lines around her eyes. This, she thought, is what a "banker" looks like. She and her ilk had become objects of hate and vilification; their effigies were being burned on the streets and caricatures disembowelled and bloodied in newspaper cartoons. It was hardly surprising. Contagion had spread from the city to the countryside; from Iceland to Asia. Bailouts seemed to be given to large financial institutions rather than cash-strapped individuals. The economy was shrinking; the pound was falling further. Few seemed safe. Even the great Swiss banks UBS and Credit Suisse needed help. Hong Kong stocks were crashing; Russia, South Africa, Pakistan and Argentina were unable to raise money. But no one was prepared to take responsibility for the crash, nor were there any apparent consequences for those in the world of finance. Small investors were losing their houses and savings, while leading financiers boarded private planes bound for exclusive estates to conduct secret conversations.

Tying her hair back into a ponytail, Blaze put more foundation on her scar and applied a dab of colour to her pale lips. Imagining an increasingly angry mob demanding retribution on Wapping's streets, she changed into jeans and a T-shirt. She didn't blame anyone for resenting her privileges, particularly when her own fortune was riding the rapids of the financial turmoil with relative ease. Her portfolio had been liquid and largely unaffected by the collapse in share prices. With many stocks now undervalued, she had the opportunity to buy at rock-bottom rates. Banks were unlikely to lend; and for those, like her, with reserves of cash, it was a buyers' market. Some companies' value had plummeted; others, with strong underlying assets, would recover. If Blaze got the timing right, she'd make a fortune. Her only issue was what to buy.

She took the Tube and stopped at the gym on her way to the office. The place, normally full of City types, was empty. The attendant handed over a towel and a bottle of water.

"Bloody ghost town. Most of the businesses round here have gone under," he said.

As she ran on the treadmill, she imagined the deathly quiet of Sleet's offices and, for the first time, allowed herself to feel a frisson of superiority; let him laugh at and mock her now. All her predictions had come good.

At 7:20 a.m., Kerkyra Capital's reception area was deserted. An unknown security guard checked her pass and let her through. Neither her PA nor TiLing was there to meet her. Blaze took the lift to the seventeenth floor. The doors opened and she gasped. The floors were littered with empty champagne bottles and, in the centre of the office, there was a huge paddling pool full to the brim with something that looked like Vaseline. Cigarettes were stubbed out on carpets, walls and furniture. Desks were smeared with the residue of white powder. Empty glasses were strewn across tables. There was an eerie silence, broken only by the ticking of falling stocks shown in red on the huge television screens. A government minister was being interviewed on breakfast news: "We will never appreciate how close we came to a collapse of the banking system." On the monitors, stocks and currencies fluctuated as investors shifted their investments between markets. Blaze looked up at a sea of red figures and saw that the Far Eastern prices were tumbling.

Hearing a noise behind her, she turned to see a young man, tie loosely around his neck, suit dishevelled, playing a computer game. He looked familiar but she couldn't immediately place him; he had her hair colour and, as he looked up, she saw a rough-hewn version of her brother's face and realised it was her nephew.

"I know who you are," Ambrose said. "I've seen you around."

"What are you doing here?" Blaze asked, confused.

"I'm Sir Tom's assistant," Ambrose puffed with pride. "Didn't you come to the party? It was epic, four days non-stop." He hesitated and laughed. "Come to think of it, you weren't invited."

"Why aren't you at school?"

"Sir Tom says school's a waste of time."

"He went to school," Blaze pointed out.

"Sir Tom says—"

Blaze had heard enough. Ignoring him, she walked up the corridor and into the Chairman's office, a cavernous room with large picture windows on three sides. At the far end, sitting behind a huge desk, Sleet was looking at a computer screen. Glimpsing Blaze, he raised a hand but didn't bother looking up.

"Scott, I presume," he said. "Why haven't I made that joke before?"

"What the hell's going on?"

"I had a little celebration," he said, tapping his keyboard. "Thanks to you, I made an absolute killing—I'm up 34 per cent and rising. I've been buying all sorts of bargains at rock-bottom prices and selling the dogs that won't bark."

"What?" Blaze couldn't believe what she was hearing.

"The funny thing is, your presentation made sense. I couldn't say that out loud or people would have taken their money out of the Kerkyra funds, but I mirrored your portfolio exactly. On the day of the crash, I shorted some bank stocks, building societies, CDOs. The more the market went down, the more cash I made."

"So you deliberately misled our clients while privately following my advice?"

"I didn't want to risk losing their fees, did I?"

"That's outrageous."

"It's called business: I was hedging my bets. If you'd been wrong, I'd have made money on fees on their portfolios. Win-win, baby."

Blaze tried to keep her voice level. "Do you have any scruples at all?"

"Let me think about that for two seconds—one, two, no." He laughed loudly and leaned back in his chair. "Boy!" he called. "Piece of scum?" Ambrose came hurrying through the door. "Have you said hello to Aunty Blaze?"

Ambrose turned red.

"Why do you let him address you like that?" Blaze asked her nephew.

He didn't reply.

"Get me a coffee. Fucking run and get me a coffee," Sleet shouted at the young man. Ambrose turned and ran up the corridor.

"Why humiliate someone like that?" Blaze's face burned with indignation.

"Don't you remember how old we were when you did the same to me?" Sleet grimaced. "I can't tell you how sweet revenge feels."

Blaze looked at him. "That was different."

"How is she?"

"Who?" Blaze wondered if Sleet had gone mad.

"Anastasia."

Blaze could hardly believe it. The living Anastasia had been containable, a figure in a far-off country, but in death she was all-pervading, affecting every area of Blaze's life.

"She died."

"Died? What do you mean?" Sleet rose from his chair.

"Dengue fever."

"No!" Sleet advanced towards her, his arms waving.

Blaze, alarmed, took a step backwards. "I didn't know you kept in touch."

"I thought about her every day." Sleet's shoulders slumped and his bottom lip quivered. The tip of his small, bulbous nose had turned red. "Leave, now." He pointed towards the door.

Blaze walked across the trading floor. Reaching her office, she stepped gingerly over two used condoms and swept several cigarette stubs off her keyboard. Hoping to find calm and clarity in market indices, she turned on her computer.

"Blaze?" TiLing stood in the doorway. "I tried to warn you but your work mobile was switched off."

"Were you part of all this?" Blaze looked at the detritus on the floor.

TiLing shook her head. "I wasn't invited."

"Come in and sit down, if you can find anywhere." Blaze couldn't keep the weariness from her voice.

Carefully removing two pieces of pie and a glass from a chair, TiLing did as asked.

"I'm finished here." Blaze gestured around her office.

"Things are getting better. Congress has guaranteed $700 billion of toxic debt. The British government is introducing packages worth £500 billion," TiLing said. "We'll clean up this room and get back to normal."

Blaze was staggered by her colleague's naivety. "The FTSE has just had its biggest ever fall, down 21 per cent. The Dow's had its worst week in history. Iceland's three largest banks have collapsed. Goldman's and Morgan Stanley have had to change their status just to stop the flow of redemptions."

"The Americans will never let the global financial systems collapse. I hear they're pumping money into the European market." TiLing stood her ground.

"They feel responsible—for now. But the Fed can't maintain this course politically."

"It's not in America's interest to let the world burn."

"They'll save a handful of banks and their hundred best companies; the rest will be hung out to dry."

TiLing shook her head. "It's a blip."

Blaze looked at her, dumbfounded. "How can you be so sure?"

"I read history at university; everything is cyclical."

Blaze didn't answer immediately, but rearranged the pencils on her table into neat lines. "It's not just the crash, TiLing. I've had enough."

"Is this about your father?" TiLing asked. "My mum died last year and the whole family went a bit mad." She fought back tears, remembering her mother.

"I'm sorry, you should have told me." Blaze had no idea about the personal life of her closest associate.

"I did and you gave me a week's compassionate leave."

"I did?" Blaze vaguely recalled a feeling of irritation when TiLing wasn't around.

TiLing wondered if Blaze knew that she lived with her father and extended family in a small flat in London's Chinatown. That her elderly parent worked in a dim sum bar although his arthritis was putting his job in jeopardy. TiLing's salary paid for three younger brothers' fees at university or business school. One day, hopefully not too far off, her siblings would repay her investment in their future, but for now she desperately needed Blaze to carry on. Standing up, she took a folder from her briefcase and put it in front of her superior. "I've come up with a plan, a way for us to get out of here and start again." TiLing ran around the desk so she was beside Blaze. "I've got it all worked out. We'll start a hedge fund, build on your extraordinary reputation. People are longing to invest their money with you."

"It's not that simple," Blaze said.

"It is! All we need is a name, a few desks, an attitude and an area of specialisation. We'll need some private equity and then we're off."

Blaze hesitated. "For the first time, I'm having doubts about staying in finance. This used to be fun, making money for its own sake, but now I've seen the destruction, the damage caused by this mayhem, I don't think I can do it again," she said, thinking of Kitto.

"You are a conviction investor. You've been proved right," TiLing urged, trying to keep her voice level. "I have a line of hopefuls waiting to invest with you; there's £400 million on the table."

Blaze got up and went over to the window. "I have a young woman staying with me, the daughter of a friend. The other day she suggested we did something together. I couldn't think of a single thing to do in London, a place I've lived for most of my adult life. In the end I took her to the Tate because we'd had an office party there last year." She turned back to her colleague. "How old are you, TiLing?"

"Thirty-one." TiLing paused. "Next birthday."

Blaze laughed. "So young."

TiLing looked offended.

"You're the most talented person in this office," Blaze continued. "You'll have no problem finding another job."

TiLing went around the desk and stood face to face with her boss. "I work for you because you are one of the bravest, most ethical and talented investors of your generation. People listened to you and they'll listen again. If you walk away now, you'll be remembered as the woman who couldn't hack failure or success."

"That's unfair."

"So make it untrue."

Questions rattled around Blaze's brain. Was she strong enough, talented enough to start her own business, or would it expose her lack of emotional intelligence and swamp her in an administrative quagmire? Maybe she was a maverick investor who needed the comfort of a large organisation in order to function? Blaze ran her hands over her face and, tracing the bumpy edge of her scar from below her eye to her jawline, tried to consider other options. There were unlikely to be many jobs on offer in the City. What else could she do? Her entire career had been in this world and tailored to suit her narrow set of skills. She wasn't a good enough mathematician to return to academia and she was too intellectually inflexible to retrain in another discipline.

Then TiLing delivered her last shot. "If you don't do it, the same investors who want to back you will give their money to Wolfe."

Blaze's breath caught in her throat: Wolfe had taken enough.

She sat back down at her desk and, picking up a pencil and a piece of paper, began to doodle; with Moonshot Wharf plus all her share options and cash in the bank, she was worth nearly £10 million. Not for the first time, the thought occurred: as she had no children or other dependants, what was she saving or making more money for? Her own needs and desires were minimal; she had no interest in yachts, art or expensive holidays. Why risk starting a new business? On the other hand, what was there to lose?

"Why do you want to make money?" she asked her adviser.

TiLing didn't hesitate. "For all the obvious reasons: freedom and opportunity. I'd send my younger siblings to the best universities; get the top medical care for my father; and set up home with my boyfriend."

As she listened, Blaze doodled with her pencil. Without thinking, she drew a rectangle and then some windows. There followed a river, trees and a garden full of flowers.

"Where's that?" TiLing asked.

"Home," Blaze said and, in uttering that word, realised her purpose. Her father, though estranged, had made her the guardian of Trelawney. Twenty years had passed since their last meeting, yet Enyon still believed in his daughter and her ability. A lump rose in her throat. To restore the house was a Herculean task, but Blaze had to try and honour her father's wishes, live up to his expectations. Turning the piece of paper over, she began to make some more calculations.

"What are you doing?" TiLing asked, wondering if her boss was having some kind of breakdown; in the five years they'd worked together, Blaze had never drawn childish pictures or mentioned home.

"I need to make at least £2 million a year," Blaze said. "The roof alone will cost twenty."

"The roof?" TiLing's worst fears were being confirmed.

"We'd have to fix the plumbing and the wiring as well."

TiLing put her hand against the wall for support.

Looking down at the scribbled figures, Blaze crystallised her plan: she was going to create a foundation in Trelawney's name which would pay for repairs now and in the future.

"Do you think we can charge the standard two and twenty fees?" she asked.

"Why not?" TiLing said, her spirits rising.

"You believe we can raise £400 million?"

"By the end of the week."

Blaze took the pieces of paper and tore them into tiny shreds.

"We need a billion."

TiLing let out a low whistle. "That might be difficult in the first year."

"But doable?"

TiLing shrugged. “Money follows success.”

Smiling, Blaze looked at TiLing. “We’ll call the business Moonshot Capital. I will invest all of my own money. No one can accuse me of not having my own skin in the game.”

“All? Are you sure?” TiLing asked, wondering again about Blaze’s state of mind.

“One hundred per cent sure,” Blaze replied, meaning it. “We start tomorrow.”

TiLing punched the air.

16

The Letter

MONDAY 27TH OCTOBER 2008

Later that day, an envelope addressed to Blaze was delivered to Kerkyra Capital. Bound in red tape, it had the words *Private and Strictly Confidential* across the top. Opening it, Blaze saw a handwritten letter and a sheaf of official-looking papers. She closed her office door and tore open the envelope.

Blaze,

I have spent the last few weeks thinking desperately how to exonerate my behaviour and do something to make you think a little better of me. It's true that I shorted Acorn's stock with one thing in mind—to make money—that's what we do—but, as lame and unlikely as it sounds, I had no idea that your brother was Viscount Tremayne. For the first time in my professional life, I have seen the human impact of one of my investment decisions.

Owing to the idiocy of losing the respect of a woman whom I'd like to know better, I have, since then, recalibrated the ethics of my investment policy. I am not a romantic man but, from the moment I first saw you, I felt that our destinies were linked. I so enjoyed our afternoon in the country that, after you left, I was tempted to drive to London at breakneck speed to meet you off your train at Marylebone.

I have taken steps to mitigate my actions and to put right the damage caused to your brother. Enclosed are legal papers showing that I have bought and written off his debts up to £1 million. I have no idea about his specific financial circumstances but hope that this transfer of the profit I made from Acorn will mitigate some of his present hardship.

Please don't see this as a cynical attempt to salve my conscience or as a means of seeking a lever of control. I don't imagine my gesture will right the wrong committed or put things on a better footing between us, but I do hope it will be seen as an acknowledgement of my failings and the negligent way that members of our profession treat others.

Finally, you might ask why not do this act anonymously? Only because in the course of trying to uncover the identity of the creditor you would have wasted time and possibly exposed yourself and your brother to speculation and gossip. The paper trail enclosed in this letter is untraceable.

Sincerely,
Joshua Wolfe

Twenty-four hours later, Blaze, after many attempts, replied.

Dear Mr. Wolfe,

As predicted, your actions and your letter have caused some confusion. Suffice to say for now that I will do my best to repay you as soon as possible.

Yours sincerely,
Blaze Scott

17

Propositions

SUNDAY 30TH NOVEMBER 2008

Jane chased the horse all the way from the rose garden to the river. Most of the time, Milly was a biddable creature who came when called and liked to have her ears scratched. Today, fortified by eating the last of Jane's favourite plants, she was intent on escape. Neither Jane nor Milly could move particularly quickly over the sodden ground and they skidded and slipped in the mud. It had rained almost constantly since the funeral; the river had burst its banks and most of the meadow lay under water.

From an upper floor of the castle, Toby and Arabella watched their mother lunge for the horse's collar. Milly easily evaded capture; Jane stumbled and fell face first.

"Do you think she's gone mad?" Arabella asked. "I mean, like more mad than usual?"

"She is talking to herself a lot," Toby said, watching his mother pick herself up and set off at a determined pace towards the departing horse. About ten yards farther on Milly stopped and Jane made another grab for the animal's collar. Milly jumped to one side; Jane slipped and fell again. This time she didn't get up but sat in the mud.

"Is she crying?" Toby asked, trying to read his mother's facial expression from a distance.

"I can't see. Do you think we should help her? Or stay well away?"

"I think she might be laughing," Toby said, as his mother fell on to her back and flailed her arms around beside her. Even Milly stopped to see what was going on.

"Thank God, the washing machine's working again," Arabella remarked.

"Let's hope she cleans up before Blaze arrives."

Below them, Jane got slowly to her feet and walked back towards the castle. Milly, thinking of feeding time, followed her mistress.

"Who needs television with a mother like ours?" Arabella asked. "Maybe we could become a reality TV show like *The Osbournes*? I can see it now: *The Trelawneys of Trelawney.*"

Toby didn't laugh; he found his mother's growing eccentricities increasingly worrying. She had shown up at the parents' meeting the week before in a floor-length multicoloured skirt unearthed along with the photographs from the attic trunk. It hung off her hips and dragged along the ground.

Thanks to Blaze's intervention, there was now hot water in the castle and the radiators were working. Once again, there was decent food in the fridge and Mrs. Sparrow, fully reimbursed, had been promoted to Cook. Arabella had held a fake funeral for the death of mince, and she and her brother vowed never, under any circumstances, to eat it again. Clarissa had finally agreed to take meals in the kitchen with her grandchildren, but Jane often missed lunch or dinner. When she wasn't in the office reclassifying the unpaid invoices and preparing long and highly detailed spreadsheets for her sister-in-law, she was making new prints, bent over the attic press or her sketch pad. Once her designs had been full of colour, but now her palette was limited to blacks and greys. Bucolic scenes were replaced with a swirling mass of insects, serpents, ivies, briars and twisted trees, reflecting both her mood and outlook on life. Jane had papered these to her bedroom wall.

"Like totally fucking creepy," Arabella had commented. Even Toby, normally supportive of his mother's work, had shuddered. The bugs were menacing and the snakes so real it seemed they might slither out of the papery world and into theirs at any moment.

Today, as Jane had often told her children over the last few weeks, was D-Day: they'd find out whether they had to leave Trelawney. The house belonged to their aunt until Ambrose came of age and she would be likely to want to enjoy it.

Toby checked his watch and saw that it was already midday.

"She better clean up."

"Do you think the wicked aunt will chuck us out?" Arabella asked. Their first and last sighting of Blaze had been through the rain at Enyon's funeral. Under her thick black hat and raincoat, the most memorable feature was a splash of red lipstick. Arabella had already packed her favourite possessions—a microscope Tuffy had given her, the skeleton of a rat found in the attic and a photograph album—into a small bag.

"Mum says we'll be given a few weeks' notice to find somewhere else," reassured Toby.

"Where will we go?"

Toby shrugged. "She went to see a housing trust and put our names on a register."

"Will Blaze chuck Gran out too?"

"It's not like she's shown any interest in her since the funeral, is it? She hasn't been down once."

They both looked at Jane walking back through the overgrown garden, past the Venus fountain and the 8th Earl's grotto. Milly followed at a safe distance, unsure whether to surrender to capture.

"Blaze is a hedge-fund manager," Toby said.

"A real one? Like on the news?" Arabella could hardly contain her excitement.

Toby nodded.

"So she's, like, really bad?" Arabella whistled. "We could shoot her and be heroes?"

"If we kill her we'll just be murderers."

"But lots of people will cheer."

"There are different kinds of City people, all on a spectrum of evil. I don't know where she falls."

"Do you think she was one of the ones that did for Dad?" Arabella's eyes followed Jane, who had now put a halter on Milly and was leading her back past the decimated rose garden. Horse and owner were splattered in mud. "Maybe she ruined Iceland or Ireland."

"I wish Dad was here," Toby said.

Arabella bit her lip. They tried not to mention Kitto in front of their mother as it led to copious tears.

"Do you think he'll come back?"

"I want the old Dad." The last time the children had seen him, he'd stared out of the window seemingly oblivious to their presence.

"Has he had a breakdown?"

"He should be at home." Toby clenched and unclenched his fists, unable to understand why their mother had excommunicated their father.

A black chauffeur-driven Mercedes swept up the drive.

"Perfect timing." Toby shook his head in disbelief. The car stopped outside the front door. Jane rounded the corner at the moment Blaze stepped out, pristine in a black trouser suit. From their second-floor window, the children could make out the flash of their aunt's red nail polish and matching red lipstick, the awkwardness of the greeting followed by Jane leading Milly towards the barn, and Blaze walking purposefully through the front door.

"She looks like Cruella de Vil," Arabella said. "Do you think we should hide Pooter?"

"He's hardly a cute spotty puppy."

"Shall we go downstairs and protect Mum?"

"I'm going to meet Celia."

Arabella's face fell. "I thought she'd finished with you?"

Toby winced but didn't reply.

"I hope she does." Arabella didn't mean to be unkind but, with her father and eldest brother away, Tuffy at a conference somewhere in America, her mother distracted and her brother obsessed by his girlfriend, she was mostly alone and bored. She liked her grandmother but had heard more than enough stories about the old days.

Jane had made an effort to tidy her office, but the desk was covered with papers and folders, the filing cabinets were still exploding with documents and the bookshelves bowed under the weight of ledgers and directories. On one wall there was a huge estate map dated 1938. Most of the time Jane didn't notice it; but, following Blaze's glance, she was painfully aware that nearly all of the fields were now in other people's ownership.

"Have you seen Kitto?" Blaze asked.

"The children saw him last week," Jane said, wiping dust off a chair and pushing it in her sister-in-law's direction. Blaze took a white handkerchief out of her pocket and cleaned the seat carefully.

"He's not doing well."

"I suppose that's my fault?" Jane asked.

Blaze ignored the remark. "He'd like to see you."

"Too late for that."

"He gave her up for you, Jane; isn't that enough?"

Jane brushed the top of the desk, sending little clouds of dust up into the air.

"Anastasia took everyone else's heart—why couldn't she leave my husband's?"

Blaze agreed with her sister-in-law, but didn't want to add to the hurt. "If you knew all along, why was it such a shock?"

Jane hesitated and looked out of the window. When she finally answered her voice was barely audible. "There's a difference between knowing and accepting, between suspecting and acknowledging." She pushed her shoulders back and cleared her throat. "I went to the local council to enquire about housing. There are eight thousand on the waiting list. As a deserted bankrupt wife with three school-age children, I'm about number five thousand. If I become a heroin addict, my chances would be better."

Blaze didn't react.

"There were forty jobs advertised for shelf stackers and till managers at the new Tesco outside Launceston. Three hundred and seventeen people applied. I got rejected before interview."

Taking her briefcase from the floor, Blaze snapped open the locks and brought out three neatly bound folders which she placed on her knee.

"You see, I find myself in a bit of a bind—sort of up shit creek without a paddle. I have no one else to blame, of course. Should have had a Plan B—should have seen the whole thing coming." Jane was trying hard to push the lump in her throat back down. "Your brother and I," she hesitated, "we were the wrong people for the job. Turns out we couldn't run a bath, let alone an estate." She stole a look at her sister-in-law; Blaze was fiddling with the edge of one of her folders. "I'm sorry you've been left with the mess," she concluded.

"I'm only the regent. The castle belongs to your son."

"We have been woeful custodians."

"Something of an understatement." Blaze didn't need to conduct her sister-in-law's performance review; she was desperate to get back to London. The incorporation of Moonshot Capital, as TiLing predicted, had been easy. So too had enticing clients; the fund had quickly reached its target. What Blaze hadn't anticipated was Sleet's fury and vindictiveness. His star manager had defected, taking with her many of Kerkyra's clients, including Spalding Trust, an insurance company which had placed £250 million with her and promised, subject to performance results, to move another £750 million over by early 2009. Sleet had tried to stop banks from handling Moonshot, threatening to withdraw any Kerkyra custom from those who dealt with it.

Her other issue was as pressing: the challenge of finding something in which to invest. There were opportunities, but the market was volatile. Because Moonshot was largely liquid, it was making minimal performance fees. With her mother, Jane and her niece and nephews to support, as well as Wolfe's loan to Kitto to repay, Blaze needed to generate money.

"Can you clear some space?" She pointed to the desk.

Jane hurriedly piled some files on the floor.

Blaze put down the three folders: green, red and blue. On the front, typed neatly on white stickers, were the headings "Past," "Present" and "Future." The last one was worryingly slim and contained, as far as Jane could see, only a few pieces of paper. She remained standing; it didn't seem right to sit down without asking. It was her sister-in-law's house now.

"As you correctly summarised, this is one huge mess."

Jane nodded. "Could you give us a couple of weeks to find somewhere else? I don't mind taking Clarissa. We've become used to each other."

Blaze looked at her in surprise. "I don't want you to go."

"You don't?"

"I want to offer you a job."

"Job?" Jane wondered if she'd heard correctly.

"The house needs a full-time live-in caretaker and manager. I'm offering you the position. The salary is £45,000 per annum plus health insurance and a contribution to a pension."

Jane slumped into a chair.

"Before you accept, you should hear my plans."

Jane didn't trust herself to speak without crying; her children would have a home, there'd be food on the table and, best of all, she thought guiltily, she wouldn't have to lose her printing press.

Blaze cleared her throat and opened the files. "I've been through the estate accounts, such as they are, past and present. In its simplest form, before any repairs, excluding food and any luxuries, your annual overhead has for some years been approximately £245,000. While in some ways this has been admirably parsimonious, it was also woefully short-sighted."

Jane tried to concentrate.

"I have asked three building companies—two local and one national—to quote for putting the roof right, and the cheapest estimate is in excess of £25 million. There's also the plumbing, rewiring, central heating and other factors to consider. All in all, we'd be looking at a capital investment of over £50 million spread over five years."

"There is, as you are aware, debt of over £1 million," Jane said.

"That's been taken care of," Blaze replied, thinking of Wolfe's letter.

"Taken care of? You paid it off?" Jane asked in amazement.

Blaze shifted uncomfortably in her seat. "Let's just say a guardian angel."

"You are so kind." Tears spilled out of Jane's eyes.

"Let's go to the kitchen. It's so cold in here I can't concentrate." Blaze hoped that a change of scene would help banish thoughts of Wolfe from her mind. Picking up her three files, she strode out of the room.

The sound of her sister-in-law's heels clack-clacking on the flagstones jolted Jane out of her stupor and she followed. It was Mrs. Sparrow's day off and the kitchen table was covered in the remnants of the children's breakfast: badly cut slices of bread and honey, unwashed pans, plates smeared with egg yolk and bacon rinds.

"Kids," Jane said apologetically. Taking a cloth, she wiped the end of the table and righted two chairs for them to sit on.

Blaze continued with her theme.

"In addition to repairs, there's also the issue of inheritance tax."

Jane felt her spirits drop. "I thought about serving teas."

"You will be. And lunches. And breakfasts. We are going to sweat this asset."

"Sweat the asset?"

"It's about time the house contributed. To date it's been a drain on income. Time for it to pay." Blaze smiled and pushed across the folder labelled "Future." "Have a look. I'll make coffee."

Jane opened the file and flicked through a series of pages, but the numbers swam in front of her. Fix on the cream teas, she told herself.

"I worked out that I could make a hundred scones for 20 pence each and sell them for £3," she said, shoving the folder away.

"That isn't going to cover the cost of heating, is it?" Blaze asked. "Can I get back to the bigger picture?"

Jane nodded.

"To prevent the inheritance-tax liability arising and provide a public benefit, the house has to be open to the public for at least thirty-one days a year. The problem is how to get anyone to come to this part of Cornwall. There are five National Trust houses nearby with superior collections."

"None as beautiful or as old."

"I'm not the one who needs convincing. All the other houses are, by and large, in good condition; they have been looked after. This one hasn't and I can't afford to put it right. I am wealthy, but not that wealthy."

Jane felt her spirits dive again.

"Even if I had the money, I wouldn't give it to you." Blaze's first concern was repaying Wolfe the £1 million. She had put her apartment on the market, but had not had one viewing. "My proposal should bring in hundreds of thousands of visitors, each paying £8, and employ many local people. It will take a few years to generate a full income, but at least Ambrose will inherit a viable business. With time, there'll be enough money to gradually replace the roof, the wiring and install central heating. In the short term, I'll set up a small foundation whose purpose will be solely to loan the house funds for basic repairs."

"Why would you do all this for us?"

It was a question Blaze had asked herself many times over the last few weeks. Her father mainly, but also perhaps pity for her brother and sister-in-law and the challenge of overcoming impossible odds. There was another factor: the opportunity to return to Trelawney with her head held high.

"Please read this." Blaze pushed another piece of paper across the table. By the second paragraph, Jane burned with anger: Blaze's idea was to open the house exactly as it was; Trelawney would stand as a cautionary tale of what happened to aristocrats who failed to work and overlooked the realities of change and progress. It would be a testament to an anachronistic and antiquated system, and visitors would be invited to see the degradation of a noble dream as well as its history. The decline and fall of the House of Trelawney would mirror the history of Britain; like the country, Trelawney was a shadow of its former self, a mere elegy and an effigy. Visitors would walk with wonder: viewing the sky through gaping holes in the roof, crunching fallen plaster underfoot, observing the inhabitants at rest and play. Anyone who felt moved to could contribute to a restoration fund.

"Is this your idea of a joke?"

Blaze looked surprised. "Of course not."

"You want to put me and my children and your own mother on display like animals in a zoo and parade our failings before the public?"

"That's not how it's meant." Blaze shifted uncomfortably in her seat, aware that her approach might seem insensitive.

"That's how it damn well looks." Jane leaned across the table, propelling the sheet of paper back towards her sister-in-law. "I would prefer to starve and live on the streets than accept this." She stood up and walked to the door.

"Jane," Blaze called. "Please wait."

Jane stopped but didn't turn around.

"The disintegration of the house began long before you arrived. Nothing has been spent on it since the 1900s when labour became expensive."

"Kitto inherited a going concern," Jane said quietly.

"A going concern. Going, not staying."

"I love this place; I have let it down."

"Trelawney is just a film set for our dreams and fantasies. Take away the script, the razzamatazz, the people or prestige, the power or money, and it's just bricks and mortar."

"It's more than a simple story," Jane replied. "It's a way of life. It's where I live with my children."

"You call this a life?" Blaze looked around the kitchen in amazement.

"You ought to leave." Jane clenched her fists so hard that the knuckles turned white.

Blaze shoved her chair back and rose to her feet.

"I'm going to offer Mum a room in my flat or sheltered accommodation. I will also look after Kitto. He needs psychiatric support, possibly primary residential care. I won't throw you out of here—it's your home. Do what you like with it until your son comes of age. I will inform the solicitors of my decision." Taking up her briefcase, Blaze left the kitchen and walked towards her mother's apartment.

Opening the door to Clarissa's rooms, she was hit by a wave of heat; there was a burning fire and three fan heaters. Bowls of freshly cut flowers sat on each surface, and the dining table was set for one, with two wine glasses, two knives and fork, and fine bone china.

"Oh, it's you," Clarissa said, appearing from her bedroom. "I can't believe how long it is since you've been. I might have died." She let out a sniff.

"Things have been tricky at work—you might have seen all the stuff on the news?" Blaze saw that the flat-screen TV had arrived.

"Business and shares don't affect us in Cornwall." Clarissa went over to the chair nearest the fire and sat down.

"I wish you were right," Blaze said, thinking about the queues of anxious savers she had seen on the news outside one of Acorn's branches in Launceston.

"Poppycock."

Blaze changed the subject. "Are things a bit more comfortable now?" She was hoping for a tiny thank-you or at least an acknowledgement of her generosity.

"I don't like the carers."

"Why?"

"They're foreign."

"Is that so wrong?"

"I have to explain things all the time. The other day I asked for Gentleman's Relish on toast and a bottle of Berry Brothers Good Ordinary Claret. The woman had no idea what I was talking about."

"Those are slightly arcane requests." Blaze suppressed a smile.

"You said they were highly trained."

"They are qualified caregivers."

"I want a new one."

"You're on your eleventh person. It's not that easy to get people to come to this part of the world."

"What about a local girl?"

"We advertised and no one answered. They don't want this kind of work." Blaze fought to keep the exasperation out of her voice. "I want you to come to London."

Clarissa leaned over and poked the fire hard. "I hate London; a noisy, smelly place."

"I can organise proper care there—with English people—and you can live in my flat."

"What is a flat?" Clarissa asked, looking perplexed.

"It's—oh, never mind." In the small butler's pantry off the drawing room, Blaze could see a pretty young woman heating up some lunch for her mother.

"I only like living somewhere surrounded by my own land. Looking at other people's property would make one feel ill. The answer is resolutely and absolutely no."

The carer came out of the pantry holding a steaming bowl of soup. "Ladyship, like lunch?" she said in a thick Polish accent.

"Magda, how many times do I have to tell you: 'Luncheon is served, Your Ladyship,'" Clarissa corrected her.

"Lady Luncheon served," Magda said sweetly.

Clarissa turned to Blaze. "Do you see what I mean? It's too much." Then she turned to Magda. "My name is not Lady Luncheon, nor is it Lady Dinner or Lady Bedtime or Lady Pills."

Magda smiled, put the bowl on the table and asked Blaze, "Soup?" Blaze shook her head and, looking at her mother, enquired, "What does it matter if she gets your name right or the correct title?"

Clarissa drew herself up tall. "I may be the only one left who flies the flag of standards, but fly it I will." She went over to the long mahogany table and sat down. Blaze sat next to her.

"I worry that you'll get lonely here."

"Life without your father is exceedingly dull. I turn round to say something to him and realise he isn't there." Clarissa gulped hard. "Then I remember he never will be. I can't tell you how odd that feels after sixty years."

Blaze reached a consoling hand towards her mother but it was ignored. Clarissa blinked several times and then raised a spoonful of soup to her lips. "Is she trying to burn my mouth? Magda, Magda, too hot." Magda came out of the pantry again.

"What's wrong, Lady?"

"The soup is too hot."

"You want chill soup?"

"I want soup I can drink without a fatal injury." Clarissa pushed the bowl away.

"It will cool," Blaze said.

"I'm too near death to wait for soup to cool. I could go at any moment."

Magda took the soup bowl back to the pantry. Blaze heard the fridge open and the sounds of an ice cube being popped out of a plastic holder followed by a splash. Seconds later Magda appeared with a melting cube sitting in the middle of the soup. This time there was no sweet smile, just a look of resignation. Turning around, she went back to her kitchen.

Clarissa regarded the ice cube with disdain.

"She was on the wrong side in the war," she said in a stage whisper.

"She's Polish, not German," Blaze countered.

"She was one of the Poles who tried to murder your father and did for my brothers."

"She would not have been alive."

"You want to leave me with a murderess." Clarissa's lip trembled. "All alone in this forsaken place without your father."

Blaze felt exhausted. "Come back to London with me, please."

"Now you're trying to take me away from my home." Clarissa had recovered her composure and adopted her most imperious expression. "I will not be moved." She raised the soup spoon to her lips and took a sip. "Now it's too cold." She put the spoon down and pushed the bowl away. "I worry about Jane; she has let herself go. You must have a word with her, darling, or when Kitto comes back from his holiday he won't recognise her."

Blaze looked at her mother. Did she think her son was on holiday or had she invented this fiction to protect herself from reality?

"Don't you think it's about time you found a husband?" When things became difficult, Clarissa used Blaze's marital status as a weapon.

"Not this again, Mum."

"You might find a nice widower. The Plantagenet-Parker girl nabbed a grieving marquess when we thought she was far too long in the tooth and broad of girth to find anyone."

Blaze stood up. She knew exactly where this conversation was going.

"You can't handle the truth, can you?" her mother taunted.

I am a husk of a woman, childless and sad, Blaze said to herself.

"You are childless and sad," Clarissa said, holding out her cheek for her daughter to kiss. "What is a woman without a man?"

Still a woman, Blaze said under her breath.

"A husk, a mere husk."

Though Blaze had been expecting this, her mother's words stung.

"Magda, Magda, see Lady Blaze out, please," Clarissa called.

"I can see myself out," Blaze said, picking up her coat and briefcase.

"I'm trying to train the girl. It's for her own good."

Magda came out of the pantry, wiping her hands on a tea towel.

"All I ask, Blaze, is that you find me one, just one, decent member of staff." Clarissa looked hard at Magda.

"You want resignation?" Magda asked.

"You see, you see." Clarissa's voice rose. "They are so temperamental."

"Magda, please don't go," Blaze said. "You are doing a brilliant job. My mother is in mourning and not herself."

"I am entirely myself. Who else would I be? The man in the moon?" Clarissa retorted.

Blaze leaned down and kissed her mother. "I'll see you soon."

Clarissa looked forlorn. "Do you have to go, darling?"

"Things are difficult at work."

"Please don't stay away too long. I am bound to die. Next week, if I'm lucky."

You'll outlive all of us, Blaze said to herself and, pushing the door open, stepped out into the courtyard. As she headed towards her car, she caught a glimpse of Jane bent over the sink, scrubbing something. Blaze walked past the window and down the cobbled path. She was glad that Jane and her mother had been so difficult; it made the unlikeliness of a return to Trelawney easier to bear. Without her sister-in-law's involvement, her idea to open the house to the public would never work. Let them all live there and manage the decay. Blaze would send enough money for them to get by.

18

The Festive Season

SUNDAY 14TH DECEMBER 2008

For as long as anyone could remember, the Earls of Trelawney had held an annual New Year's Eve party in the Great Hall. In days of plenty, up to seventy-five guests stayed in the house while several hundred billeted in nearby stately homes. It often took an hour to disgorge all the guests from their carriages and footmen had to run up and down the waiting line with hot-water bottles and mulled wine to stave off boredom and cold. To justify the journey, the Earls put on a terrific show: there were minstrels, acrobats and orchestras; the finest chefs were brought over from Paris and the best wine from Bordeaux. At the start of the twentieth century, dance bands were flown in from America. As the money ran out, the bands became a record player; wine came from a box; the guest list was pruned; and dinner became peanuts and crisps.

Jane longed to cancel, but pride spurred her on and she was determined not to be the first Countess to break the tradition. The main problem was who to ask—she dreaded the gossip and endless questions about the whereabouts of her husband. In the end, she resolved to put on a bit of a show. Between Blaze's modest stipend, Tuffy's rent and the children's odd jobs, she had saved enough money to hire some large speakers (her budget didn't stretch to a local band), two kegs of beer and some crates of wine from the local cash and carry. Mrs. Sparrow helped her bake pasties and tarts.

For the first time in the castle's 800-year history, Jane was inviting people who lived in the village.

"Don't expect me to come," Ambrose said.

"This is 2008," Toby replied. "Times have changed, you know."

"Is this a ploy so your girlfriend can feel at home?" Ambrose mocked.

Toby took a swing at his brother.

"Boys!" Jane said. Having all three at the castle tested her patience to the limit. None could drive; all were bored. No wonder generations of Trelawneys had forced their children to ride, hunt, sail, shoot and partake in endless rural pastimes. It was a way of keeping them occupied. Once upon a time Jane had tried to limit social media and computers; now, at the first sign of trouble, she suggested FIFA.

"What do you do when you sneak off with Great-Aunt Tuffy?" Ambrose asked his sister. Arabella longed to explain, but knew it would be met with incomprehension and ridicule. Tuffy's latest paper, "Lyme disease as a lead indicator of climate change," to be presented at a scientific conference in Birmingham early in the new year, would make the connection between warmer weather and the spread of infectious illness. Over the last five months, she and Arabella had been monitoring the significant increase in ticks and fleas on dead rodents and carrion, and correlating this to a rise in global temperature.

"Why don't you ask Taffy?" Jane asked.

"She's called Tuffy and she wouldn't be seen dead at a party."

"Maybe she could hop in and have a bite?" Ambrose roared at his own joke.

"I'm sure she'd jump at the chance." Toby couldn't resist teasing his sister.

"Fuck off."

"Language, Arabella, language," Jane remonstrated.

Toby held up his hands in mock horror. "Bit late for that."

"Shall we ask the Plantagenet-Parkers?" Jane said, keen to keep the peace.

"No!" The children were united in that at least.

"The Beachendons?"

"Those three chinless wonders? No way."

Jane put down her pen and paper. "So you do the guest list then. I don't know anyone."

"We'll just ask the village," Toby said firmly.

"I'm going to Courchevel," Ambrose announced.

"Who's paying?"

"My friend Mohammed's dad is taking us in his plane. All we have to do is bring underpants."

"You lucky bastard," Arabella said. "I want to go to the Caribbean."

"Courchevel is in France, you twat—it's a ski resort."

"You'll be cold in your underpants."

"I don't know anyone who lives in the village," Jane interrupted.

"You know the Sparrows," said Toby.

"They're not coming."

"Why not?"

"Cross Mrs. Sparrow didn't say." Jane knew that Gordon had forbidden his wife to come; Glenda might have to take the Trelawneys' money but she would never accept their hospitality.

"What's for dinner?" Arabella said, hoping that Mrs. Sparrow had left something; Jane could murder the finest ingredients.

"Is the same vicar there?" Jane asked.

"He left years ago, it's a woman now."

"Does Mrs. Grundy run the corner shop?"

"Her son John took it over."

"Has Dad got a ski jacket?"

"Look in his cupboard."

"Thought you only had to bring underpants."

"What's the name of the family who moved into the rectory?"

"Jenkins."

"Did you know there was a war called Jenkins's Ear? Might be a relation."

"Who'll draw me an invitation card?"

"Only children draw cards."

"You *are* children."

"*Top Gear*'s on in five minutes."

"My turn for the chair."

"Last one gets the floor."

A mad scramble, two upended chairs, a thrown punch, a spilt glass, followed by the clatter of footsteps on the stone floors, and then absolute quiet. Jane sat at the table, resting her head on her forearms. She felt so tired. Too tired to upright a chair, let alone give a party. Why didn't Kitto come back? Surely if he loved her enough, he'd ignore her anger and make everything OK. Thinking about her husband brought a fresh wave of tears, too many to wipe away.

Eleven days later, on Christmas morning, Jane rose early to put the turkey in the oven. She went to let out the chickens, feed the livestock and tend to Milly. It was, even by Cornish standards, filthy weather. Heavy, freezing rain blew up the estuary at right angles to the house. The horse stood with her head between her front legs in the far corner of the field, refusing to hear Jane's call. Having caught the animal, Jane decided to bring her into the kitchen as a Christmas treat.

Ambrose was the first child to emerge. He walked into the kitchen in a pair of new slippers, hand-embroidered by his mother with the family's crest.

"What the fuck is the horse doing in here?"

"It's cold and wet outside."

"It's a fucking horse."

"If you'd seen her, you'd have taken pity."

"It's not house-trained or hygienic." On cue, Milly lifted her tail and delivered a large, steaming turd.

"I'll have that out of here in a jiffy," Jane said, opening the cupboard beneath the sink and bringing out a dustpan and brush.

"You think this is funny and a bit eccentric, don't you? But it isn't funny. It isn't cool. It isn't hip. It's just depressing, squalid and filthy. I wish you could see it through a normal person's eyes." Ambrose's voice cracked. "You think I don't bring people home because I'm snobbish. Wrong. I wouldn't subject anyone I like to this place."

"You don't mean that, darling."

The veins beneath Ambrose's temples stood out and his face had gone as red as his slippers.

"Look at your daughter. She's feral. Runs around with a mad old woman collecting fleas. Poor Toby's in love with a girl who'll leave him for a boy with central heating. No wonder Dad walked out."

Jane was torn between wanting to shout at or comfort her son. "Ambrose, have a cup of tea."

"What is the role of any parent if it isn't to help equip their children for the future?" He looked around the kitchen. "Is this the world you want for us?"

"You have been given so many advantages," Jane said, feeling aggrieved that her eldest couldn't appreciate the sacrifices made on his behalf. "We sent you to one of the best schools in England in the hope that you might get an education and contacts. But you've squandered those opportunities."

"What was the point in doing exams? My future was set, mapped out. The prison of inheritance, of duty and 'standards.' I am trapped."

Jane thought he might cry.

"This family hates and resents me for my so-called good fortune. As if it's my choice to have been the firstborn, to have been left with this total dump."

Jane made a move to hug him but, sidestepping her, he put his foot into Milly's turd. There was an ominous, audible squelch.

"For fuck's sake," Ambrose said, hopping around on one foot while he ripped the dirtied slipper off the other. "Sleet says the aristocracy is finished, over, done with," he spat out. "He's right."

"He doesn't sound awfully nice, your Mr. Sleet."

"He's the most brilliant man in the whole world. I have finally found someone to admire." Ambrose took a step towards the door. "You never liked me as much as the others. You made that perfectly clear from the day Toby was born—you thought I was a bit square, a bit bourgeois, like your own parents." His voice wobbled. "I no longer care what you think. I don't want to be like you or Dad: I'm going to make it. I'm going to be like Sleet." He kicked off the slipper he was wearing. "I'm off to London."

"It's Christmas Day, there are no trains," Jane said, wishing she too could run away.

Ambrose shrugged. "I'm probably not the only saddo trying to get away from home." He stuck his thumb out like a hitchhiker. "Happy Christmas." The door slammed behind him.

Jane wondered if she should run after him, try to offer some words of reassurance, but she knew that, even if she found him, they were both too hurt and angry to put things right. Hopefully the journey to London would be grim and long enough for Ambrose to reflect on what he'd said and think of his parents and home in a more flattering light. She scooped the horse dung up in the dustpan and gave the floor a half-hearted wipe with the dishcloth. Unhooking the hay net, she led a reluctant Milly out of the kitchen, along the corridor and down the drive to the field.

Forty-three people accepted Jane's New Year's Eve drinks invitation and the first to arrive, on the dot of 8 p.m., was Clarissa, accompanied by Arabella.

"Toby, darling, get me a stiff gin. Three fingers," Clarissa told her grandson.

"It's wine or beer only," Jane said.

"I'll have one small glass of red wine." Clarissa pursed her lips. "Who's coming? I hope you've asked the Plantagenet-Parkers and the Beachendons."

Jane braced herself. "Actually we've asked the village."

"The village? I don't understand."

"The neighbours."

"Very funny, darling." Clarissa took a sip of wine.

Jane looked at Toby and shrugged.

The next guests to arrive were Mary Clark with her husband and two children. They were followed by John and Marsha Grundy and his mother who was commonly known as Mrs. G.

"I do wish the Plantagenet-Parkers and the Beachendons would hurry up," Clarissa grumbled as she watched the other guests, none of whom she recognised, throng through the front door.

Mark and Celia Sparrow arrived. Toby brought them over to meet his mother.

"Why are they using the front door?" Clarissa asked.

"People aren't mingling," Jane said nervously.

The guests had split into two groups, both largely silent. In the middle, with her back to the fire, stood Clarissa, staring stonily ahead.

"There's been a bit of trouble in the village," Mark explained. "Seems that John Grundy's wife Marsha has been carrying on with Ted the publican. Ted's wife smashed the windows of the corner shop."

Jane put her hand over her mouth to suppress a smile. Looking over at the diminutive John Grundy, she tried to imagine him at the centre of such drama.

Taking a bottle of white and a bottle of red, one in each hand, Jane advanced towards her guests.

"You are most welcome here," she said. "Happy New Year."

The alcohol ran out by ten o'clock, the conversation some time before. Couple by couple, the guests sidled away, some thanking Jane for her hospitality, others simply nodding in her direction.

"That was a terrific success," Clarissa said, unable to keep the triumph out of her voice. "Next year, I'll do the guest list."

"Feel free."

"You're tight."

"Not nearly tight enough," Jane retorted.

"Arabella, walk me home before there's a scene." Clarissa held out her arm.

The room was spinning slightly. Looking up, Jane was sure that Van Dyck's horse winked at her. She winked back and laughed. She needed another drink. It was hours till midnight and she had to keep going. She picked up the bottles one by one. They were empty. She eyed the door to the corridor and walked determinedly towards it. One foot, two foot, one foot, two foot, whoopsie. She must have tripped, for she found herself flat on the floor. Ouch. That knee again. Pooter's licking my cheek. Sweet Pooter. He understands. Who's picking me up? Strong arms. Is it Kitto? Has he come back? I miss you, darling K. Thank you for coming back. Oh dear. It's not you. Suppose you never could carry me. Big girl Jane. It's you, handsome Toby. Stinker of a party, wasn't it. Absolute stinker. Remind me never to do that again.

When Jane woke, it was dark. Reaching for her phone, she saw that it was 5 a.m. How did the saying go? The darkest hour is just before the dawn. Curled up in the foetal position, Jane considered her options. Kitto didn't want her; one of her children had already left home and the other two would follow soon; she was friendless, jobless and hopeless. With no other choice, she texted Blaze a message. *If offer open, I will be your manager. Grand opening April 1st? Jane.*

19

Sleet Hall

WEDNESDAY 31ST DECEMBER 2008

Blaze was facing pressure from Ayesha to accept an invitation to Sir Thomlinson and Lady Sleet's New Year's Eve party.

"The papers say that it will be the party to end all parties," Ayesha said. "I can't believe that you'd put a little work issue before my happiness."

"The man is trying to ruin my business and my reputation."

"So hold your head high, put on your best frock and show the world that you are bigger than his idle, unfounded taunts."

"If only it were just vibes, but he's run a campaign against me in the press and is using every trick, including bribery, to persuade my most important clients to move their funds."

"Then treat the party as a platform to refute and as a stalking ground to find more clients. By skulking in corners, being invisible, you are letting him win."

Eventually Blaze conceded and, at 8 p.m. on New Year's Eve, a chauffeur-driven car arrived to collect the two women from Moonshot Wharf. Ayesha came out of her room swathed in one of Blaze's floor-length shearling coats. Her eyes were ringed with kohl and her lips were stained a deep pink. Her long auburn hair was pinned around her face like a burnished halo. The effect of the black coat and the fine pale face reminded Blaze of a Renaissance Madonna.

"You look extraordinarily beautiful," she told her niece.

Ayesha smiled graciously. "Your costume suits you." She had found Blaze a fitted deep-red camisole and matching voluminous trousers that tied tightly at the ankles. The colour showed off Blaze's creamy skin. "Try these on too." Ayesha clipped two snake-shaped bangles on to her aunt's upper arms and fitted a cobra-style pendant around her throat.

"Where did you find these?" Blaze laughed.

"Southall Market. It's Little India—you can find anything there."

"How did you get my size?"

"I took one of your shirts with me. The tailor copied the measurements but I made him take them in a few inches. What's the point of all that running if you don't show off your body?"

"Can I see what you're wearing?"

"When we get there."

Blaze's phone beeped.

"Another text from him?" Ayesha teased. "And you thought that was it."

"We should go," Blaze said, wanting to change the subject. Wolfe was in regular contact and recently she had started returning his texts.

"To think how mortified you were after the first date," Ayesha continued, remembering finding her aunt curled up on the sofa after a sleepless night.

"It was a disaster." Blaze couldn't tell Ayesha what had happened.

"So why did he send flowers?"

Pulling on her coat, Blaze wanted to read Wolfe's text but was embarrassed to appear keen.

"Aren't you going to read it?"

Blaze looked at her phone. *My New Year's resolution is to spend more time with you, JW.* She tried not to smile or blush and failed on both counts.

Ayesha laughed and clapped her hands together. "You've gone as pink as a newborn rat."

Blaze read the text again. "He didn't put an X at the bottom."

Ayesha snorted. She opened the door of the apartment and pressed the button for the lift. Blaze double-locked the front door and set the alarms behind her. In the lift, she stared at her telephone.

"Yesterday he used an X," Blaze said, scrolling through Joshua's texts as the two women rode down to the ground floor. Then she laughed at herself. "Imagine if he could see me now. A middle-aged woman panicking about an X."

The air outside was biting. Ayesha shivered and buttoned up her coat. Their chauffeur jumped out of the car and opened the rear door. Ayesha nodded imperiously and settled herself into the back seat.

"Destination as advised?" the driver asked.

"Yes, please," said Blaze, sitting next to her niece.

"I think you're in love," Ayesha teased.

"I hardly know him! We've had one dinner, two letters, eight phone conversations and eleven texts." Blaze stopped and said quickly, "Not that I'm counting."

"If Mark doesn't text me every day, I feel sick," Ayesha replied. "I don't care if the others fall off a cliff."

"Is he your boyfriend?" Blaze asked. Mark spent a lot of time at the apartment but he never stayed the night.

"He is my true love," Ayesha said softly. "Aunty, whoever this man is, you look ten years younger and fifty times happier than when I arrived in London. I have a whole car journey to get information out of you."

Once Blaze started talking about Wolfe, she couldn't stop; facts and feelings tumbled out in no apparent order. Her mind, normally incisive and orderly, was scrambled by reawakened emotions. She felt idiotic and elated as she told Ayesha about their phone calls. Most of the time their conversation hovered around neutral subjects like investments, market fluctuations and political events, until the tension became too much and they'd lapse into silence, both caught up in longing for more intimacy.

"Why hasn't he made another move?" Ayesha asked.

Blaze wriggled in her seat. "I'm not ready." How could she explain that her desire to see him was swamped by a paralysing fear of losing control and of being rejected.

"What is it you like most about him?"

Blaze thought for a while before answering. "He's so clear about who he is and what he stands for. Joshua doesn't try to prove anything or seek confirmation. It sounds arrogant, but I find it reassuring."

"His parents must have adored him. That kind of confidence only comes with unconditional love," Ayesha said wistfully.

Blaze leaned over and took her niece's hand. "You must miss your mother."

"Of course."

"And your stepfather and half-brother?"

"My stepfather tolerated me because he loved my mother. My brother, as the youngest, was horribly spoiled, mostly by me." Her face contorted. "He's only twelve. When I get my own house and husband, Sachan will live with me." She hesitated. "That's why I am in such a hurry to sort out my life and create a home. I want Sachan to have the best of everything."

"And what do you want?" Blaze asked.

Ayesha laughed. "Power." Then she grinned widely. "And I intend to get it."

Blaze didn't doubt her.

The car made its way through West London and out onto the M4 towards Newbury. Ayesha broke the silence.

"Who is this Thomlinson Sleet?" she asked.

"He used to follow your mother around at Oxford. Once he climbed up the drainpipe and through a window to give her a rose."

"Oh, one of those," Ayesha said dismissively.

"There were so many climbing suitors that the dean moved her to a ground floor in an inner courtyard."

"She was lucky to have the opportunity to drive men mad."

At the gates to Sleet Towers, two full-grown elephants stood guard, ridden by frozen-looking mahouts. The elephants' heads and trunks were intricately painted and the animals swayed restlessly from foot to foot.

"I didn't come all the way to England for this," Ayesha said crossly. "Every wedding in India has an elephant."

They gave their names and invitations to a young man who handed them each a small parcel with their initials inscribed in italics on the front. Ayesha tore the wrapping off hers immediately, to find a map of the party, a dance card and a gold pencil. Opening up the dance card, she laughed.

"Sleet has reserved the first dance with me already! How charming." She smiled knowingly.

Blaze grimaced, hoping his interest in Anastasia's daughter would quickly wane. Her own dance card was empty and, she suspected, would remain so the whole evening.

Their car joined a long line of chauffeur-driven vehicles. After a quarter of a mile the cars stopped and guests were asked to climb aboard a golden train. Inside they found mini bottles of champagne and hand-peeled gulls' eggs. There were two other couples in their carriage: a well-known American senator and her husband and a pop star whose last great hit was in the 1970s. They made hesitant introductions to one another, but their small talk was abruptly ended by a loud whistle. Outside a heavy fog descended and the windows were lashed with violent waves. The carriage rocked from side to side and Blaze grabbed hold of the edge of her seat.

"We're at sea!" Ayesha called out.

"We're in Berkshire!" But, looking out of the window, Blaze saw that they were indeed bobbing around on a huge ocean. To the left was a great whale, held down by tree roots, and, striding across its back, a young man wearing golden trousers brandishing a cutlass. Nearby a boat tossed on frothing waves until it came close enough for the young man to jump aboard.

"The Seven Voyages of Sinbad," Ayesha said, her eyes wide with amazement. Around them, in tableaux vivants, scenes from Sinbad's life were re-enacted as their carriage moved on. The sea calmed and they passed a huge egg which cracked open to reveal hundreds of writhing, slivering snakes; across a spit of land, a mermaid rose from the depths of a lagoon and diamonds rained from the sky. For the entire train ride—neither could tell how far they went or for how long it lasted—Blaze and Ayesha were transfixed. How was it done? Theatre, trickery or technology?

The train stopped. A young woman swathed in a gauze-like material shot with gold thread introduced herself as Scheherazade and led them along a tunnel lined with fresh rosebuds. To the left and right actors performed scenes from *1001 Arabian Nights.*

"Are they having real sex?" Ayesha exclaimed. "Look at those two—I think they are." Blaze looked straight ahead; she didn't need any more reminders of Sleet's vulgarity.

The tunnel ended and the guests found themselves in front of Sleet Towers, a low-slung, red-brick, Queen Anne-style mansion. Projected on to its vast façade were more scenes from the *Arabian Nights* while classical music blared out from huge speakers. Protected from the cold by a domed glass entrance stood hundreds of dwarves, painted gold and holding flaming torches.

"This is revolting. Complete exploitation," Blaze said.

"It is magnificent," Ayesha corrected her.

From out of the darkness stepped more young women, their faces hidden by delicate veils of chiffon, to take Blaze's and Ayesha's coats. Blaze gasped when she saw Ayesha's "costume." The top half of her niece's body was bare, hand-painted with snakes, ghouls, djinns, wild horses and various couples in states of erotica. Two heart-shaped discs covered her nipples. Her breasts, though small, were perfectly rounded and pert; her figure lithe and curvaceous. Slung low over her hips were diaphanous trousers made from the softest silk that shimmered around her bottom and legs.

"What do you think?" Ayesha asked, whipping around.

Blaze didn't know what to say so she simply nodded, speechless. It was simultaneously erotic and audacious, and yet far too delicate to be considered vulgar.

"I went to Covent Garden and made friends with the set designers at the Royal Opera House. The company was supposed to be doing the scene painting for a new production of *Giselle* but preferred the challenge of my body. They've done a good job, haven't they?" Ayesha shimmied in front of Blaze. Around them fellow guests and helpers stopped and stared, stunned by her nakedness, frozen by the beauty of the apparition. Blaze recognised the look of horror on other women's faces; their weeks of preparation rendered insignificant, their efforts eclipsed.

"Fuck me sideways," a voice boomed. Blaze turned to see Sleet striding towards them.

"You've got a nerve coming here, Blaze," he said. "Walking out of my company, stealing my clients and now eating my food."

"Supping at the devil's table," Blaze agreed, with a fixed, disingenuous smile.

"Pity you can't find anything to invest in," he sneered. "I hear your clients are getting restless." As he spoke, he jabbed his fat finger in her face.

Blaze burned with rage and was about to answer when Ayesha, unseen until then, came to stand between her aunt and Sleet. The tycoon's mouth opened and closed; his finger dropped, his eyes widened.

"I don't believe you've met Anastasia's daughter, Ayesha? Ayesha, this is Thomlinson Sleet."

Ayesha looked him straight in the eyes and said in a low, husky voice, "You're not someone I'd forget."

Blaze could hardly believe what she was seeing and hearing; Ayesha had inherited her mother's wiles. The past flashed through her mind: memories of Anastasia using a combination of coquettishness and beauty to fell admirers, condemning Jane and Blaze to the status of permanent wallflowers.

"You are not leaving my side all evening," Sleet said, recovering his senses.

"What will your wife have to say about that?" Ayesha asked.

"Lady Sleet just walked out on me! Said I worked too hard and only the chef understood her needs."

"Are you devastated?" Ayesha opened her eyes wide.

"I certainly am: a good chef is harder to find than a wife."

Blaze took her niece's arm and dragged her away from Sleet. "The man is an absolute creep. You mustn't have anything to do with him," she whispered.

Ayesha looked at her condescendingly. "I can take care of myself."

"Not this one, Ayesha, please." Blaze glanced over at Sleet who was grinning lasciviously at the young woman.

Extracting herself from Blaze's grip, Ayesha went back across to

Sleet. "I don't know how anyone could leave you," she said, raising her beautiful eyes and gazing into his. "Will you show me your house?" she asked. They walked away, leaving Blaze on her own.

Entering the first marquee, Blaze looked up to see acrobats flying above the guests on trapezes made from brightly coloured ribbons. Scanning around, she recognised four captains of industry, three newspaper editors and their proprietors, two former cabinet ministers, a clutch of rock stars, a bevy of A-list film stars and even a Nobel prizewinner (chemistry). I am, she thought, the only person here who is not famous.

Standing alone by the bar was a well-known misanthropic hedge-fund manager, Christof Kempey, whom Blaze had met at various conferences.

"Who knew that Sleet had this kind of address book?" she said.

"He doesn't—the guests are either for hire or here on business."

"What about the politicians?" Blaze asked.

"Sleet makes significant donations to all parties, guaranteeing access to the PM and the Cabinet, as well as Leaders of the Opposition, 24/7. The film stars are less expensive and the hacks can be bought for a free glass of anything."

"I feel naive."

"These events are useful. You might pick up a deal or a tip on the way to the bathroom."

"On that note, how have you fared in the recent turmoil?" Rumours abounded that Kempey Capital Partners, his eponymous hedge fund, had been heavily invested in UBS and HBOS.

"The shittiest year of my life. I'm down 45 per cent and am haemorrhaging clients."

"What are you going to do?"

"You seem to have all the answers, Blaze—you tell me. I take my hat off to you for predicting all this."

A waiter appeared, offering Château Lafite 1961 or vintage champagne. Blaze took the former, Kempey asked for a vodka.

"I called it right, but don't seem to be capitalising on the results. Everything looks precarious; things can go much lower." She took a sip of wine; it was like liquid silk. The claret made the drive worthwhile.

"There's the Governor of the Bank of England talking to the Chancellor—shall we go and ask what they're planning next?"

Blaze followed Kempey over to a small banquette where the two men sat deep in conversation.

"Are you going to drop interest rates?" Kempey asked without any introduction.

The Governor smiled tersely. "I can't divulge information like that."

"Throw a desperate man a bone, why don't you?" Small beads of sweat broke out on the hedge-funder's forehead.

The Governor and the Chancellor didn't react.

"You've got to do something," Kempey said, his voice rising.

"One of the things this crisis has shown us," Blaze chipped in, "is how little governments and central banks can actually do. Your only options are to print money to try and stimulate the economy, or lower interest rates even further, but what will that achieve in the long run?"

"You're Blaze Scott?" the Chancellor asked.

She nodded.

"Next time you see a crisis approaching, please can you let us all know?" He laughed half-heartedly.

"I tried but no one would listen. You wrote me off as a mad doomster."

"What do you think's going to happen next?"

Blaze could hardly believe it: the Chancellor of the Exchequer was asking her opinion on the economy. "I don't see anything positive in the short term. Banking systems are teetering. I hear bad news from Bank of America and Anglo Irish, and the consequences following the collapse of Lehman's will be long and painful. House prices are falling, unemployment rising."

The Governor and the Chancellor exchanged weary looks. They were interrupted by a waiter riding a prancing white stallion, expertly balancing a tray of shots. The horse danced on the spot but not a drop of vodka was spilt. Kempey took one, downed it in a gulp and then helped himself to two more. The horse trotted off and behind it came a troop of barely dressed harem dancers offering canapés.

The Chancellor shook his head. "This is surreal."

"Where have you put your money?" the Governor asked Blaze.

"Mostly in cash or gold. I've made some investments in India. Long-term, things will pick up."

The Chancellor, a veteran of many governments, smoothed his trousers. "Memories are short. We've been here before in 1973 and 1987, to name a few."

"Don't forget the dot-com crash of 2000," Blaze added.

"How can you be so blasé?" The sweat ran down Kempey's face; he looked on the verge of tears.

The Governor rose slowly to his feet. "I'm going to find my wife." He walked off towards the bar.

"I ought to seek out the Leader of the Opposition," the Chancellor said.

Kempey went in search of a bar, leaving Blaze on her own.

Taking another drink from an acrobat perched on the back of a black horse, she walked into the next-door tent, which was lined in midnight-blue velvet. The ceiling had been made to look like the night sky—she identified Orion's Belt, the Little Bear and Perseus—while the walls mimicked an Islamic palace under moonlight. Guests stared in wonder, faces upturned. There was another doorway, and Blaze stepped through it into a colourful bazaar serving food from all corners of the globe. She saw the newspaper editor Leo Seville deep in conversation with a well-known African dictator, and a perennially perky soap star talking to the leader of UKIP. Blaze knew all by name, but none well enough to approach, and she decided to keep going, hoping to find Ayesha.

The next room had been transformed into a frozen cave, the floor covered with shaggy sheepskin rugs. In the centre there was a huge, naked sleeping woman carved from ice and her pudenda was a trough of caviar. Vodka spurted from both of her breasts in perfect continuous arcs. A minor member of the royal family stood on his own, shovelling spoonfuls of caviar into his mouth.

"Might as well," he said to Blaze. "Don't want this stuff to go to waste."

"We're making music while Rome burns," Blaze said.

The Royal looked at her blankly.

"Suetonius told the story of Emperor Nero playing a violin while his city was on fire."

"Can't follow what you're saying," the man said, stuffing his mouth. "Have some." He offered Blaze a soup spoon of black shiny eggs.

Blaze shook her head. The festival of excess, the sheer waste and opulence, was sickening and she felt partially responsible. Sleet had made money from her predictions and those ludicrous profits were on full, appalling display.

"If I were you, I'd just get on and enjoy it. The world might end tomorrow," the Royal said.

Blaze had to get out, and quickly. First, she had to find Ayesha. Hurrying through tent after tent, she saw a famous rock band, perhaps the world's most famous, was playing live. Below the stage there was a dance floor and in the centre, moving like a flame in a gentle wind, was Ayesha. Next to her, Sleet stamped and gyrated, rolls of fat undulating, sweat pouring from his face and under his armpits.

Blaze marched across and shouted into Ayesha's ear. "Let's go home."

Ayesha shook her head.

"I need to get out of here," Blaze said desperately.

"Take the car. I'll find my own way." She threw a look in Sleet's direction and winked.

"Ayesha, you are better than this."

Ayesha threw back her head and laughed. Turning away from her aunt, she shimmied towards Sleet.

Blaze, smarting, walked out of the marquee and through the other tents towards the exit, where she found her coat and bag. Reaching into her pockets, she searched for the card with her driver's number. She found nothing. She looked in her bag. Her heart sank. There was an attendant with a walkie-talkie and Blaze asked him to radio for the driver of a black Mercedes.

"Do you know how many black Mercs there are out there?" he laughed. "What name might it be under?"

"Scott," Blaze said, fighting feelings of desperation, unable to face one more minute at the party.

The attendant shrugged unhelpfully. "I'll put it out on the radio but most of the drivers are asleep in their cars."

"Don't worry, I'll find him." Blaze headed outside into gusts of snow, now falling heavily. Flakes landed like cold slaps on her nose and cheeks. Her heels sank into the wet ground and within a few steps the bottoms of her silk pantaloons were drenched. The waiting cars were on the other side of the park, some quarter of a mile distant. Flinging off her gold-strapped shoes and hitching up her long coat, she set off down the driveway, gravel cutting into the soles of her feet. The physical pain paled next to the memory of Ayesha dancing with Sleet; Blaze tried to ignore a deep sense of foreboding.

In the distance, the bright lights of a car came towards her. It was moving fast, but slowed and came to a stop about ten feet away. Blinded, she put her hands in front of her eyes. The driver got out and approached, his silhouette made fuzzy in the falling snow. Blaze tried to get out of the way by stepping off the road into the verge, but her feet slipped and she fell to her knees, suctioned to the ground by wet mud. The man held out his hand; she took it and, with his help, stood upright.

"Are you OK?" he asked.

The voice was unmistakable. "What are you doing here?"

"I've been asking myself the same question all evening."

"I didn't see you."

"I searched all over for you."

Blaze, bedraggled, snow- and mud-spattered, was glad that her coat hid the fancy-dress outfit. What bad luck had led to this chance encounter with him of all people? She wiped her face and ran her hands through her hair to try and straighten it. "I'm not at my best."

"You must be cold."

Her teeth were chattering.

"The car's warm." Walking over to the Land Rover, he opened the passenger door and helped her climb in. From the front seat, he leaned into the back, found a blanket and placed it over her legs, then turned the heater up high.

"Where would you like to go?"

"If I could find my driver, I was going to ask him to take me to the nearest station. My niece will need the car later," Blaze said in hope.

"A train at nearly midnight on New Year's Eve?" He glanced at her out of the corner of his eye. Blaze said nothing, aware how ridiculous she must appear. "I'll drive you back to London," he said.

"It's out of your way."

"I came tonight in the hope of seeing you." He put the car into gear and headed towards the exit.

They drove in silence for about half an hour; the only noise was the slapping of wipers on the windscreen and the hum of the radiator above the engine. In a small village they saw the lights of a pub and outside a few hardy people huddled under a makeshift awning smoking cigarettes.

"I have an overnight bag in the back with a clean set of clothes," he said. "Why don't we stop for a whisky and you can get changed?"

"I would like that," Blaze stuttered, feeling the wet silk of her trousers clinging to her thighs and stomach. Every part of her was cold.

He stopped the car a little way up the road from the pub and, leaning over the seat behind him, took out a small holdall. Blaze opened the door and, stepping into the snow, gave an involuntary yelp.

"Put your arms around me," he said, getting out and coming to her side of the car.

She clasped her fingers around the back of his neck and let him scoop her up in his arms. His jacket smelled of hay, with a slight tang of mothballs. His face was roughly shaven and she felt the bristles against her cheek.

The pub was full of revellers and the walls were covered with Christmas decorations. The landlord stepped out from behind the bar. Blaze's companion let her down gently.

"It's past closing time; we're only allowed to serve residents," the landlord explained.

"Do you have any rooms left?" the man asked.

"Only one. It's small and at the back. £50."

"I'll take it."

"What's your name?" the landlord enquired.

"Wolfe—Joshua Wolfe."

By the time Blaze had changed into Wolfe's jeans and jumper and returned to the bar, her hair roughly towel-dried and face free of make-up, he was sitting on a small sofa by the open fire. On the table there were two tumblers, a bottle of whisky, a pot of freshly brewed coffee and many packets of salted peanuts.

Waking up in the small bed, in an unfamiliar room the following morning, Blaze tried to piece together the sequence of events. Had they drunk the whole bottle of whisky? Did they really dance with strangers around the bar? Did he kiss her first or did she kiss him? She remembered the feeling of his caresses on her neck, his fingers on her thighs, the urgency of their lovemaking, but all those sensations had merged. Now she lay watching his sleeping face, the rise and fall of his chest, his mouth slightly open, his right arm thrown behind his head like a child, and was filled with a feeling of contentment; she had only known him for three months, but felt as if she'd loved him for decades. She let hope in—hope for a different kind of future and another long-lost dream: the longing to make someone else happy.

Carefully, so as not to wake him, she wriggled out of bed and went to the bathroom. Looking at herself in the mirror, she was pleasantly surprised. There were dark smudges under her eyes and her hair was tousled beyond help, but she noticed a softness around her mouth and a rosy hue across her cheeks. Even her scar looked less vivid. Her naked body was lithe and firm, and she turned to the left and right to admire herself, thankful for the hours of training in the gym. Her reverie was broken by a loud ping and, turning around, she saw his mobile phone flashing on the cabinet. She wondered what the time was: early for someone to be messaging. The phone pinged again. Don't look at it, she told herself, and then picked it up. You're only checking the time, she thought reassuringly. Taking the Nokia in her hands, she saw that it was 7:40 a.m. Put the phone down now. She pushed the button and two messages flashed up. Both were from someone called Amanda. The first one read: *Morning. Can't wait to see you. XX.* The second said: *Really can't wait.* Blaze felt the energy drain from her body. She slid down the wall and sat on the floor, cradling her thighs. Of course there was an Amanda, she thought miserably. There was bound to be a Laura and a Cassandra too. How could she have been so naive? To him, she had been nothing more than a New Year's Eve conquest. She washed her face with cold water and tried to smooth her hair before going back into the bedroom to gather her clothes.

Wolfe opened his eyes and smiled sleepily. "Are you coming back to bed?" he asked, pulling down the sheet for her.

"I have to get going," Blaze said coldly.

He sat up. "Has something happened?" He looked confused. "Last night was so . . ." he hesitated, ". . . so lovely."

"Glad it was for you," Blaze countered. "I was drunk."

Wolfe recoiled. He's certainly a good actor, Blaze thought, looking at his bereft expression. She pulled on her harem pants and picked up her damp, long coat. "I'm going to ask for a taxi."

"It's too early—I'll take you wherever you need to go." He got out of bed and looked for his clothes. "I don't understand. What's going on?"

"Who's Amanda?" Blaze turned to face him.

Wolfe stepped back. He looked incredulous. "Have you been reading my texts? Snooping into my private business?" His face flushed with anger. "I don't like people who do that."

"Your phone was in the bathroom; the messages flashed up."

Wolfe shook his head and started getting dressed. "This is the second time you've seen the absolute worst in a situation and jumped to a conclusion; once again you've played judge and jury and found the accused wanting. And I have not even been allowed a trial, let alone the opportunity to make a statement." He pulled on his trousers and slipped his sweater over his head.

Blaze stood by the door with her arms crossed. How typical of a man to go on the offensive; it proved her worst fears.

"I can't be with someone who sees the negative in everything and catastrophe at every turn." Stuffing the rest of the clothes into his overnight bag, he picked it up with one hand and held open the door for her with the other. They walked downstairs in silence. He had prepaid the bill with a credit card and stopped to hand the room key to a young girl wiping the bar. This time he didn't carry her or open the passenger door of the Land Rover. Blaze got in beside him and he drove, his eyes fixed on the road ahead. After seventeen minutes they arrived at Reading Station.

"Do you have money for a ticket?" he asked.

Blaze nodded and opened the door.

"Wait." He turned towards her. "For the record, Amanda is my ex-girlfriend. I was with her for nearly seven years. She was and is a very important and much-loved person in my life. She recently had a child on her own and asked me to spend a few days over New Year with her. I have few significant people in my life but those I love, I will die for. She is one of them." He hesitated. "I'm not a philanderer and I don't end up in bed with random women. I'm sorry that you have such a low opinion of me." His face was impassive and stony. "Happy New Year, Blaze."

Blaze slid out of the car, burning with shame and regret. Before closing the door, she looked at him. He was right; for the second time, she had assumed the worst: first with Molly and now with someone called Amanda. The first time, he'd given her a chance; now her jealousy had snuffed out any hope.

"I'm sorry."

Wolfe didn't answer. He put the car in first gear.

Blaze closed the door and watched the Land Rover pull away. She stood there for ten minutes, maybe more, just in case he changed his mind and drove back to find her. When it was clear he wasn't coming, she turned and walked into the station.

20

Seeds

SATURDAY 17TH JANUARY 2009

When Arabella came down to breakfast, she found her mother hiding underneath the kitchen table.

"What the hell are you doing?"

"I thought you were the vicar."

"Why would I be the vicar?"

"He's always lurking."

"It's seven in the morning; he'll be having breakfast. Which is something that Toby and I would like to do too."

The day before, Arabella had passed her mother running from the Mistresses' Wing to the kitchen door with a wastepaper basket over her head.

"I'm incognito," Jane had hissed.

Then there were the culinary fads. One week, Jane had cooked only Mexican food, before switching to Greek. Neither had been a success. Driven by hunger and necessity, the children borrowed a cookery book from the library and worked their way through the recipes. Occasionally their mother came to meals, but often she stayed in her office shuffling through endless correspondence, bills and paperwork. She spent most nights closeted in her studio printing new, even more morbid, wallpaper designs.

Arabella had stopped going to school. Her mother hadn't noticed and her brother was too wrapped up with Celia to care. Instead she spent her time with Aunt Tuffy, whose latest research project involved feeding caterpillars the leaves of marijuana plants grown in the fourth ballroom.

"When will you see results?" Arabella asked. The experiment had been going on since the month before Enyon's funeral and had been repeated through many life cycles of caterpillars.

"Butterflies sequester and store toxic substances from their larval food-plant to use as part of their chemical arsenal. Cabbage whites store mustard oil from cabbages and put it into their caterpillar eggs to make them less palatable to predators. Monarch butterflies use poisons from milkweed, aphids like cardiac glycosides and swallowtail butterflies prefer aristolochic acids for the same purpose."

Arabella could hardly contain her excitement. "What will the marijuana reveal? Why not use a simple cabbage?"

Tuffy looked at her thoughtfully. "I might make a scientist out of you yet. You're asking the right kind of question. Marijuana is pungent, potent and easy to grow. I'm interested in two things: can we identify plant compounds that bring about changes in colour and might the same compounds smell so awful that they scare a predator away?"

"And if you could?"

"Imagine if there was a pill to repel mosquitoes? Think how many millions of lives could be saved. Or if we could genetically modify a wheat or grass seed with a compound that would render wild animals repulsive to ticks or fleas."

"Using nature to fight nature without having to invent anything new."

The older woman nodded. "As so often in life, the answers are right in front of us." Unused as she was to human company, Tuffy could see that something was troubling her great-niece. "Are you going to tell me what's wrong? If not, go away." Although she sounded cross, Arabella understood that Tuffy was trying to be kind. She told her about Jane's recent behaviour.

"Your mother is taking measures to stop people from bothering her," Tuffy said. "She has to decide if she values friendship over productivity. Both require a significant investment of time."

"Have you got any friends?"

Tuffy thought about this question as she moved seven bright green caterpillars from one box to another. "It's been a great relief to find the company of insects and animals far more interesting." She looked at her niece and smiled. "Now make yourself useful. Fetch down those specimen jars on the top shelf and in your best handwriting copy out the following names."

For the first time in over forty-six years of marriage, Gordon and Glenda Sparrow were sleeping apart. Every night she asked him to come back to their marital bed; his answer was always the same.

"While you work for the enemy, I'll have nothing to do with you." Gordon's anger, humiliation and grief had made him irrational. As far as he was concerned, Kitto was responsible for Acorn's bankruptcy and the loss of Gordon's savings and job. At the age of sixty-five and in the present climate, he was unlikely to find other work. Mark had offered help, which neither grandparent would accept. It went against everything they believed in; penury would be preferable. If Glenda could have found work elsewhere, she'd have taken it. Unlike her husband, she didn't blame Kitto. He was an irresponsible ass but not a bad person. She bore Gordon's fury in case it made him feel better, less powerless. Her heart broke for her husband and his shattered dreams. It was Mark who persuaded his grandfather to create an activist group of former employees and shareholders of Acorn to lobby the government and the bank's creditors, hoping that proactivity would give Gordon a sense of purpose. Mark drove from Bristol to Trelawney three evenings a week to teach the older man how to use a computer and search for other people who had lost their savings. Glenda didn't think it would do any good but was, at first, pleased that Gordon had an outlet for his rage. But the interest became an obsession and grew into a mania; sometimes she came downstairs in the middle of the night to find her husband hunched over the laptop (lent by Mark), stabbing the keyboard with two fingers.

She comforted herself that Gordon had a cause, even if it didn't have an effect.

Gordon's network began to spread. He found associates in Cornwall, but also as far afield as Scotland and Scandinavia. Then he began to research their legal position and case law. The once-pristine kitchen was turned into his centre of operations. In the past he had picked flowers for his wife; now he made notes—pages and pages of notes—which were piled into neat stacks. Glenda's domain shrank to a small corner around the kettle. If she watched television (always alone), the volume had to be almost inaudible so as not to disrupt the Skype calls Gordon made to his new friends. Glenda's world had contracted; Gordon's had exploded. She no longer recognised her husband: the man who had loved nature; who could name any tree in the forest; who coaxed cuttings out of sandy soil; who would nurse an injured mouse back to health had morphed into an angry and embittered campaigner. Before the crash, Glenda had counted the hours until she returned home to her husband; now she could not wait to get to the castle every day.

Jane stood at the sink, trying to make headway with the washing-up. Looking out of the kitchen window, her hands in soapy water, she saw a single rose trembling on a branch, a splash of colour against the January gloom, and she smiled. It was bound to be a good omen. This fleeting moment of pleasure was dashed by the sight of Magda, head down, coat on, suitcase in hand, marching determinedly towards her. Jane didn't need to be told what had happened. Magda was just one of a long line of carers—eleven in six months—driven to resignation by Clarissa's rudeness. The agency had been absolutely clear: "Magda Pawlokowski is the last person we will send you. There aren't many who are prepared to live in the back of beyond and even fewer who will put up with such a cantankerous old woman." Jane had been to five different agencies. She had even registered under a fake name; news, it seemed, spread quickly in that part of the world and the House of Trelawney was on a blacklist.

The kitchen door swung open and Magda entered, brandishing a sense of righteous indignation like a sword.

"Enough! Lady is too rude."

"What happened this time?" Jane turned and wiped her hands on a tea towel.

"Food too hot, food too cold. Food too salty, food too sweet."

"Would you like a cup of tea?" Jane hoped she could calm Magda down and persuade her to stay. The alternative—looking after her mother-in-law herself—was too bleak to contemplate. She leaned her face against the windowpane, hoping the glass would cool her hot brow and wondered if she had the emotional resilience to cope with any more upsets; she felt that one more problem would tip her into insanity.

"Taxi," Magda said firmly.

"We could increase your wages?"

"Taxi."

"An extra day off?" Jane was running out of ideas.

"Taxi."

"Please, Magda, please." Jane wondered if going down on bended knee would help. At that moment she was prepared to consider anything.

Magda shook her head. "Taxi."

Jane drove Magda to the station and, once alone in the car, took out her phone and sent Blaze a message. *Last carer has walked out. Your mother, your problem. Jane.*

21

Black Monday

MONDAY 19TH JANUARY 2009

Looking at the downward market movements on her computer screen, Blaze saw that the value of her stocks was falling. Since Moonshot Capital's inception in October, most of her investment decisions had gone the wrong way: her fund was losing money on crude oil, Apple and bank stocks. Their biggest position, £75 million in an Indian telecom business, had turned out to be the worst performer; Blaze had been correct in predicting that the Indian mobile-phone market would expand quickly but wrong in assuming that the providers would make money; that investment halved in value. She pushed back her chair and took a sharpened pencil and piece of paper from her desk, then went back over her calculations.

Moonshot Capital had raised £500 million, but Blaze had made two mistakes: the first was to invest in the wrong companies, the second was to leave £200 million in cash. Her competitors, Sleet and Wolfe, had made big bets, mainly by shorting ailing companies, and were up 10 and 12 per cent respectively. Her self-confidence was wavering: had she lost her touch? Why was she, known for her steely, unemotional persona, suddenly so indecisive? She tried to attribute it to her father's death but the real reason was that, since New Year's Eve, Blaze had thought of little else but Wolfe, going over and over the events and coming to the same conclusion: she had thrown away her greatest, perhaps her only, chance of happiness.

Looking through the glass window of her office to the trading floor, she saw six pinched, worried faces. She called TiLing on the intercom.

"Do you have a minute?"

TiLing tore her eyes away from the screen and came in, closing the door behind her.

"Have you seen the latest results?"

TiLing nodded.

"Have I lost my touch?"

TiLing leaned against the door and shook her head. "You've lost your concentration. You are physically present but mentally absent. In the past you thought deeply, you researched and interrogated decisions, ran the ideas and strategies through computer simulations, debated their worth and rehearsed outcomes. Recently you have been whimsical and illogical, making the craziest decisions against your colleagues' advice. We're sitting on £200 million of cash and our investors want to see some return. They could make more money by sticking it in a high-yield-interest bank account."

Blaze was silent; TiLing was right. "Who's that?" she asked, pointing to a new face in a corner of the back office.

TiLing looked over her shoulder. "An intern," she said distractedly. "Joe Smith or Jones or something."

"Why do we need an intern?"

"We took him on as a favour for a friend of a friend." TiLing wished Blaze would focus on what really mattered.

"What happens if he's a spy?" Blaze said, looking at the young man.

"If only we had something to hide."

Blaze picked up a pencil and began doodling on a piece of paper. This time she drew clouds hanging over a stick woman.

"My mother's carer walked out. I've been trying to find a replacement. You've no idea how difficult it is to persuade people to go to Cornwall."

Overcome by frustration, TiLing sprang across the room and smacked her hand on the desk. Blaze jumped.

TiLing leaned towards her. "Please, can you concentrate on business during office hours? On Friday, during the investment committee, you wittered on about cream teas and burial sites. This morning you bought more Microsoft shares when it's perfectly obvious that few will buy new computers during a recession. Last week, our analysts advised that the Indian government's decision to issue licences to eight new mobile-phone providers would lead to a tariff war and margin pressure; you ignored the advice. Even though there's an oil glut, you went out and bought more crude."

"Those investments will come good." Blaze hoped the doubt in her mind wasn't audible. "We have to play a long game."

"Spalding are thinking of switching back to Kerkyra," TiLing replied. The insurance company's decision to move to Moonshot had been their biggest triumph; if word got out that Spalding had lost confidence, others would be bound to follow.

"It's a few weeks into the new year. Why are they so skittish?" Blaze asked.

"If you haven't noticed, the markets are in free-fall." TiLing couldn't believe she was having to explain this to Blaze, of all people.

She handed Blaze a letter.

Blaze recognised the headed paper; it was another of their major investors. *Your decision to stay underinvested and long in cash is lamentable; you're looking like a one-trick pony, able to call a crash but unable to navigate a recession. I'm out.* It was signed Jim Treherne, Kingsland Asset Management, who had put £25 million into Moonshot Capital.

"Is this a joke?" she asked, knowing that it wasn't.

"Three guesses where he's moved his money?"

"Kerkyra," Blaze said.

TiLing nodded.

Blaze looked across at the intern who was talking into a phone with his hand cupped over the receiver.

"I want that man's CV. I don't trust him."

TiLing's desperation eviscerated any politeness. "Stop thinking about an intern, start thinking about where to put our money. Three other clients are threatening to switch to JW Inc."

At the mention of Wolfe's company, Blaze flinched. She had left several apologetic messages on his voicemail, but he hadn't returned any of her calls. Knowing TiLing's eyes were on her, she turned away towards the window. The large office block on the opposite side of the road, once a hive of activity, full of traders and stock pickers, was now empty. Empty buildings were like ghost ships of former businesses. In their street there was only one whose lights were on: Barclays Bank. Blaze got up and, leaning her head against the cool glass, tried to think. She had to make a decision, any decision would be better than none; it was time to get back in the market and behave like a conviction investor.

"What do you want to do?" TiLing asked.

"We're going to make a big investment. I'm going to raise £1 billion, using all of our assets as leverage," Blaze said in a bright but unconvincing tone.

"There is no liquidity in the market and, with our performance, who's going to lend us more money?" TiLing replied, thinking about Sleet's ongoing campaign to discredit Blaze.

"Do you remember Helmut Myer of PNB?"

"The Prussian bank?"

Blaze nodded. "I saw him at Sleet's party; he told me to come to him with any good ideas."

"I'm looking forward to hearing those." TiLing sat down wearily on the small sofa in Blaze's office.

"We have to take a risk and be bold. Fortunes are never made on the back of timid decisions." As she spoke, Blaze ran through a list of investment ideas. She didn't like any of them in particular.

"For months you've been saying there's nowhere safe to put our money. How are you planning to rework the narrative?"

Blaze looked at the building up the road, at the hum of activity in Barclays, wondering why she hadn't considered it before. "We're going to buy bank stocks."

"They're riddled with problems."

"Governments learned their lesson by letting Lehman's go down. Bush has pumped billions into the economy; Obama will follow suit. There's no way they'll let another big institution fail." Blaze felt a bubble of excitement rise in her chest.

"Look at their balance sheets. Banks are mired in debt after years of reckless decisions. Even if central banks prop up the rotten businesses, they can't control the share prices. My strong recommendation is that we use our liquidity and diversify from our existing bank holdings." Frustration propelled TiLing to her feet. It took all her resolve not to punch the wall.

Although every word her colleague said made sense, Blaze couldn't agree. "The G20 will create fiscal stimuli and institute programmes of quantitative easing. They'll slash interest rates and pour more money into the economy."

"What's happened? Where's this new strategy come from?" TiLing couldn't understand why Blaze, so timid in recent weeks, had changed her mind.

"I've been thinking about the macro situation—the U.S. government provided the Bank of America with another $20 billion and the British government put £500 billion into the economy in October and are considering doing more. The rest of Europe, bankrolled by the U.S, are bound to follow suit. We must buy as much as possible, markets are certain to rise." Blaze turned around to face TiLing and spoke in a low, determined voice. "I am going to take a big position in Barclays."

"Barclays?" TiLing spat out the name. "It's not worth the paper its shares are written on. If you remember, we bought £5 million worth at 150 pence per share at the end of last year. As of today, they are at 90 pence."

"It was worth over 500 pence a share; the government can't let it go down."

"The share price can and will go a lot lower," TiLing argued.

"This is exactly the time to double our holdings; triple or maybe quadruple them. We can make up our early losses. We have to be bold, hold our nerve."

TiLing was exasperated. "You're crazy. Where the hell did you get that idea from? Look at the balance sheets, listen to the rumours about their results. Barclays are bust, Blaze. They are overleveraged, have bought badly and are run by people who put their own bonuses before their shareholders' interests." This time she couldn't contain her irritation and, slamming her hand on Blaze's desk, sent a pot of pencils flying.

But Blaze had made up her mind. "I'm going to put another £1.4 billion into the market."

"If you do this, I'm leaving," TiLing said.

"That's your decision." Blaze's tone was icy.

TiLing shook her head sadly and left the room, closing the door hard behind her. Through the glass panel, Blaze saw her address her team. There was a brief discussion and then all six employees packed up their possessions and made their way out of the office, one or two throwing their erstwhile CEO a reproachful glance. Before he departed, the intern made a call, all the while his eyes on Blaze. TiLing was the last to leave. Turning to Blaze for the final time, she shrugged and didn't smile.

Blaze put in a call to Helmut Myer and outlined her plan; she'd provide security of all of Moonshot's remaining assets in return for a loan of £1 billion. One hour later the banker got back to her: PNB would lend her £600 million at LIBOR plus 1.3 per cent. They were expensive terms but Blaze had no alternative. The credit line was opened and at 4 p.m. she bought £400 million worth of Barclays shares at 82 pence per share. It was an audacious move but she felt confident. The markets closed with Barclays down a fraction at 81.29. She ran off any misgivings in the gym, pounding on the treadmill for an hour and a half. Later she ate a pizza and drank half a bottle of wine in the local trattoria, watched a suitably vacuous romantic comedy on her PC, curled up on the sofa opposite her desk and went to sleep. She felt wretched for TiLing and her team, who had given up other jobs to join Moonshot Capital; but this was the nature of a business that valued money over security and excitement over ease.

Sleet and Ayesha were having lunch on his boat, moored near Antibes. The young woman had accepted his invitation to join him in the South of France on condition that he provided a suite at the nearby Eden Roc hotel and agreed that this trip, like all their other meetings, was chaste. Sleet had to concede Ayesha was playing an enticing game. The week before he had bought her the entire new Prada collection; her thanks was a short message. Three days later he followed up by sending her an exquisite Monet sketch of the River Thames, which she acknowledged briefly. Now she sat opposite him, refusing the glass of vintage champagne, caviar and truffles, toying instead with a small green salad, her beautiful face composed in a perfect study of boredom. Sleet was amused by her game: he knew he'd win in the end. His intention had been to seduce and then abandon the girl; as the daughter of Kitto and Anastasia, it was what she deserved. For now, he was enjoying her spirited defence but knew she wouldn't hold out for long: penniless little nobodies never could.

Sleet had come a long way from Delaware. All the scars of his early childhood had been expunged. He had, through hard work, self-belief and achievement, changed his circumstances and risen like a phoenix from the ashes of impoverishment and the paucity of opportunity. Scholarships had carried him from an undistinguished one-room school to Yale, Oxford and Harvard Business School. Acumen landed him a job first at Goldman Sachs, and determination and complete lack of any personal scruples led to his success as an activist, stripping company after company of their fat and positioning them as slimmed-down, money-making machines.

He used the profits to build a spectacular collection of Impressionist paintings. He had a yacht, a plane and seven houses scattered across the most desirable parts of the world. His suits were cut by the best tailors, his food prepared by the greatest private chef. But something was missing: however hard he tried, however much money he made, he seemed to lack that elusive, desirable and unquantifiable accolade—class; and however low the Trelawneys sank, they exuded and oozed insouciant, effortless style and utter certainty about their place in the world. He slavishly copied their idiosyncrasies, employing a man just to wear out the elbows of his cashmere jumpers; he wore a watch, like Kitto and his father, on the outside of his shirt cuffs; he bought a pair of engraved Purdey shotguns and took enough lessons to pass as an excellent shot. There were certain mores he couldn't adopt: the aristocracy's apparent disdain for cleanliness, and an unwavering affinity with Labradors and Scotland.

Since that moment of utter humiliation at Anastasia's feet, Sleet had been determined to eradicate the Trelawneys' sense of superiority and his own feeling of inferiority. Bit by bit he bought land and had amassed as much as the Trelawneys owned at their zenith, including parcels of their former estates. He had shorted Acorn's stock, partly to make money but mainly to ensure that Kitto was forever unemployable. He hired the dunderhead Ambrose just to belittle him. Through his spy Joe Smith, posing as an intern at Moonshot Capital, he kept tabs on Blaze: it turned out that she was good at prophesying loss, incapable of capturing any upsides. It wouldn't be long before he bankrupted her and took over Moonshot; it was all a question of waiting and he had become good at waiting.

Looking across the lunch table, he saw that Ayesha was texting on her mobile phone.

"Who is more important than me?" he asked, unable to keep the irritation from his voice.

Ayesha put the phone down. "No one is more important than you," she said and then, to his surprise, leaned over the table, took his head in her hands and kissed him on the mouth for the first time. Sleet grinned broadly and tried to grab her by the wrist.

"Let's go to my cabin."

Ayesha shook her head. "I'm not that kind of woman."

"What kind are you?" Sleet failed to hide his disappointment. The prize was so near and yet so damnably elusive.

"I am a virgin and will stay one until my wedding night."

Sleet's mouth fell open. This was the last thing he'd expected. "You're nineteen. Even my fifteen-year-old daughter has—"

Ayesha held up a hand to silence him. "I don't need to know."

Sleet sat back and laughed. He had to admire her gall. Marriage was absolutely not happening; it was far too expensive and he had enough heirs; no way was he wasting more than a few days on this girl.

Ayesha stretched slowly, unfurling each of her long fingers and limbs, all the while looking Sleet directly in the eye. She knew exactly what he was thinking but, unlike him, she knew the outcome.

"I'm going back to the hotel now. For a little nap in my room. Why don't we go dancing tonight?"

"I have to return to London, to work," Sleet said.

"What a pity. I don't need to be home until tomorrow. Be a poppet and send the plane back to get me." Without waiting for an answer, she blew him a kiss and walked off towards the yacht's tender for a ride back to shore. Ayesha knew she was playing a high-risk strategy; she could only keep Sleet at bay and interested for a finite amount of time. Climbing down the steps into the waiting speedboat, she offered a silent prayer. *Let's hope you trained me well enough, Mummy darling.*

Blaze woke early the following morning in her office and took a hand shower in the bathroom. She wiped her face clean of yesterday's make-up and put on a coat of bright red lipstick. She made a cup of coffee and, opening her desk drawer, took out a bottle of vodka. Pouring a tot into the steaming black liquid, she offered herself a toast in the glowing computer screen. "Here's to success," she said with little enthusiasm.

She played a game of solitaire on her PC until the markets opened at 9 a.m. Barclays' shares had started at 82.21 pence. She punched the air; she'd made a couple of million overnight. The tide had turned. Barclays was coming back—and so was she. Tapping codes into her computer, she spent the remaining £600 million of borrowed money on more Barclays stock and sat back to watch. For the first hour, the market reacted to her investment and Barclays rose to 113 pence as others followed her lead. In less than sixty minutes, her stock rose further; on paper she made several more million. Her spirits soared further. But shortly after 11 a.m., the picture changed and the price started to slip. Sitting with eyes fixed on her computer screen, Blaze watched in horror as her money evaporated before her eyes. Within an hour, Barclays had fallen to 72 pence; over the next two hours, she lost £43 million. The shares closed at 67.34.

She left the office in a daze. Drunk on fear and adrenalin, she wandered aimlessly along unknown streets. It was nearly midnight when she got back to her apartment. A bottle of wine and two sleeping pills later, she fell into a fitful sleep. As dawn broke, she got up and went to the gym. Two hours of running and weights failed to calm her nerves. At 9 a.m., when the markets opened, she received the first of many calls from Helmut Myer—what did she think was happening? The telephone rang incessantly: worried clients seeking reassurance; reporters, tipped off by someone, circling like vultures. By Wednesday night, Barclays shares had dipped to 61 pence. By Thursday they had fallen to just under 55 pence. Helmut Myer rang every thirty minutes: PNB needed urgent additional security or they would require her to sell shares to limit their losses.

"If you sell out now," Blaze said, "my clients will lose all of their money. The only thing to do is sit tight and wait for recovery."

"If you can raise another £100 million, we will wait a few days."

Doug Smith, the CEO of Spalding Trust, was equally nervous.

"How did you know?" Blaze asked, wondering how Moonshot's investors were so well informed.

"Sleet's been helpful" was the invariable reply.

At 10 a.m. on Friday, with Barclays' share price still falling, Helmut Myer issued an ultimatum. "We need a margin call by 4 p.m. or we are calling the loan."

Blaze hadn't slept for three nights. In a frantic attempt to save her company and her investors' money, she contacted every person she knew, bar Sleet or Wolfe, praying she would find someone willing to commit enough money to keep Moonshot afloat. No one was interested. All she'd worked so hard for, the sacrifices she had made and the future of Trelawney were in peril. Worst of all, she had promised her clients a safe haven and had let them down. Her heart twisted when she thought of the pensioners at Spalding—the lady from Newcastle who'd sold her house, the small farmer in Wales who'd taken out a mortgage on his property in the hope of getting out of debt.

There were two people left on her list. With a heavy heart, she picked up the phone and punched in a number.

"I've been waiting for this," Sleet answered. "My friend Helmut is very upset."

"So I don't have to explain what I need," Blaze said. As she spoke she could see her ghostly reflection in the window.

"I'll put up £100 million."

Blaze exhaled slowly. "Thank you."

"You haven't heard my terms," Sleet added.

"I'm listening."

"In return, I get 100 per cent of Moonshot and your head on a platter. The moment the ink is dry, you're out."

Blaze couldn't believe what he was asking. "I created this company."

"See it as saving your reputation."

"And what happens to me?"

"You can go back to Cornwall and lick your wounds. If the share price recovers, you'll get some of your money back. Eventually." He let the syllables of the last word roll pleasantly and slowly around his mouth.

"You are a bastard."

"I told you that I'd own you. There's no escape," he said.

"Is revenge worth all this money?" Blaze asked incredulously. The deal was hardly risk-free for Sleet; if Barclays didn't recover, he stood to lose up to £100 million.

Sleet, as if reading her mind, burst out laughing. "I could lose a lot more and enjoy the ride. Just be grateful you have the clothes you're wearing and your licence. My lawyers will be with you at 4 p.m. with the necessary paperwork. Sign up or sink." He laughed again. "Oh, and by the way, I'm taking your niece out to dinner again tonight. We're getting on well."

Blaze's heart lurched. "I'll kill you."

"Have fun trying." Sleet hung up.

Blaze sat in front of her computer watching the share price fall to 50, then 49 and then 48 pence. Wolfe was the only person who could now help, but he wasn't returning her calls. For the sake of her shareholders, she had no choice but to accept Sleet's deal. Looking around her spartan room, she saw how little imprint she had made or left. Through the glass, in the empty outer office, the computers were like gravestones glowing in neon light. The only hints of former human occupation were cardboard coffee cups, balls of paper, a pizza box and an old tennis ball. In her own room, there were no framed photographs or lucky mascots to take home, only a laptop and her phone. A few might remember her as a one-trick pony—the perils of following your own conviction. Twenty years earlier she had arrived at Paddington Station with £50; today she was leaving her office with even less. Her licence to trade would almost certainly be rescinded by the Financial Services Authority.

Sleet's lawyers arrived at exactly 4 p.m., carrying the relevant paperwork. Blaze, numbed by humiliation, signed in the necessary places. Opening up her desk computer, she typed in a code that automatically transferred everything to Sleet's account. She took off her high-heeled shoes and, putting them into the bin next to her desk, slipped on a pair of trainers. Her life in the City was over. She double-locked the office door and left the keys at the front desk. She felt nothing: neither despair nor fear.

The weekend, behind locked doors at Moonshot Wharf, passed in a blur of vodka and sleeping pills. Saturday must have slipped into Sunday which became Monday or maybe Tuesday—she didn't care; she had nothing to get up for. When Ayesha finally shook her awake, Blaze tried to fight her off, but the young woman was determined.

Ayesha put a cup of coffee on the bedside table.

Blaze sat up in bed and rubbed her eyes. "What day is it?"

"Tuesday. You smell and look terrible. You're going to have a shower now. There's a man here to see you."

"The bailiff," Blaze said.

Ayesha ignored her and, pulling her out of bed, marched her to the bathroom. Blaze let herself be washed and dried.

"You look like a bag of bloody bones," Ayesha grumbled, forcing her aunt's limbs into a white silk shirt and a pair of black trousers. She combed Blaze's hair and pushed her into the living room. "I'm going out. You two need to talk." Taking her bag, she walked out of the apartment.

Blaze looked up. Sitting on the edge of her large white sofa was Joshua Wolfe.

"While you were sleeping, Barclays' shares climbed to a high of 84 pence."

Blaze couldn't hear what he was saying; all she wanted to know was why he was in her apartment.

"Why have you come?" she asked. An acute hangover seemed to have shrivelled her brain and made her tongue too large for her mouth.

"Barclays' directors published a letter claiming to have £17 billion over and above their debt. The bank is back on the road. You were right." Wolfe remained seated. His voice was calm but his eyes roved around her face.

Blaze hoped she looked better than she felt. "Lucky Sleet. You should congratulate him. I sold out to him on Friday. He owns everything, even this apartment." She grimaced. "I have only my own recklessness to blame. I'm out, finished."

"You're far from finished." Wolfe got up from the sofa and took a step towards her. "I bought Moonshot yesterday morning for £1. Sleet didn't want it; buying your business was simply a means to humiliate you. The company is still operational. Helmut Myer is prepared to continue with the loan."

Blaze looked at him, dumbfounded. "Why?"

"Because I believe in you. Buying Barclays was a good decision, even if your timing was off by a few days. You bought too early but your judgement was correct. By the end of the week, you'll make back your money and, if your hunch is right, you'll treble the value of your investment by the end of the year. Sleet will look an idiot for selling at the bottom of the rout." He hesitated. "I will make sure everyone knows it; he can't be allowed to behave like he did with no consequences."

Wolfe was now so close that Blaze only had to raise a hand to touch his. She clenched her fists to stop herself. "You didn't return my calls."

Wolfe shrugged. "I was angry. Hurt. And I suspected you were calling me about business, not about what happened." He took another step forwards. "Blaze, come back to work. Moonshot is your fund. I will be a hands-off investor. Your portfolio will be one of many on my books."

Now it was her turn to feel disappointed; Wolfe was only here on business. Blaze shook her head. "I'm done with the City."

"You're one of the best, Blaze; you can't walk away." His voice rose slightly.

Blaze smiled at him. "I am pleased that you've made your money back and grateful that you came here to tell me. You've saved me from the ignominy of being struck off and, more importantly, my clients won't lose their investments. But my heart's not in it any more. I used to love taking risks but when I bought the Barclays shares, something had changed: my pulse didn't race; my nerves didn't fizz. I did it because a sixth sense told me, not for the thrill of the chase. To be a great investor, you have to be a gambler and be prepared to risk everything: for me, the excitement of winning and losing has gone."

"You were right!" Wolfe insisted.

"I don't feel vindicated, just empty."

"You're tired. Take a few weeks off. Get your mojo back." He wanted Blaze to look at him, but she stared at the carpet, tracing an invisible pattern in the wool with her toe.

"Selling Moonshot didn't frighten or appall me. I felt an overwhelming sense of relief: I was finished, it was over and I wouldn't have to fight any more."

"Without you, there won't be Moonshot."

"My number two, TiLing Tang, is steady, professional and knows the portfolio as well as I do." She paused. "I behaved appallingly to you—imagined the worst, stamped my foot like a child. Why have you done this? Why take the risk?"

Wolfe shrugged. "I believe in you."

"As an investor." Blaze tried not to sound too sad.

"As a person as well."

He reached over and, taking her hand in his, traced her lifeline with his finger. "It took a bit of time to calm down but I'd like to see you again."

Blaze looked at him and smiled. "Thank you," she said with sincerity.

He leaned in and tried to kiss her.

"I'm sorry, Joshua, but I can't do this." Blaze stepped backwards and pulled her hand out of his.

Wolfe, unable to hide his disappointment, closed his eyes and rubbed his forehead with his hands. "What are you going to do?" he asked after a few moments.

"I'm going home. I'm going to Trelawney."

22

Hot Chocolate

WEDNESDAY 18TH MARCH 2009

Ayesha found the red-fronted tea room in a small alley off St. James's between a sandwich bar and a dry cleaner's. The interior, all brass and red velvet, was supposed to look like a *fin de siècle* Parisian café, but all the details, from the Formica tabletops to the fluorescent lighting and the fake wooden floor, were wrong. A frieze of poorly painted can-can dancers covered one wall and on the other, for no apparent reason, was a poster of the Eiffel Tower in the snow. Spray-painted gold lettering on the window announced that this was *Chou Chou, La Maison de Thé.*

Tony sat waiting in a corner, dressed in a bright pink shirt and white silk cravat, with his steel-grey hair as perfectly swirled as an ice-cream cone. "Darling, you look even more beautiful than when I last saw you." He got slowly to his feet, holding out his arms and kissing the air on either side of her cheeks. "You have inherited the best of your mother's and your father's genes. Anastasia's looks were astonishing but almost too other-worldly. The Trelawneys have added a certain earthy sensuality."

Ayesha smiled happily. "If it's not too indelicate to ask, how old are you?" she enquired.

"Far too old to tell the truth. Now, let's order." They sat side by side on a scratchy velveteen banquette. *"Garçon?"* Tony said to a bemused-looking youth.

The waiter, dressed in black jeans and a red T-shirt, tipped his name badge in Tony's direction. "My name is Stanislav, not *Garçon.*"

Tony turned to Ayesha and shrugged. "The young today are so ill-educated. Imagine not being able to understand restaurant French, particularly when you work in 'Chou Chou.'" He puffed out his cheeks with indignation. Stanislav handed over a leather-bound menu containing four pages of drinks.

"I know this place is hideous, but I'm a chocoholic. I recommend Valrhona, Atacama or Chilean," Tony said. "The Toblerone is simply revolting. What will you have, darling?"

"Can I have them all mixed together?" Ayesha asked.

Tony laughed. "Of course!" He checked that Stanislav was listening. "Two hot chocolates made from your best reserves, with fresh cream and sprinkles, Stan."

Stanislav regarded Tony with ill-disguised irritation.

Leaning back in his seat, Tony scrutinised his great-niece. "Now tell me about yourself."

"I've turned into a frightful swot. Blaze has persuaded me to sit the Oxbridge exams. I don't want to go, but if Plan A doesn't work . . ."

"Plan A?" Tony raised his eyebrows.

Ayesha looked at him from under thick black lashes.

"I'm interviewing prospective husbands. Only the seriously wealthy need apply."

Tony clapped his hands together. "How delicious—a proper project. Do you want him rich, stinking rich or oligarch rich?"

"Somewhere between the last two."

"Any candidates?"

"I have been on a few viewings," Ayesha admitted.

"Any offers?"

"There's a Colombian, a Texan, a strangled Duke of Something or Other and a repulsive hedge-funder who thinks I am the reincarnation of my mother."

"Did he know your mother?"

"They met at Oxford and he never recovered. He calls me Anastasia by mistake."

"Creepy." Tony shivered. "Do you like him?"

"I like the opportunities he's offering."

"How cynical."

"The alternative is to get a job."

"That would be frightfully dull," Tony agreed.

"I have to make money so that I can marry the love of my life, Mark, who unfortunately is not nearly rich enough to look after me."

"Can't you live happily ever after in a garret?"

Ayesha threw her hands up in horror. "Out of the question." Straightening the hem of her skirt, she added, "He will be a great success, but unfortunately time has yet to catch up with his invention; he's teaching computers how to think."

"What a perfectly appalling thought," said Tony. "You should stop him immediately."

"He's a genius and so full of integrity," Ayesha insisted. "He'll make sure no harm comes to the human race."

Tony seemed unconvinced. "So you marry the squillionaire and leave him for the love of your life?"

"I might have to have a child to secure the alimony."

"What happens if the sprog takes after its father and you're left with a vulgar baby hedge-funder?"

Ayesha shuddered at the thought of a miniature Sleet: ginger-haired, flat-footed and corpulent. "Then I might not fight for custody."

"You are funny. Much funnier than your mother."

Ayesha looked at him seriously. "Marrying me will cost him a billion."

Tony looked back in astonishment. "That is a fantastical fantasy; odds against, I'm afraid."

"My mother assured me that with the right level of determination, you can get what you want."

"It didn't work for Anastasia!" Tony had visited many Indian palaces and found the princes, nawabs and maharajas to be as desperate and impoverished as most of the English aristocracy. In both cases, external grandeur barely masked the internal decay. "I went to Balakpur in the 1950s; it was frightfully shabby even then," he said, remembering miles of dusty corridors, a ballroom ceiling strung with Christmas decorations and a bad-tempered maharaja bemoaning the lack of pheasants in his kingdom. "I thought your mother married below her station. Looks like hers could ensnare anyone. Why did she do it?"

"Because of me. My arrival spoiled everything, limited her choices." Ayesha fought back tears. "Her nickname for me was 'The Little Millstone.' "

Her face hardened. "She made me promise to put it right."

"Put what right?"

"Everything. And I will."

Something about Ayesha's tone unsettled Tony: an eerie, icy single-mindedness. He'd never understood women; men were so simple by comparison. Centuries of absolute power had dulled the male brain, whereas women, forced for so long to cajole and manipulate, had evolved into far more complex and capable beings.

"Do you miss Anastasia?" he asked.

"I do my best to remember the good bits." She hesitated, as if searching for something positive. "I miss her clarity."

"That's an odd thing to say."

"If Mother was here, she'd know how to manage my situation."

"Did you love her?"

Ayesha played with the edge of the white paper tablecloth before responding. "My childish longing, fuelled by books and fairy tales, for what a mother should be obscured what she actually was. That fantasy of a kind, maternal woman took precedence over the actual person. It's far easier to live with an idealised version. No one wants to admit that their mother wasn't a very nice person; it might be contagious or genetic."

Tony leaned across and put his gnarled old hand over her exquisite white fingers. "I like you very much."

Ayesha's eyes filled with tears. "Thank you," she whispered. "I haven't had much practice at being popular."

Their drinks arrived: tall glasses topped with mountains of cream. Tony shovelled a large spoonful into his mouth, letting it melt slowly between his teeth and down the back of his throat.

"So what did Anastasia have planned for you?" he asked.

"She left clear instructions," said Ayesha.

Tony raised an eyebrow.

"She wanted revenge."

"On who?"

"That would be telling." Ayesha smiled enigmatically.

"Your mother has gone; why bother?"

"Perhaps we never stop trying to please our parents." She smoothed out imaginary creases in the tablecloth and changed the subject. "What do you think about Blaze's idea to open Trelawney to the public?"

Tony looked thoughtful. "For eight centuries our family has enjoyed being waited on. Maybe this is divine retribution. I wonder how many teas they'll have to serve before the novelty wears off."

"The local council are insisting on a steward in each room."

"There's nothing left to steal!"

"It's to protect the public from falling plaster and rotting floorboards. The place is a health hazard."

Tony scraped the residue of chocolate from the bottom of his glass and licked his spoon. "It does make one sad. The point of Trelawney is its utter other-worldly fabulousness. It was built to amuse the elite, not to entertain the masses."

"Blaze wants to make it into a viable business so the next generations can stay there."

"Why would anyone want to run, let alone live in, a theme park?" Tony snorted. "I can't see Ambrose making a go of it."

"Is he so dreadful?" Ayesha had met Jane's eldest briefly at the funeral, but had not heard a lot about him except that he liked sport.

"He was born with a charm bypass on a highway to nihilism. I can't think of many good things to say about him."

"He's not very handsome," she said, remembering the flat-footed, auburn-haired young man walking behind the coffin.

"Not very anything, sadly."

Ayesha burst out laughing. "I wish I could spend all my time with you."

"A little bit of Tony goes a long way."

Tony paid the bill and together they walked out into St. James's, past the palace, and crossed through a pretty rose garden into the park. A group of French schoolchildren chased a pigeon half-heartedly. Two nannies dressed in uniforms pushed old-fashioned Silver Cross prams. Tony walked stiffly with the aid of a silver-topped cane. His well-cut cashmere coat had been darned on one cuff and Ayesha noticed that his shirt collar, just visible beneath a white silk cravat, was also frayed. She had heard that he was almost penniless and lived in a bedsit off the Earls Court Road. Blaze was allowed to support him, but only as far as the poverty line.

Short of breath and wheezing slightly, Tony sat down on a wooden bench out of the wind.

"Are you lonely?" he asked abruptly. "I have never met a beautiful woman who isn't. Beauty is the most terrible curse. It makes the person into an object, something to stare at or possess. The first time I met poor sweet Marilyn Monroe, she was having dinner alone in the Bel-Air. No one wanted to talk to her, they just wanted to gawk. I went over and asked to join her. She fell on me like a camel coming across an oasis in a desert. I have never seen anyone look so grateful."

"Was she lovely?"

"You know how cherry trees have that one perfect moment when all the blossom trembles in a slight breeze? When the colour shimmers in the spring sunshine? That was her—but all the time—impossible to take your eyes away." He looked up at Ayesha. "Your mother had the same quality. The first time I saw her was in the library at Trelawney. She wore a red shift dress and her hair hung around her face like a halo. The whole room went silent. I remember feeling terribly sorry for her. Shall we walk a bit farther?"

They reached a small and incongruous vegetable garden opposite the back entrance to Number 10 Downing Street. Apart from a few rows of cabbages and beetroots, most of the beds were empty, neatly raked and prepared, waiting to be sown or planted.

Ayesha glanced around to make sure no one was listening. "I need your help on two important matters."

Tony seemed delighted. "I am all ears."

"You are an art dealer, aren't you?"

"I like to think of myself as an adviser."

"I need to sell something: a Monet sketch of the Thames below Westminster."

Tony looked keenly at her. "Did you steal it?"

Ayesha was horrified. "I was given it!"

"If it's the one I'm thinking of, I know the owner."

"It was a gift," Ayesha said quickly.

"He's not the man I'd choose for my daughter." Tony noticed that the young woman looked away guiltily.

"You must not tell Blaze: do you promise?"

Tony shuddered, thinking of Thomlinson Sleet pawing his niece. "What were the conditions of the present?"

"He said the painting was an 'appetiser' of things to come."

Tony grimaced. "No wonder you want to get rid of it."

"I need the money to invest in a technology company called Apple." She hesitated. "My friend says it will be even bigger one day."

"You're playing the markets?"

"I want to be rich." She corrected herself. "I am going to be rich."

Tony laughed. Ayesha didn't.

"Your Aunt Blaze knows about investments. Why don't you borrow from her?"

"She's wiped out."

"So the rumours are true." Tony shook his head in disbelief.

"Moonshot Wharf is on the market. The apartment is crawling with estate agents."

"How is she?" He tried to imagine Blaze without the armoury of her professional life.

"She's gone to Trelawney to look after her mother. I am home alone until the place sells."

In the distance, they heard the sound of wings beating against water and turned to see two swans, one black, one white, fighting on the nearby pond. Ayesha and Tony stood side by side, watching the battle play out.

"Your picture is worth about £800,000, but only to the right client. Unfortunately the former owner is the biggest collector of Impressionists; he outbids everyone else."

"Can we put it in an auction? Maybe he'd buy it back?"

"I don't think he'd be too amused to see his present flipped so quickly."

"So sell it privately. I'll take a lot less for it," Ayesha said firmly.

Tony started to walk slowly in the direction of the Mall. "One of the worst things about ageing is that if you stop, there's a danger you might never get going again; muscles seize up and then every tiny movement is uncomfortable. I used to ski and run after tennis balls, now a short stroll is a second-by-second choice between pain and paralysis."

Ayesha slipped her arm through his and they continued towards Admiralty Arch. It was bitterly cold and the end of Tony's nose dripped. A fierce wind whipped across Trafalgar Square and they sheltered behind one of Landseer's monumental lions.

"Will you sell my picture?" Ayesha asked.

Tony nodded. "I'll see what I can do. Now let's go to the blessed National Gallery. At least it'll be warmer."

Circumnavigating Nelson's Column, they went up the flight of stone steps into the museum, where there was an exhibition of paintings by the Renaissance master Andrea Mantegna. The two stood side by side in front of a picture of St. Sebastian, a beautiful young man tied to a Corinthian column, every part of his body stuck with arrows.

"He looks so gloomy and resigned," Ayesha said. "He should be furious and writhing in agony."

"His faith gives him courage and forbearance."

"This old art is so dreary. All martyrised men and long-suffering women. If I have to look at art, I like something understandable like a soup tin or a misty bridge," Ayesha said with finality.

"I've never had communion with a soup tin or a bridge," Tony said.

"How many human pincushions have you spoken to?" Ayesha pointed at Sebastian.

Tony felt it was his duty to try and impart to the next generation some of the knowledge accumulated over a long and rather pointless life. In his opinion, a love of aesthetics differentiated man from beast.

"Warhol and Monet are so obvious. Mantegna has real profundity. Every part of the painting has a hidden meaning. Think of it as the difference between a pop song and a symphony. One is all synthesised and catchy; the other's intention and significance deepens and expands over time."

Ayesha gave a fake yawn. "Who has the time to lie around listening to old music? Pop songs might be bad but they're mercifully short."

Tony was insistent. "Try to put yourself into the picture, to imagine yourself as the subject."

Ayesha let her eyes roam around the painting. "I am never going to be a martyr!" she pronounced. "I'm going to come out on top of every situation." She walked away from St. Sebastian dismissively.

Tony refused to be defeated. Taking her by the arm, he led her to another picture. "This one is much more fun. *Triumph of the Virtues,* painted in 1502."

Ayesha had to admit that it was rather entrancing; her eyes roved over the strange semi-human creatures masquerading as vices; other-worldly beasts emerging from a putrid pond. Nearby, Diana the Goddess of Chastity was about to be raped by a lascivious centaur watched by truncated gremlins. Fat baby angels fired bows and arrows from the sky and a beautiful Goddess Minerva strode through their midst, driving away the wicked with golden locks and a giant spear.

"A great improvement on the gloomy old Sebastian," she pronounced, and Tony felt a tiny lurch of hope.

"It must have caused a scandal?" She bent down to look at the date. "It was painted nearly six hundred years ago!" She let out a low whistle.

"I suspect mankind has always had venal proclivities." (Tony smiled to himself. Why do the young think they are the inventors of bad behaviour?) "It was one of a series of paintings commissioned by the young Marquise of Mantua, Isabella d'Este, for her private rooms."

Ayesha looked bored.

(The only way to get her attention is to make this all about her.) "She was very beautiful, imperious, only fifteen years old when she got married. She used her station and wits to become one of the most powerful women of her time."

Ayesha turned back to the picture.

(Bingo, I've got her again.)

"I'd like to have met her," she said.

"She was a brilliant monster."

"Sounds like Anastasia."

(Like mother, like daughter.)

"Isabella ruled her court with a rod of iron, commissioning many of the great artists: Leonardo, Michelangelo, Titian, Raphael, Giorgione and, of course, Mantegna. She was one of the greatest patrons of the Renaissance."

"Why isn't she better known? I've heard about the Medici, the Borgias and so forth."

"I've never understood."

"Almost certainly because she was a woman written off by male historians as an inconsequential wife."

"Possibly." (Never get between a feminist and their cause.)

"Did artists paint her?" Ayesha asked, examining a particularly odious-looking beast at the bottom of the canvas.

"She rarely liked her own portraits; had most of them destroyed."

"I love pictures of myself," Ayesha said.

"Artists must be clamouring to paint you." (The narcissism of youth is so amusing.)

"Not yet," she replied. "Maybe I'll make Isabella my role model." She thought for a while before adding, "It would be fun to be her reincarnation and commission the greatest artists of the day."

"What a good idea." (Oh, to be back in that wonderful intermission between the uncertainty of childhood and the disappointment of maturity.) "You'll need a lot of money and power."

"I will have both," Ayesha said confidently.

Tony laughed. (This young woman is going to learn a few bitter lessons.)

As if reading his mind, she replied, "Watch me."

Tony wished he was younger and had more energy: Ayesha was the most exciting person he had met for many years. Too bad he wouldn't be around to witness the spectacle of her ambition and arrogance.

"I'm going to learn everything there is to know about art," she announced. "And you are going to teach me."

Before he could remonstrate, she was on to her next topic. "There's a second matter we need to manage." She hesitated. "It concerns Blaze's love life."

Tony held up his hands. "A lost cause, my dear. I've been pushing dusty dukes and cadaverous counts her way for years. She simply isn't interested." They had reached the gallery's Central Hall and he leaned against an old iron radiator, drawing the tepid warmth into his frozen bones.

"She's met someone."

Tony raised an eyebrow. "Pray tell."

"And it's requited."

"And I suppose she's pushing him away with all her might?"

"How did you know?"

"She is hopeless and stubborn." Tony closed his eyes to think. "What can we do?"

"We're going to arrange a 'spontaneous' meeting. She mustn't know about it or she'll back out."

"I suppose you have it all planned?"

Ayesha smiled knowingly. "Of course, I need your help."

Tony looked at her glowing face and felt a distinct sense of foreboding. He had played Cupid before with Blaze and, on each occasion, the arrows ended up embedded deep and painfully in his own flesh, like those in St. Sebastian's torso. He and Blaze were the same: some are born lucky; others just have to bear their lot.

Ayesha's phone rang. She looked at the screen and frowned.

"Who is it?" Tony asked.

Ayesha pulled a face. "I have to go."

"Where, why?" said Tony. "What about Blaze?"

His niece kissed him on the cheek. “Unfortunately, this is a summons I have to obey.”

“I can’t imagine you kowtowing to anyone.”

“It’s only lip service; part of a master plan.” She waved and ran down the stairs towards Trafalgar Square.

23

Curtains

WEDNESDAY 22ND APRIL 2009

Blaze was staying in her mother's apartment at Trelawney. The upper-floor bedroom had been hand-painted in the 1930s with bouquets of lily-of-the-valley wallpaper. The silk curtains, though massively faded, had been handwoven using the same flowery motif. A small double sleigh bed was placed to the side and on the opposite wall there was a dressing table whose glass surface was covered with hairbrushes, hand mirrors and powder compacts, all embossed with the initial "T." Above the window was a curtain pole and on it an earlier resident had carefully placed a handleless saucepan to catch the rain which made its way through the ceiling during heavy showers. In the far corner of the room, a second vessel, formerly used as a chamber pot, was strategically positioned beneath another hole. Blaze was used to cold, but hated the sound of mice scampering across the floorboards and along the rafters above her head. There was only one bathroom in the Mistresses' Wing; access was through her mother's suite.

Next to Blaze's bedroom there was a study. From her desk, overlooking the back entrance to the castle, she had a perfect view of the comings and goings at Trelawney. By the time her own alarm went off at 6:30 a.m. and she drew her curtains, her sister-in-law was already awake. Blaze could see down into the kitchen where Jane made breakfast for her children. This morning, as on every other, she would then carry any kitchen slops down to the hen house, followed by Pooter, the bucket held as far as possible from her body to avoid spillage onto her jeans. If Blaze stood up and craned her neck to the left, she could just make out the corner of the cowshed and the stables, Jane's next stop, where she would help Jim, the farmhand, let out the animals and muck out their sheds.

In bad weather, Jane wore a woollen hat and an old oilskin over a tweed jacket. In good weather, she wore much the same. Blaze noticed that, most of the time, Jane was alone. Late at night, Blaze could see a single lit window in one of the servants' wings and wondered what her sister-in-law did up there. It hadn't occurred to either of them to salve their boredom and isolation by becoming friends; both were firmly locked into their respective positions of mutual mistrust.

"Shall we continue with the Trelawney history?" Clarissa asked most nights. "Where's your notebook?" Blaze kept the red-backed journal and a pen close by in case her mother wanted to recount another story. For Clarissa, recording these snippets of family history had become an obsession. No detail was too arcane, no meander through minor characters too ephemeral, and she took cues from random events or thoughts. The previous evening, inspired by beef and Guinness pie for supper, she'd recounted the time when the 5th Earl had slaughtered his entire herd of cattle to provide a feast in honour of his only daughter's wedding to the second son of the King of England. Nobility from as far afield as Scotland and Ireland had been invited for the great event but, the day before, a flash flood washed away the bridge across the Tamar and half the guests were stranded at Tavistock. Undeterred, the Earl floated the carcasses upriver and a huge banquet was held in the town square.

Another evening, Blaze and her mother had been sitting by the fire when a spark flew from the grate and nearly set the carpet alight. This reminded Clarissa of the 16th Earl, a man so drunk and debauched that he liked to build conflagrations in the middle of the ballroom and dance naked around them attended by local beauties. Inevitably, the ceiling caught fire and the Elizabethan wing nearly burned down. His heir, a more prudent and sober character, fully restored it and added a fine baroque extension. For Blaze, writing down her mother's memories was easier than talking, more restful than thinking.

When she wasn't with Clarissa, Blaze read newspapers and watched the news obsessively. Britain was formally in a recession. Neither the programme of quantitative easing begun in March nor the G20's global stimulus package of $5 trillion had any effect on local lives. Unemployment was rising steadily; small and large businesses were failing. While RBS and Lloyds shares had fallen dramatically, Barclays had risen to more than 200 pence. Blaze's original investment was secure, but she didn't want to liquidate it yet, believing that the bank was undervalued and the stock could rise further.

The impact of the recession was stark and plainly visible in Cornwall. High streets were deserted and shops abandoned. Only the cheapest supermarkets and charity shops were thriving.

TiLing had been made the CEO of Moonshot Capital and she and Blaze spoke most days. Officially, Blaze had nothing to do with the company, but her former number two lacked confidence and sought her advice; based on her own market research in Cornwall, Blaze encouraged TiLing to buy shares in the low-budget supermarkets and pubs, Morrisons and Wetherspoons. Sleet had made even more by shorting ailing banks and mortgage brokers but, as this practice had been subsequently banned by the Financial Services Authority, she wondered where her nemesis was putting his money.

Most of all, she thought about Wolfe. He haunted her days and nights. Three months had passed since their encounter at Moonshot Wharf, and no word. Late one night, fortified by a bottle of wine, she decided to telephone him. It rang for a long time; she was about to cut off the call when she heard his voice.

"Hello?"

Blaze opened her mouth but no words came out.

"Hello?" he asked again.

Overcome by embarrassment, she hung up. Then she looked at the phone in amazement. What was happening to her? How could she let a man she hardly knew rob her of her sense of self and decorum? It had to stop. Refilling her glass, she made a toast. "Here's to the end of self-pity, madness and sadness. Here's to being a single, independent, capable, healthy woman. To making the most of life."

Moonlight had turned the track into a silvery ribbon stretching from the house all the way to the escarpment. Pooter ran in front, his head down and tail waving from side to side, as steady as a metronome. Jane took care where she walked—a few nights before she'd tripped over a fallen branch and skinned her knee. By the time she got home, an hour later, the blood had hardened into her jeans and ripping them off had been more painful than the original hurt.

The midnight walks began after Kitto's departure; Jane's inner demons felt more manageable outside. In the first few months she walked around the garden, but had recently ventured further afield, taking the lane towards the escarpment or following the river towards the sea. The colder the weather, the easier the journey; tonight, unseasonably chilly even for April, created perfect walking conditions and her boots crunched on frozen grass.

Winter had stripped the trees. New leaves were beginning to unfurl and, backlit by the moon, their canopies of bare branches quivered like lace fans in the breeze. An owl called, low and mournful. Was it looking for a mate or warning others off its hunting ground? Jane wondered if birds, like humans, sent out confusing signals. She was thinking of Blaze, so obviously lonely and yet aggressively keeping everyone at a distance. Jane hardly saw her but, from the glow of the light in her bedroom, knew her sister-in-law kept similarly strange hours. For the time being there was oil in the tank, the butcher and grocer turned up and Mrs. Sparrow's wages were paid, but Jane lived in fear of Blaze withdrawing support.

The incline grew steeper and the frosty air caught inside Jane's lungs. In the distance she saw an unmissable streak of black and white: a badger working its way along a fence line. She hoped that Pooter hadn't seen it; she didn't fancy the dog's chances. Since Kitto had left, the Labrador had gone into mourning and spent hours sitting by the kitchen door, waiting for his master to come home. Any crunch of tyre on the gravel sent him into paroxysms of excitement and, with the realisation that the car belonged to another, he slumped inconsolably by the Aga. Jane knew how he felt. If it weren't for the children, she might just lie down and never get up.

Blaze couldn't sleep. She sat at her desk listening to the BBC news bulletin. More cases of swine flu had been identified: maybe, she thought, I will get it, die and everything will be a lot simpler. Checking her watch, she saw that it was 2 a.m. and her sister-in-law had not returned. The last thing she needed was anything to happen to Jane. Blaze's admiration for her tenacity and hard work had grown by the day; it would take six people to replace her. Pulling a pair of trousers over her nightdress, Blaze went downstairs, grabbed a thick coat and some boots, and opened the back door. The air was biting cold. Two hours earlier, she had seen Jane set off towards the escarpment and, following in her footsteps crystallised in the freezing ground, she walked for half a mile up the track. The moon was bright and she didn't need a torch to see. Two hundred yards ahead she caught sight of an unusual shape in a rut. At first she thought it was a sheep or small cow lying down, but the closer she got, she realised that it could only be a person. Then she heard a gentle keening. She ran, slowly at first, but when the cry became louder she speeded up, sure that Jane had fallen and hurt herself. When she got within fifteen yards, she saw her sister-in-law rocking backwards and forwards holding Pooter's body in her arms. Blaze sank to her knees beside her.

"What happened?" she asked, leaning over to stroke the dog. Pooter was warm to the touch, but inert.

"He was fine," Jane sobbed. "Then he seemed to jump into the air and landed on his back. He let out a yelp and collapsed. I ran to him; he licked my hand and went limp." She cried harder. "He was my friend, my only friend. I can't bear it. I can't." She rested her face in the animal's coat. Her whole body shook. Blaze didn't know what to do, but instinctively leaned forward to stroke her sister-in-law's back. After a few minutes, Jane raised her head and, wiping her tear-stained face, looked at Blaze.

"Will you help me take him home?"

"Of course." Blaze nodded and, standing up, took off her coat. "Let's wrap his body in this. It will be easier to carry."

"Won't you get cold?"

"This is warm compared to my bedroom—they never insulated the Mistresses' Wing." She bent down and laid her coat on the ground. Jane got stiffly to her feet and together they folded the garment around the dog's body. Jane took the front end, Blaze the back, and they walked slowly down towards the house. Pooter was surprisingly heavy and they had to rest several times. They reached the back door and lowered the dog on to the flagstones.

"Would you like a hot drink?" Jane asked.

Blaze nodded. "Maybe we should bring him just inside?"

Jane smiled gratefully. "Let's put him in the cold store. Tomorrow I'll bury him in the rose garden. He used to love it there." She burst out crying again. "I haven't cried for months—and now this. I wonder if I'll ever stop. Maybe it's easier to mourn the loss of a dog. Oh, God, how can I tell the children? After all that they've been through." Her voice rose to a wail and she took vague swipes with the back of her hand at the tears and mucous streaming down her face.

They brought Pooter in and Blaze unrolled him from the coat and put a large blanket over his body. The dog's eyes were open, liquid brown and trusting. His tongue lolled out of the corner of his mouth. Jane bent and kissed his head. Blaze held her sister-in-law's arm and led her along the back corridor to the kitchen. "Sit down, I'll put the kettle on."

Jane sat at the table staring into the middle distance, too tired or overwrought to do or say anything. When the tea came, she blew on its surface, enjoying the warm steam on her cold face. After a few minutes she asked, "What do you do all day?"

Blaze sat down opposite and took a sip of tea. "I listen to the news obsessively, watch what's happening on the stock markets and transcribe Mother's history of the house and its inhabitants." (She missed out the hours spent thinking about Wolfe.)

"Your mother must be so happy to have an audience," Jane said. "I was too busy."

"We assumed she had no hobbies or interests outside our father's life, but she spent years researching and thinking about the different incumbents. Some of her recollections are slight and only give an insight into the family or social life; others reflect the history of the country or the times."

"I can't imagine you having the patience to sit through her long-winded explanations."

"Maybe I've got to that age when a woman turns to God, gardening or genealogy."

They both laughed spontaneously and then regarded each other, remembering old jokes, bygone ease. "I think God deserted me some time ago," Jane said.

"God who?" Blaze asked and they both giggled.

"Perhaps we could use some of the stories when you open the house?" Jane suggested.

Blaze looked at her. "That's a wonderful idea. It would animate the rooms and be much more interesting than passing out written sheets. Do you think we could persuade Mum to tell a few?"

"Try stopping her."

Glancing up at the wall, Jane saw that it was already 3:30 a.m. Only a few hours until she had to get the children up for school. "I need to try and get some sleep." She pulled herself up to standing. "Thank you for helping me tonight."

"Thank you for letting me," Blaze said in return.

Jane closed her eyes and breathed deeply. Maybe, she thought, I have lost a dog and regained a friend. “Why don’t you come by tomorrow? We can have lunch.”

Blaze nodded. “I’ll have to look at my diary; it’s so full.”

“Mine too.” Jane laughed. “Come at one.”

“I look forward to it,” Blaze said and, with a shy smile, turned and walked out of the kitchen.

24

Red Tape

TUESDAY 12TH MAY 2009

Even though the temperature in the dining room at Trelawney was just above freezing, the Plymouth District Local Planning Authority's senior officer was perspiring; for John Acre, this case was an unusually exciting break from his normal roster of shop signs and building codes. His number two, Penny Cuthbert, was supposed to be taking notes but was entirely distracted by her surroundings.

In preparation for the visit, Jane had made an effort to clean and polish one end of the thirty-foot-long, rarely used, mahogany dining-room table. The huge open fireplace was spattered with bird droppings, and she had not dared light a fire in case the nest (or nests) lodged somewhere in the flues ignited. Trelawney could only open to the public with the local authority's agreement; and Acre was the person to convince. Jane wished that Blaze was there to help argue their case but, with the cost of preparations for the opening of the castle rising unremittingly, her sister-in-law had taken a job advising a company specialising in ethical investments and was working three days a week in its offices in Bristol. Since Pooter's death, the two women had begun to spend time together, either over a meal or going for a walk. Both wondered, separately, if their friendship had been rekindled from old embers or by the sparks thrown off by loneliness. Either way, it didn't matter; they were grateful for glimmers of light on their dark interior worlds.

"This is like Hagrid's room from *Harry Potter,*" Cuthbert had said when Jane showed them in earlier that morning. Unlike her boss, Cuthbert was clearly feeling the cold and her long, thin nose ran constantly.

"Have you filled out form 67ART1?" Acre enquired.

"Which one is that?" Jane asked, flicking through the many papers on the table. She'd had no idea that opening a house to the public would involve so many forms.

"It's green," said Cuthbert. "A kind of hospital green."

Jane spread the papers out like a fan and found three pale, sickly-green forms. "Is this it?" She held one up.

Acre studied it. "No, that's the 69ART2.3. It relates to sewage. We'll discuss your septic tank later. I have a list of things to talk about." He waved a piece of A4 paper with two columns of "topics" numbered from 1 to 64. Words like "access," "safety" and "regulations" swam into view. Stifling a feeling of panic, Jane shuffled through the documents in front of her. She must stay calm.

"This?" She held out another.

Acre smiled. "Yes. Now let's see if you've checked the right boxes and filled it in correctly." He had a high-pitched nasal voice that reminded Jane of a mosquito circling its prey. His eyes flicked greedily down the form and alighted on paragraph 9 of section C, clause 4. "I see that this one is blank," he said triumphantly. The insect has landed, Jane thought, suspecting he was only interested in faults and omissions.

"And which section is that?" Jane was determined to keep her temper in check; on the occasion of Acre's last visit, she had snapped at him, a tactless move given his power over their future plans.

"It's the section on bats."

"Bats?"

"Yes, bats."

"What about them?"

"Whether you have any, what kind and whether the public might disturb them."

Jane had heard about the power of bat protection societies and decided to tread carefully. "I'm not a bat expert."

"You will need to consult one."

"What will they tell me?" Jane tried to keep her voice neutral.

"For a start, what kind of animal you have," Cuthbert piped up. "There are the crevice-dwellers like the common pipistrelle, the soprano pipistrelle, Nathusius' pipistrelle, Brandt's or the whiskered bat. But you are more likely to have the roof-dwellers like the serotine, Leisler's, Daubenton's or, if you are lucky, a barbastelle."

"Too much detail for now, Ms. Cuthbert," Acre said, unable, nevertheless, to suppress a hint of pride. Jane wondered if they were sleeping together and entertained visions of them both carefully folding their beige suits and drip-dry shirts on the back of the chair before engaging in frantic copulation. She forced herself back to the present.

"Actually, it is relevant because some, like the brown and grey long-eared bat, need flight space in the roost while others, like the great horseshoe, need flying access as well." Cuthbert smiled lovingly at her supervisor. They *are* sleeping together, Jane thought.

"But as you know, Mr. Acre, none of the proposed visitors will venture above the ground floor. That leaves two between the public and any bats."

"That is not the issue."

"Perhaps you could explain what the issue is?" Jane was confused.

Acre, hardly able to suppress a smile, turned to his number two and, with the excitement of a father asking his child to play "Chopsticks" at an adult party, suggested that she might like to enlighten their client.

"In this country, due to a decline in bat numbers during the last century, all species are protected by the Wildlife and Countryside Act of 1981," Cuthbert said. "There is also the Countryside and Rights of Way Act from 2000, the Natural Environment and Rural Communities Act 2006, and we are awaiting other amendments in the forthcoming Habitats and Species Regulations."

"And what does all this mean?"

"It is, therefore, illegal to deliberately or recklessly kill, injure, capture or disturb bats, or to obstruct access to bat roosts or damage or destroy bat roosts, whether occupied or not." Cuthbert took a deep breath and smiled broadly.

"So it makes no difference if the roosts or the properties are occupied?" Jane asked.

"None whatsoever."

"This house is eight hundred years old; what happens if there's a bat roost from the fifteenth century—is that protected?"

Cuthbert turned to her supervisor for clarification.

"I think we look for reasonably recent occupation."

"What does it matter if we're not going upstairs?" Keep calm, Jane reminded herself. Don't antagonise these people; imagine you are on the same side.

Cuthbert leaned forward with excitement. "Like you, I thought bats lived upstairs but actually they live wherever it suits them. We found bats in a downstairs toilet once, didn't we, Mr. Acre?"

"We did, Ms. Cuthbert." Acre nodded. "So next you need to consult your local SNCO."

Jane wrote this down. "What does it stand for?"

"It is short for Statutory Nature Conservation Organisation."

"How do I get in touch with them?"

"Yellow Pages."

"Or the internet. There's a very interesting website—the Bat Conservancy Organisation's portal," Cuthbert said.

"And then what?" Jane's heart sank.

"If there are any building works pertaining to the opening, you will need an S80 demolition notice completed by you and an S81 issued by the building control officer at the local authority."

"Is that you?" Jane asked.

"Oh, no. That's Len Beamer," Cuthbert said.

"Len Beamer retired," Acre corrected her.

"So he did. Who took over?"

"They haven't appointed anyone yet."

Cuthbert turned to Jane. "You've no idea how convoluted the appointment processes have become. It can take months and months to fill one position."

The door burst open and Aunt Tuffy stormed across the room holding a plastic bag and a fork. "Don't mind me," she announced cheerfully.

"Tuffy, we are in a meeting," Jane said.

"Won't be long." Tuffy went over to the fireplace, sank to her knees and started to scrape some of the ivy away from the hearth. "Quite amazing how quickly it grows."

"What's she doing?" Cuthbert asked.

Jane shrugged, hoping her worst fears wouldn't be realised.

"Excellent," Tuffy said and, taking the plastic bag, carefully placed it over something in the fireplace.

"What are you doing?" Cuthbert asked Tuffy, as the elderly woman slowly got back on to her feet.

Tuffy triumphantly waved the specimen bag. "Arabella told me where to find an excellent *Xenopsylla cheopis.*"

"Can I see?" Cuthbert stood up and approached.

"I really wouldn't," Jane said weakly.

Cuthbert leaned forward and stared into the bag. Seconds later she screamed and jumped backwards.

"Dead rat!"

"Of course it's dead! Do you think I'd be stupid enough to try and catch a rat with a fork and a plastic bag?" Tuffy shook her head in amazement.

"I wondered what that sickly smell was." Cuthbert went and stood behind Acre's chair.

"It's heavenly, isn't it? The smell of a decomposing body and the certainty of lots of maggots and fleas." Brandishing her spoils, Tuffy walked out of the room.

Cuthbert, now pink in the face, straightened her shoulders and, mustering her most professional smile, returned to her seat.

There was a long silence before Acre cleared his throat. "I hope you don't think this is inappropriate, but would you mind my asking, Lady Trelawney, where your husband is? It's irregular to conduct these kind of meetings without the owner present."

"Do you mean without the owner or without a male?" Jane asked.

Acre shifted uncomfortably in his chair. "This is 2009, Lady Trelawney—I am not making any sexist judgements."

"Do you know that when my mum wanted a TV licence, her dad had to sign the form? That was only in the 1980s," Cuthbert said.

"Thank you, Ms. Cuthbert," Acre replied. "Now, if you don't mind telling us where His Lordship is."

Jane looked at her hands and then at the family portraits. She was unsure how to answer the question. Stuck for a good alternative, she settled on the truth. "I haven't got any idea."

Acre and Cuthbert exchanged knowing glances.

Jane didn't trust herself to say anything rational. "I'll be back in five minutes," she said and ran down the corridor, through the hall and into the third drawing room. Here, some distance from Acre and Cuthbert, she screamed loudly. She went on screaming until she felt calm enough to walk back to the dining room.

"We thought we heard someone shouting," Cuthbert said.

"The ghost of the 7th Countess," Jane whispered.

Cuthbert looked around nervously. "Are there many?"

"Ghosts? Hundreds. It's like living in a permanent cocktail party," Jane replied. "The 7th Countess has developed a passion for hoovering and it's been a great help. Like having unpaid staff."

Cuthbert considered this remark from an employment law point of view. "That would be a hard tribunal to bring."

Jane crossed her hands over each other and looked across the table at the two guests. "Today is the day we intended to open Trelawney to the public. But today, like many preceding days, we are mired in bureaucracy. Let me reiterate what we are and what we are not trying to achieve: we don't wish to disturb bats, or to endanger anyone's life by falling masonry or inhaling mould or any other kind of injury; we want visitors to share in the history of this great place; and we want to train and employ local people by creating new businesses. Imagine if we gave young people something to do other than smoking crack at the village bus stop. Unemployment in this area is rising fast and, for young women in particular, there are few job opportunities. We're not asking you or any other government departments for grants towards this project. We want to give something back." Jane hesitated. "But our dreams are being thwarted by pieces of red tape. Tell me, Mr. Acre and Ms. Cuthbert, what would you suggest we do?"

Acre and Cuthbert sat silently for a moment.

"We respect your intentions, Lady Trelawney," Acre said. "But it's a matter of health and safety. You need to do some repairs."

"No!" Jane's voice rose and she struggled to catch it but, like a ball thrown too high, it slipped away and out of her reach. "No, no, no."

"No?"

"No." Jane breathed in deeply. "The whole point of the exercise is to show people what happens to buildings, to families, to society if they're left untended. Nature takes over." She got to her feet and, going over to the wall, tugged at a bit of ivy. The plant, as she suspected, was deeply embedded and to pull it even harder might bring down a chunk of plaster. "You see, we humans think we are in control but we're not. Nature is waiting patiently and, at the first opportunity, she'll pounce." Jane lunged towards Cuthbert, who screamed and held her hands up in self-protection. She continued with her theme. "It's the same with people. My husband's forebears enjoyed uninterrupted wealth and privileges for eight hundred years. Without money and prestige, they've been returned to their natural state. Now they are no better, no different to animals."

Acre and Cuthbert looked at each other wearily.

"The thing, Lady Trelawney, I don't get," Cuthbert's expression was earnest, "is what are people going to see? There's nothing to look at. Why would anyone pay to walk around an empty house?"

"It's a cautionary tale," Jane said, echoing Blaze's words and remembering how, only weeks earlier, she'd wanted to murder her sister-in-law for this preposterous suggestion.

"I don't think anyone wants more of those. It's been a terrible year. Only yesterday they laid off fifty people at Tesco's in St. Austell. All anyone wants now is fantasy and entertainment." Cuthbert pursed her lips.

Looking at the bovine Cuthbert with her shiny, moon-like face, Jane saw that the local council officer was correct. The crash and the recession had given everyone more than enough reality; who really wanted yet another story of decline and fall? The house's purpose, if it had one, was as a purveyor of fantastic illusions. That said, neither she nor Blaze had come up with any viable, affordable alternatives. Yoga studios, five-star restaurants, B&Bs, hotels, amusement parks and things of that ilk required enormous investment.

Straightening her shoulders, Jane mustered her best smile. "Where have we got to?"

"You'll need a SAG."

"Sag like my spirits," Jane said, attempting a joke.

"SAG as in Safety Advisory Group," Cuthbert corrected. "They will help with risk assessments, emergency planning and damage limitations."

Jane felt the last drops of hope ebb away.

"You'll have to consider signage, traffic management, first aid, PR, admission costs, online and manual ticketing," Acre added.

"And facilities. We recommend one toilet per hundred lady visitors and one per five hundred males," Cuthbert said. "And one per seventy-five disabled people."

"We have a total of eight—or maybe it's seven—working bathrooms in the whole house," Jane replied. "We can't afford to add any more."

"And you'll have to manage all this without disturbing the bats."

"The dear, dear bats," Jane said without any irony.

25

The Auction Room

THURSDAY 25TH JUNE 2009

"Why have you brought me here?" Blaze asked Tony, looking around the auction house whose rooms were hung with works of art from all periods. A large marble statue of Aphrodite, the Goddess of Love and Beauty, was placed near a painting by Picasso of a priapic Minotaur. On another wall there was a drooling dog painted by a justifiably forgotten Victorian artist displayed next to a metallic Jeff Koons balloon rabbit.

"I thought you should leave the wilds of Cornwall and see a bit of real life," Tony said. Even though it was lunchtime, a DJ with bulbous headphones stood by a deck in the centre of the room spinning vinyl records; rap music boomed out of huge speakers. A couple of sinewy women danced in front of a Damien Hirst spot painting and a reality TV star posed for photographers by an Andy Warhol screen-print of a soup can. The waiters and waitresses, all better-looking than the guests, handed out trays of bite-sized burgers and Bellinis.

"You call this real life?" Blaze laughed. It was the first time she'd been to London for many weeks and she'd been instantly overwhelmed by the cacophonous noises and malodorous smells. With only a month to go before the opening of the house, she and Jane were working around the clock. But Tony had been insistent and, as she hadn't seen her uncle for a long time, she'd agreed to make the long journey.

"You should approve," Tony told her. "The sale is in aid of those who were wiped out by the crash. All the works have been donated by hedge-fund billionaires."

Blaze hadn't heard about the event and wondered what else she had missed out on during the last few months of self-imposed purdah.

"I think it's extremely bad taste, very Marie Antoinette 'let them eat cake,'" he said. "Do they think they can salve their consciences and solve a problem by offloading art bought from the spoils of other people's misery?"

"At least they're trying to do something." Blaze felt guilty; she hadn't done anything.

"Let's go somewhere quieter," Tony said, taking his niece's arm.

Finding a smaller room with a bar at one end, he helped himself to two glasses of champagne, handed one to Blaze and then groaned. "Alert at three o'clock: the Duke of Swindon with some new parlourmaid."

"That's one of his daughters," Blaze said, recognising Lady Ophelia's distinctive carrot-coloured hair and strawberry-tinted face.

"She looks like a parlourmaid."

"You are such an odd mixture," Blaze laughed. "A committed socialist one moment, a rampant snob the next."

"Capriciousness is the preserve of the old. So marvellous to be able to let random thoughts pour from the mind to the tongue without pause or retribution." He downed his champagne in one and, taking another full glass, scanned the room. "Where is she?"

"Who?" Blaze asked.

"Ayesha said she was coming."

Blaze had also neglected her niece who, since the sale of Moonshot Wharf in March, had moved to a flat in Marylebone and refused all offers of financial assistance.

"Oh, no," Tony said. "Here comes a frightful human hazard." He tried to duck behind a Henry Moore sculpture, but a man, dressed in a white linen suit with orange shoes which matched his complexion, clapped a hand on his shoulder. The newcomer's smile was disingenuous, his irritation palpable.

"Anthony, I hear you are trying to steal my client."

"Maurice Sutchnot, meet my niece Blaze." Tony smiled faintly.

Maurice nodded in Blaze's direction and leaned in closer to Tony. "What's your explanation?"

"Is Willoughby Bruff only allowed to buy works from you? I sold him a Monet sketch," Tony said smoothly. "Where's the harm in that?"

"You let him have it for well below the market value," Maurice chided. "That kind of bargain-basement price fucks it up for the rest of us. Now he keeps asking for reductions in everything."

Tony shrugged.

"It was so cheap I thought it must be a fake." Maurice loosened the collar of his shirt and wiped his hand over a sweaty forehead.

"If you knew more about art, you'd know it is a great sketch and mentioned in all the catalogues raisonnés of Monet's work." Tony sipped his champagne with apparent nonchalance, but Blaze could tell her uncle was uncomfortable. "Besides, that sketch elevated your client's portfolio."

Maurice took a step closer to Tony and hissed, "I've put together a first-rate collection for him."

"Poppycock and piffle. You've flogged him a mass of aspiring artists one has nearly but not quite heard of. The Monet adds cachet to that bunch of also-rans."

Blaze thought Maurice might strike her uncle. His face turned pillar-box red and sweat bubbled from his nose and forehead. He straightened his shoulders and, in a voice loud enough for most of the room to hear, said, "How's your Earls Court bedsit, Tony-boy? You must come and stay at one of my houses near St.-Tropez."

Tony put his head to one side and thought for a minute. "The south of France had its best moment in the 1950s; now it's full of the oleaginous in search of oligarchs—perfect for you!" Turning his back on Maurice, he led Blaze towards a minor Impressionist painting. Two small red spots had appeared on his cheeks. "Let's get away from that horrible creature," he said.

"Is the art world always this pleasant?" Blaze asked.

Tony didn't answer immediately. "I'm too old for this game." His voice quavered.

"I can see why: that man was the bitter end." Blaze leaned over and gave her uncle a kiss on the cheek.

Tony stopped. "In any other era I would have been dead at least a decade ago. Instead, because of medical progress, I am condemned to a life of genteel poverty and decrepitude, permanently trying to get enough money together to pay the rent. Most of my friends are dead, and those that are living can't remember who I am or hear what I'm saying. I'm too old to fuck or digest my food. I have to pee so many times during the night that I might as well sleep on the loo."

Blaze had never heard her uncle speak like this before nor had any idea of the extent of his penury or desperation.

"You still give pleasure, make people laugh."

"Like an old clown." Tony pulled the corners of his mouth downwards.

"You only had to ask," she said, knowing how feeble it sounded.

Tony patted her arm. "Pride is the only thing I have left."

A gong sounded and a uniformed steward announced that luncheon was served.

Blaze groaned. "I thought you and I were eating alone."

Tony didn't answer and Blaze followed him to another room where two long tables were set.

"There she is," Tony said delightedly, as Ayesha sashayed across the room towards them. As she moved, the crowds parted, conversation stopped. She was dressed in a white wool suit, nipped in sharply at the waist. The hem stopped halfway down her thighs and her slim bare legs were accentuated by four-inch stiletto heels, while her auburn hair, teased into thick burnished curls, bounced on her narrow shoulders. The total effect was expensive, elegant and highly provocative.

"We did it! We got them both here," Ayesha pronounced. She and Tony exchanged happy glances.

"What are you plotting?" Blaze asked suspiciously.

"You'll see." Ayesha laughed. "Blaze, come with me." She took her aunt by the arm and, leading her to the far table, pointed to an empty chair. Blaze's heart sank. She knew that the next few hours would be torture: a slow death by polite and insincere conversation. She sat down and introduced herself to the man on her left, the head of a minor stock-broking firm who immediately started talking about his passion for golf. Blaze wondered how quickly she could escape. She was aware that the person on her right had arrived, but didn't turn to introduce herself for a few minutes. When she did, she came face to face with Joshua Wolfe.

"Why are you here?" she asked, unable to think of anything else to say.

Wolfe laughed. "I'd forgotten how charming you could be!"

"I wasn't expecting to see you." She was flustered and knocked over her water. Wolfe leaned forward and righted the glass.

"I donated my William Nicholson painting." Following his gaze to the opposite wall, Blaze saw the beautiful still life which had hung in his spare bedroom. Glancing along the table, she saw Ayesha and Tony watching her sheepishly. Blaze shot them a furious look.

"Are you interested?" Wolfe asked.

"In the painting?"

"That's what I meant," he said, smiling. "But I could extend the question."

"I . . . um . . . I . . ." Words deserted her.

Wolfe put his hand on hers. "It's worth selling it, just to sit next to you."

"You didn't return any of my calls," she said, knowing how pathetic this must sound.

He leaned towards her and whispered something in her ear.

Later, on the train back to Cornwall, Blaze tried to remember what they had talked about. She knew they hadn't mentioned investments, nor had they made any effort to talk to anyone else. After the first course, their knees had made contact and, somewhere between the main course and pudding, they pressed the sides of their bodies against each other. At quarter to four, long after most of the other guests, including her relations, had departed, they left the auction house, found her a taxi and he came with her to Paddington Station. They kissed on the platform until the guard blew the whistle, and then through the open window. He ran after the train, making her repeat the promise to meet again after the house opening.

26

The Opening

SATURDAY 18TH JULY 2009

Squinting through one eye, Jane watched the faintest halo of light glow behind the tattered curtains. A heavy blanket of silence hung over the house and she guessed correctly that it was not yet 5 a.m.; even the fox cubs were sleeping. Within half an hour, the litter would tumble out of their earth, the wood pigeons would commence their early-morning cooing and hordes of bees and other insects would feast on dewy fronds of wisteria outside her window. Most mornings, she allowed herself the luxury of counting in the dawn chorus, picking out the different songs: the deep milk-bottle throttle of the bittern, the staccato shout of the warbler, the babbling curlew, the chatter of the mistle thrush or the fruity melodic call of the blackbird. This morning she went through another list: of things to do, to check, to manage before the grand opening at midday. She let her hand stray to the other side of the bed, felt the cold, empty patch where her husband once lay and wondered if she would ever get used to sleeping alone.

Trelawney was not ready. In its heyday, it had taken a retinue of nearly one hundred staff to prepare for a single house-party. Over the last weeks, Jane and Blaze and two hired hands had worked night and day but their tasks were never fully completed. The original ambition—to open at least fifteen rooms to the public, each one representing an episode in the family's history—had been scaled back significantly and, of the planned seven rooms, only three were ready. Jane hoped that neither John Acre nor Penny Cuthbert would be there with their notebooks, checking off all the health and safety issues that hadn't been addressed.

She forced herself out from under the warm, threadbare linen sheets and, swinging her legs over the side of the bed, felt for her slippers. Although it was July, the long winter was hiding in the brickwork and the walls were still cold. It would be mid-August before any warmth wormed its way through the bricks and mortar to the inside. She ran a bath in the enormous cast-iron tub resting on lion's paws made for the 19th Earl. He'd been seven feet tall and, with the castle's antiquated plumbing, it took twenty-five minutes to fill halfway. Kitto had made a "shortener" out of bricks so that Jane could lie down without sinking. The enamel under the brass taps was stained green by years of Cornish residue and for the first few minutes the water ran a peaty brown. Jane turned on the hot tap and stepped back to avoid the explosion of water; if only she had the luxury of time to enjoy this new phenomenon. After ten minutes, when the level was only ten inches deep, she crouched in the ancient bath and splashed herself energetically. Then she found a clean pair of socks and knickers and pulled on yesterday's clothes: jeans and a Fair Isle jumper. She'd forgotten to charge her phone the night before and left it by the bed. Opening her bedroom door, she tripped over the red rope put there as a deterrent to keep visitors out of the private areas of the house, and landed flat on her face.

Lifting herself up slowly, one leg at a time, one hand on her lower back, the other on the banister, Jane rubbed her sore shins. These days it seemed that few parts of her body didn't ache; it was almost inevitable that her shins should join her neck, back, forearms and temples in a constant thrum of pain. Steadying herself with one hand on the wide mahogany balustrade, she went down the staircase to the hall. The evening before, Toby and Arabella had cut armfuls of elderflower, guelder rose, ragged robin and gunnera. Maybe, she thought, their visitors would presume that using wild flowers was a deliberate affectation.

In the kitchen she was surprised to find Blaze already at the table, poring over a history of the castle.

"I'm sorry you're looking after Clarissa. Let's hope a new carer turns up soon."

"I've offered the agency twice the normal salary. Perhaps avarice will triumph over umbrage."

Jane grimaced, thinking of Magda's and the others' fury at the way they'd been treated.

Blaze pushed away the ancient guidebook written for guests by a bored and largely illiterate Countess before the First World War. "She advises 'changing before each meal and after every activity.' Can you imagine living like that? There wouldn't be time to do anything else." Blaze looked more closely at Jane and suggested, "Perhaps you should find the hairbrush?"

Jane ran her fingers through the knotted curls. "So many things to remember."

"Have you done your homework?" Blaze asked.

Jane shook her head. "Milly escaped again last night and, by the time I'd caught her, I had to start making scones. It was past midnight when I started reading up on the family; three sentences in and I was fast asleep."

Blaze's spirits sagged; persuading her family to act as tour guides was certain to lead to disaster.

"Can't I do slavery rather than the Wars of the Roses—at least you have fewer dates to remember?" Jane pleaded. "I can never remember if it was in 1491 or 1481 when the Trelawneys came to the rescue of Queen Margaret and Henry VI." While she could recite the names of every queen who'd died in childbirth and match any great work of literature to the relevant reigning monarch, Jane had always had difficulty with dates.

"It was 1471 and our lot were bloody useless—most of the population favoured the House of York."

"I get so muddled between Henry VI and Richard III."

"They were enemies. Richard was the York king supposed to have murdered his nephews in the Tower of London to secure the crown."

"Oh, he was that one."

Blaze got up and looked out of the window at the ruined garden. "Why are we doing this? Perhaps we should just let the house go."

The two women remained silent for a long minute.

"We've been through this argument too many times," Jane said eventually. "We can't just give up."

"The castle won't let us," Blaze said. "It's in control, pulling our strings."

"Will you help me with my speech?" Jane asked, wanting to stop this line of conversation. A few nights earlier, Blaze had told her about a psychic she consulted regularly who predicted that Kitto would return and Trelawney would be restored to its former glory and more. It was baffling and worrying that a rationalist, so adept with numbers and calculations, would entertain such fantasies.

Blaze sat down and taking a piece of paper, scribbled down some notes. "You take the visitors to the bloodied standard and hold it up. 'This,' you tell them, 'is Richard's standard and it was his blood spilt when he was cut down at the Battle of Bosworth in 1485.' "

"How do we know it's his blood?"

"For over five centuries this is what the family has believed."

"Bosworth is nowhere near here."

"The 12th Earl fought on the side of Henry Tudor."

"Which one was he?"

Blaze groaned. "He became Henry VII. Jane, I don't think you should do this."

"To think I got a first-class degree in history. Where has all that knowledge gone? Did I lose a bit more with the birth of each child? Can the brain regenerate?"

"It retains information that is strictly necessary," Blaze said kindly.

"Like how to start a boiler, mend an engine and solder a handle back on to a broken pan." Jane got up and went to fill the kettle.

"Maybe you should talk about the trials and tribulations of life as a contemporary countess." Glancing at her sister-in-law, Blaze saw that Jane's head was bowed and her shoulders were shaking. Was she laughing or crying? It was far too early for either. Blaze wondered if she could tell her to "get a grip" or sneak out of the kitchen without comment?

"Sorry, I know you hate tears," Jane said.

"You've got to be strong."

Jane lifted up her head and, reaching for the dirty tea towel, wiped it across her face, then turned to Blaze. "I'm going to pack my bags and write the children a note. It's for the best."

"Please sit down," Blaze said. It was 6 a.m.; she was already exhausted.

"My mind is made up," Jane said, blowing her nose loudly into the tea towel.

Please let there be another clean one, Blaze thought.

"I'm not sad. I am angry. I've had enough. This isn't my real home; it never has been, never could be, but I've given it my whole life, my inheritance, and have never received a single word of thanks. Before I'm totally past it, while I have enough strength, I'm going to leave this hellish prison, this ghastly family, and start again. I will go to my Cousin Lynn's and get a job."

"Please, Jane, sit down. It's too early for all this."

Jane, her face swollen and red, her chest heaving, slumped onto the bench seat in front of the window. "I've been trapped by my children but you could be in London having a life."

Blaze didn't answer immediately. "You're not the only one whose life is upside down."

Jane looked up in surprise. "I thought your business was recovering?"

"Who said anything about business?"

"You've met someone?"

Blaze was about to answer when there was a loud knock on the back door. Both women looked at the old clock on the wall. It was 6:15.

"Are you expecting visitors?" Blaze asked.

"Only the debt collectors." Jane rose to go to the door.

"You better wash your face first."

Jane hurried over to the sink and turned on the cold tap. While she splashed her face, Blaze walked down the stone passage to the back door. Opening it, she saw a large man with a ruddy face, black hair and a fluorescent yellow jacket.

"Dick Dawson, leader of the Cornish Brass Band. We're playing here later. Is the Countess around?"

"Hello, Dick," Jane called from behind Blaze. "I was expecting you at midday."

Looking beyond Dick to the gravel drive, Blaze saw a large dustcart with three men leaning against its silver sides.

"We were on the rounds so I thought I'd drop by and see what music you wanted."

"What are the choices?" Jane asked. Her face and hair were wet and she ran a sleeve over her chin and nose.

"We have three melangeries. One for funerals, one for weddings and one for other stuff."

"We better have the other stuff," Jane said.

"What is that?" Blaze asked.

"Kylie, the Beatles, Sheena Easton and a bit more Kylie."

"What about some traditional Cornish songs?" Blaze suggested.

"Kylie goes down better," Dick said.

"Kylie it is then."

Dick nodded. "We'll need a place to change. And some crisps."

"Just crisps?"

"Beer would be nice to wash them down."

"Bitter?"

Dick nodded again. "And £100 cash up front."

After the dustmen had gone, Blaze turned on her sister-in-law. "A hundred pounds is a hell of a lot of Kylie! What were you thinking? We could have put the money into hiring three extra helpers for the day."

"It'll be festive."

"It'll be cringe-making."

Jane giggled. "You sound like the thirteen-year-old Blaze."

"That's how old we were when Kylie first sang."

"In our teens."

"We were already twenty!"

"That ages her."

"And us."

In the kitchen Jane put the kettle back on the Aga to boil. "We never finished the conversation."

"Coleridge was interrupted by a man from Porlock, you by a Kylie-playing bandleader from Truro," Blaze said. She didn't want to discuss Wolfe.

"What's that supposed to mean?" Jane asked.

"Don't you have some more scones to make?"

"I've made five hundred."

"Cornish pasties?"

"Fifty." Jane hesitated. "What if no one comes?"

"We'll be on carbohydrate overload for many weeks."

"It's not funny."

"Am I laughing?"

Jane took out a crumpled list from her pocket and read aloud: "7 a.m.—lock Milly in her stable. Feed ducks and hens. 7:30 a.m.—wake up children. 7:45 a.m.—finish laminating notices. 8:15 a.m.—hang bunting outside doors. 9:15 a.m.—take food to orangery and set up tables, chairs, cups and saucers. 10:00 a.m.—check ropes. 10:30 a.m.—check ticket barrier, tickets, petty cash, route maps and loo paper."

Blaze stood up and walked across the room.

"Where are you going?"

"I have a few chores of my own." She stopped at the door. "And please wash that tea towel."

"Why won't you enter into the spirit of the thing?" Celia asked. "For fuck's sake, this is your house and family."

"These whiskers itch like crazy." Toby's face was obscured by a stick-on walrus moustache and long sideburns. He wore a pinstripe suit and a black frock coat, slightly moth-eaten, found in one of the attic rooms.

"John Rolfe would have had lots of whiskers."

"What was Pocahontas doing here?" Celia went behind a curtain and Toby heard the sound of ripping fabric. "Didn't she live in America?"

"According to Gran, she stopped off for a night on some country-wide tour. What's that noise? What are you doing?"

Celia stepped out from behind the curtain.

"I don't think Pocahontas would have worn that," Toby said. Celia had torn off most of the minidress, leaving her midriff bare and the skirt revealingly short. In recent months, he'd noticed her flirting with others, particularly Roberto Syson—a boy in the year above, captain of the football team, a lead guitarist in a band; someone whose natural attributes Toby admired and could never begin to equal. He knew too that his insecurity irritated Celia, who was far happier in the role of huntress than comforter.

"Celia, I love you," Toby declared. He had never uttered those words to anyone apart from his mother.

"Sweet," Celia replied, and gave him a pat on the head.

"Sweet? Is that all you can say?" Toby felt as if Pocahontas's tomahawk had been lodged in his heart. "Why are you with me, Celia?" Even before the words had left his lips, he knew it was the wrong thing to say; it was so un–Roberto Syson.

"Don't get heavy." Celia was beginning to find Toby a bore, always wanting to hold her hand and stare into her eyes. They were only sixteen, not old people. "Come on, Toby—let's get our act straight," she said, pulling down the hem of her dress. "You never know who might be watching."

Both of them, simultaneously, thought of Roberto Syson.

In the Mistresses' Wing, Clarissa stood in front of the long mirror looking at her own reflection. "Are you sure the ermine works with the tulle?"

"You look extraordinary," Arabella said truthfully. It was her turn to look after Clarissa, a job that no one ever volunteered for. Her grandmother wore a floor-length gown in white silk covered in layers of white tulle embroidered with tiny flowers. On her feet were matching handmade white silk court shoes also embroidered with flowers. Her hands and forearms were sheathed in kid gloves and around her shoulders was a stole of ermine.

"You don't think I look emancipated?"

"Emaciated?" Arabella suggested.

"Wallis Simpson said one can never be too rich or too thin." Clarissa turned to the left and right. "It's at moments like these that one appreciates self-restraint—the joy of keeping one's figure. I wore this to my coming-out ball in 1946. I've been keeping it to wear in my coffin." Due to her failing eyesight, Clarissa couldn't see the liver spots splashed over her back and arms. Nor did she notice the papery veined skin hanging in folds over her bony chest or the bald patch at the back of her head. In the last few years, she had lost over a third of her body weight and the dress had become far too long. She took her shoes off to reveal toes twisted by bunions. Protected by her own vanity, she saw only the young debutante with the creamy bosom and the cascading golden hair.

"I don't suppose *Debrett's* has advice on appropriate attire for the occasion of opening one's house to the public, but I am not too old to be the belle of the ball."

"The visitors will want to see what a proper countess looks like. They'll want you to play the part."

"I don't need to play anything."

Looking at her grandmother, Arabella was glad that she hadn't asked any friends; they'd have laughed.

"What time is it now?" Clarissa asked.

"It's eleven-fifteen, so we should go to the main house in about fifteen minutes."

"We must not be late for Her Royal Highness."

"I've never met a real royal," Arabella said.

"When I was a gal, Amelia wasn't considered top drawer." Seeing Arabella's puzzled look, she added, "Minor royal, I'm afraid."

"Why did you have to be afraid?"

"No one gets it any more," Clarissa said in despair. "Now, dear child, I have to powder my nose. I will meet you in the drawing room."

HRH Princess Amelia had not been to Trelawney for thirty years, but she remembered the grand weekend house-parties for up to forty guests, based around a summer ball or shooting or hunt meets. On one notable occasion her cousin, the young Queen, had danced the night away to a fifty-piece swing band flown over from America. The same evening, the young Duke of Maddingly had proposed to a sheikh's daughter and the leading debutante of her day, Lady Serenetta Dunn, had ridden naked on a white horse through the ballroom. The Trelawneys had the reputation for throwing bigger and better parties than anyone else in the West Country. They had to, to justify the long journey from London.

The Princess had been surprised and delighted to receive Clarissa Trelawney's letter. Forcibly retired twenty-two years earlier for calling the Ghanaian ambassador something inappropriate, she missed her former life and was bored to tears in Kent. On the long (very long) drive across the south coast of England, she replayed old memories and wondered how many people would be at Trelawney for the weekend. It was well known that the family had fallen on hard times, but their wealth had been so enormous there was bound to be a bit of a show. As her car made slow progress up the A303, she looked out of the window for signposts to her youth. Every twenty miles she saw a turning to a stately home; there was Hellingham Hall, bang smack in the middle of Tedworth country in the county of Wiltshire. It had a second-rate hunt (miles of Salisbury Plain) but a jolly field of dashing young men. A bit farther on there was a sign to Barrowby and she could just see the Palladian house's riot of chimney tops peeking over a medieval oak forest. She remembered a particularly violent game of Freda in which a billiard ball knocked out the front teeth of the leading debutante of 1955. The exquisitely beautiful Miss Henrietta Fletcher-Lawrence had been earmarked for Lord Devonly, but had been so disfigured by the accident that she only bagged a baronet.

As the car drove through the West Country, the Princess recalled days out with the Cattistocks and the Portmans in nearby Dorset. She thought about her great love for the Marquess of Salisbury and the weekends spent in the misery of unrequited love at Cranborne. They passed a sign for Mapperton and she remembered an ill-advised liaison with the younger son of the Hinchingbrooke family. It was too too sad, the Princess thought. Most of the great houses had gone; thank heavens for the Montagues and the Cecils. The rest had given up and their ancient seats were now hotels or outposts of the National Trust. It had been such fun. All her own children and grandchildren did these days was slave, slave, slave in order to snatch ghastly holidays on mosquito-ridden beaches. They had shown her the photographs. Even the very rich didn't know how to enjoy themselves any more, going from one identical-looking cabana to another, ticking off location after location like a night at bingo (not that the Princess had ever played bingo but her butler loved it).

The Princess thought back to her own holidays: a week with Nanny at West Wittering and then Scotland for the Glorious Twelfth. Mummy would never have "done" abroad. Daddy couldn't have gone anywhere; the wars had seen to him. Lost one arm in the First and both legs and all his marbles in the Second. Poor poor Daddy. Princess Amelia could just remember the end of the conflict. They had been sent to their uncle's estate in Norfolk. It had been such a hoot. Hundreds of children running about, long beautiful summers and no beastly school. After it ended, though, things became dowdy and England shrank into a dingy brownness. She remembered the rations which arrived in jam jars each week. Half a pound of butter and sugar for a whole seven days. Endless Spam. The rare treat of a boiled sweet.

As they drove on into Devon, she wondered if Kitto Trelawney had kept his looks. Of course he'd married for money and she hoped the beauty genes had survived another generation of dilution. He had, like the best of his class, been perfectly languid. She recalled him dressed in a scuffed velvet smoking jacket, leaning against a fireplace, a cigarette held aloft in long, thin fingers. The car skirted the edge of Dartmoor, which looked like the Serengeti: great swathes of grassland scattered with wild animals and the odd crooked tree. In the cleft of a valley, she saw a picture-perfect village: little white houses around a stone church. She remembered a wonderful "boneshaker" with Enyon Trelawney in the back room of a public house. They had been hunting when a storm broke. Separated, accidentally on purpose, from the rest of the field, they sought shelter in the appropriately named Queen's Arms. Enyon paid the publican to close off the private room and they had made love on the stripped-pine table. She remembered him shouting "Tally-ho!" at the *moment critique.*

The outskirts of Plymouth began before the moor ended. Looking out of the window, the Princess noted a new business park: a collection of glass and steel set in a latticework of tarmac roads. The next cluster of ugliness was a shopping centre, a huge 24-hour supermarket surrounded by other outlets. One place to overfeed the population and another to provide ever larger pieces of elasticated clothing. In my day, she thought, no one was overweight and no one was anorexic.

Plymouth had taken a pasting in the war. The Germans had blasted the heart out of the beautiful city. As the car bypassed the centre, navigating an endless series of roundabouts, the Princess remembered the rubble-strewn streets and slums. In the 1960s she had opened a new block of flats and wondered if the monstrosity was still standing. Thank heavens for her Cousin Charles; at least someone understood how to build houses.

As the car left the outskirts of the city, the Princess felt the muscles in her neck relaxing. Back to open country, to the beautiful, unwrecked England which she loved so much. Her driver asked for a "comfort stop." She wanted to go herself but feared the headline: PRINCESS PISSES AT PETROL STATION. That said, she wondered if anyone would recognise her these days.

Another forty miles on, they turned off at a small sign to Trelawney and were immediately plunged into a canopy of dappled darkness. The trees joined branches overhead and the banks of the road, once an ancient cart track, grew narrower and steep-sided. The retaining walls, made from granite and stone, were lined with an electric green moss dotted with ferns and lichen. Almost improbably, trees had taken root in great boulders. The car slowed to cross a narrow bridge and, from the window, Princess Amelia saw a merry, twisting river, its blue clear water rushing over huge rocks towards the nearby sea. The road widened and the car passed through an ancient forest of stunted oaks, one of the last in England. In a clearing she spotted a herd of fallow deer arranged in a fan around a handsome stag. In the distance the estuary glinted in the sunlight and, beside it, the most magnificent house in southern England came into view. A knot of emotion caught in the Princess's throat. " 'I vow to thee, my country,' " she hummed under her breath. " 'Entire and whole and perfect, the service of my love.' "

A couple of miles farther, and the car turned left towards a pair of ornate iron gates. The Princess looked at them closely. Once entirely covered in gold leaf, they were now rusty and broken. One of two Trelawney griffins remaining on top of the gateposts had been beheaded. On a large noticeboard was a hand-painted announcement. *House open today. 12 noon. First time EVA. £8.*

Next to the sign was a makeshift camp, with a banner hanging from the other gatepost. On it, in large red writing, were the words: *For 8 centuries the Trelawneys robbed from the poor to feed the rich. Stop them! We won't forget Acorn.* In his hand a man held up and shook a home-made placard: *Get Kitto.*

"What do you think all that is about?" Princess Amelia asked her driver.

"Something to do with the bank that went bust, Your Highness." The chauffeur straightened his shoulders. "Viscount Trelawney was Chairman when it went down."

"I never understood why he had to take that job," Princess Amelia said. "He was only bred to ride and shoot; anything commercial was bound to end in trouble. Stop the car."

"Are you sure, Ma'am?" The driver looked at his employer in the rear-view mirror.

"One has a duty to explain to the governed how things work. Otherwise how will they ever learn?" Princess Amelia looked expectantly at her chauffeur who, remembering his place, put on his cap and leapt out of the front seat to open her door. Holding herself erect, and wearing a smile of utmost condescension and superiority, she stepped out of the car and walked purposefully towards the man.

Gordon Sparrow recognised her immediately. It took every cell in his body to counteract the inclination to remove his cap and bow deeply to a member of the royal family, a relative—albeit distant—of the Queen. But he did resist, reminding himself that this lady was part of the establishment that had let him and his family down so badly.

Princess Amelia presumed a man of his age would recognise her and be overcome, as so many had been before, by a mixture of gratitude (for her family's contribution to society) and servitude (for their supremacy). From the flicker of his eyes, she knew that he knew exactly who she was. A quick scan over his face and body revealed all she needed to know about him. The bulbous nose (too much beer), the ferrety eyes (inbreeding some generations back), the calloused hands (manual labour), neatly darned jacket (a protective wife lurking nearby) and the hard-set mouth (serious umbrage taken). Princess Amelia was a clever woman who, had she been offered a scintilla of education, might have enjoyed a career in the civil service or teaching. Instead she had been trapped in the yoke of her class and the expectation of her relations and their subjects. Used to being listened and deferred to, she saw an opportunity to prove not only her superior lineage, but to bring comfort to a member of the flock who had strayed.

She stood up straight, tucked her handbag under her arm and, placing her feet slightly apart, spoke from her stomach, just as her elocution teacher had taught her nearly seventy years earlier.

"Good afternoon, my good man. Are you forgetting what the Trelawneys have done for this county? All the houses and jobs and leadership?" she said imperiously. "I'm sure your family has relied on their good grace for many generations."

Gordon snorted. "Good grace? Blinking *dis*grace."

Princess Amelia was disconcerted by his rudeness. "Really," she said, taking a pace backwards. "I would ask you to mind your language."

Gordon looked at the ground; he had gone too far. A lack of deference was one thing; rudeness to a royal personage was unforgivable. What would Glenda say? He dropped his chin to his chest. "Forgive me, Your Royal Highness."

The Princess nodded graciously; one had to be gentle with the lower classes.

"We trusted them to know what to do," he said quietly. "Or at least, if they didn't know, to admit it." He hesitated. "Kitto Trelawney thought his title was a good enough qualification. He knew nothing about finance, but he took the job, the salary and let us all down. I've lost the shirt off my back, will probably lose the roof over my head. Worst of all, I've failed my missus." He fought back tears.

"I hear Kitto Trelawney is not doing so well."

"People like that will always come out on top." The bitterness had crept back into Gordon's voice.

The Princess decided to change tack. It was her duty to defend the ruling classes to the bitter end, but also to provide a *tour d'horizon* for those with less understanding of how things actually worked. She decided to help the poor man get a grip on what was really going on. "I blame Europe. If we hadn't gone into the Common Market, we'd all be better off."

Gordon nodded. "I agree with you there. We elected MPs to protect our dignity and offer long-term benefits and they simply handed it all over to some faceless Gerry on the Continent."

"All this crisis has done is expose the absolutely useless, self-serving wops." The Princess knew this kind of talk had got her into trouble before, but she couldn't help herself. "If only Lilibet was in charge."

"Lilibet?"

"Her Royal Highness Queen Elizabeth."

Gordon was surprised that he and the Princess shared so many opinions.

"The only politician who talks any sense," she continued, "is that Nigel man."

"Farage?"

"Frightfully common, but at least he says it like it is."

"Or as he'd like it to be." Gordon thought the UKIP leader was a little toad, but decided to keep quiet.

"Now, if I might suggest," the Princess concluded, "you put away your placards and go home and write letters to Brussels."

"I wouldn't know who to write to."

"Exactly my point. Faceless bureaucrats can hide behind upstanding members of the aristocracy. Don't be angry with Kitto. His worst crime was naivety." She leaned in towards Gordon. "Go home, sir, to your wife. Take your fight, use your energy and acumen on a bigger stage."

She saw that her words had hit their target. The Trelawneys would have no more trouble from this man or his grievances. Princess Amelia nodded at him and, with one last regal curling of her mouth, walked back to the car. Her chauffeur, who had been standing alert in case of an "incident," bowed slightly and opened the door for her. Settling herself into the back seat, she smiled graciously. "You may continue to the castle."

The drive was pitted with enormous potholes, some deep enough to lose a sheep, and the car creaked and groaned over the unstable ground. It used to be quicker by horse, the Princess thought. Silly old progress never got anyone anywhere faster. Just a lot of hype and nonsense.

Gordon slowly packed up his banners and placards. The Princess was probably right; the fight was bigger than Kitto Trelawney. He had been myopic and small-minded; Gordon Sparrow was going to bring down the government.

When she arrived at the main entrance to Trelawney Castle, the Princess found the place strangely deserted. A fire had been lit in the Great Hall and someone had put out a small table with a notice taped to the front saying *Tickets.* She wondered where the butler had got to and asked her driver to go to the servants' entrance to enquire. Standing by the fire and looking around, she saw that the Van Dyck was still there—things could not be that bad. Minutes later a harassed woman dressed in jeans and a Fair Isle jumper appeared carrying a bucket of freshly cut wild flowers. The Princess assumed she was a gardener and nodded politely in her direction.

"Oh, goodness—one of my children was supposed to be keeping a lookout for you. Hope you haven't been here long," the woman said.

"Moments." The Princess was well trained.

The woman plonked the bucket of flowers on the floor and, wiping her hands on her jeans, advanced towards the fireplace.

"Jane Trelawney; we met many years ago at my wedding."

"Your wedding?"

"I'm Kitto's wife."

The Princess looked at her aghast. What had happened to the pretty, pink-faced young woman she remembered? This one was haggard and far too thin.

"Why don't you come into the kitchen for a quick cup of tea before the hordes arrive?" Jane suggested.

"The kitchen?"

Jane smiled understandingly. "Or I could bring you a cup of tea here."

"I would like to powder my nose," Princess Amelia said.

"Of course. You could use my bathroom—not very neat but it's the nicest," Jane replied, hoping she had remembered to make her bed and tidy her knickers away.

They were about to set off towards the Great Staircase when they heard the click-clack of a pair of heels and a tremendous rustling.

"Amelia, darling, is that you?" Towards them, backlit by mid-morning sun, came Clarissa, her white silk gown with its layers of embroidered tulle swooshing from side to side.

"Clarissa?" Princess Amelia said hesitantly.

"You are such an angel to come all this way. I will forever be in your debt." Reaching Amelia, Clarissa bowed into a deep curtsy. Unfortunately her knees were enfeebled and she sank to the floor. Jane came to the rescue and hoisted her mother-in-law to her feet. Arabella, who'd been lurking in the shadows, took the opportunity to introduce herself.

"I'm Arabella, you're my first royal." She hesitated. "Would you like to see my collection of live insects?"

Amelia smiled icily. "We prefer communion with humans or quadrupeds." Then, turning to look at the now upright Clarissa, she asked, "I didn't realise it was fancy dress?"

"I thought the occasion merited something a little special. I wore this dress the night we first met at Buckingham Palace in 1946." Clarissa had also put two round circles of rouge on her cheeks and smeared the tops of her eyelids with a turquoise shadow. Her white papery hair was a bit lank on the left, where she had obviously lain the night before.

Blaze walked into the hall and looked at her mother. "What are you wearing?"

"I am dressed for the Royal Court not the Law Court, if that's what you mean," Clarissa said, eyeing her daughter who had chosen a smart black trouser suit, black high heels and a white silk T-shirt.

"Mum, you can't wear that."

"Why not?"

Blaze wanted to tell her mother that she looked like a cake left out in the rain. In the light, the dress had yellow age stains and the neckline was far too low for its incumbent's figure.

"Because you will show me up," Princess Amelia said. "I am, I believe, your guest of honour and, as you know only too well, Clarissa, I must not be upstaged."

Clarissa's hand flew to her mouth. "You are right, of course. How silly and thoughtless of me not to think of that. I'm a bit out of practice down here. Will you give me ten minutes to change?"

Amelia nodded graciously. Blaze mouthed thank you to their distinguished guest and followed her mother back to her wing.

"I really must powder my nose." Amelia's urge to pee was almost uncontainable. It must have been six hours now. She remembered the nasty bladder infection poor Cousin George got after a day-long inspection of the troops. It had taken months to get him right again.

At twelve noon, the band who were installed beneath the massive portico outside the Great Hall struck up with Kylie's "Spinning Around." It was a perfect English summer's day and overhead a gulp of swallows swooped and weaved in eddies of warm air. Clarissa returned wearing a sensible wool suit. A long line of visitors stretching all the way from the front door to the far distance waited patiently. Toby and Arabella held a long piece of ribbon across the entrance and Princess Amelia stepped forward with a pair of kitchen scissors to cut it.

"I declare Trelawney Castle open to the general public for the first time in eight hundred years."

Clarissa was the first to clap, followed by the family and then by those who could see what was happening.

"Family, take your places in the rooms, please," Clarissa commanded, before turning, with Arabella's help, to make her way towards the Great Staircase.

Arabella, who had been given the job of managing the ticket desk, explained to the first couple that the entrance fee was £8—unless you were from the village of Trelawney, over seventy or under eleven, in which case it was reduced to £3. "Under-fives get in free. For an extra £2.50 you could also get a home-made scone and a cup of tea."

Looking up the line of waiting people, Jane thought there must be at least five hundred, maybe more. If half were full-paying adults, they'd make enough to cover the rope. Out of little acorns great oaks grow, she thought, repeating one of Kitto's maxims, and the absence of her husband made her throat swell and close. Don't cry now. Not now.

"Come along, Jane, take your place," Clarissa nagged.

Feeling the crib sheet in her pocket, Jane made her way up to the grand salon, where the bloodied standard hung.

On the landing halfway up the Great Staircase, Clarissa took her position. To avoid any strain on her grandmother's voice, Arabella, self-appointed technical adviser, had set up an old karaoke machine with a microphone. Clarissa looked down into the motley crowd below: a woman trying to get a double buggy up a small stone step; a little boy running his mucky fingers along the edge of the marble hall table; an oriental couple (Japanese or maybe Korean) dressed in identical grey plastic mackintoshes and matching ankle-high wellington boots; two gum-chewing bleach-blondes in their mid-twenties with stocky swains who thought "house opening" meant a new pub. Arabella bounded up the stairs, turned on the karaoke machine and handed the mike to her grandmother.

"Good afternoon, ladies and gentlemen." Clarissa stopped. Her voice caught and she was surprised by the tremor of emotion fluttering in her heart. It couldn't be nerves, she thought. She had made many speeches in her day—at the WI, local fetes, opening the new hospital in Truro, announcing the winner of the Trelawney dog and flower show, and supporting her husband when he tried (and lost three elections in a row) to become a local MP. She cleared her throat and looked down at the floor. She noticed out of the corner of her eye that her audience, sensing a minor disaster, was paying attention.

"Ladies and gentlemen," Clarissa repeated, "welcome to my family's home." Her voice sounded strong and surprisingly young. Her heart rose. Once again she was being looked at and listened to. Glancing down at the assembled crowd, she smiled graciously.

"There has been a Trelawney on this site since 1073. The history of the family is about custom and continuity, about evolution, not revolution. Some might blame us for being snobby and out of touch—let them. I am proud for upholding standards, for keeping the flame of my forebears alive."

She pointed to a huge flagstone. "If you look down there, that was the first stone laid by Enyon de Lawney in 1086. Imagine how many footsteps have worn it away. In the first one hundred years, the family slept with its animals. Cows, sheep and horses were an early form of central heating. As my husband's forebears accrued a fortune, they enlarged the house. Some of you might recognise those magnificent Gothic-style pillars and round-headed arches to my left. They were almost certainly built by the same stoneworkers who transformed Durham Cathedral at the end of the thirteenth century. A century passed and more money accrued: if you look upwards at the remarkable hammer-beam ceiling, it will certainly remind you of Henry VIII's hall at Hampton Court—he copied us. To my right, those huge windows, three storeys high, which lead onto the knot garden, were designed by Robert Smythson, who later in the sixteenth century created Hardwick Hall for Elizabeth, Countess of Shrewsbury. The interior, a fine example of British baroque, was remodelled by Inigo Jones, who put in the Minstrels' Gallery. The family were, you won't be surprised to hear, loyal to the Crown, and after Jones had worked on buildings for Charles I and James I, my husband's ancestors decided to employ the royal architect. Perhaps, though I haven't thought of it before, this is where the term 'keeping up with the Joneses' originated from."

Clarissa laughed at her little joke and looked down at her audience;

to her horror each and every one looked bored. A few stared blankly around, one or two checked their watches, the children lay on the floor or were being forcibly restrained by their parents. A couple had actually wandered off in a different direction. A spotty youth was texting on his phone. At first, Clarissa was deeply irritated, but this was followed by an uncommon emotion: fear. If she couldn't interest these people in the house, who could? And then what would happen? They'd all be turfed out. Trelawney would crumble into dust. Clarissa knew she had to inspire and infect them with love for this wonderful building. If she didn't, her whole life would be declared void and pointless.

"Come closer," she called to the Japanese tourists and the woman with the double buggy. "I was eighteen when I first set eyes on Trelawney. It was 1947; the war had recently ended. I had spent five years on a remote estate in Scotland, sent there with my sister and a nanny for safekeeping during the bombing. My marriage was to all intents and purposes arranged; the season had stopped during the war and there were no opportunities to meet young men. The good ones were away, fighting. I met my husband once at a small cocktail party in London; the next time was at our wedding in Claridge's. There was no honeymoon in those days; we were still on rationing. Our wedding cake was tiny, since there wasn't enough sugar, let alone ground almonds to make marzipan."

A girl of about twelve put up her hand. "No sweets?"

"Goodness, no. That explains why no one was fat."

"Did you meet Hitler?" another child asked.

"No, but my husband's Cousin Unity knew him well and her sister the Duchess of Devonshire had tea with him."

"Really? We're doing him in history," a boy called out.

"Apparently he had a very common brown apartment and nasty little napkins with 'A. H.' embroidered on them." Clarissa beamed. She was happy to share important historical insights.

"What did you think when you first saw the house?" the lady with the buggy asked.

"It was raining so hard that all I could see was the car windscreen wipers. Just as well, for if I had realised how large it was, I might have run away. I remember coming into this hall and all the servants, thirty-two in total, were lined up in uniform waiting to curtsy or bow to their new Countess."

"What did they all do? I'd love to have thirty-two servants," someone said.

"It was lovely having help, but also like running a small and inefficient business. There were constant rows, people coming and going, the cooks were extremely temperamental."

"My nan was your lady's maid," a middle-aged woman said.

"What was her name?"

"Sarah."

"Sarah what?"

"Dawson."

"Oh, Dawson—of course I remember her." Clarissa looked at the woman keenly. Dawson was one of the maids her husband had got pregnant. "Was your father or mother her firstborn?"

"My father was number three."

Clarissa felt mightily relieved. She hated meeting Enyon's illegitimate progeny.

"When I arrived," she continued, "there were two men whose job was just to fill up the log baskets, one to brush our top hats; there were clock winders and under-butlers."

She came down from the stair landing and walked over to a huge wooden chest. "Who's feeling strong? If we lift up that lid there'll be many treasures inside." A fit-looking lad tried and failed. His father stepped forward to help him. In the end it took three to heave up the heavy oak lid studded with metal spikes.

"My husband could do that on his own," Clarissa said proudly. "He was one of the strongest men in the whole county." She bent down and looked inside. "Let's play lucky dip. Who wants to pull something out?"

The Japanese tourists edged their way to the front and gingerly reached into the dark interior. The man took out a red wooden ball; the woman chose a wooden box full of counters.

"Who knows what these are?" Clarissa asked.

She was met with blank faces.

"This is a croquet ball—to be played on the front lawns with long mallets, metal hoops and small holes. Pull out something else." She waited until a little girl opened a box with brightly coloured circles inside. "These discs are for baccarat, a game introduced to Cornwall by Queen Victoria's son, the then Prince of Wales. It was made illegal, because so many aristocrats lost all their worldly possessions on the gaming table. The 22nd Viscount gambled away an estate the size of Wales in one evening." There was a gasp from the crowd.

"Gran, Gran?" Arabella fought her way to the front. "You have to finish your talk now; the next group is waiting to come in."

Clarissa looked crestfallen. "We are just getting going." Her audience nodded.

"You can come back tomorrow or next weekend," Arabella said.

"Yes, do come back—it was such fun meeting you all," Clarissa added graciously.

Arabella steered the visitors up the Great Staircase and into the main ballroom where Jane stood waiting beneath the bloodied standard. She had changed at the last minute into clean trousers, but had not realised that the waistband, now several sizes too big, was in danger of falling down to her ankles. Unable to find a belt small enough, she had tied a piece of orange baling twine around her middle to keep it up.

Jane waited for the crowd in front of her to settle. She wished her nerves would do the same.

"Good afternoon. I am Jane, Countess Trelawney, and this flag, known as the Bosworth Standard, was a memento from the Battle of Bosworth in . . ." She froze; she simply couldn't remember if it was 1485 or 1585. Or was it 1464 or 1525? It could even be 1920, for all she knew. She tried to quell the sense of rising panic. Clearing her throat, she started again. "This bloodied standard is supposed to be smeared with Richard III's blood when he was killed at the Battle of Bosworth." All facts flew from her head and she tried to remember what and who Richard had been fighting. She took out Blaze's notes but the figures refused to come into focus. The crowd began to fidget and two of the children splintered off from the group. A pair of Japanese tourists looked at each other in bemusement. A woman with a buggy bent down to wipe snot from her child's nose. Jane opened her mouth to speak, but the words seemed to stick somewhere between her brain and her throat. Beads of sweat formed on her neck and temples. Members of the audience talked amongst themselves.

"You might well ask what the Trelawney family were doing at Bosworth." A male voice from the back of the room rang out loud and clear.

Jane, startled, looked up.

"To know the history of my family is to understand the history of England. Since the first dwelling was built on this site in 1086, the Trelawneys have involved themselves in the key moments of our island story." The crowd turned to look behind them. Standing in the doorway was Kitto.

"Let me through, please," he said and, working his way through their midst, went straight up to Jane and stood next to her, his shoulder touching hers. "Most powerful families hang on to power and wealth for a few generations—ours is unusual, we have survived for twenty-six. Why? By cleverly and ruthlessly backing the winning side, even if it meant switching loyalties at appropriate moments. Take this episode—Everard Trelawney supported Richard III for 700 of his 777-day reign; but, seeing the tide turning, he switched and fought for Henry Tudor who became Henry VII."

"How do we know it's his blood?" someone asked.

"For over five centuries this was what the family believed. We have never had it DNA-tested, but maybe we should. Perhaps, with science's extraordinary advances, we'll be able to re-create Richard."

"Bosworth is nowhere near here," another voice piped up.

"You are absolutely right but, although there was no Great Western Rail, no M4 or M5, the family did manage to get out a bit." There was a titter in the crowd. Kitto felt a tiny splash of water on the back of his hand. Looking down, he saw Jane's head was bent and, from the quiver of her shoulders, assumed she was crying. He whispered into her ear. "Are you OK—do you need to get out of here?"

Jane didn't trust herself to speak—the bubble of anger building up inside her chest had become so large that she had to fight for breath.

How dare her husband presume that she needed his help, how dare he take over her presentation without permission? Kitto, oblivious, carried on with his talk.

"If you look over here," Kitto said, pointing to a wall covered with family portraits, "you'll get some idea of the many generations." Above him, placed like peeling postage stamps blackened by time and woodsmoke, hung his ancestors. Even the frames, ornate and once covered in gold leaf, had lost their sheen. The earliest portrait, of the 11th Earl, was a two-dimensional depiction of a warty man in heavy red velvet robes. He looked out as if surprised by their attention, his right eyebrow arched, a sneer on his lips. The 11th Earl reminded Kitto of his own father and, thinking back to the day of the burial, he shivered slightly. He spoke more quickly; all he wanted was to talk to his wife, to reassure her, to tell her how he'd missed her. That morning he'd woken up and felt quite differently. A fug had lifted and his head had cleared. His only thought was to get back to Jane, to Trelawney and his family, and beg their forgiveness.

"I wonder how many of you know where your grandparents are buried, let alone your great-grandparents or their parents?" The crowd before him shrugged and tried to think that far back.

"I have no hope of forgetting my past. Each and every one of my forebears has been painted at least once. Their remains are in the burial ground on the top of the escarpment a few miles from here."

"So no escape?" someone called out.

Kitto shook his head ruefully. "It can feel like a heavy burden indeed. As if all those eyes are trained on me."

"Why's the lady so red in the face?" a little boy asked, pointing at Jane.

"She gets terrible hay fever," Kitto said. Jane clenched and unclenched her fingers.

"Now, look up at the lady and gentleman in the middle." He pointed to a woman in an elaborate silk dress, low-cut and off the shoulder. While her bosom was barely covered, her arms were encased in an explosion of white taffeta and around her neck was a huge diamond hung on a simple velvet ribbon. "That is the 17th Viscountess Trelawney, my great-great-great-great-great-great-grandmother. In her day, she was a famous actress and a mistress of King Charles II. She was a commoner, the daughter of a fishmonger from Essex, so it caused a huge scandal when my ancestor decided to make her his wife. I'm sure you agree, she was a beauty. Underneath is inscribed 'No man breathing can have more love for you than myself.' She died out hunting and he buried her with that enormous diamond around her neck. As you can imagine, there have been times when the family was tempted to dig up the body, but my ancestor foresaw those problems and only he and the gravedigger knew where she was interred."

As Kitto spoke, he felt Jane's breathing steady. Looking at the crowd before him, he saw with relief that they were listening to his every word. "The ugly old bat on his other side was his second wife, the daughter of a wealthy businessman, hence a more successful financial alliance, though apparently loveless despite the fact that eight children came of it."

"Hello, Dad." Arabella appeared. "What the fuck are you doing here?"

The crowd looked bemused.

"Family joke," Kitto explained. "We always greet each other like this."

"No one tells me anything." Arabella looked both angry and tearful.

"Is it time for the group to move on?" Jane found her voice.

Arabella nodded.

"Would you show them where to go, please, darling," Jane asked.

Arabella hesitated but, seeing her mother's expression, turned reluctantly to the visitors. "Please follow me to the library where my Aunt Blaze will tell you about another aspect of the family's history." Shooting a look at her parents, she led the way out of the ballroom.

When everyone had gone, Kitto looked at Jane. "I have been the most absolute fool and rotter. I can't begin to tell you how sorry I am."

Jane gazed up into his earnest face. She saw that his hair had streaks of grey and there were new lines around his eyes and mouth. He was noticeably thinner. None of this or his apology made any difference; Jane pulsated with fury.

"You can't just waltz out one minute and canter back in the next.

Life doesn't work like that," she said, walking towards the door. Kitto, unused to seeing his wife angry, struggled for something to say.

"Jane, Jane, wait, please," he pleaded. Jane stood still, but didn't turn around to face him. Kitto looked at his wife's back: at her limp, slightly dirty hair, her trousers bunched about the ankles. Clearing his throat, he said, "I can't do the business of life without you. You are my rock, my friend, my love. I'm so sorry that it's taken me this long to realise what I had and what I hope and pray I haven't lost."

Jane listened to these words, the ones she had wanted to hear for so long—perhaps their whole marriage—but the sentiments hardened rather than melted her resolve. The silly fool; his absence had set her free—she could manage perfectly well without him. For the last twenty years her greatest fear had been him leaving; and she had clung to him, squeezing the oxygen out of their love. His absence had achieved the opposite of everything she'd feared. The last months had made her realise how strong and capable she actually was.

From her silence, Kitto understood it was too late. "I'll go. This is your home. Indeed, seeing everything today—what you have managed—is humbling. I would never have thought of doing this or got it together. You've given the old place a purpose." He walked past her towards the door and the staircase beyond, hoping she'd call him back, but Jane didn't move; there was nothing to say.

As Kitto went down the stairs, Arabella ran after him. "Dad, stop, what's going on?"

He turned towards her. "Your mum doesn't want me here."

"Do you blame her?"

He shook his head.

"Things have changed," Arabella said.

"I just hoped she might still love me."

"Only thinking about yourself." His daughter's face was twisted with pain.

"I'm so sorry, Arabella. I haven't been well."

"There you go again: me, me, me." Arabella clenched and unclenched her fists and took a step towards her father. For a moment Kitto thought she might hit him.

"We don't need you, Dad. We're doing OK. Mum's getting better. She doesn't cry so much any more. She's beginning to eat again and two days ago she actually laughed. I'd forgotten what that was like."

"It's one of the sweetest sounds," Kitto agreed and carried on down the stairs towards the Great Hall, where there was another group of visitors listening intently to his mother. Unable to face Clarissa, he veered left and opened the door to the servants' staircase.

"Where are you going?" Arabella called.

"I'll stay in the pub tonight. Look after your mother. Whatever you think of me, please remember that I do love her, and you and your brothers. Maybe one day you'll forgive me; some people grow older but forget to grow up."

"You can say that again."

Arabella watched the door close behind him. Turning around, she saw Jane standing at the top of the Great Staircase. Her mother looked as pale as the white plaster ceiling.

"I don't think I can quite face another group, darling."

"Go and lie down. I'll take the next lot straight to Aunty Blaze. Can I bring you anything?"

Jane shook her head and, holding on to the wall for support, made her way along the passage to her bedroom. She didn't bother to undress, but lay down on her bed and fell immediately into a deep sleep.

It was, without question, the worst day of Toby's life. Dressed in stiff tweeds, his fake moustache aggravating an outbreak of acne on his upper lip and cheeks, he had performed, over and over again, the part of the stuffy, charmless preacher husband while Celia took the opportunity to use the role of Pocahontas to flaunt her curvaceous body in a sensual dance in front of groups of strangers—for the obvious delight of Roberto Syson, who stayed through three performances. Many hours later, Celia left, pretending to be tired but clearly bound for a secret assignation. Watching her go was like reliving the car crash in slow motion: the lorry coming closer and closer, the screech of tyres, the tearing sound of metal on metal, the vicious bite of the seatbelt against his shoulder and torso, the screams of his grandparents, followed by utter darkness.

He lay with the lights turned off in his bedroom. The curtains were drawn, but the early-evening sun spilled through the tears in the fabric and cast mocking beams across the floor. A piece of wallpaper had come unstuck and quivered in the breeze. The tap in his basin dripped. Outside, the rooks cawed to each other, a mournful song of broken promises and hearts. Toby knew he had lost Celia and that life without her made no sense at all. He would have to lie there until he died.

The door burst open and his sister stood there, clouds of auburn hair framed by the light on the landing.

"Guess what? Dad came home. And I told him to go away," she said triumphantly.

Toby squinted at her, unable to react; the news couldn't penetrate his obsession.

"Mum's in bed asleep, so Aunty Blaze tried to make us dinner, but it's so disssssgusssssting that she's offered to buy us all something at the pub. So you've got to get up now, because the Princess and Gran are waiting."

"The Princess?" Toby sat up. That was his private name for Celia; perhaps she was downstairs rather than in Roberto Syson's arms.

"Princess Amelia is still here. Her uppity chauffeur said it was against EU rules to drive more than seven hours in one day so he couldn't take her back to Kent tonight. She tried to fire him on the spot, but of course she can't drive her own car so she has to spend the night here until she can go home tomorrow."

Toby sank back into his pillow. The wrong Princess.

"Get up!" Arabella pulled at her brother's sheet. "I'll tell you a secret. Dad's at the pub." She looked at Toby, who hadn't moved a muscle. "And the special tonight is chicken korma."

27

An Afternoon

FRIDAY 31ST JULY 2009

He met her at the station. This time there were no misunderstandings; both of them knew why she had come and what would happen. He drove with one hand on the wheel, the other holding hers. She shimmied over to his side so that their shoulders touched and their bodies collided at every bump and turn. Three times he stopped just to take her face in his hands and look into her eyes.

Parking the Land Rover by the barn, he took a blanket and basket out of the back and, without speaking, they walked hand in hand up the hill to the high meadow. The late July air was warm and scented. Some of the fields had already been harvested, ploughed and tilled. The hedgerows were tangled with wild flowers. Wolfe laid out the blanket on the ground and took Blaze in his arms, stroking her face and her neck with his lips. Wordlessly, he unbuttoned her shirt. She wriggled her hips slightly to help him free her jeans and underwear. He unclipped her bra and her breath caught in her throat as he kissed her breasts, her stomach and then her inner thighs. She rose to her knees and pulled his T-shirt over his head while he removed his jeans. Pressing their naked bodies together, they made love urgently, rolling off the blanket and into the grass.

Afterwards, they crawled back onto the rug and lay naked, side by side, warmed by the sun, their fingers and legs entwined. Raising himself on to one elbow, Wolfe kissed her face tenderly—her eyelids, her cheeks, her scar, her mouth, her throat—without taking his eyes off hers.

"I love you," he said, again and again.

"I love you too," she replied, knowing she had never uttered four words so sincerely. Happiness ripped through her. Rolling on to their sides, they looked into each other's eyes. They made love again.

"I'm not letting you out of the valley this time," Wolfe said when they were done. "Tell me you're staying?"

Blaze hesitated. "There are still things to sort out."

He sat up quickly and looked at her. "What does that mean?"

Blaze squirmed under his gaze. She'd wanted this for so long and yet, now it was happening, she was seized by panic. "I'm not ready," she said, unable to articulate her true feelings: the fear of being vulnerable and of caring too much.

He shook his head in astonishment. "Not ready? How many more miscommunications, periods of silences, weeks apart do we need? This is ridiculous." The last syllables caught in his throat.

Blaze sat up. "It came out wrong," she stammered, trying to correct herself.

But Wolfe had heard enough. "Love is about actions not words. If I didn't know about Trelawney, I'd assume there was someone else."

"Of course there's no one else," she retorted. She reached out to take his hand, but he turned away from her. She half rose to her knees and tried to keep her voice level. "We've only just opened the house and it's beginning to take off. Visitor numbers are picking up; there's a lot more to do. And then there's my mother."

He sat up and searched for his T-shirt. "What is it with you?" he asked, his voice uneven. "The moment we get close, you pull away."

"You froze me out for months," Blaze exclaimed, irritated that he was putting all the blame on her.

"I thought, when you finally agreed to come here today, you had made a decision." He stood and started putting on his jeans. "I can't be with someone who puts their family's past before their own future." His voice was flinty.

"I have to settle my ghosts; I have to save Trelawney." This, they both knew, was only partially true.

He was quiet for a moment or two. "I really care for you, but I can't wait indefinitely," he said, low and determined. "And I can't cope with your vacillations; it's too painful."

"I don't know what's wrong with me," Blaze replied miserably.

"It's simple—you don't love me enough." He turned his back to her.

"You are so wrong." Blaze got to her feet, naked, and walked towards him, catching his arm with her hand.

He shook her off. "I didn't know it was possible to love another human being as much. I want to lay my whole self down before you, to protect you, to adore you, to love away your past hurts. There's literally nothing I wouldn't do for you."

"Joshua, please don't," Blaze said. "I love you. You must know that."

He shrugged his shoulders and walked off down the hill.

"If you really loved me, you'd give me more time," she called after him.

He stopped and looked back at her. "Another false horizon?" He laughed dismissively. "You prefer to be miserable in familiar territories than risk happiness in an unknown world. You care about your insecurities more than people. I fell in love with a brave woman, not a coward."

Blaze remained silent; stung by his words, unable to think of any reply, she watched him walk away. The sun was still hot but she shivered violently. She found her scattered clothes and pulled them on. Below, she heard a car ignition and saw his Land Rover driving off up the lane. Clutching her shoes, she ran across two fields, grazing her feet on the sharp-edged golden stubble. She reached the farmhouse and sat down at the kitchen table to wait. Five minutes later, there was the sound of a car approaching. Her spirits soared: he had come back. She darted outside, but instead of Wolfe she saw a middle-aged woman.

"You must be Blaze. I'm Molly. Joshua asked me to take you to the station." The woman had a kindly face. "Are you ready to go?" She was holding Blaze's bag, left earlier in the Land Rover.

Blaze nodded miserably and followed Molly outside. Later, she couldn't remember if she'd spoken a word on the way to Haddenham.

Blaze went back to Trelawney and moved out of the Mistresses' Wing into her old childhood bedroom and waited for him to call. For the first week, Jane, without asking what had happened, looked after her like a mother tending to a sick child. She made Blaze soup and boiled egg and soldiers, never commenting when the food lay uneaten or sentences remained unfinished. Blaze resigned from her job in Bristol and threw herself into manual labour. She worked harder than anyone; there wasn't a task she didn't volunteer for, a chore that was beneath her. In the mornings she swam in the estuary until the water turned her extremities numb. At dusk she ran up the hill to the burial ground—all in a desperate, failed attempt to banish him from her mind.

28

Pools and Butterflies

MONDAY 17TH AUGUST 2009

Kitto and Toby walked through Plymouth to Tinside Lido. Built in 1935, it was one of the few landmarks that the Germans hadn't bombed during the war. Only open for the summer months, the lido was, on this baking-hot Monday, surprisingly quiet. The blue striped pool glistened in the late-afternoon sunshine and gulls wheeled and shrieked overhead. A few hundred feet offshore, as if pinned against an azure sky, were the white sails of a small flotilla. On the horizon there was a huge tanker, bright red and blue, bound possibly for America.

"We might even get to swim," Kitto said, looking at the pensioners lined up along the sides of the lido in their deckchairs, sipping tea from Thermos flasks and taking sandwiches out of cling-film wrappers. Toby, who hadn't wanted to come, glanced around nervously. His greatest fear and most ardent wish was to run into Celia. At school she'd been surrounded by a gang of protective girls. At 4 p.m. each day, Roberto Syson met her at the gates on his 800cc motorbike.

Toby had brought his swimming trunks, but hoped Kitto would not make him swim. He'd spent most of the last weeks in his room, curtains closed, and had no wish to bare his white body.

"We used to come here as children, with Nanny," Kitto remembered.

Toby was amazed. "You grew up by a lake, a river and an estuary."

"Nanny said it was dangerous and muddy!"

Toby surveyed the municipal pool. "Dad, why are we here?"

"I wanted to spend time with you. Make up for all those missed opportunities."

"It's a bit late!"

Kitto's shoulders sank. "I'd like to try." Toby decided swimming was easier than talking and ran to the changing rooms. Minutes later he emerged and dived straight into the deep end. It was unheated and the water's iciness knocked the breath out of him. He shot to the surface, gasping for air and respite, his arms flailing, and made for the side. Kitto sat on the edge laughing.

"Isn't it incredible? The cold makes every cell in your body feel alive."

Toby couldn't speak but in that moment, all of his senses on fire, he knew for the first time since Celia's departure that he could survive without her and the constant thrum of misery would abate. Kicking away from the white-tiled side of the pool, he forced himself back through the water and swam two quick widths. Rapidly his body adjusted to the temperature and he could feel blood coursing from his heart through his veins. Soon the feeling returned to his hands and feet. Lifting his face out of the water, he laughed, intoxicated with the sheer joy of being alive. He pretended to be a seal, lacing his body up and under the surface, plunging down to the depths and propelling himself with a great whoosh to emerge in front of his father. Kitto took off his trousers and, stripped down to his boxer shorts, jumped in beside Toby and the two ducked and wrestled. At first the onlookers were annoyed, but soon got caught up in their exuberance, remembering their own parents and childhood.

Later, his skin puckered and blueish in tone, Toby shivered himself dry in the last embers of sunshine. He refused Kitto's offer of a towel or jumper; he wanted to revel in the goosebumps, to make up for the hours lost that summer wrapped in melancholic inertia.

They walked through Hoe Park and up to Sutton Harbour.

"There's nothing good to say about this place," Kitto said, looking at the concrete office blocks, cheap fast-food takeaways, the clusters of bored young people by the bus stops, tired mothers leading crotchety children and old men disappearing into basement betting shops.

"Have you seen Ayesha?" Toby asked. He could never mention his half-sister in front of his mother.

"She wants to go to Cambridge to study History of Art."

"I thought she wanted to read biophysics?"

"Your Great-Uncle Tony has converted her to aesthetics."

Toby let out a low whistle. "Lucky her." Then his shoulders slumped. "I seem to be the only one in the family with no calling, no idea what I want to do."

"You'll find your way." Kitto looked fondly at his younger son. "Perhaps you have to learn to care a little bit less about things and learn to put yourself before others?"

Toby smiled at his father gratefully; since losing Celia, his self-esteem had collapsed.

"I'll walk you to the bus stop," Kitto said.

"Why don't you just come home?"

"I have to wait for your mother to ask."

"You grew up there," Toby said crossly, wondering why his father was living in a small bedsit in Plymouth.

"People make houses and I realise that my home is wherever Jane is."

Toby didn't say anything. He thought grown-ups could be pretty stupid.

Sitting in the bus on his way back to Trelawney, Toby wondered if his brother would ask them to stay on when he inherited in December. The thought of leaving the castle was too painful to contemplate. Toby had read enough literature, watched enough television, had enough friends, to know that his family life was eccentric and dysfunctional, yet it was his world. He could not imagine opening his curtains without looking down on to the wildly overgrown garden below or beyond it to the glinting estuary. Or going to sleep without the music of creaking pipes, scuttling mice or the wind chasing around the battlements. The best day of his life so far had been the announcement five years earlier that there was not enough money for him or Arabella to return to boarding school. The two of them had unpacked their trunks, hardly daring to look at each other or scream their delight out loud in case the decision was reversed.

The view softened as the suburbs gave way to rolling green fields and occasional glimpses of the sea, snatches of dark blue against distant hills like purplish bruises in the dusky light. Bad weather was coming in from the west and Toby could see the scratch marks of rain on the horizon. The bus dropped him at the turning to Trelawney and, getting out, he slung his swimming bag over his shoulder and took a shortcut alongside the river. He stopped for a moment to look at the icy water careering over large, moss-covered boulders and, out of the corner of one eye, glimpsed the blue flash of a kingfisher. Crossing a small stone bridge, he climbed up the old cart track, cobble-bottomed and steep-sided, made hundreds of years earlier by farmers taking their produce to market. Trees grew out of the banks, their roots entwined amongst great granite slabs. The tops of the branches had grown into each other, transforming the track into a cool, dappled tunnel. At the top of the hill, Toby emerged into a field and turned left. The air smelt of newly cut grass and silage and he felt the early-autumn chill settling over the fields.

Rounding the next corner, he looked down at Trelawney and his heart swelled. Most of the buildings were dark, but he could see light spilling out of the dining room and Great Hall windows. He could just make out a diminutive figure—his mother, perhaps—carrying an armful of cut branches in through the front hall. Damn his brother for inheriting. Toby knew that Ambrose would never love Trelawney as he did. For his elder brother it was merely a birthright.

Ambrose would treat Trelawney as a weekend home and let the place decline even further. If the house were Toby's, he'd dedicate his entire life to saving it. Walking down the hill, he realised that there were some who left and some who stayed; some who were bound to live their lives away from their place of origin. Arabella, Ayesha, Ambrose and Celia were wandering spirits, but he was a stay-at-home type. He'd do everything—anything—to remain at Trelawney. This was his calling.

While Ambrose hadn't been granted the gifts of either imagination or intelligence, the meaning of the dream which woke him night after night was clear. However much he'd drunk, irrespective of the amount of exercise or narcotics taken, at some point in the small hours he awoke, crushed and pinioned under the collapsed walls of Trelawney. He struggled to sit up, trying to push the masonry off his chest, clawing at his nose and mouth to clear away the dust. Repetition offered no comfort: each time was more real than the last; each dream took longer to recover from.

He was often, as on this occasion, woken by panic attacks. Fighting to regain his equilibrium, he went to the shower and stood letting the hot water wash away the sweat. His body heaved with the effort of catching breath. He never knew how long the attacks would last; sometimes they were short, at other times interminable. The doctor had prescribed Xanax and beta blockers, but nothing worked. After twenty minutes he left the shower and walked dripping wet to the kitchen sink. He poured a glass of water and downed it before pouring and drinking several more. Looking out of the window, he judged it was about 4 a.m. There were a couple of lights on in neighbouring apartments and he could see a woman getting ready to leave; she must work on a Far Eastern trading floor, where the day started at five. Ambrose had been assigned to the Real Assets department and was currently shadowing "Mad Moose," a trader who specialised in coffee and nuts. As a younger man, MM had spent weeks at a time navigating ports in Africa or rivers in South America to secure the best deals. Now so much was done on computers and the trader could only follow what was happening on the ground on Google Earth, complaining bitterly and constantly about the erosion of his "real skills." After work, with no friends in London, Ambrose spent his meagre wages at the gaming tables and bars in Soho. A good night was defined by how little he lost at poker and whether he could walk without falling over.

Though he didn't have to leave for work for a few hours, Ambrose was reluctant to go back to sleep. He made a cup of instant coffee and sat at the table looking out over Docklands, down at the concrete pathways where ant-like figures hurried towards the Underground, knowing that soon he'd join that well-worn path: another little insect. He dipped a digestive biscuit into the brown liquid. There was an art in not letting the wheat and sugar dissolve entirely. If he got the first dunk wrong, it was a bad omen for that night's card game. He left the biscuit a fraction too long and a chunk disintegrated. Frustrated, he threw the coffee away. He couldn't afford to lose any more money this month.

Ambrose lived his life according to a series of bizarre, ever-changing superstitions, ranging from melting biscuits to cloud formations, enabling him to avoid any direct responsibility for unfortunate or unforeseen outcomes, such as his girlfriend's recent departure, his inheritance, his failure to pass any A levels, his losses at the gambling table or extra pounds gained. He was a blamer, swamped by choice and privilege, and were it not for the internship at Kerkyra Capital, he'd have continued to muddle on through a miasma of self-pity. Exposed only to Kitto and his ilk, and the unworldly masters at school, he'd had no idea that men like Thomlinson Sleet existed. To him the hedge-funder was the acme of all things admirable: fabulously wealthy, unbearably narcissistic and utterly uncompromising; a higher form of being. Sleet knew all about hero-worship and how to exploit it; the trick was inconsistency. At one moment he was crushing, the next he showered the younger man with gifts and opportunities. Ambrose mistook the attention for genuine concern, never guessing that he was just a pawn in Sleet's master plan.

He was living in one of Sleet's staff flats: small, white and impersonal. There were only three steps from the kitchen unit to the bed and two more to the bathroom. What it lacked in size, it gained in functionality. Unlike Trelawney, water came out of the taps, the lights worked, the surfaces were easy to clean and the air conditioning kept the temperature constant. Best of all was its absolute anonymity; there were four hundred flats in the building and he'd never need to know the name of another person. At home, people knew each other's business; he was judged and found lacking. He would, with Sleet's help, prove them all wrong. He would be the 27th Earl of Trelawney and no one would ever forget him.

Arabella and Tuffy sat side by side at the table, the great-aunt calling out specimen names while her niece typed the results into a computer. This data collection was to be part of an addendum to Tuffy's paper linking warmer weather to an increase in insect-borne diseases.

"Why did you never have children?" Arabella asked.

"Can't abide the little creatures."

Arabella fought away tears. "I'm a child."

Tuffy snorted with laughter. "I put up with you because you are a person, not a child."

Arabella wiped her nose on the back of her hand.

"Don't move," Tuffy said, jumping up and fetching a Petri dish from a cupboard. Arabella froze as instructed. Taking a small wooden spatula, Tuffy carefully scraped the snot from Arabella's wrist and put it into the dish.

"What do you want that for?"

"Waste not, want not." Tuffy carefully labelled the dish and put it into her fridge, which contained only things of scientific use.

"What was your childhood like?" Arabella asked.

"Boring, boring, boring."

"But you lived here!"

"It was a different time. It took a nursery maid a whole hour just to put on the layers of petticoats, and then there were the hundred brushes of the hair, morning and night, not to mention the agony of ringlets and ribbons; a prize cow had nothing on us. Then I spent the morning with a governess learning to sing or sew. It was absolute torture, especially as my brothers were flung outside on horses or with guns."

"Bet Uncle Tony wanted to swap."

Tuffy laughed. "He had his story, I had mine."

"I've never believed in stories," Arabella said.

Tuffy shook her head. "Our ability to tell, create and believe in stories is *Homo sapiens*'s most powerful weapon. It's how we organise ourselves, how we control each other, how we justify our decisions. If we didn't have them, we'd be like fleas or rabbits or any other member of the animal kingdom, beings just trying to get through the day." She got up and filled the kettle by the sink. "Religion is just a story. Waitrose tells a better story than Lidl. Most things you learn at school are irrelevant, but you've been assured they're important. You buy your car from one company over another because a salesman told you a better tale about its gearbox or revolutions per minute."

"I don't see what that's got to do with us?" Arabella said.

"Look at your grandmother trying to keep the past alive by retelling all those family histories over and over again, trying to convince anyone who'll listen that it did matter. Your poor father lacks panache and showmanship and can't persuade anyone to follow him. Your brother Ambrose doesn't have any imagination—his whole world stops at the end of his nose."

"How do you know so much about him?"

"Times change; types don't. Every family has an Ambrose. It's bad luck when his kind is the son and heir."

"I don't understand how this affects Trelawney. The castle's been here for eight hundred years; surely it will just go on." Arabella accepted a cup of tea from her aunt and blew on the surface to cool it down.

Tuffy ignored this remark, stood up and reached for a file on top of her desk and began looking in it for a piece of paper. "I know I put the results in here," she said, flicking through the index.

"I don't know why we have to let visitors tramp around the place," Arabella continued. "Mum only sold forty-five cream teas last week; the deep freeze is full of leftovers."

"Here it is!" Tuffy found what she was looking for and started to transcribe a series of numbers from one piece of paper to another. "It takes enormous willpower and self-belief to cut the umbilical cord, to begin another story. Most of us practise natal homing—I've taught you about that. Your parents and Blaze can't imagine a different kind of life."

Arabella nodded. "Salmon are prepared to die in their journey upstream just to get back to their place of birth. Sea turtles are compelled to lay their eggs on old stamping grounds even if those places have been built over." She thought for a moment. "But there's no evidence that humans, unlike other members of the natural world, are driven by geomagnetic impulses of olfactory cues."

Tuffy sat back in her chair and looked at her niece. "You have the makings of a scientist. You've proved my point: we come back because we want a sense of an ending."

Arabella stared into her tea. "Why did you never leave?"

"There weren't many options in those days. Marriage or being a governess. Both seemed appalling."

"What's wrong with marriage?" Arabella asked, but couldn't think of anything to say in its favour.

"I preferred study to the business of loving."

Tuffy put down her cup and, picking up two butterfly nets from behind the door, handed one to Arabella.

"If we're lucky, we'll find some orange-tipped *Fritillaria* on the escarpment. Now that the rain's stopped, I think they'll be back."

Arabella jumped to her feet. The pursuit of insects was far more interesting than this endless chat about Trelawney. They left Tuffy's rooms and went out past the big house. The sun was setting, but heat shimmered over the horizon. Harvested fields were dotted with bales of straw. There was one lonely white cloud, perfectly fluffy and round, as if a child had drawn it on a neon-blue sky. The two of them walked in companionable silence.

"Did you always like animals better?" Arabella asked.

"Gosh yes!" Tuffy said. "They are so uncomplicated and free of pretensions."

"Do you ever get lonely?" Arabella tried to imagine a life without her school friends or family.

"With so many billion creatures all around me? Hardly!" Tuffy bent down and turned over a fallen branch to reveal hundreds of woodlice, ants and worms which had made their home in the bark and in the damp ground around it. She and Arabella crouched down side by side and watched the insects. After a while, Tuffy carefully replaced the moss and stick. Then she stood up and looked at her niece.

"I'll only ever give you one piece of advice, dear Arabella. Make work your friend—it will never let you down, never leave you and, the more love and attention you give it, the more rewards you'll receive. Now for goodness' sake, stop all this incessant questioning. We need to hunt butterflies."

Although she sounded fierce, Arabella could see that her great-aunt was enjoying the conversation and this made her happy. She had had a miserably lonely summer. Toby had hardly left his bed and her mother, aunt and grandmother were obsessed by visitor numbers and cakes. Most of the time she couldn't follow what Tuffy was talking about, but she understood enough to know that her aunt's world could become her world and the thought filled her with excitement.

"There's one," Tuffy yelled, as a fragile orange and white butterfly hovered over a bush about thirty feet in front of them. Wielding her net like a sword, Arabella charged through the prickly gorse in search of her prey.

29

The Birthday Party

SATURDAY 5TH DECEMBER 2009

"You are cinematic gold, Ma'am," Damian Derbish told Clarissa as she finished her last piece to camera.

"Derbish, how many times do I have to tell you that the Queen is 'Ma'am'; I am 'Your Ladyship'?"

The documentary producer hit his forehead with the palm of his hand. He had come to the castle on a whim in July after the local paper had singled out Trelawney's opening as the event of the week and the Dowager Countess as a national treasure. He made a small filler for the regional news which, thanks to Clarissa's performance, had been picked up by the BBC's *News at Six.* For Damian, who had spent his entire career bumping along in local television, this was a game-changing moment; he envisaged a prime-time international series, *The Trelawneys*, with spin-offs including a feature film (he had already mentally cast Meryl Streep as Clarissa). He had also designed his own range of merchandise: the Trelawney Teaset and the Trelawney Twinset. This eccentric aristocratic woman would lift him out of his small flat in downtown Plymouth to a detached house on the edge of Dartmoor. The family would upgrade their car from a Skoda to a 2004 series X5 BMW.

Clarissa loved the camera, loved that hundreds more people had come to Trelawney since her debut on *BBC One South West.* She liked walking up Launceston High Street and once again being recognised for who she was. One lad asked for her autograph. She declined, of course. At least someone in the family was trying to keep the roof on. Since her TV appearances, the weekend visitor numbers had risen from a few score to several hundred. The magic break-even point—the amount of footfall the house needed to meet the oil bills and start a minor repair programme—was a thousand paying adults a day, three days a week for six months a year. Blaze was still meeting the shortfall but, although her investments had recovered, she'd made it clear that this arrangement was not indefinite.

I will not let Trelawney go down, Clarissa thought, even if it means looking faintly ridiculous in old ball dresses and exaggerating my pronouncements. Damian was a perfect foil who, in normal circumstances, she would not have given one iota of attention to, but he'd do for now. When I have my own television show, she pondered, I will demand a better kind of producer. If only her old friends William Holden and James Stewart were still alive. Jimmy had said she'd make a great star. "Aren't I one already?" she'd asked him coquettishly. He'd kissed her hand. "The rest of the world deserves to see you in close-up," he'd replied. Oh, those had been the days, the good old days.

"Where is my stole?" Clarissa asked.

"Ginny, Ginny, quick—get Her Ladyship's fur," Damian told his assistant who was also the cameraman, the sound operator, the driver, the tea-maker and the editor. Ginny Barloe, aged thirty-two, had her own (largely unprintable) thoughts about Clarissa Trelawney and her airs and graces. She had voted for the local Communist Party in 1997, and again in 2005, with the sole aim of getting rid of people like the Dowager Countess, who thought they were different, a cut above, merely because some ancient ancestor had managed to buy a title. She agreed to go in search of the mangy white fur if only to escape her boss's sycophancy. Leaving the Great Hall, she heard Damian start up again.

"My Lady, I have shown the rushes to the Head of News South West and he agrees that we could edit your pieces together and put out a whole half-hour feature."

"A half hour?" Clarissa said coldly.

Damian wiped the sweat off his brow. "Maybe we could make a fifty-minute programme?"

Clarissa turned away to hide a look of delight and stared out of the window. Behind her she could hear Damian's heavy breathing; he wanted the limelight as much as she did. She counted to ten, partly to let him suffer, partly to ensure that her voice didn't betray even a smidgeon of enthusiasm.

"One has a lot to say."

Damian could hardly contain his excitement. "Of course, it would mean having access to a few family events, behind-the-scenes kind of things."

"There are no 'behind the scenes.' This is my life."

"We would need to add a bit more texture, a bit more layering."

"I thought this was about me?" Clarissa wheeled round to face him; two red spots had appeared on her papery cheeks.

"We need to see you in context. The great matriarch. The keeper of the flame and, if you don't mind me saying so, society's ethereal beauty."

Clarissa nodded graciously. Damian was desperate for her to agree. Without the other members of the family on board, he'd never get a longer commission. The old lady on her own could sustain a twenty-minute film, but fifty was a stretch too far. His hope was that, once the cameras were rolling, the cracks in the family's guard would slip and reveal their dysfunctional behaviour. Even though the film crew had spent less than three days in the castle, he had picked up many tantalising snippets of information. The sudden appearance of an unknown granddaughter. The cook's grandson, a boy made good, who was part of the largest tech company in south-west England. The elder grandson and heir, soon to turn eighteen, who never came home. The heartbroken younger grandson, who hardly left his room all summer. The granddaughter whose spare time was spent catching fleas with a mad old aunt. Then there was Blaze, who dressed only in black and white silk and smoked thin cigarettes with gold tips. The recent return to the marital bedroom of Kitto, which seemed directly linked to his wife's growing irritation with everything and everyone. "You couldn't make it up," Damian had told his senior producer. "You couldn't, and you don't have to."

"Your daughter and daughter-in-law have been quite reticent about appearing before the camera," he said now, thinking of how Blaze left the room when he entered and refused to answer any direct questions. Jane simply went bright red and clammed up. Kitto wafted around the place wearing a beatific smile.

Ginny came back carrying a slightly bedraggled white fur wrap.

Clarissa inclined her head and turned so that Ginny could place the ermine around her narrow shoulders. Against her family's advice, she had worn her white tulle and taffeta coming-out dress this morning. Damian, she noticed, had shivered with excitement when she made her entrance.

"It's Ambrose's eighteenth tonight," Clarissa said. "Maybe you could film guests arriving. Everyone will be coming."

"Thousands?" Damian asked.

Clarissa looked at him in surprise. "Everyone who is anyone: about sixty people."

Ginny snorted loudly. Clarissa glanced in her direction.

"Hay fever," Damian explained quickly to the Dowager Countess and, turning to Ginny, gestured crossly towards the door.

"She can't help it; she was badly bred." One of the great advantages of old age, Clarissa knew, was no longer bothering what anyone thought of her. In her twenties she'd cared deeply; in her forties she had given up minding; in her sixties she realised that people were so self-absorbed they never gave a damn; and now, in her eighties, she saw that shock tactics were the only certain means of gaining attention.

"Filming the birthday party might be amusing. Tonight Ambrose officially takes the reins," she said.

"Are you expecting any dramas?"

"Don't be so silly. Things will continue in the Trelawney way."

Clarissa imagined her grandson's grateful homily to his beloved grandmother, his determination to go out into the world and restore the family fortunes, while Damian fantasised about drunken aristocrats and outlandish antics. Ginny hoped she could get home in time to watch *Match of the Day* with her girlfriend.

"Should I talk to the Earl and Countess?" Damian asked, trying to sound unconcerned.

Clarissa hesitated. "Come to my apartment at seven. We can go together. And for goodness' sake tell your assistant to wear something appropriate." Without saying goodbye (goodbyes were frightfully common), she walked out of the hall, down the passage and towards the Mistresses' Wing. Looking up at the heavy blanket of cloud, she decided it was too cold to snow. She put on the fur boots and thick coat that Blaze had bought her but hurried towards her apartment nonetheless; it was almost impossible to defrost the old bones. As she crossed the courtyard, a small shiny-headed man wearing a suit and carrying a briefcase hailed her.

"Are you a mugger?" Clarissa asked forthrightly.

The man was clearly freezing cold and had been standing there for some time. "I'm trying to find Lady Louisa Scott," he said.

"Why do you want her?" Clarissa enquired.

"She's won the Caldicot Prize for Biology for work on the connection between disease and warm weather. The Academy are desperately trying to locate her."

"Does it come with money?" Clarissa had never heard of the award.

"About £250,000."

Clarissa looked astonished "All that from catching insects?"

The man looked appalled. "She's one of our most eminent scientists."

"She's a flea-trapper."

"Could you tell me where to find her?" The man had had enough of this arrogant old woman.

"Tuffy lives down there. Turn right by the bins and it's the first door on the left."

"Thank you."

"And if you do find her, remind her there's a party tonight and she's expected."

Kitto had moved back into the castle in September. Jane was unsure whether she wanted to stay married, particularly as the man who had returned to the house was noticeably different; the new Kitto lacked confidence and sought constant reassurance. Jane didn't have the time or patience to indulge his neediness.

She spent the morning cleaning the dining room, unused since Acre and Cuthbert's visit in May. More ivy had forced its way through panes of glass, shattering the fragile barrier between out and indoors; the floor was covered with bird droppings and something had eaten a large hole in the corner of the old Turkish carpet. Kitto sat in the corner, reading a book of poetry.

"How long would it take for nature to claim back her land?" Jane said, as she pulled the strong suckers and long fronds of ivy away from the walls.

"She's winning already," Kitto replied. Tearing out and setting fire to a page of his book, he held it in the chimney breast and, as he feared, the flame didn't draw properly. "I think birds have nested in the flue. Shall we risk a fire?"

"It's a choice between death by asphyxiation or hypothermia."

"Everyone should keep their coats on."

"Poor Ambrose—we want to try and put on a good show, don't we? His birthday must be memorable." Jane missed her son, who had not been home since last Christmas.

Taking his wife in his arms, Kitto kissed her forehead.

"Did I tell you how proud and grateful I am? You did what I never could and put the heart and soul back into this place."

Jane smiled up into her husband's battered face. Since his breakdown, Kitto looked both older and younger; there were deep lines scored around his eyes and mouth and yet his expression, once wry and knowing, had been replaced by an aura of innocence. In the past, he had roamed from room to room, thought to thought, aloof and aloft, hardly seeming to take anything or anyone in. He'd spent his hours outside with his gun or scribbling poetry into a red exercise book. On the odd occasions that friends visited or they opened a decent bottle, he became loud and animated but these events had become increasingly rare. Now

Jane woke up every morning to find him staring at her in gentle wonder. He followed her around like a disconsolate dog and, at dinner or walking in the garden, he held his wife's hand gently, as if it were a small wounded bird.

"It's been a group effort," she said, trying to wriggle out of his embrace; she didn't have time for smooching. "I could never have done it without Blaze or your mother."

Kitto stroked the back of her head. "The old place has a real chance of washing its face."

"We'll have to sell an awful lot more scones to make that happen," Jane replied sadly. Although the takings from entrance fees and the sale of food had risen to nearly £500 a week, that was far short of the £1,000 needed to keep the place fully functioning. With winter approaching and Trelawney closed to the public until spring, she was already worrying about refilling the oil tank. At least Ambrose had left school and there were no more fees. His A-level results had been so disappointing that university was unlikely. It was a relief that Thomlinson Sleet had given him a job.

"Shall we dance?" Kitto asked. "It's been so long."

Jane looked up and stroked his face. "We have an awful lot to do, darling. Shall we dance later, after dinner and speeches?" She stepped away from him.

"Let's seize the moment!" Kitto leaned forward, took Jane by the waist and gyrated his hips against hers. "I'm hearing the Rolling Stones's 'Wild Horses.' "

"I'm seeing sixty for dinner, beds to make, pies to be cooked and tables to be laid."

"All work and no play makes Jane and Kitto a dull girl and boy." Kitto held his wife more tightly. Jane pushed him away firmly. For years she'd dreamed of such entreaties; now they were beginning to grate. Once, she had seen his lack of affection as a failing on her own part. If she'd been prettier or more sophisticated, or if she'd been Anastasia . . . His indifference stung, but this new neediness was cloying, like a cheap, all-pervasive perfume. It followed her like a reproach from room to room. Was this how she'd made him feel for the last twenty years of their marriage? Had he too shrunk from her baleful expressions and reproachful stares? As she predicted, Kitto stood there with his arms limp and tears threatening to fall.

"You don't love me any more," he said.

Here we go again, Jane thought to herself.

"Don't be silly. I love you madly but it's our son's eighteenth birthday and I need you to help me get ready."

Kitto nodded.

Jane handed him a broom. "Start from that end and work your way down to the door. Small strokes, so as not to send the dust flying everywhere."

"Where are you going?" Kitto asked.

"Nowhere. While you do that I'll be right here polishing the table." She held up a duster and a tin of wax.

The door pushed open and Tony walked into the room. He was wearing a lilac linen suit and white shoes and carried a small leather suitcase.

"We weren't expecting you until later," Jane said, going forward to kiss him.

"My favourite uncle," Kitto chipped in.

"You only have one," Tony pointed out, laughing at the old joke. "Now, who wants a snifter?" Opening his case, he produced a bottle of sherry and put it on the table. Kitto hollered in delight.

"We have so much to do." Jane failed to hide her irritation.

"We used to have people to 'do.' "

Jane flushed. "If you're looking for that kind of weekend, might I suggest the local pub?"

Tony saw that he'd overstepped the mark. "It was a joke in poor taste."

"It was unkind."

"That too. I am sorry, Jane."

Jane scooped some beeswax onto the table and began to polish. Tears of frustration fizzed behind her eyes: the whole lot of them, she thought, were hopeless. One wanted to drink, the other to dance, her mother-in-law was constantly searching for her close-up, and her eldest son had texted to say he was arriving at 6 p.m. with a girl and an announcement and to get out the champagne. Thank goodness for Blaze and the other children. At least there were some sensible people in the house.

"Kitto, old boy, get some glasses please," Tony asked.

"Why don't the two of you go to the kitchen and I'll be along when I'm done." Jane rubbed strenuously with both hands.

"Because I've something to tell you both. It's important."

Cancer, Jane thought, that's all we need, more bloody drama. She kept on polishing. Hopefully he only has days to live and won't take too much nursing. Where the hell am I going to put him? And how will we keep him warm enough? Will the NHS send out carers or will I have to do that too? She could feel anger building up like waves gathering strength on a shoreline. Damn this bloody family; why do they always assume I'll do their bidding on their timetable?

Kitto returned with glasses. Tony unscrewed the top of the sherry bottle and carefully poured three shots. Jane noticed that his hand shook—definitely cancer, she thought, or dementia: that would be worse; a slower death. She imagined nappies and social services, saw herself retrieving a lost Tony from ditches or schoolyards. With any luck he was about to ask them to sign papers for Dignity or Digitas or whatever that place was called in Switzerland where they euthanised people.

"Jane, dear, you've been polishing the same two inches for the last ten minutes," Tony said. "Why don't you put down the cloth and sit for a moment?" Looking at the table, Jane saw that there was only one tiny area which shone and gleamed.

"Have a drink, darling, you deserve it," Kitto said.

Yes, I bloody well do, thought Jane and, picking up a glass, drank the sherry in one long gulp. Tony and Kitto exchanged glances.

Tony pulled out two chairs: one for Jane, the other for himself. Noticing that they were covered in dust and mouse droppings, he took a silk handkerchief from his top pocket and flicked it over the leather seats. Then he topped up Jane's glass and sat down slowly. Once Jane and Kitto were also sitting, he cleared his throat.

"I'm here to talk about inheritance."

Jane and Kitto looked at each other wearily. Tony rarely lost an opportunity to tell others how shabbily he'd been treated.

"It was just the way things were done," Kitto said.

Tony held up his hand to silence his nephew. "As you might remember, the only thing I inherited from my father was a book."

Here we go again, thought Jane. How many times have I heard this tale of woe? Clarissa had become so tired of the lament that she'd stopped inviting Tony to any family occasions. The first time he'd come back in twenty years was for his own brother's funeral.

"The thing is that it wasn't any old book. It was the *Landino Dante,*" he said with a great flourish.

Jane and Kitto were none the wiser.

"I take it from your expressions that you don't know what the *Landino Dante* is?"

They shook their heads.

"Have you ever heard of Cristoforo Landino?" Tony sighed; how could people survive such ignorance? Where was the joy in a life of philistinism? "He was one of the greatest humanist scholars. He lived and worked in Florence for Piero di Cosimo de' Medici and taught the young Lorenzo. He wrote philosophical dialogues and poems under the pseudonym of 'Xandra,' but it is his commentaries on the *Aeneid* and *The Divine Comedy* for which he is famous."

Jane wished that Tony would hurry up. But Tony wasn't in a rush; he'd spent the last decade wondering what to do with his most precious possession.

"The so-called *Landino Dante* was printed in Florence in 1480—it is excruciatingly rare. Possibly the rarest and most sought-after book in the Western world."

Jane glanced surreptitiously at her watch and ran through her mental checklist. Pick Arabella up from piano practice; Ambrose and girlfriend arrive on 6 p.m. train; pies into oven; ice cake; put kegs of beer into Great Hall; wash hair. Thank goodness she'd remembered to buy some sparkling wine from the cash and carry.

"Have you heard anything I've said?" Tony asked.

Jane pulled herself together. "You were telling us about the book."

Tony proceeded slowly, as if he were talking to two children. "The designs are close to Botticelli: the execution was by Baccio Baldini."

Jane looked longingly towards the door.

"The only known copies of the book contain only two engravings. This one has twenty-four."

"That's fascinating," Jane said, trying not to sound too bored.

Tony couldn't believe that the two of them were so uninterested. He'd hoped to delay the moment of vulgar revelation, but could see there was no alternative.

"Several years ago, one dislocated page from a later edition made £75,000 at auction. This version could be worth millions."

Kitto let out a low whistle. "So why haven't you sold it?" He knew Tony was impoverished.

"I was saving it for the proverbial rainy day."

"Good for you, darling Uncle," Kitto said with enthusiasm. "Maybe you can upgrade your bedsit? Buy somewhere decent to live?"

"It's a studio flat," Tony replied huffily.

Jane walked to the door. She was pleased for Tony; at least someone had got something useful from the house.

"My intention is to give it to Ambrose as a birthday present, with certain conditions of course. I'd like him to mend the roof of the Great Hall and restore the Grinling Gibbons woodwork, my favourite thing in the whole of Trelawney."

Jane, suddenly all ears, came back to the table and sat down. "Oh, Tony, that is exceptionally generous."

Kitto went over to his uncle and threw his arms around the older man's shoulders. "It's the most marvellous thing I've ever heard. Let's crack on with that bottle of sherry."

Blaze was packing her suitcase; Ambrose's eighteenth, his accession to the ownership of Trelawney, seemed like an appropriate time to go back to London and pick up the pieces of her life. She didn't know her nephew but knew enough to guess (correctly) that they would not get on. She needed to get away from the house and begin again with no traces of the past, no reminders of Wolfe. Since leaving his farm that day, she had entered into a state of emotional numbness. She moved through her own life like a spectator, standing aloof from events and feelings. The second any memory threatened to return, she displaced it with some new activity.

She was proud to have been part of the operation to resuscitate the house. Visitor entrance fees and cream teas would never bring in significant revenue, but she had drawn up a business plan for the next thirty years which, with careful management, would cover the overheads and leave enough for a modest programme of repairs. Under her scheme, the house would be publicly accessible, three wings would become desirable residences on long, full repairing leases, and the eighteenth-century stable block would be turned into commercial units and let to local businesses. Meanwhile, the park would be put to work as a venue for rock concerts, horse trials and county fairs. Once they raised enough money, the Edwardian wing would be restored and turned into a residential centre for cooking, yoga and self-improvement courses. Built by her ancestors to entertain the few, Trelawney would become a place to delight the many; henceforward, the so-called elite would be at the service of what her mother liked to call the masses. Blaze was not a believer in *Schadenfreude,* but it occurred to her that her family were now at the mercy of the descendants of those whose hard labour had created their success. To keep a roof over their heads, Kitto and his children had to ingratiate and cajole. Once upon a time the family had seen it as their right to order and punish; now their only hope was to serve and delight.

Over the last nine months her investments had recovered: the Barclays shares had trebled; Microsoft, Apple and the price of oil were all rising. Although Indian telecoms were still in a state of flux, one of the women whose micro-businesses she had financed had turned out to be an extraordinary force in the newly emerging world of social media. This had inspired Blaze to set up a not-for-profit company which made small loans to help individuals start or grow a business. Grants started at £25 and increased to many thousands. The criterion for lending was based on the ethical standards of the start-ups. In only a few months she had funded a clean-water company in an African village and financed enough solar panels to bring light to a school in India. Part of her motivation was to use her skills for the greater benefit of humankind, but she was also keen to work in any area which never brought her into contact with Joshua Wolfe.

Sitting on the edge of her bed, Blaze listened to the familiar noises—the groaning of the pipes and the creaking of the boards—and, over the top of the base notes, Jane shouting at Arabella to do something and Kitto singing a refrain from *Don Giovanni.* She thought ahead to the sounds of her London life: a single key turning in the lock; one pair of footsteps on the stairs; Radio 4 on a Saturday morning; the long, silent nights. She imagined looking around her apartment: a single cup on the draining board; the imprint of a solitary body on the left-hand side of the bed; one pair of knickers hanging up to dry; a quarter of a pint of milk in the fridge; one umbrella in the hall; one set of keys on the side table; one apple, one banana and one pear in the fruit bowl. If she got cancer—when she got cancer—who would collect her ashes?

There was a sharp knock on the door. Blaze flipped the lid of her suitcase closed.

"Come in."

Jane opened the door and crossed the room in three great bounds. "You're not going to believe what's happened. It's a bloody miracle," she said, jumping from foot to foot. Catching sight of Blaze's suitcase, she stopped.

"Where are you going?"

"Home."

"Oh, Blaze, has something happened?"

"Now Ambrose is coming of age and the place is getting back on its feet, it's time for me to go. I can't squat forever like a cuckoo in your nest."

Jane seemed suddenly to deflate. Her shoulders dropped and her head sagged. "Please don't go. Please. I need you."

"No, you don't. You've got Kitto back and all your children. And Trelawney."

"Haven't you enjoyed being here?"

"Yes, I have." Blaze surprised herself by the vehemence of her answer.

"Then stay. I can't do this alone."

"You can. You know you can. Over the last six months you have become a powerhouse. There's nothing you can't do. You'll be running a major company soon."

"Don't go," Jane pleaded.

For a minute Blaze didn't reply; she was touched by her sister-in-law's entreaty. "Much as I would love to, Jane, I can't fold my life into yours or put the clock back to my younger days. I won't be far away, I'll visit often."

Jane came and sat down next to her on the bed and put her arms around Blaze's waist. The two women held each other close.

"What were you about to tell me?" Blaze asked.

"Uncle Tony has a book. Not just any old book. He wants to give it to Ambrose as a birthday present in the hope that he'll set up a foundation with the proceeds. It'll be a kind of endowment and the income will go towards Trelawney."

A few months earlier Blaze would have found Jane and her uncle's naivety maddening. How could a book make a dent in the overheads? She smiled at their unworldliness. "Where did this book come from?"

"It's the one his father gave him the day he was asked to leave Trelawney and make his way in the world."

Like others, Blaze had heard the story hundreds of times.

"No one ever thought to ask what the book was," Jane continued. "Even Tony didn't bother to look at it. It stayed in brown greaseproof paper at the bottom of his cupboard for over thirty years. One day, on an impulse, he unwrapped it."

"Don't tell me—it was studded with precious stones and inlaid with gold?" Blaze said sarcastically.

"It's more valuable than that. Tony thinks it might fetch a few million at auction."

Blaze laughed out loud. "Oh, come off it. Tony lives like a pauper. If he had anything valuable, he'd have sold it."

"That's what I thought." Jane produced two clippings and handed them over. Blaze turned towards the window to get a better light. Entitled "The World's Greatest Missing Treasures," the first article was from *The Times,* 27th February 2007, and listed priceless objects or artefacts that many longed to find. At the top was the Amber Room, made by the baroque sculptors Schlüter and Wolfram in the early eighteenth century for the Prussian King Frederick William; when the Russian Emperor Peter the Great had admired it, Frederick gave it to him as a gift. Blaze read on quickly, taking in missing masterpieces by Leonardo da Vinci, crown jewels, Fabergé eggs, a menorah from the Second Temple and, at number 28, the *Landino Dante.* The second article had the headline: HAS THE WORLD'S RAREST BOOK FINALLY APPEARED? Speed-reading, she saw that the *Landino Dante* was "thought to have been discovered in an Irish nunnery, but scientific tests proved it was only a copy. Even so, this rare facsimile fetched £750,000 at auction, bought by the Gates Foundation and put online for all to admire."

She put the articles down. "It doesn't prove anything."

Jane leaned over and pointed to the penultimate paragraph of *The Times* article. "You remember the standards—one from Bosworth and the other from Naseby? If you read the diary of the 17th Earl, he says that he came home with two things: the bloodied standard and a 'charming tome.' "

"I am not convinced."

Jane looked hurt. "Talk to Tony yourself. He says it's been independently valued by two major auction houses and the world's leading expert on manuscripts."

"I wouldn't spend the money yet." Blaze got off the bed and went over to the window. It was nearly six o'clock and completely dark outside. The beams of two torches made a zigzag pattern across the park and she knew it was Arabella and Tuffy returning from an insect-hunting trip.

"Do you want a hand getting dinner together?" She changed the subject.

"It's pretty much done. The guests will be arriving soon." Jane ran her fingers through her straggly hair, wondering if there was time to wash it. "The best thing about the last few months has been rekindling our friendship. I don't think I can bear to lose it again. I don't care if Tony's book is a fake, or if it's only worth 20p; I want you to stay with us."

"I have to build my own life and I like seeing Ayesha."

"Is she going to university?" At the thought of Ayesha, a knot of jealousy tightened in Jane's stomach. She had yet to reconcile herself to her husband's illegitimate daughter.

"She's behaving mysteriously. Said something about reading History of Art at Cambridge."

"Like mother, like daughter. Anastasia never showed her cards either."

"Isn't she coming tonight?"

"Apparently not." On an impulse, Jane took her sister-in-law's hand. "Thank you, Blaze. For rescuing me. Not for the first time." Silently they both thought back to their childhood when plain Jane Browne had been befriended by the most popular girl in school.

After Jane had left, Blaze went into the bathroom to brush her teeth and get ready for dinner. She looked back at herself in the mirror. These months in the country suited her. Her cheeks were tanned, her hair softer and the scar on her face seemed less livid, or maybe she was finally getting used to it. She pulled the skin tighter around her jawline and let it go—at least that part of her body was taut and defined. To her surprise, the inexorable onset of ageing didn't depress her; indeed her spirits felt remarkably, almost confusingly, light. She brushed her hair and put on a thin coat of pale pink lipstick. Coming back to Trelawney had helped her finally to leave.

Waiting until Damian and his assistant were stationed at the bottom of the stairs with their camera turning over, Clarissa made as grand an entrance as she could manage. Wearing a couture ball gown of pink shot silk designed for her in 1956 by Dior, she slowly inched her way down the centre of the Great Staircase. Arabella had offered to hold her arm, but Clarissa preferred to risk injury than share the limelight, particularly as her granddaughter, dressed in a short skirt and heavy boots, was not suitably attired. The assembled guests watched, transfixed, as the Dowager Countess of Trelawney creakily walked downstairs, keeping her gaze fixed on an unknown point in the middle distance, her mouth frozen in a beatific smile. It was her gloved hands, flapping awkwardly from side to side in an attempt to maintain balance, that most remembered. They were the prelude to the inevitable tumble that most foresaw and a few prayed for. Clarissa reached the bottom without mishap and, waving regally to her guests, paused dramatically in front of Damian's camera.

"You look splendid tonight, my Lady," the producer said.

Clarissa agreed wholeheartedly.

"Tell us, in your own words, about the guests?"

"Just a few neighbours."

"From the village?"

"Don't be silly!" Clarissa let out a little laugh. "We don't ask hoi polloi."

"Hoi polloi?"

"Commoners."

Damian couldn't believe she was saying this on film. He'd get that BMW now.

Behind him, Ginny snorted. He made frantic hand signals to quiet her.

"Our nearest neighbours are the Castelrocks from St. Rush. You'll see Cleo over there." She pointed to an elderly woman wearing a tiara, a tired dress and a pair of gumboots on her feet.

"Get the shots," Damian hissed at Ginny. The camera panned away from Clarissa towards the guests.

"I notice a clergyman is present."

"That's the Bishop of Truro. Only Jane Austen invited vicars to her parties."

"There seem to be a lot of dogs," Damian remarked, looking at ten or so animals, of different sizes and breeds, running around between the guests.

"Most of my friends prefer four-legged to two-legged beasts, so it seemed churlish not to ask them."

"Who else is here?"

Clarissa pointed to two old ladies sitting side by side on a bench, both with pudding-bowl haircuts and wearing identical dark green corduroy suits. "That's Lady June Marchmont and her companion Alice. As you can tell, June's not the marrying kind; nor, one assumes, is Alice. About six of the dogs belong to them. I drew the line at their bringing their horse. The man over there in the lilac linen suit is my brother-in-law, Anthony Scott."

"Is he the marrying kind?" Damian couldn't resist asking.

Clarissa ignored the remark. "The slender young woman over there with the tiny husband is a second cousin once removed. The man with a face as red as a tomato is another relation, Windy Swindon. The ludicrously dressed so-called huntsman is a decorator called Barty St. George: he's a party fixture; people are said to adore him. Over there is Tuffy, who you must have read about; it turns out she is quite the thing in the biographical world."

"The biological world—yes I did read about her." Damian hesitated. "You must be proud of your family, seeing them here after so many centuries?"

"One is proud of winning a flower show or the Cheltenham Gold Cup; family is a thing you have to put up with. You hope to respect them, even like them, but it's better not to set the bar too high."

"We finally agree on something," Ginny said, poking her head out from behind the camera. "My lot are shits until they want money."

"Tell me about Ambrose," Damian said. The camera swung round to pick out a young man with one arm around a pretty girl's waist while the other held a bottle of champagne from which he swigged. Ambrose was wearing jeans, an open-neck shirt and a velvet jacket. He shared all his father's features—the auburn hair, hazel eyes and pale skin—but, while the effect on his father and aunt was striking, it didn't work on Ambrose's face. His mouth was slightly too thin and set in a permanent sneer, his eyes too close together and his hair too thick. He had neither his brother Toby's gentleness nor Arabella's enthusiasm, and he had also inherited Jane's father's stout figure. None of this troubled the firstborn since he knew, with a deep-seated certainty, that he was better than most.

"It's a pity for him, and for the family, that he wasn't born in the late eighteenth century. I worry whether the boy has the skills needed to navigate his inheritance."

"Or lack of?" Damian suggested.

"Quite."

Their conversation was interrupted by a loud banging. Kitto had taken off his shoe and was thumping it against a wooden chest. Once he had their attention he climbed the stairs to a half-landing and addressed his guests.

"Thank you all for coming to celebrate this wonderfully auspicious occasion, Ambrose's coming of age. As most of you know, I can take little credit. Jane is the one who deserves the praise. She bore three wonderful children, she brought them up and, most surprisingly of all, she put up with me and with my family." Kitto paused, his voice breaking slightly. "I would like you all to raise your glasses to Jane: my wife, my friend and saviour."

"I thought tonight was about me!" Ambrose shouted. He was already drunk. There was a smattering of nervous laughter at his intervention. Kitto raised his glass and ran down the stairs to Jane, took her hand and kissed it. Everyone clapped. Jane looked at the floor. Clarissa, who disapproved strongly of public displays of affection, tutted. Kitto turned around and ran back up.

"As most of you know, it's a huge challenge trying to maintain large houses. My parents were the last generation to have the money to live like Trelawneys. Some of you remember the lavish house-parties, shooting and hunting weekends, the balls and other festivities. Without a huge fortune, that kind of life was unrealistic and, some might say, anachronistic. When Trelawney was at the centre of a large mining or agricultural empire, it was more sustainable, but its use as a sybarites' den seems hardly palatable. What were my family thinking? Living like kings and queens while England burned?"

"I think you should stop filming now," Clarissa said to Damian. Neither the producer nor Ginny had any intention of switching the camera off. The evening was turning out even better than they had dreamed. Damian pondered suitable titles for his new series: *The Decline and Fall of the British Aristocracy*? Or maybe *The Last Gasp*?

Seeing that the red light was blinking, Clarissa spoke a little louder. "You will not use any material without my permission." Damian smiled, hoping that the microphone was picking up her angry words.

"I am hardly innocent," Kitto continued. "I bought into the rules and way of life. In the name of history or standards—or was it self-interest?—I repeated not only a great mistake, but a cruel and foolish custom. When Jane and I took over the house, I asked my sister Blaze to leave. My parents had done the same to my Uncle Tony. My grandfather and his father followed the tradition too, but that doesn't justify any of our actions. Simply repeating customs and adopting past traditions are the preserves of the lazy and the unimaginative." Kitto didn't look at his mother, but most of the audience did. Clarissa pitied her son. He had learned nothing.

"The great irony is that the two most wronged people in this room have put these injustices behind them and have returned to save the family's reputation and the roof," Kitto resumed. "Blaze is using her business acumen to restore dignity and purpose to Trelawney, while Tony is about to make an extraordinary announcement." Smiling at his uncle, Kitto beckoned for him to come up onto the landing.

"Hang on, hang on." Ambrose pushed Tony out of the way and walked up the stairs. When he was level with his father, he turned to face the guests. "Thanks, Dad, for the speech. Very touching. Thanks, Mum—you put me off mince for life." He burped slightly and ran his hand over his mouth. "So, as you know, today I'm eighteen. Wahey for me." He started to clap and looked expectantly at the assembled crowd. Damian panned the camera around and caught people applauding in a desultory fashion.

Ambrose took a swig from the bottle of champagne and continued.

"I witnessed first-hand the misery of living here. Of being cold all winter, of the boiler running out, of my mum in tears of exhaustion, of Dad disappearing off to London on a Monday morning. It was fun living in a house where no one cared if you broke anything, until there was nothing left to break. Then I saw this place for what it is: just the dregs of a former life."

The guests looked at each other nervously, wondering if it was some kind of joke.

"Let me say this in plain English. I don't want some money-gobbling-shithole-bollocks of bricks. I loathe this house. I detest my family. I'm out."

There was an audible intake of breath followed by a muttering. Clarissa sat down heavily on the only available chair. Jane and Kitto reached for each other's hands. "No!" They stared at the floor, aghast. Tony's legs wobbled and he leaned against Blaze for support.

"Jolly nice of Aunt Blaze and Great-Uncle Tony to offer to help. But it's not necessary. I've sorted the whole thing." Ambrose drained the bottle. "I've done what should have been done years ago. I've sold the place. Lock, stock and smoking barrel. Signed the deal today." There was a stunned silence. Kitto stared at his son and then at his wife. Damian whipped the camera round in time to see Clarissa tumble to the floor in a deep faint. Toby pushed past the guests to tend to his grandmother. Ambrose shrugged.

"I know it's a bit shocking. We've had eight hundred years to get used to being here, but I want to live. Let me repeat that. I want to live. Look at my parents—Dad's gone a bit loopy and Mum's totally tonto. It's not a great advert, is it?"

"You have no right to pronounce on my life," Jane said, making her way to the foot of the stairs.

"You tell him," Windy Swindon bellowed. "Stinking little toad letting the side down."

"Like anyone gives a flying fuck what you think," Ambrose shouted back. "You overblown, overfed child molester."

"I'm going to shoot you!" Swindon strode towards the young man but fell over one of the dogs and ended up on his knees.

Damian inadvertently squealed with joy.

"You're done for!" Swindon hauled himself to his feet.

Ambrose held his hands up. "Oh, shut up, you old bore!"

Swindon, unused to being spoken to in that manner, hesitated.

Ambrose stamped his foot to get everyone's attention. "I want to introduce you to Trelawney's new owner. He's been waiting patiently in the wings for the last hour."

He ran up a few stairs to the library door and, opening it, said, "Come on out."

Ambrose stood back and the unmistakable figure of Thomlinson Sleet stepped out on to the staircase. Blaze's hand flew to her mouth. This had to be an elaborate joke. Kitto turned to his sister. "Did you know?" Blaze shook her head.

Sleet walked nonchalantly down the stairs, waving one hand. Dressed in a large navy-blue cashmere coat with two scarves wrapped around his neck, he looked like a man who had lost his way from Bond Street.

"Welcome to my house!" he said cheerfully. "Never thought an upstart like me would get the keys to the castle. For those who don't know about my past, I was one of those abandoned babies. Found in a phone box in Delaware, parcelled out around foster parents, but eventually adopted by a nice old childless Catholic professor and his wife. I met the Scott family at Oxford and to me they seemed like glamour incarnated. I wanted what Kitto had—" he paused "—and now it looks like I've got it." He spoke with gusto and certainty, but his voice cracked and he had to clear his throat. "Some things took longer to win than others. For those of you who are worried about Trelawney's future, don't be. I'm rich. Ask Blaze—she helped me. I've got enough money to gold plate the fucking roof. And I probably will."

"Who is this frightful man?" Lady Marchmont asked Alice.

"It must be a party trick. They'll have strippers later." Her companion pursed her lips into a thin, disapproving line.

"Disgusting," Lady Marchmont said.

Sleet stopped and dropped his voice. "I didn't buy this place as a status symbol. I bought it as a wedding present for the love of my life. It's what she wanted most in the world and it was my duty to give it to her."

Blaze swallowed, trying to remember the woman's name. Trish? Jackie? She thought they'd separated, but apparently not. Sleet looked back up the staircase and called, "Come out, my darling."

Damian's camera and sixty pairs of eyes swivelled to follow his gaze. A few moments later, a sylph-like figure appeared, wearing a simple red slip, her auburn hair shining in the candlelight, her legs bare, her feet in delicate gold sandals.

"My lords, ladies and gentlemen, may I present Ayesha, Lady Sleet."

Blaze felt her heart lurch. Jane's mouth slackened. Kitto froze. Clarissa, now back on her feet, leaned heavily against Toby. Uncle Tony tucked the *Landino* volume into his satchel, out of sight. Windy Swindon let out a long, low, appreciative whistle. Damian mentally accepted the BAFTA for best documentary feature.

Mark Sparrow shoved forward through the crowd and ran up the stairs. Reaching Ayesha, he stared up at her, his despair palpable.

Ayesha gazed back down at him, but her expression remained blank.

"Who is that?" Sleet asked his bride. She didn't answer. Mark stood rooted to the spot until Glenda Sparrow appeared from a side door and, hurrying through the guests and up the staircase, took her grandson firmly by the arm and pulled him away.

Then Blaze ran up the stairs and stabbed her finger in the younger woman's face. "What on earth are you doing?" she asked.

"Fulfilling a promise to my dying mother," Ayesha replied in a low voice.

"What promise?"

Ayesha didn't answer.

Putting his arm protectively around his wife, Sleet steered her down the stairs and across the room.

Seeing Ambrose, he reached forward and gave him a clap on the back. "Clear your desk first thing on Monday. I want you out."

Ambrose looked at him in amazement. "You said we were partners."

Sleet laughed. "Who'd trust someone who fucks his own family over?"

Turning to the guests, he said, "We're off to South America to continue our honeymoon. The builders move in shortly, so enjoy the place till then."

He led his new wife to the front door. Ayesha kept her eyes on the floor, her gaze soft. It was impossible to tell what she was thinking.

Outside, the guests could see a gleaming car and a chauffeur holding open the door. Ayesha slipped into the back seat and pulled a rug over her knees. Sleet went round to the other side and got in next to her. Moments later the car growled into life and everyone watched the tail lights disappear up the driveway.

30

The Coffee Shop

TUESDAY 9TH MARCH 2010

Glenda waited for Mark in a coffee shop in Exeter, looking at the pastries held captive in overchilled glass cabinets; biscuits the size of Frisbees catching germs on hastily wiped counters; frazzled immigrant workers steaming up milk for bored-looking locals. This chain had real lamps and low-slung armchairs; maybe that was the point—to make people feel familiar in a home from home, although she couldn't imagine many wanting fringed lamps and flock wallpaper. The tea, milky and tasteless, had cost £2.25, which Glenda thought was daylight robbery, although it was worth paying to see her grandson who had not been back to Trelawney since the night of the party.

"What brings you here today?" Mark asked, bending down to kiss his grandmother. Her call had come out of the blue. "Is Grandad OK?"

"He's fine. I had a bit of shopping to do." It was a disingenuous excuse and they both knew it. Anything Glenda wanted, and quite a bit more, was available in Plymouth.

"Would you like a top-up?" he asked, heading towards the counter. Glenda handed over her empty cup. She'd got here an hour early; the traffic and parking were a worry and she hadn't wanted to miss a moment with her grandson. She had sat there watching people and rehearsing what she was about to say. She'd promised Gordon not to mention anything "personal," but it had been ridiculous to think she could drive all the way here to talk about the weather. The truth wouldn't kill him; it might set him free.

"How have you been?" she enquired when he returned with another cup of tea for her and a black coffee for himself.

"I've been busy. We had a big order from Apple. We're hiring a hundred extra people and have taken over a new factory."

"Glad the recession isn't hurting you. You should see the queues around the job centre every Monday morning—it's heartbreaking. I blame those bloody foreigners coming over and undercutting our workforce."

"It's the fallout from the financial crisis, not the immigrants."

"I can see who's working and who isn't."

"My business couldn't survive without skilled workers from abroad." By far the most talented members of his team were either immigrants or first generation to the UK.

"I'm not talking about the boffins."

Mark didn't say anything—it was useless trying to explain the principles of net migration to either of his grandparents.

"Look, there's one." Glenda pointed to a man of Indian origin mopping the floor of the coffee house.

"He was almost certainly born here. His grandfather probably fought alongside your grandfather in the war."

"The people of this country are revolting."

You can say that again, Mark thought.

"They're not going to stand for it."

They'll just lie down and moan on and on, Mark said to himself. "Tell me about Grandad," he said out loud, changing the subject.

"Your grandad's got a new lease on life since he set up the Acorn action group. Our kitchen has become the front line in the battle to recover the value of everyone's investments. There's a constant stream of people coming in and out. They're going to court, or so they say, to try and get their money back."

"But the money's gone."

"Your grandad says the government bought Acorn at a knock-down price and it owes the shareholders compensation."

"That sounds fair enough."

"One janitor against the great and the good: can you see that happening?"

"At least he's no longer camped outside the front gates threatening to kill Kitto Trelawney."

"I don't recognise my husband any more," said Glenda. "He talks about nothing else, he thinks about nothing else."

"Do you blame him? He lived for his dream of retirement."

"He took a risk. If he'd done as I said and just kept the money in a deposit account, all would be well, but he wanted to be clever, he thought he could play the markets. There's consequences for him just like there was for Kitto. He lost it all too."

Mark leaned across and put his hand over his grandmother's. "I'm making money. Why don't you let me treat you and Grandad to a nice cruise? Get you out of England for a bit?"

"He'd never go. He's fighting on behalf of all the widows and the dispossessed."

They sat in silence for a while, watching a woman trying to persuade her child to eat a biscuit rather than her car keys. At another table a young couple were making out, seemingly oblivious to the rest of the world. Mark looked at his watch.

"I should get back."

"What are you making?"

"We're creating a piece of software that can recognise faces."

"Isn't that what eyes are for?"

"Robots don't have eyes."

Glenda shivered. "You're giving me the collywobbles. It's not right to give machines eyes and brains—who's going to police them?"

"It's the future, Gran, whether you like it or not."

Glenda shifted in her chair.

"I saw Lady Trelawney in the market the other day. Her Uncle Tony sold an heirloom and bought her and Kitto a little house by the sea in St. Garaway. She's set up a workshop outside St. Austell and her wall-paper is selling all over the world. Aunt Tuffy has paid for Arabella to go to a posh school to study biology, so it's only Toby at home now. He seems to have put Celia behind him and is going out with Mr. Fogg's daughter."

"The weird hippy preacher?"

Glenda nodded. "I'll have another tea for the road, please."

Mark went over to the counter.

When he returned to their table, Glenda continued with the news.

"It looks like every builder in Cornwall is working on the castle trying to make it habitable. You can hear the banging and clanging for miles around. Sleet wants it 'state of the art,' whatever that means, and now he's trying to get selected as the Conservative candidate for Plymouth Moor. Even though there's a waiting list of twenty good locals, he's bound to get it."

"He's American. It wouldn't be allowed."

"He's got dual nationality now."

Glenda took a quick peek at her grandson's expression; he hadn't asked her to stop talking.

"Of course the Dowager Countess won't move out of Trelawney—she's got rights, apparently. Sixty years' continuous habitation, so the builders are working around her—lucky she's so deaf and determined. She's still doing her reality TV series. Do you ever watch it? It was on BBC One but ratings fell and it's been moved to BBC Two. She carries on like Posh Spice, changing her clothes frequently and yabbering on about standards, and she has two thousand followers on Facebook. If you ask me, it's revenge on her husband."

Mark glanced at his watch, but Glenda was determined to continue.

"You're too young to remember Enyon in his prime. He was the best-looking man in Cornwall, maybe in all England. All the women loved him. Girls used to throw themselves at him and he loved catching them. The Countess knew what was going on. There was no point trying to stop the hanky-panky; she knew he wouldn't ever leave. Then *she* came along." Glenda stopped and waited until she had her grandson's attention. "She was so young and so beautiful."

Mark looked at her. "Who?"

"Anastasia." There, Glenda thought, I've said it—finally let the secret out.

"What are you talking about?"

"Anastasia wasn't in love with Kitto; she was in love with his father and he with her."

"Gran, that's rubbish." Mark pushed his cup away and looked towards the door. Glenda leaned over, looked to the left and the right and then in a low voice told him, "You forget who changed the sheets, who did the laundry, who had to sneak Anastasia out past his wife's bedroom in the morning."

Mark stared at his grandmother in astonishment. "Did Kitto know? Or her friends?"

"Lady Blaze walked in on them one afternoon. The shock damn nearly killed her; her beloved father with her best friend. She tried to tell her mother, but Clarissa slapped her and called her a liar. Blaze left the house the following morning and never came back. Told everyone it was about a bedroom, but if you check the timings, she had gone long before Ambrose arrived."

"What did Clarissa do?"

"Nothing at first. She mostly did nothing. Thought the infatuation would burn itself out, but then Anastasia told her she was pregnant and that she was keeping the child. Enyon said he wanted it too. You should have heard the palaver! Clarissa told him that she'd tell Kitto and Blaze and bring down the House of Trelawney."

Mark exhaled slowly, letting out the air with a soft whistle. "How did she persuade Anastasia to go?"

"Clarissa and Enyon received her in the library, together. The Countess told the girl that Enyon didn't love her any more. They were going to give the baby a settlement. Same as she did with the others."

"How did you know all this?"

"I was sent to pick Anastasia up off the library floor. She was curled up in a ball and couldn't move. I brought her back to our place and your grandad and I looked after her for a couple of weeks—she had nowhere else to go."

"What did the Trelawneys do?"

"Enyon shut himself up in his study for months. Wouldn't eat or see anyone. Clarissa said it was because he missed Lady Blaze." Glenda drank the last dregs of her tea. "I thought she might—you know—get rid of the baby, but she was adamant about keeping it. One morning I took her a cup of tea and she'd gone. Vanished. No note. Nothing. And then the phone call, followed by news of a daughter."

Mark ran his hands through his hair, wondering if Ayesha had any idea. There were so many things about the young woman he couldn't understand. How or why she'd married one man while professing to love another, for a start.

"How old was Anastasia when it began?"

"About sixteen."

"What about Kitto and her? I thought that was supposed to be the great love affair?"

"It was a front to throw people off the scent. Poor Kitto fell in love with her, of course."

Mark grimaced. "The old man should have known better."

"I think they loved each other."

"Who is Ayesha's father?" he asked.

"Enyon."

"So Ayesha is Kitto's sister, not his daughter?"

Mark pushed his chair back, suddenly overcome with longing for his erstwhile girlfriend. "Why are you telling me all this, Gran?" He started looking in his pocket for his keys. He rose to his feet, but his grandmother put a hand on his forearm.

"You're not the first man to lose his heart to a young woman. There's no shame in it."

"I don't want to talk about it. You wouldn't understand." He was clearly intent on going, but Glenda wasn't letting him off that easily.

"Sit down."

Mark slowly lowered himself back into the chair.

"If you'd have fallen for any other girl from any other family, I'd have told you to follow your heart. Not this one. Ayesha is half Trelawney and wholly unwanted. I'm told her mother hated and abused her; blamed her for everything. Poor child suffered a triple rejection: from her father before she was born, from her mother when she was born and now from her father's family when she came back here. What does that do to anyone?"

Mark was silent. He'd been devastated by Ayesha's unexpected marriage to Sleet, but believed she had been driven by circumstance into making a foolish decision. He would wait for her; she was worth waiting for.

"You're too good, too principled for them. The Trelawneys didn't last eight hundred years by being nice or being the best."

"We are going to be together," Mark said.

Glenda's heart sank. Had she inflamed rather than doused her grandson's passion? She saw herself as an ordinary woman who had lived an ordinary life, hardly venturing from one small patch of England, rarely challenging the attitudes handed down by generations of her own family. Yet she felt certain that Mark had the ability to make a difference and to change society. Glenda didn't understand technology, but she knew there was going to be a revolution and that her grandson had an important part to play in it. She chose her next words carefully.

"I don't blame you for loving her. But Trelawney will destroy her like it has the rest of them. That place is more than just bricks and mortar; it's rough magic."

She glanced at him out of the corner of her eye; he was listening.

"You have a calling, Mark, a bigger purpose than love. You are already a bridge to the future, providing jobs and skills to a part of the country forgotten by most. You can't throw it away for one woman and you can't look backwards. Stay away from that house and that family and all that they represent; they'll bring nothing but heartache."

Looking at her grandson, she saw that her words had hit their target. They sat in silence for a few minutes. Glenda checked her watch and made a move to get up.

"It's your grandad's birthday on Saturday. It would mean the world to him if you'd come for dinner."

Mark met her eyes and smiled. "You are a remarkable woman."

"That's a yes then?"

He nodded.

Before he could change his mind, Glenda stood and, picking up her bag from the floor beside her, bent down to kiss her grandson on the cheek.

"You better bring a bottle of fancy wine. We could use something a bit special."

31

One Day in May

WEDNESDAY 26TH MAY 2010

"Did you know that Coco Chanel gave this to Enyon's mother in 1928? At the time she was carrying on with his cousin, the Duke of Westminster? Coco was a Nazi supporter—so was Bendor, I suspect, but that was hardly unusual in the British aristocracy. They still can't abide Jews or Arabs. At least they're even-handed in their anti-semantics."

"Anti-Semitism," Damian Derbish corrected her.

Clarissa ignored him and slipped on the Chanel tweed jacket. The red light of the camera blinked and she knew she was expected to perform.

"After the war we wouldn't have dared throw anything away. For us, a coat had to last a lifetime." She checked the small clock on the side table and looked at Damian. "Hold on to your hat; it's about to start."

Seconds later, the walls of the Mistresses' Wing shook violently. Damian, carrying his video camera, got to his knees and crawled under the dining-room table, certain they were experiencing an earthquake.

"Man up, Derbish," Clarissa called over the infernal noise, "it'll only last a few minutes. They do it every morning at six o'clock. Part of their tactics to get me out of here." She raised her right hand in a clenched fist. "One shall not be moved."

To Damian's relief, he got the shot, albeit from a bad angle. He could use subtitles over the din. Later, Clarissa could do a piece to camera explaining how the Sleets were trying to drive her away using a dawn chorus of drills, the severing of pipes and the blocking of drains. Nothing could be proven; it was all the accidental by-product of major restoration work. The Dowager Countess had been offered and had refused alternative accommodation: Trelawney was her home and she'd leave feet first.

The ratings for the series, *The Last Stand of the Countess Trelawney*, had been falling steadily. There were mutterings that it might not be recommissioned if the viewing figures fell below a million. Now in its sixth consecutive month, it was due to be moved from BBC Two to BBC Four. Damian had achieved the longed-for promotion and had swapped the Skoda for a BMW, but he was now living in his semi on the outskirts of Plymouth. He hoped the christening would provide a much-needed fillip.

The drilling stopped after ten minutes. Putting her fingers to her temples, Clarissa tried to massage the headache away.

"Some might call this a form of Chinese torture?" Damian suggested, holding the boom close to Clarissa's mouth.

"The night after the family left, in February, the pipes burst and water poured down all the walls from the tanks in the roof to the basement. Some think places are inanimate objects, without feelings, but the house of Trelawney was lamenting the departure of the last Earl. Long after the fire brigade turned off the pipes, the water kept coming. Explain that!"

"I can't."

"That's what I said." Clarissa flipped open a small compact and powdered her nose. There was a grease spot on her white silk shirt and the collar had frayed. She carefully positioned a chiffon scarf to cover the stain.

"Were you surprised to hear about the pregnancy?" Damian asked.

Clarissa didn't answer immediately. She'd learned from watching her rushes over and over again that pauses could either be eliminated through editing or used to powerful effect. Anticipating this question, she had thought of many responses and even more ways of delivering them. She also knew that, unless her utterances were reported in the press and social media, her television show would be cancelled. She had inhaled the oxygen of publicity and found it intoxicating; there could be no return to the thin air of anonymity. In the days when breeding meant something, those lamented long-lost days of deference, Clarissa had been used to being stared at, revered and admired. Now the upper classes had been replaced by the vaguely famous; A, B and even C listers were more highly valued than the crumbling aristocracy. Her types, once the acme of society, were now has-beens. As she prepared to speak, she squared her shoulders and stiffened her resolve. Bugger discretion, she thought, and, taking a deep breath, turned and faced the camera.

"I was absolutely horrified. The girl had prospects, real prospects."

"You must be happy for her?" Damian asked, adjusting the focus to a close-up.

"Happy for her? Do you have children?" Clarissa sounded incredulous.

"Two: a girl and a boy. I love them both," he said.

"Children are overrated." Clarissa made sure that her delivery was precise and dismissive. She imagined this short clip being replayed on all social-media platforms.

"Why did you have them then?" Damian asked.

Clarissa hesitated. There were so many things she could say, so many ways to shock, but she decided to tell the truth. "That was the arrangement. I got the ring, the status, the house, and he got the heir. I can assure you that, after two, I shut up shop. Enyon wanted more, but nothing, nothing was going to persuade me to go through all that again." Watching Damian's face told her that it had been the right approach; the producer's mouth hung open with astonishment. "Do you know Kitto wanted to know if I had breastfed him." She laughed.

"What did you say?"

"None of his bloody business."

Damian wanted to punch the air. Another series was in the bag. Quivering with excitement, he tried to keep the camera steady.

"The problem for the younger generation," Clarissa continued, "is thinking they are entitled to happiness." She snorted derisively. "Happiness! They should try living through a war; we were grateful to be alive.

This generation starve themselves willingly, go to horror films and freeze off their fat, but have no idea what it's like to be hungry or cold or frightened." Taking a fluffy brush with a head the size of an apple, she dusted her nose and neckline with violet-scented talcum powder and took a last look in the mirror. Slowly she got to her feet, one hand on the table for support, the other on her achy back.

"Don't you love your children even a little bit?" Damian asked.

"Why is everyone so hung up on love? It's just a biological twitch to try and make things appear better. Ask Tuffy—she says we're just animals with pretensions."

"I want to make sure your audience fully understands what you are saying."

Clarissa considered the hundreds of thousands of people who tuned in to watch her programme; maybe some of them had feelings for their children and she mustn't risk outright alienation. "One is fond of one's offspring—" she paused "—at times."

"Shall we have another baby?" Kitto asked Jane at the breakfast table.

"Gross," Arabella said, pushing away her cereal bowl.

"That's disgusting," Toby agreed.

"We're not that old," Kitto said.

"You are far too old." Arabella ran her hands through her tangled hair. "Besides, the thought of you two having nookie is revolting."

"Nookie? That doesn't sound like a future scientist speaking," Kitto teased his daughter. "Shouldn't it be copulation or reproduction?"

"That's enough." Jane stood up and cleared the plates.

"Sit down, darling, for a while longer. It's so rare to have Arabella and Toby here at the same time. If only half-term could last all the way to the summer holidays."

Two days into half-term and Jane was already looking forward to her offspring returning to their respective establishments. "I've got to be at work in half an hour, as well as preparing for the naming ceremony and an invasion of your family." She stacked the plates noisily on the sideboard.

"It's not till the weekend. Relax, Mum," Arabella said.

Jane bit her lip. It was easier to ignore than ignite.

The kitchen was similar to Trelawney's except on a lilliputian scale. Jane had painted it the same electric pea green with a border of daisies and had found an old dresser in the local auction house. There was a Rayburn and a smaller pine table. The floors were also made of stone but, as this house was only two hundred years old, the hearth was less pitted and worn. Outside, the façade and garden were kept severe and clean by constant salt blasting. Nothing grew except for pockets of stonecrop or flatweed. Jane had tried to plant a climbing rose on the sheltered side of the house but the wind ripped it out. On stormy nights, the house heaved and shook in the violent winds. Kitto found it romantic; Jane wished she shared his enthusiasm.

"Does she know who the father is?" Arabella asked.

"Of course," Jane replied, although she had no idea.

"Is he coming?"

"Not as far as we know." Jane ran through the mental checklist of chores ahead. Instead of sitting around and gossiping, she wished one of them might lend a hand.

"It'll be hard bringing a baby up on her own," Kitto said. "Why don't we offer them a bed here? With Arabella going to boarding school and Toby at agricultural college, there'll be two empty rooms plus the spare."

"You can't give away my room to a strange baby," Arabella said crossly. "I need somewhere to go in the holidays."

"I don't want to lose two homes that fast," Toby added.

"We will not be offering your bedrooms to anyone," Jane said firmly. Far from fearing the empty nest syndrome, Jane couldn't wait for them to go. She had spent far too long being someone's wife and mother.

"I was trying to be kind." Kitto reached out for her hand. Jane sidestepped the gesture and started to wipe down the surfaces.

"Perhaps you could apply for the position of manny?" she suggested.

"What's a manny?"

"A male nanny."

"That would be funny. I can just imagine Dad forgetting to feed the baby because he had a new idea for a poem."

"Leaving it in the supermarket because he went off into one of his daydreams."

The children laughed at their father's increasingly long roster of eccentricities. Jane wished she was more patient with Kitto. Coming back from work at the end of a long day, she'd often have to go out again to try and track him down on the cliffs or tucked away on a distant beach where he'd forgotten the time or the way home. Like a child, he refused to wear jumpers or coats, and, when it was cold, it took hours in front of a burning fire to stop his teeth from chattering. They shared a bedroom at the cottage; there weren't enough spares to allow the luxury of separate quarters. She loved her husband, but her feelings were more maternal than matrimonial.

Jane's studio now employed seven people. Orders for her hand-printed wallpaper had grown substantially in the last six months, with commissions coming from America and the Far East. She had taken the press from the attic at Trelawney, dismantling it one part at a time, and reassembled it in a disused garage in the nearby town. Blaze encouraged her to outsource her designs to a factory capable of mass-producing wallpaper, but Jane refused; part of the integrity of her work was seeing the process through from start to finish. Her aim was not to get rich (although her family sorely needed the money); she was an artisan for whom the making was as important as the product. To speed up the process and reduce the administrative burden, her young assistants helped fulfill the orders and prepare the press. Bright colours had returned to her practice and her designs were full of joy and movement. Those who looked closely might see the same animals and trees appearing in each composition. No one stopped to ask if they were representations of real people. Jane was glad; the designs were still her private biography, her way of making sense of the world.

Arabella unfurled her legs and, propping her toes up on the table, started painting her nails.

"That stuff stinks," Toby complained.

"Not as much as you." Arabella smiled mischievously at her brother. "You are such a square. It must be Mr. Fogg's daughter."

"Very funny."

"Does she have you in the crypt?"

"Arabella, that's enough," said Jane.

"Fucking weird that your father-in-law is christening the baby."

"He's not a vicar, he's a preacher. And it's a naming ceremony, not a christening," Toby explained again.

"Why?" Arabella asked, putting the last touches to her nails, each one a different, gaudy colour.

"Something to do with respect for the child's father," Jane said, wishing she understood.

"He's abandoned her, why should she care?" Arabella danced around the kitchen to air-dry the polish. Now nearly seventeen, she had lost any vestiges of teenage awkwardness and become a radiant beauty. Clouds of auburn hair framed a porcelain-white face. Her eyes were a shade brighter than the usual Trelawney hazel and her lashes were heavily fringed. She had her father's deep-red bow-shaped mouth and her Aunt Blaze's long legs.

Toby pushed his chair back.

"I'm going for a walk. Dad, do you want to come?"

"Yes. Jane, why don't you take the morning off work and come too?" Kitto asked.

"I've got seven orders for Japan to make and ship out. Then I want to start cooking the food for the weekend."

"It'll go off by then." Unsatisfied with one of her toenails, Arabella wiped the polish off and started again.

"Where's Great-Uncle Tony going to sleep?" Toby asked.

"He's found a B&B up the road," Kitto said. "He's being very mysterious, refusing to come to lunch on Sunday."

"I need to go to Tuffy's; will you drop me?" Arabella asked.

Jane nodded, swallowing feelings of irritation. "Be quick." At Trelawney there had always been a place to hide. Their new house was so small that you could hear a cough two rooms away.

"What can I do to help?" Kitto asked.

"You could make supper?" Jane suggested.

"Is there anything to cook? What would you like? Do I need to go to the shop?" Kitto asked.

Jane was about to explain, but realised it would be quicker to do it herself.

"You two go for a walk. I'll pick up some food on my way home." Putting on her coat, she checked her face in the mirror and gestured to Arabella to hurry up.

"Mum, my shirt's not clean. I need it for tonight." Toby pulled a favourite T-shirt out of the laundry basket.

"You're all old enough to do your own washing." Jane walked out of the house, shutting the door firmly.

"Mum, wait!" Grabbing her shoes in one hand and her satchel in the other, Arabella, barefoot, rushed after her mother.

Two days later, early on Friday morning, Tony checked his pocket for his train ticket and looked around the studio room for the last time. He had made his bed carefully, put away the single cup and the saucepan, and turned off the gas at the mains. The day before he'd taken the last of his clothes to the Distressed Gentlefolk shop in Pimlico. Most assumed that, as a member of the aristocracy and habitué of yachts and palaces, Tony lived in a similar style to his many friends and relations, but this room, eighteen by thirty-four feet, had been home for twenty-seven years; he wouldn't miss one thing about it. The last thing he did was to wrap up his only remaining valuable possession, a sketch by Whistler, in brown paper, his christening present for little Perrin. Taking a last look around his former domain, Tony considered the negligible impression he'd left on the world; a sybaritic life capped by a nonentity's death. He doubted anyone would bother to write, let alone read, his obituary. His greatest achievement was two mentions in friends' biographies: one misspelt as Antonio Scott, the other amongst a litany of party-goers. His lovers were all dead and his conversational style, once feted, belonged to another era. If the point of humans was to procreate and extend their own race, he had failed in that too. Of his family, only Blaze would remember him with genuine fondness, silently invoking his name when she drank a Bloody Mary or saw another in a white linen suit. It was too late to mind, let alone do anything about it.

Closing the bedsit door, he posted the keys back through the letter box and went out through the front entrance into Earls Court. Walking down the side street, he thought back to the days when one had to step over prone bodies and navigate pools of vomit. Not so any more; even this part of London was semi-gentrified. The Australians had moved out to Muswell Hill, the drunks to Lambeth. The bankers would never get here; the houses weren't grand enough and the constant rumble of the M4 and the Underground would prey on the nerves of their emaciated wives.

At the corner of Cromwell Road, Tony was nearly knocked off his feet by thundering juggernauts. He held on to a lamp post with one arm, clung to the brown-wrapped parcel with the other and waited for the kindly yellow light of a free taxi. When one pulled up, the driver hopped out to help him in.

"Thank you," Tony said, holding the man's arm.

"Shall I put your seatbelt on for you?" the cabbie asked.

"I can manage that, just." Tony smiled at him.

"Where to, guv'nor?"

"Paddington Station, please."

The taxi driver indicated right and soon they were heading towards the station.

"Going to see family?" the driver asked.

Tony's heart sank. He couldn't bear the chatty ones. Didn't they understand that private transport was an opportunity for peace? He wanted to take a last contemplative look at the city which had been his home for sixty years.

"I'm going to a christening," he said, not wanting to be rude.

"You must have seen a few of those?"

"More than I care to remember. I suppose it's touching that people want to go on having children." Tony looked at the taxi's dashboard and saw three family photographs.

"I know what you mean. Our Sarah's expecting her fourth and she hasn't got a pot to piss in." The cabbie shook his head. "We do what we can to help, but there are eight other grandchildren, all needing something. There's too many people on the planet already."

Tony didn't reply, hoping that silence would stem his driver's incessant chatter.

"So where you going to?" the cabbie asked.

"Cornwall, the county where I was born."

"Never been there. Keep saying to my missus we should go."

Tony smiled. "It's lovely, if a bit wet."

"Will you stay long?"

"For the rest of my life," Tony replied.

"No luggage. Not even a holdall?"

"All taken care of," Tony said. "Just this," and he held up the parcel.

"You're my kind of fellow. Whenever my missus goes anywhere, she has to take a huge suitcase. Even if it's a day trip to see one of the children."

Mercifully the traffic wasn't too bad and the taxi bowled through the park. Though it was early in the morning, there were plenty of people out. Blossom clung to the trees and the grass was lush green.

"What's the baby called?"

"Perrin."

"Odd name."

"It's a traditional Cornish girl's name."

"So it is a girl! One never can tell these days and one shouldn't presume. I've got granddaughters called Ray and Charlie. Bloody confusing, if you ask me."

Which I didn't, Tony thought. He stared fixedly out of the window, hoping the man would stop talking. A group of horse riders went past: two little girls led by a gum-chewing battleaxe in a black fitted jacket. If the dreaded Clarissa had been there, she'd have wound down the window and told the woman that tweed was for hacking, black was for hunting. Tony sighed with relief—he'd only have to see her once more.

At Paddington the cab driver helped him out and Tony made his way to Platform 5 and the 9 a.m. train to Parr. He'd booked a single seat, facing forward. It didn't take long to pass through suburbia and into the open countryside. Resting his face against the cool, grimy window, he watched the counties pass and the distances between towns grow as he sipped the free tea and ate the complimentary biscuits. He checked his wallet for the tenth time. The £20 note was still there. The following day, after the ceremony, he'd take a taxi to the cliffs above Lantic Bay. From there it would only be a short walk. His last steps to freedom. He felt no fear, no regrets or any excitement. He'd had enough of this life; better to end it on his terms while he was mobile and continent. Blaze and Jane had both offered to take him in, but after sixty years of independent living he was too old to try and adapt to new rhythms. He'd had a good life—not the one he expected or even wanted, but interesting enough. Recently he'd begun to feel tired. Every day was a battle against aching limbs. The simple act of putting on his socks took a whole hour. He couldn't be bothered to read or go to his beloved National Gallery any more. Most of his friends had shuffled on. The best thing that had happened over the last year was exploring London's museums with Ayesha. Unlike most of his family, she had the "eye." On the whole, Trelawneys were heathens. He liked them well enough, but they were still heathens.

Ayesha lay on the deck of the *Lady S,* staring into Mustique's azure waters. The boat was one of the best things about being married to Sleet, not least because the farther it went, the less she had to see of him. He had flown out for the weekend and she could hear him shouting into his phone, ordering his broker to buy this or sell that. In the first few months of their marriage, Ayesha had feigned interest in his professional life; now she checked the stock market only to see how much his net worth had increased. Thank goodness she had married a man with a talent for making money; he was going to need it. The bills for restoring Trelawney came in thick and fast: the latest estimate had increased from £25 to £32 million to fix and furnish. The roof would be £15 million and that was long before they addressed the six miles of plumbing, the twenty-seven miles of electrical rewiring or thought about underfloor heating. Ayesha was determined to make Trelawney the best possible version of itself.

Her thoughts turned to her mother's story about being excommunicated by the family when they found out she was pregnant.

"How could they?" Ayesha had asked incredulously. "You were so young."

"I was an ugly, inconvenient secret." Vengeance had been her dying wish. Ayesha promised to fulfill her mother's last request. She was surprised how easy it had been.

Sleet marched along the deck towards her. He was wearing swimming trunks covered with ducks and matching yellow Topsiders. His stomach and thighs wobbled in different directions.

"You look very Palm Beach, darling," she said.

"Is that a compliment?" Sleet could never tell if his wife was teasing. He couldn't, for that matter, understand her. If she spoke, it was careful, modulated and enigmatic. The fourth Lady Sleet might bankrupt him, but he'd never get bored of her.

Ayesha took out her iPhone and, scrolling through the photographs, showed Sleet a picture of a Lalique bracelet: a pansy made of diamonds and sapphires.

"I sent it to the baby as a present from us," she said.

"I thought you weren't speaking to the mother."

"It's not the child's fault."

"Did you fly the whole way to London just to choose it? The fuel for the jet would have cost more than the knick-knack." Sleet was annoyed that his wife's trip to London had happened when he was on the West Coast.

"I had other things to do," Ayesha said mysteriously.

"Most husbands and wives share information."

Ayesha didn't answer. She stood up and put on her bikini top. Sleet had no idea that she and Mark had spent forty-eight blissful hours in London, taking a short break in their lovemaking to find a present for the baby. She wondered how her husband would react to the news if she won a place at Cambridge to read History of Art or if she told him that her beloved brother Sachan was arriving to live with them the following week.

"Where are you going?" Sleet asked.

"For a swim," she said.

"I've only just got here," he replied mournfully.

"And we've got three whole lovely days together." Ayesha bent down to kiss her husband's head. Three whole days, she thought. God help me.

32

The Naming Ceremony

SATURDAY 29TH MAY 2010

Looking down at the tiny baby suckling at her breast, Blaze wondered if her heart might explode. How was it possible to love anything so much? She'd never liked babies and hadn't wanted one of her own. Now this unexpected, perfect creature had blown apart an orderly life and rewired every aspect of her emotional being. Only a few weeks old, Perrin already had a thatch of auburn hair. As she sucked, she made little snuffling and squeaking noises and thumped her tightly curled fist against her mother's breast. Once in a while she raised a large blue eye upwards and let it roll backwards in its socket like a drunk on the verge of unconsciousness. Bending down, Blaze kissed the downy head and breathed in the milky scent.

She had seen the baby's father once since the child's conception. He had accused Blaze of tricking him, treating him like a sperm donor and deliberately, cruelly ignoring his principles. He did not believe it was an accident: why hadn't she taken precautions? But it had never occurred to Blaze that she might conceive—having babies was something that happened to people with steady periods and partners. The discovery had been a complete surprise. Hospitalised after passing out in the street, she'd woken up in a ward to be told that she was five months pregnant. The routine blood test also revealed that the foetus had a higher-than-normal chance of being born with Down's syndrome. The doctor suggested an amniocentesis and showed her the long needle to be inserted through her stomach into the womb.

"It comes with a risk of self-induced termination," he said matter-of-factly.

Blaze, stunned by the news, looked at him blankly.

"The way I put it to patients is that you have to choose between death by a car or plane crash?"

"I don't understand."

The doctor cracked his knuckles and leaned across the desk. "Having a baby with Down's is one outcome; losing it with this procedure is another."

Every latent maternal instinct came rushing to the fore: Blaze didn't care if the baby was born with Down's or with thirty fingers; all that mattered was protecting, nurturing and bringing it safely into the world. She had never been more certain of or more committed to anything. No one was going to stick a needle into her unborn child's secret space or endanger its chances of survival. Giddy with love and a sense of purpose, she had rushed from the doctor's waiting room back to her flat in Maida Vale.

Perrin took herself off her mother's breast and fell into a deep sleep. Blaze laid her daughter over her shoulder and rubbed her back until the infant let out a huge, contented belch. Downstairs Blaze could hear the sounds of her family getting ready to leave for the ceremony, which was due to start at 4 p.m. With any luck the baby would sleep through the short service and wake only for her late-night feed. To her astonishment, Blaze never minded being woken—any excuse to look at Perrin, to hold her and look after her. During the week, Blaze took the baby to her office in Islington from where she managed her micro-financing company. The business had grown quickly since its inception six months earlier and now employed eleven full-time people investing in hundreds of small start-ups across the world.

She was glad to be out of the City. Each day brought news of more endemic toxicity. The Securities and Exchange Commission had accused

Goldman Sachs of willfully defrauding investors through the sale of sub-prime mortgages. A court-appointed examiner charged Lehman Brothers with knowingly manipulating their balance sheet. In Ireland, a former chair of the Anglo Irish Bank was arrested for suspected fraud. The uncoupling of cause and effect, the blanket denial of culpability and consequences, reflected attitudes in much of the industry. The billions of dollars of quantitative easing being pumped into America and Europe seemed only to prop up large businesses instead of reaching those individuals or small companies most adversely affected. Blaze was sickened by what she saw, but also aware that less than a year ago she'd have regarded the turmoil as an opportunity to look for interesting investments. Perrin had reset her ethical barometer; now she feared for her daughter's and the next generation's future.

There was a gentle knock on the door and Jane's head appeared.

"We should leave soon, it's nearly three fifteen." Jane looked at Blaze and her sleeping child and smiled. "I love seeing you as a mother."

"I still can't believe it."

"Shall I hold her while you get ready?" Jane stepped forward to pick up Perrin, who was now dressed in the Trelawney christening gown: yards of beige-coloured lace, worn by two centuries of the family's new babies.

"It's only now I've added to the family that I feel part of it," Blaze said, fastening her nursing bra and slipping on a burgundy cotton dress. She put on a pair of flat shoes and tidied her hair in the mirror, leaving her face free of make-up.

Blaze walked across the room and felt the damask curtains. "I recognise these."

"Ayesha threw most things out. Whatever we could fit in here, we took."

"Have you seen her?"

Jane shook her head. "I rehearse what I'd say."

"How does your speech go?"

"Pretty short." Jane hesitated. "It starts and ends with one word."

"Which one?"

"Bitch."

Blaze laughed.

"I'm not joking," Jane said crossly.

"She sent Perrin a present."

"I hope you sent it back."

"Certainly not; I made her husband millions."

Blaze looked at her sister-in-law thoughtfully. "I thought when we lost Trelawney that the family would disintegrate and there'd be no reason to see each other and nothing to come home to. But it turned out that, far from being the interloper, you are the family's heart. The one who's keeping us all together. Where you go, we'll follow. Thank you."

Jane smiled weakly and looked out of the window at the white horses dancing across the seascape and the gulls wheeling above the water. Once she'd have been happy for this accolade; now it made her feel trapped.

"Mum, we've got to go," Arabella called up the stairs. Outside, Kitto honked the car horn. Blaze took her baby in her arms and the two women made their way carefully down the narrow painted stairs.

"Do you wish Perrin's father was here?" Jane asked, turning off the kitchen light.

"Yes, but at least he's part of her. I see him in her smile, in her eyes." As Blaze spoke, her voice broke; she missed him.

Jane looked at her. "I'm so sorry, darling."

"You can't have everything." Blaze shrugged and coughed to clear her knotted throat.

"Mum, get a move on," Toby shouted through the letter box.

Jane opened the door and let Blaze and the baby out first. A gust of wind blew the two women's dresses up above their heads and they stood, knickers on display, in front of the house.

"Standards, darling," Blaze yelled through the material which entirely covered her head.

"Standards," Jane echoed.

In the car Clarissa turned her head away and under her breath muttered, "I think I might disown all of you."

"What then would be the point of living?" Kitto asked.

Clarissa couldn't answer.

Kitto leaned towards her and gave his mother a kiss on the cheek. "All we have is family."

They drove in convoy to the tiny chapel at St. Madryn. The former church was set in an ancient wood behind a crescent-shaped white sandy beach named Petroc. Hidden from sight by rolling dunes on one side and a huge granite rock on the other, it was only accessible by a steep mossy track lined with ferns and lichen. Once the private domain of a Cornish queen, it had been deconsecrated in the 1970s and was now used for secular ceremonies and parties.

"Why do we have to come to this frightful dank dingley dell?" Clarissa asked, as she tottered down the steep path, clinging to Toby's arm for support. "We have a perfectly good church of our own where Trelawneys have been buried, baptised or married for at least seven centuries." She was secretly relieved that none of the locals would witness this event and that Enyon hadn't seen the arrival of his beloved daughter's illegitimate baby. How pathetic of Blaze to fail to get the father to marry her.

"The Sleets would never let us use it. The church is part of Trelawney," Jane said.

"I don't see what that's got to do with it," Clarissa trumpeted. "I have rights."

"What's wrong with doing something different?" Tony asked, trying to keep upright as his thin-soled shoes slithered on mossy stones.

"Change for change's sake is ridiculous. Just because something is new, it doesn't make it better," Clarissa snapped. "There are lots of churches, why go for hocus-pocus?"

"Blaze didn't want to offend the baby's father by having a Christian ceremony."

"Is he a Druid?" Clarissa asked. "Or worse? Come to think of it, what could be worse?" She thought a bit. "Actually I can think of many more awful alternatives." She shuddered theatrically.

The family made their way down the path, which was lined with banks of buttercups, campion and valerian. "This must be the best year ever for wild flowers," Kitto said and, unable to contain his excitement, danced with abandon in their midst. Arabella and Toby exchanged weary looks; their father's behaviour was becoming increasingly erratic.

"Waltz with me, my darling," Kitto called out to Jane, who pretended not to hear.

Blaze cradled Perrin in her arms. "I will make a great life for us," she whispered in her tiny ear. "You won't want for anything or anyone, I promise you."

Rounding the corner, the family saw that the windows of the chapel were glowing and candle flames danced behind brightly coloured stained glass. In the gloaming light it looked like a tiny ship on a sea of wild flowers. Mr. Fogg, the master of ceremonies, a vicar turned preacher, pushed open the heavy, studded oak door and stepped forward to welcome them. Clarissa held out her hand imperiously. Toby cringed; it was the first time his girlfriend's father had met his family and, far from being worried about their reaction, he was concerned what Mr. Fogg might think of them. Jane broke with tradition and kissed the preacher; Arabella dug her toes into a crack in the paving stones and tried not to giggle; Tuffy, who hated meeting new people, looked the other way; and Blaze, shifting Perrin to one arm, clasped Mr. Fogg's dry, warm hand.

"The organist was indisposed at the last minute," he said apologetically. "But it's not a total loss; Miss Fox's left arm is playing up and the organ's a bit flat."

"My organ gave up years ago." Tony said.

"Anthony," Clarissa remonstrated.

"I've lived in Cornwall for forty-five years and never knew this chapel existed," Kitto said.

"It dates from the early sixth century," Mr. Fogg explained. "It was founded by a Welsh princess named Madryn, elder daughter of King Vortimer of Blessed of Ghent. The spring is supposed to have healing qualities."

"Exactly what this family needs," Jane said. "Perhaps we should all get blessed here; come out the other end fresher and better people."

"Don't tell me the father's a Jew?" Clarissa said in a stage whisper.

"I've noticed an interesting type of Polytrichum by the wall," Tuffy said, holding up a large wedge of moss. "How many variants are there here?"

"I must admit I don't know. My speciality is divinity," Mr. Fogg confessed.

"Or is he a you-know-what?" Clarissa asked, putting a hand to her scrawny bosom. "A Ninth-day Adventurist?"

"You're missing out on a whole world." Tuffy was aghast, unable to believe the man's willful and woeful ignorance.

"Gods of different varieties are my universe," Mr. Fogg said, clasping his hands together in supplication.

"And those so-called varieties don't spread as far as nature?" Tuffy snorted and, turning to Arabella, asked, "Did you bring some specimen bags?"

"Of course." Arabella nodded and pulled copious plastic bags out of her pocket.

"Who wants smelly old moss?" Toby said, wanting to ingratiate himself with his girlfriend's father.

"Oh, no. He's a Pentecostal Mormon," Clarissa groaned. "Or an Epicurian."

"There are over a thousand different species of moss in Great Britain, many undiscovered. They are our heritage, the first visible colonisers of our ancient land," Tuffy explained.

"We used to call moss nature's underpants," Tony said.

"Mosses can hold many times their own weight in water; it's like a miniature cooling and humidifying system," Arabella told Tony.

"Pity my underpants couldn't do that—it would have saved a great deal of trouble."

"Do you think we should crack on with the service?" Kitto asked. He had forgotten to wear a jumper or jacket and, although it was late May, the chapel was cold and draughty.

"Don't tell me: the father's a Buddhist—the baby will grow extra limbs and sit around cross-legged all day." Clarissa leaned against the wall for support.

Mr. Fogg checked his watch surreptitiously. He'd hoped to be home before the nut roast was polished off by the little Foggs, but the service was running half an hour late already. In an attempt to hurry things along a bit, he handed out the small red books and an adapted Church of England christening sheet.

"Please take your seats," he said firmly. The family shuffled into the two front pews. Luckily the church was small and the lack of a full congregation was barely noticeable.

Mr. Fogg took his place by the font, rearranged his duffel coat and bobbly hat and announced, "We will sing number twenty-three, which is on page thirty-four of the little red book. You'll recognise it from the popular version by Yusuf Islam, formerly known as Cat Stevens."

"The father is a Muslim!" Clarissa proclaimed.

Clearing his throat, Mr. Fogg led the singing in a thin reedy voice.

"Morning has broken,
Like the first morning."

"I refuse to sing a Muslim song," Clarissa said, snapping her hymn book shut. "Or a Jewish or a Catholic one, for that matter."

"It was written in 1931 by an English poet Eleanor Farjeon, set to a traditional Gaelic tune," Kitto told his mother.

"I like 'I Vow to Thee, My Country' or a good psalm."

Toby looked at his girlfriend's father in consternation; he couldn't help wondering if she'd develop the same bulbous nose and wild ear hair.

Tony sang loudly and badly; this was his funeral as well as Perrin's baptism and he was determined to enjoy his last contact with his family and a Higher Power. He missed the pomp and formality of a traditional church service but supposed that God, if there was one, would overlook today's eccentricities. Clarissa thought about Enyon and their perfect marriage; Tuffy and Arabella were lost in dreams of moss. Only Blaze didn't sing: her throat hurt with the effort of not crying her heartbreak to the rafters. She felt lonely and afraid, daunted by the task of raising Perrin on her own and haunted by memories of her brief time with Wolfe. Jane, seeing her friend's face, leaned forward and put an arm around Blaze's shoulder.

When the song was finished, Mr. Fogg beckoned the family up to the font. Made in the thirteenth century from a single piece of local granite, it had a criss-cross pattern on the outside and the well was covered with an intricately carved iron lid.

"In naming a child, a Higher Power calls us out of darkness into His marvellous light. To follow this light means absolving our sins and rising to new life." Mr. Fogg was sure that the motley crew before him were thinking about other things, but he lived in hope of reaching one stray lamb. Out of the corner of his eye, he saw the old uncle wipe away a tear and wondered if it was too late to draw him into his flock.

"The water is a symbol of a Higher Power washing away our sins in an act of forgiveness." Mr. Fogg beamed—it was his favourite line in the service.

"Total tosh," Clarissa tutted.

"Amen," Kitto said, looking furiously at his mother.

"A-women too," Arabella added, remembering that feminism was an active cause. Toby kicked his sister.

Mr. Fogg pondered what it was like to be part of this family, brought low by time and ill fortune. Who would have thought the mighty Trelawneys—builders of counties, castles, battalions and businesses—would be reduced to such inconsequential circumstances? The community had talked of little else for the last few years. He thought of an appropriate passage from the Bible and was tempted to say it out loud, but decided against it. *In the sweat of thy face shalt thou eat bread, till thou return unto the ground; for out of it wast thou taken: for dust thou art and unto dust shalt thou return.* He looked at his watch and realised that the nut roast was in the oven. Closing his eyes, he imagined the smell and his taste buds began to twitch.

"Who's doing the reading?" he asked.

Arabella stepped forward. She'd been told to write a poem but, while finding the sentiment was easy, rhyming and metre had refused to coalesce.

"All that matters is that we don't harm the planet.
Every living thing is equally important."

"Is this Shakespeare?" Clarissa asked waspishly.

"Well said," Tuffy exclaimed.

Arabella pursed her lips and continued.

"A blade of grass is as significant as an elephant.
A flea is as necessary as a horse."

Clarissa shuffled in her seat. "The world's gone mad. What's wrong with the Lord's Prayer?"

"Shut up and listen, Clarissa!" Tuffy shouted.

"I've been longing to tell her that for years," Tony guffawed.

Arabella straightened her shoulders and continued.

"'Mice have as much right to live as men.'"

"That's very beautiful, Bella," Kitto said.

Clarissa snorted.

Mr. Fogg wondered if anyone would notice if he cut the rest of the service short. "Will the parents and significant others step forward?"

"What is a significant other?" Clarissa asked.

"The reading isn't finished," Arabella protested.

"The great thing is to know when to stop," Clarissa said.

Blaze and Jane shuffled forward and Toby helped Mr. Fogg lift up the font's heavy lid. "Good people, will you welcome this child and uphold her in her new life?"

The Trelawneys nodded. Behind them, the door to the chapel opened and closed quietly. Tony wondered if Miss Fox had come to play the closing hymn.

"Will you be giving the child to the Higher Power?" Mr. Fogg asked Blaze.

"Higher Power?" Clarissa repeated. "Is that the name of the father?"

"I hope I'm in the right place?" a man's voice said.

Everyone apart from Blaze turned around to see who had spoken. Blaze didn't dare, in case she had misheard. Footsteps approached the font. Blaze held her breath.

"Could I hold the baby?" Wolfe asked. "Please."

Blaze closed her eyes.

"Don't forget to breathe," a voice whispered in her ear. Blaze inhaled deeply and looked up into Wolfe's face. Placing their sleeping baby in his arms, she held on to the font for support. Perrin wriggled but didn't wake.

Mr. Fogg continued with the ceremony. "Naming a child is a sign of a new beginning and becoming part of a universal family."

"We are not and never have been universal," Clarissa said.

"The cameras are not on, Mother. Can't you behave like a normal person?" Kitto snapped.

Mr. Fogg, stomach rumbling, decided to miss out the last chunks of the service; this lot would never notice. He gestured to the latecomer to lower the baby over the font and, taking a small metal cup, splashed the infant's head with water. Perrin, rudely awakened from a deep sleep, let out a loud cry of alarm.

Making the sign of a smiley face on Perrin's forehead, Mr. Fogg said, "Welcome to the world, sweet baby. May your days be happy."

"Unspeakably common." Clarissa scowled at her son, but Kitto, along with the rest of the family, was staring at the interloper, wondering if he was Perrin's father.

"Shine a light in the world to the glory of mankind." Mr. Fogg raised his voice in order to be heard over the baby's wails. Then, seeing that all attention had turned to the newcomer, he decided to use this diversion to make a swift exit. "Would you mind blowing out the candles and locking up after you go?" he said cheerfully. "Put the key under old Moses Wilson's gravestone, please. Third one down on the left-hand side." With that he was gone. Blaze and her family stayed standing, all staring at Wolfe.

"Could someone hold our daughter?" he asked.

"Oh, that's who you are," Clarissa said. "An introduction wouldn't hurt. I presume you are the aforementioned Mr. Higher Power. I am the Dowager Countess of Trelawney." She held out her hand.

"Joshua Wolfe," he said, taking it and bowing slightly before turning to the others and smiling broadly. "Sorry I was late; it was hard finding this place." Jane stepped forward, gave him a kiss on the cheek and took the baby. "Lovely to meet you." Following her lead, Kitto pumped Wolfe's hand. "You are most welcome."

"Would you mind if Blaze and I stepped outside for a few moments?" Wolfe asked the family and, without waiting for their response, he placed his hand in the small of Blaze's back and steered her towards the door. They walked in silence between the old gravestones until they reached the lip of the churchyard and stood side by side overlooking the seashore below.

"What are you doing here?" Blaze asked.

"I had a visit from Ayesha two days ago."

"Ayesha?" The situation was becoming increasingly confusing.

"She turned up unannounced in a helicopter, making an entrance and frightening the animals to death."

"What did she want?" Blaze, hurt and shocked by Ayesha's duplicitous behaviour, dreaded hearing what had happened next.

"She told me how stupid I was being. How a love like yours and mine rarely comes along and, when it does, we have to grab it and never let it go."

Blaze fixed her eyes on a point on the horizon and held on to a headstone for support; the ground beneath her feet felt as uneven as her thoughts.

"Ayesha doesn't believe in love; she likes money and status."

"She told me you were the bravest and kindest of people, that she admired you more than any living person."

Blaze looked at him blankly.

"I agreed with her." Wolfe hesitated and stepped towards Blaze as if to kiss her.

Blaze put her hand up to keep him at bay. "What happened to Ayesha?" Nothing was making sense.

"She went."

"Went?"

"In her helicopter."

Wolfe touched her arm gently. "I have been a terrible fool. Have I left it too late? Will you, can you forgive me?"

"What do you want?" Blaze tried to organise her thoughts.

"To be with you and our child."

"You don't want children; you made that clear."

"Not *any* children, but I do want ours."

Blaze didn't answer. She couldn't find the words. Joshua looked at her. After a very long pause, when no reply came, he reached over and tucked a loose strand of hair behind her ear. Blaze looked up into his face.

"It's too late, Joshua. I don't have the strength or the imagination to start all over again. For Perrin's sake, I can't take the risk; I am millimetres away from falling to pieces." Her words trailed into a whisper and she gazed at him silently, resigned. "Perhaps I loved you too much."

"What do you want me to do?" he asked, his eyes searching her face.

"I want you to go. Now. And not come back." Blaze clenched and unclenched her fingers. She felt an overwhelming tiredness; she longed to lay her head against a mossy gravestone and go to sleep.

Wolfe opened and closed his mouth. He was desperate to say something to make her change her mind, but could see from her expression that it was too late for words.

"I am so desperately sorry. I will regret my behaviour for the rest of my life." He hesitated. "Are you absolutely sure?"

Blaze's heart and body had never felt so heavy; a thousand tiny weights pulled down on every fibre, every cell. Summoning every ounce of strength, she opened her mouth. "I am sure." Turning away from her, Wolfe walked up the path towards the road.

Blaze looked out over the water at two gulls flying along the shore, their white feathers turning pink in the fading sun. She was glad he'd gone. Her love for him had been a kind of madness; sudden thoughts of him could knock the wind out of her lungs and then moments later an inexplicable current of hope would send her spirits soaring. She was lovesick: the only cure was total abstinence. And now, just when she had begun to recover from her mania, he'd come back to tell her all the things she'd been so desperate to hear. But she didn't have the strength or courage to risk a further bout of insanity. It was her duty to construct an orderly life for herself and her daughter, even if it meant forsaking a chance of happiness.

Added to which, the involvement of Ayesha, although apparently benign, terrified her. Nothing that Anastasia's daughter had done—not one single action—suggested anything kindly. There had to be an ulterior motive: of further revenge on the people whom her mother hated.

From the chapel, she heard Perrin start to cry and, impelled by instinct, she turned to go back inside.

A twig cracked loudly and she jumped. Looking into the darkening shadows, she saw Wolfe.

"Why are you still here?" she asked.

"You always needed extra time," he said. "I thought I'd wait, in case."

Blaze, bewildered, looked at him. Then, without thinking, she ran into his arms.

Acknowledgements

Writing is a solitary pursuit, but I am indebted to various people for turning an imperfect manuscript into a polished book. Sarah Chalfant, far more than an agent, was its first reader and champion. Alexandra Pringle and Shelley Wanger are peerless editors, helping make *House of Trelawney* the best version of itself. Sarah-Jane Forder's patience and skill have been transformational. Thanks also to the teams at Bloomsbury, Knopf and the Wylie Agency for their mainly invisible but always essential care and professionalism.

Mala Goankar, Jenni Russell and Magnus Goodlad were particularly astute and thorough readers. I am grateful for their suggestions and for sharing their considerable knowledge.

Thanks as well to Susan Adams, Linda Drew and Rudith Buenconsejo for their support. And to the SP for shining a torch in odd patches of darkness.

The idea for this story was sparked by the discovery of a batch of old letters, sent from India in the 1980s while backpacking with Milly Soames. Rereading the faded pages of airmail paper, I tried to imagine the last twenty-plus years without her or my other treasured friends, and from that bereft and lonely place the characters of Jane, Blaze and Anastasia emerged.

This book is also about families, but any resemblance to my own is coincidental. Indeed, I can't imagine a day without the joy and inspiration given by my daughters Nell, Clemency and Rose or the support of my sister Emmy. My father Jacob's intellect, flair and brilliance set a level to aspire to in all areas. My mother Serena, a voracious reader, thought up the title *Trelawney* and it is a great sadness that I didn't write fast enough and she didn't live long enough to read the outcome.

And finally to Yoav, who has complicated both the fictional and the actual plot in the most unexpected way.

A NOTE ABOUT THE AUTHOR

Hannah Rothschild is a writer, filmmaker and company director. Her biography of Pannonica Rothschild, *The Baroness,* was published in 2012. Her first novel, *The Improbability of Love,* won the Bollinger Everyman Wodehouse Prize for best comic novel and was shortlisted for the Baileys Women's Prize for Fiction. She writes for magazines and newspapers including *The Times, The New York Times, Vogue, Harper's Bazaar* and *Vanity Fair.* Her documentary features have been broadcast on major networks and at film festivals. She also serves as a director for a quoted investment trust. In 2018 she was made a CBE for services to the arts and to philanthropy. She lives in London with her three daughters.

hannahrothschild.com

A NOTE ON THE TYPE

This book was set in Adobe Garamond. Designed for the Adobe Corporation by Robert Slimbach, the fonts are based on types first cut by Claude Garamond (ca. 1480–1561). Garamond was a pupil of Geoffroy Tory and is believed to have followed the Venetian models, although he introduced a number of important differences, and it is to him that we owe the letter we now know as "old style." He gave to his letters a certain elegance and feeling of movement that won their creator an immediate reputation and the patronage of Francis I of France.

Typeset by Scribe,
Philadelphia, Pennsylvania

Printed and bound by Berryville Graphics,
Berryville, Virginia

Designed by Soonyoung Kwon